D0499983

THE HOT
COUNTRY

Also by Robert Olen Butler:

The Alleys of Eden

Sun Dogs

Countrymen of Bones

On Distant Ground

Wabash

The Deuce

A Good Scent from a Strange Mountain

They Whisper

Tabloid Dreams

The Deep Green Sea

Mr. Spaceman

Fair Warning

Had a Good Time

From Where You Dream: The Process of Writing Fiction

(Janet Burroway, editor)

Severance

Intercourse

Hell

Weegee Stories

A Small Hotel

THE HOT COUNTRY

A Christopher Marlowe Cobb
Thriller

ROBERT OLEN BUTLER

The Mysterious Press
New York

A portion of this book originally appeared as a short story entitled
"The One in White" in *The Atlantic Monthly* and subsequently in
the Grove Press collection *Had a Good Time.*

Another portion of this book originally appeared in *Narrative* magazine.

Published simultaneously in Canada
Printed in the United States of America

FIRST EDITION

ISBN-13: 978-0-8021-2046-5

The Mysterious Press
an imprint of Grove/Atlantic, Inc.
841 Broadway
New York, NY 10003

Distributed by Publishers Group West

www.groveatlantic.com

12 13 14 15   10 9 8 7 6 5 4 3 2 1

For Otto Penzler, who inspired and encouraged this book and the ones that will inevitably follow. And for Bradford Morrow, my dear friend and literary brother, who brought Otto into my writing life.

1

Bunky Millerman caught me from behind on the first day of Woody Wilson's little escapade in Vera Cruz. Bunky and his Kodak and I had gone down south of the border a couple of weeks earlier for the *Post-Express* and the whole syndicate. I'd been promised an interview with the tin-pot General Huerta who was running the country. He had his hands full with Zapata and Villa and Carranza, and by the time I got there, *el Presidente* was no longer in a mood to see the American press. I was ready to beat it back north, but then the Muse of Reporters shucked off her diaphanous gown for me and made the local commandant in Tampico, on the Gulf coast, go a little mad. He grabbed a squad of our Navy Bluejackets who were ashore for gasoline and showers and marched them through the street as Mexican prisoners. That first madness passed quick and our boys were let go right away, but old Woodrow had worked himself up. He demanded certain kinds of apologies and protocols, which the stiff-necked Huerta wouldn't give. Everybody started talking about war. Then I got wind of a German munitions ship heading for Vera Cruz, and while the other papers were still picking at bones in the capital, I hopped a train over the mountains and into the *tierra caliente*. I arrived in Vera Cruz, which was the hot country all right, a god-forsaken port town in a desolate sandy plain with a fierce, hot northern wind. But I figured I'd be Johnny-on-the-spot.

Anyways. That Bunky Millerman photo of me. I saw it for the second time some weeks later, after a bit of derring-do that gave me what I expected to be the scoop of a lifetime and a king beat on the other boys, who were all stuck in Vera Cruz sparring with the Army censors' over an invasion that clearly wasn't moving out of town. Seemed there'd been something else going on all this time, right under our noses. When I'd finally gotten the real dope on that and figured out how to cable it to the home office uncensored, I got an immediate wire back from my editor in chief, Clyde Fetter. He called it a knockout of a story—and it was—the only problem being his wire ended with a "but" as big as Sophie Tucker's wagging away at me: Before he could go to press with this, he needed me back in Chicago in person, as soon as I could get there.

So I found myself in Clyde's Michigan Avenue office at the *Post-Express* on a hot afternoon in May. His eighth-floor windows were thrown open to the lake but it wasn't giving us *nada*, not enough breeze even to nudge the match flame he'd just struck up. What he didn't do was cross his feet up on the corner of his desk for what has become the traditional cigar-lighting at the start of one of our big-story sit-downs. I was still attuned to ominous signs after all I'd been through lately, so I didn't miss the significance of his feet being on the floor. He had more on his mind than figuring out the front-page layout and how to ragtime up our leads. Whatever he really had on his mind was awkward enough that he went cross-eyed focusing on the end of the cigar in his mouth, and he wasn't saying a word.

"So," I said. "Is our man going to file for the Senate race?" By which I meant Paul Maccabee Griswold, the Hearst of Hyde Park, Clyde's and my überboss. He had till June 1 to file for the primary and he was getting itchy for power of a different sort. I intended the remark simply as small talk to loosen Clyde up.

"Word is," he said, without so much as glancing from the end of his cigar.

And then I saw the postcard on the cork wall behind his desk. It was surrounded by clippings and Brownie shots and news copy, but it jumped off the wall at me. Clyde was still stalling, so I circled around him and looked close.

It was me all right. Bunky had snapped me from behind as I was walking along one of the streets just off the *zócalo,* which was the main square they call the *Plaza de Armas,* and there'd been a gun battle. Bunky had it printed up on a postcard-back for me, and I sent it off to Clyde. I'd inked an arrow pointing to a tiny, unrecognizable figure way up the street standing with a bunch of other locals. In the foreground I was striding past a leather goods shop. The pavement was wide and glaring from the sun. Even from behind I had the look of a war correspondent. There but not there. Unafraid of the battle and floating along just a little above it all. Not in the manner of Richard Harding Davis, who came down for another syndicate after the action got started and who wore evening clothes every night at his table in the *portales.* Not like Jack London either, who was in town looking as if he'd hopped a freight from the Klondike. I had a razor press in my dark trousers and my white shirt was fresh. We boys of the Fourth Estate love our image and our woodchopper's feel for words. It's an image you like your editors to have of you, and so I sent this card, even though by the time I did, I'd already begun to learn a thing or two I wouldn't put in a story for the *Post-Express* or anybody else. Did the lesson of those first few days help lead me to the big story? Maybe. I'd have to think that over.

But first I pulled the card off the wall and turned it over. I'd scrawled in pencil, "After the battle notice the pretty Señorita's in this photo. The one in white does my laundry." I drew my thumb over the words, compulsively noticing the dangle of the first phrase, which was meant like a headline. I should have put a full stop. "After the battle." And I've made "Señorita's" singular possessive, capitalizing it like a proper name. Maybe this was more than sloppiness in a hasty, self-serving scrawl on a postcard. It was, in fact, true that I had no interest in the other girls. Just in whatever it was that this particular señorita had inside her. Luisa Morales.

Clyde took a guess at where my mind was. "Good thing we've got a copy desk," he said, a puff of his relit cigar floating past me.

"If I were you I wouldn't trust a reporter who bothered to figure out apostrophes anyway," I said. But I wasn't looking at him. Now that I had him small-talking, I didn't care. Something more absorbing was going on.

I turned the card over once more and I looked at Luisa, dressed in white, far away. And I was falling into it again, the lesson I was about to learn in the photo seemingly lost on me. Because what I was *not* looking at in the picture or even while standing there in Clyde's office, really, were the two dead bodies I'd just walked past, still pretty much merely an arm's length away. A couple of snipers, also in white, dead on the pavement. That's what they paid us for, Davis and London and me and all the rest of the boys. To take that in and keep focused. I got the head count and I worked out the politics of it, and I could write the smear of their blood, their sprawled limbs, their peasant sandals without a second glance. I could fill cable blanks one after the other with that kind of stuff while parked in a wisp of sea breeze in the *portales* over a glass of *mezcal.* If I got stuck finding the right phrase for the folks on Lake Shore Drive or Division Street or Michigan Avenue, I just tapped a spoon on my saucer and along came a refill and inspiration, delivered by an *hombre* who might have ended up on the pavement the next morning showing the bottoms of his sandals.

"So what became of your señorita, do you suppose?" Clyde said.

I looked over my shoulder at him. He'd drawn his craggy moon of a face out of his collar and had it angled a little like he'd just sprung a horsewhip of a question on a dirty politician.

I ruffled around in my head trying to think if at some point I'd suggested any connection to him between the one in white and the one in black. It felt like a year ago I'd sent him that story, though it was only a few weeks. But I felt certain I hadn't. "Did I get drunk and send a telegram I don't remember?" I said.

"Nah," Clyde said. "Call it a newsman's intuition."

I shrugged and looked away from him again. But I wasn't talking. And that shrug was just for show. It was all still there inside me. The whole story.

2

She more or less came with the rooms I rented in a house just off the *zócalo*. I'd barely thrown my valise on the bed and wiped the sweat off my brow when she peeked her head in at the door, which I'd failed to close all the way. These two big dark eyes and a high forehead from her Spanish grandfather or whoever. "Señor?" she said.

"Come in. As long as you're not one of Huerta's assassins," I said in Spanish, which I'm pretty good at. I figured that accounted for the smile she gave me.

"No problem, señor," she said. She swung the door open wide now, and I saw a straw basket behind her, waiting. "I'll take your dirty things," she said.

"Well, there was this time with Roosevelt in San Juan . . ." I said, though it was under my breath, really, and I let it trail off, just an easy private joke when I was roughed up from travel and needing a drink.

But right off she said. "You keep that, señor. Some things I can't wash away." She did this matter-of-factly, shrugging her thin shoulders a little.

"Of course," I said. "It's probably a priest I need."

"The ones in Mexico won't do you much good," she said.

She kept surprising me, and this time I didn't have a response. I just looked at her, thinking what a swell girl, and I was probably showing it in my face.

Her face stayed blank as a tortilla, and after a moment, she said. "Your clothes."

My hand went of its own accord to the top button on my shirt.

"Please, señor," she said, her voice full of weary patience, and she pointed to my bag.

I gave her some things to wash.

"I'm Christopher Cobb," I said. "What's your name?"

"I'm just the local girl who does your laundry," she said, and I still couldn't read anything in her face, to see if she was flirting or really trying to put me off.

I said, "You've advised me to keep away from your priests even though I'm plenty dirty. You're already more than a laundry girl."

She laughed. "That was not for your sake. I just hate the priests."

"That's swell," I said. Swell enough that I'd said it in English, and I spoke some equivalent in Spanish for her.

She hesitated a moment more and finally said, "Luisa Morales," and then she went out without another word, not even an adios.

And I stood there staring at the door she'd left open at exactly the same angle she'd found it when she came in. And I'll be damned if I wasn't disappointed because I couldn't explain to her about my name. Christopher Cobb is how I sign my stories but Christopher Marlowe Cobb is my full name and my editors right along have all wanted me to use the whole moniker in my byline, but I find all those three-named news boys—the William Howard Russells and the Richard Harding Davises and the George Bronson Reas—and all the rest—and the host of magazine scribblers and the novelists with three names are just as bad—I think they all make themselves sound pompous and full of self-importance. And it's not as if I don't like the long version of me: My mother gave me the name, after all, when she first laid me newborn in a steamer trunk backstage at the Pelican Theatre in New Orleans and she went on to become one of the great and beautiful stars of the American stage—the eminent, the estimable, the inimitable Isabel Cobb—and Christopher Marlowe was her favorite, though he didn't understand women and probably didn't like them, because he never wrote anything like a true heroine in any of his plays, and maybe that tells you something about my mother's taste in men. She did love her Shakespeare as well, and she played his women, comic and tragic, to worldwide acclaim, but she named me Christopher Marlowe and she called me Kit like they called him, and Kit it is. I just keep the three names packed away in a steamer trunk, and if Luisa Morales had only stayed a moment longer, I would have told her to call me "Kit"—everyone close to me does—though no doubt that would have meant nothing whatsoever to her, and if I'd actually explained all that about my name the day I met her, she would have thought me a madman. Which is what I was thinking about myself. I was a madman to want to explain all this to a Mexican washer girl.

3

So I beat it down to the docks, where I found out the location at sea of the German ship, the *Ypiranga,* said to be carrying fifteen million rounds of ammunition. Then I stopped at the telegraph office where Clyde had wired me. It seemed that half the Great White Fleet was also headed in my general direction, including the troopship *Prairie,* the battleship *Utah,* and Admiral Fletcher's flagship, the *Florida.* Things were getting interesting, but for now all there was to do was wait. So I ended up at a cantina I reconnoitered near my rooms.

Not that thoughts of Luisa Morales came back to me while I was drinking, not directly. I soaked up a few fingers of a bottle of *mezcal* and sweated a lot at a table in the rear of the cantina with my back to the wall and I watched the shadows of the *zopilotes* heaving past, the mangy black vultures that seemed to be in the city's official employ to remove carrion from the streets, and I thought mostly about what crybabies Thomas Woodrow Wilson and his paunchy windbag of a secretary of state William Jennings Bryan turned out to be. They complained about the dictator right next door in Mexico and his likely complicity in the murder of the previous president—not to mention his threat to American business—but when they finally found an excuse to invade the country, they grabbed twelve square miles and stopped and sat on their butts. Out of what Wilsonian moral principle? The one that let him invade in the first place but only a toehold's worth.

What principle was that, exactly? I lifted my glass to Teddy Roosevelt and toasted his big stick.

I'd done that same thing in Corpus Christi a couple of weeks earlier with a guy who knew how it would all happen. I was waiting in Corpus for my expense money to show up at a local bank. I found a saloon with a swinging door down by the docks, but the spot I always like at the back wall had a gaunt *hombre* in a black shirt with a stuffed *bandolera* and beat-up black Stetson sitting in it. He saw me look at him. Coming in, I'd passed a couple of Johnnies rolling in the dirt outside gouging each other's eyes and I didn't want to add to the mood, so I was ready to just veer off to the rail. But the guy in the Stetson flipped up his chin, and the other chair at the table scooted itself open for me, a thing he did right slick, timed with the chin flip, like the toe of his boot had been poised to invite the first likely-looking drinking buddy.

So I found myself with Bob Smith and a bottle of whiskey. He was gaunt, all right, but all muscle and gristle, of an indeterminate age, old enough to have been through quite a lot of serious trouble but young enough not to have lost a bit off his punch. He had eyes the brown you'd expect of mountain-lion shit. He didn't like being called a "soldier of fortune," if you please, he was an *insurrecto* from the old school, 'cause his granddaddy had stirred things up long before him, down in Nicaragua, and his daddy had added to some trouble, too, somewhere amongst the downtrodden of Colombia before all the stink about the canal, so this was an old family profession to him, and as far as personal names were concerned, I was to address him by how he was known to others of his kind, which was to say, "Tallahassee Slim."

I said, "There's a bunch of you Slims in all this mess, it seems."

He agreed happily, listing a few. Cheyenne and Silent and San Antonio. Dynamite and Death Valley and Deadeye. He and Birdman Slim had even spent time together with Villa last fall. Birdman was apparently Villa's one-man aeroplane regiment, having brought his spit-and-baling-wired Wright Model B down to recon and drop homemade bombs for Pancho. The plane got plugged by ground fire over Ojinaga and crashed, but Birdman Slim walked away pretty much unscathed from the wreck and beat it back up to El Paso to lick his wounds. Tallahassee Slim, after some legitimate accomplishments as a cavalry officer in the field, was appointed a major fund-raiser for Villa. He told me this simply, with an ironic shrug, not seeming to feel it was a violation of his *insurrecto* tradition. But after a stint in this capacity—mostly involving the railways and particularly those trains carrying government bullion or arms but not refusing the personal contributions of private citizens who happened to be on board—Tallahassee Slim had also come north to regroup himself and dally with some white women before heading south again. He and I traded war stories and I got around to complaining about Wilson, who I took to be a lily liver.

"Not exactly," Tallahassee Slim said, leaning a little across the table and rustling the ammunition strapped to his chest. "At least a lily liver has a straightforward position. This guy isn't one thing or another. You hear how the man talks? Teddy would put his pistol on the table and call it a pistol. Old Woody sneaks his out and calls it the Bible. He preaches about upholding civilized values, stabilizing governments, giving the Mexicans or the Filipinos or whoever a fine, peaceful, democratic life. Not to mention protecting American interests, which means the oilmen and the railroad men and so forth. And as for the locals, you simply try and persuade the bad old boys who happen to be running a country we're interested in to retire to the countryside. Problem is, the *cojones* that got those fellas into power in the first place will never let them walk away. So when it comes down to it, Woody's going to go to war. Over a chaw of tobacco, too, when it's time. Mark my words."

So we drank to Teddy Roosevelt, and I did mark those words. One thing I'd learned filling cable blanks from various *tierras caliente* for a few years already was to listen to anybody with live ammunition who called himself "Slim."

And I also lifted my glass that first afternoon in Vera Cruz to Tallahassee Slim. A couple of times. I drank *mezcal* till it was too hot to stay upright and I decided to follow the example of those who actually lived with the infernal bluster of *el Norte* and I took a nap.

4

When I got back to my rooms I found my shirts and my dark trousers folded neatly at the foot of my bed, which led me to notice a quiet babble of female voices somewhere nearby.

I stepped out into the courtyard and Luisa and two other señoritas were over under a banana tree, hugging the shade and talking low. So she saw me looking at her and she rose and stepped into the sunlight, crossing to me but taking her time.

"Señor?" she said as she approached. "Your shirts are clean, yes? Your pants are pressed just right?"

Even in the United States of America, when a girl who works in a shop or a beanery or who does laundry, for a good example, gets a little forward, you take it in a different way than you would with a girl of money and fancy family who you meet somewhere official. I've had a few blue-blood girls say some pretty cheeky things in my presence in this day and age. But the shirt-washing Señorita Luisa Morales who stood before me, as beautiful as her face was—with maybe even some granddaddy straight from Castile—she was sure no *sangre azul,* and she was already plenty forward with me, and she didn't have to get up and come over and ask about my laundry based on me just looking in her direction. So given all this, it was natural to think she was ready to spend some private time together.

I speak pretty good Spanish, but my vocabulary has some gaps. The few things I know to say in this situation I picked up in cantinas and a *burdel* or two, and though I figured she was ready for the substance of those words, I was not feeling comfortable with the tone of them. She had a thing about her that I wasn't understanding. So trying to go around another way, I said, "Why don't you come on in and we check out the crease in my pants."

She put on a face I couldn't decode. Then I said, "I speak softly and carry a big stick."

Maybe Teddy loses something in translation. Or maybe not. She was gone before I could draw another breath. I remembered those big eyes going narrow just before she vanished, an afterimage like the pop of a newsman's flash.

Right off, I had a surprisingly strong regret at this. Not just the missed opportunity. The whole breakdown. But I still had too much *mezcal* in me and the afternoon was too hot, and so I took my siesta.

By the time I saw my señorita again, it was two days later, the German ship had arrived, and so had the U.S. Navy. Bunky and I went down to the docks first thing and the German ship was lying to, just inside the breakwater, with the American fleet gathered half a mile farther out. There didn't seem to be any serious action out there and it was only a few blocks inland to the *Plaza de Armas*. So I figured I had time to write a dispatch to Clyde.

I took what I'd decided would be my usual table in the *portales* and even had a couple of beers. Bunky was off on his own with his Kodak snapping what struck him as interesting, and he swung back to me and gave me a nod now and then. He was a former war correspondent himself, a hell of a good one, but he was taking his shots with film these days instead of words, which was a damn shame. Still, he could take a good one.

So we were well into the morning and Bunky had just checked in and was about to go off again when the local Mexican general, a guy named Maass—born a Mex but with German blood and blond, upright hair—marched a battalion's worth of government troops into the

Plaza. I figured it was getting time for the off-loading of the *Ypiranga*. I was also the object of some nasty looks from a major on horseback as I finished my beer while the locals were discreetly heading for cover.

Bunky and I beat it back down to the docks, and it had already begun. I counted ten whaleboats coming in, full of American Marines, which I later learned were from the *Prairie*. No sign behind me, up the boulevard, of Maass sending his troops to meet them. I had my notebook and pencil stub in hand and Bunky took off to find his camera angles.

It all went fast and easy for our boys and for me during the next hour or so. The Marines, who numbered about two hundred, were followed by almost the same number of Bluejackets from the *Florida*, and they brought the admiral's stars and stripes with them. We took the Custom House without a shot being fired.

I was still waiting for the Mexicans to come down and put up a fight, but there was no sign of them. Meanwhile, a bunch of locals were gathering in the street to watch. A peon in a serape and sombrero called out "*Viva Mexico*" and threw a rock, and even before the rock clattered to the cobblestoned street twenty yards from a couple of riflemen, he was hightailing it away. The riflemen just gave him a look and the crowd guffawed and it was all turning into a vaudeville skit.

Then a detachment of Marines clad in khaki and wrapped with ammunition started to march through the street along the railway yards. They turned like they were heading for the Plaza. I signaled Bunky and took off after them. They were going down the center of the cobbled street, the *zopilotes* hop-skipping out of their way and giving them a look over their shoulders like these guys could be lunch. I was hustling hard and gaining on the Marines and they were passing storefronts and balconied houses. Mexicans were strung along the street watching like it was the Fourth of July.

Just as I was about to overtake the captain in charge of the detachment, I saw Luisa. She was up ahead with some other señoritas nearby but she was standing by herself and she was dressed in white and she was standing stiff with her chin lifted just a little. But I had a man's business to do first. I was up with the captain and I slowed to his pace and he gave me a quick, suspicious look when I first came up, but then he saw I was American.

"Captain," I said, and I lifted my arm to point up ahead. "You've got about two hundred Mexican soldiers waiting for you in the Plaza."

He gave me a quick nod of thanks and turned his face to halt his detachment, and at that moment I looked toward Luisa, who was just about even with me but I passed her with my next step and my next, and I slowed down, even as the detachment was coming to a halt, and it registered on me that Luisa had been watching me closely and I felt a good little thing about having her attention but at that moment the gunfire started. The crack of a rifle and another and a double crack and the Marines were all shifting away and I spun around, knowing at once that the rifles were up above, that the Mexicans were on the roofs, and Luisa had her face lifted to see and I leaped forward one stride and another and my arms opened and I caught her up, Luisa Morales, I swept her up in my arms and carried her forward and she was impossibly light and I pressed us both into the alcove of a bakery shop, the smell of corn tortilla all around us.

"Stay down," I said, and I put my body between the street and her and I realized I'd spoken in English. "They're firing from the roofs," I said in Spanish. "Don't move."

She didn't. But she said, "They're not shooting at me."

"Anyone can get hit."

"They're shooting at you," she said.

"I'm all right," I said. "This is old news to me."

A rifle round flitted past my ear—I could feel the zip of air on me—and it took a bite out of the wall of the alcove. I twisted a little to look into the street—I was missing the action—this was news happening all around me—and as soon as I did, I felt Luisa slip out past me and she was moving quick along the store line, heading away. Another round chunked close in the wall and there was nothing I could do about my spunky señorita and I pressed back into the alcove to stay alive for the afternoon.

5

It wasn't a bad spot, actually, to watch the skirmish. The Marines did a quick job of sharpshooting the Mexicans, some of them falling to the pavement below and others going down on the roofs or beating a fast retreat.

Then it was over. I stepped out of the alcove. Bunky was coming up from the direction of the docks and he was doing his camera work. I stayed with the Marines while they regrouped and tended to a couple of wounded. The Mexicans on the roofs turned out to be poor shots and the Marine captain thought they weren't regular troops. Meanwhile a scout came up and said Maass's men had moved out of the Plaza and off to the west. Later in the day the Mexicans would go over the hills on the western outskirts of town to flank the battalion of Marines in the railway yards and along the *Calle de Montesinos* by the American Consulate. The boys on the *Florida* would see what they were doing and break them up with the ship's guns and Maass and his men would all run away.

But for now the Marines mustered up and marched off toward the Plaza and I crossed onto the wide pavement in the sunlight and sauntered in the same direction. I was starting to shape a lead paragraph in my head. I passed a couple of dead Mexicans. I've seen plenty of dead bodies. My business is getting stories. You're dead, and your story's over.

Then up ahead I noticed a figure in white. I was very glad to see her. She'd gotten through the bullets okay. I headed for Luisa and she saw me coming. I was still not within talking distance and she said something to the girl next to her and moved off. I stopped. The girl Luisa spoke to looked at me with a blank face and then looked away. I'm not a masher. A little dense sometimes, maybe. I was ready to leave Luisa Morales entirely alone, if that's what she wanted.

Early the next morning, long before the sunrise, I woke abruptly to the scratch of a match. I turned my face and saw a candlewick flare up and glide to the night table, but before I could quite comprehend it all, the business end of a pistol barrel was resting coldly on my left temple. Floating in the candlelight was Luisa's face.

"You were working for them," she said.

"Who?"

"The American invaders."

I was reluctant to get into a political argument with a laundry girl who had a pistol pointed at my head. I chose my words carefully. "I'm a newsman," I said.

"I saw you with the American officer, directing him."

The pistol was getting heavier. If her weapon was cocked and her bearing in on me was unconscious, her tired hand could do something it didn't necessarily intend. I tried not to think about that. There were some other pressing issues. For one thing, her attitudes weren't adding up. I needed to talk to her about this, but I had to make the point carefully. I didn't remind her of her hatred of Mexican priests; they were all I could think of in her culture that might speak against her pulling the trigger. But I brought up the logical next thing.

"I don't think you're a supporter of General Huerta," I said.

"I hate Huerta. Do you take me for a fool?" She nudged my head with the pistol for emphasis.

"No. Of course not. But these Americans. They're here to help free Mexico of Huerta. That's all."

"Did you see who was dead in the streets?" she said.

Lying sweating in my bed, a pistol muzzle to my temple, I was still unable to set aside the impulse to deal in either the literal facts or the political rhetoric that are the goods of my trade. Rhetoric would be dangerous, and I was short on facts. I hadn't looked closely enough to identify the bodies. I wasn't saying anything, and I felt an agitation growing in Luisa. I felt it in the faint, nibbly restlessness of the steel against my head.

"Did you see who was dead in the streets?" she said again, very low, nearly a whisper.

"No," I said.

"Mexicans," she said. And she cocked the hammer.

My breath caught hard in my chest and I waited. She waited too. Weighing my Americanness, I supposed. Weighing my life. Charting a path for herself.

Then the hammer uncocked and clicked softly back into place. The muzzle drew off my skin. The candle flame vanished in a puff of her breath and I lay very still as she slipped through the dark and out of the room and out of the life she'd left for me.

6

Not that my lead paragraphs over the next couple of days were any different from what they would have been. A handful of cadets and civilians with some fatally big *cojones* sniped our boys from the Naval Academy near the waterfront and got broadsided into the next life by the five-inch guns of the *Chester* and the *San Francisco*. The Marines came ashore and pummeled their way from house to house and secured the city. We had a nifty American flag raising ceremony at the *Palacio Municipal* and suddenly our fighting boys were all done up in clean dress whites. The local officials refused to come back and govern their city, and Vera Cruz was put under U.S. martial law with us vowing to be benevolent as hell. A 7:30 evening curfew went into effect, but we lifted it within forty-eight hours. And all the while, the *Ypiranga* just sat out there in the harbor. A German ship full of arms for Mexico with the Kaiser rattling his saber in Europe. I tried to hire a launch and go out to her once things settled down, but the Bluejackets intercepted me before we could even cast off. The *Ypiranga* was unapproachable, but she was still hanging around, and the other newshounds seemed unconcerned, expecting our Great White Fleet to finally just escort her out to sea and on her way back to the Fatherland. But if we were not going to roughride our way to Mexico City, then she still felt like the best story brewing.

One potential story did come along, however, that got Luisa talking again, low and angry inside my head, even as I eventually wrote it strictly by the standards of a wrongly-assaulted, badly-misunderstood-but-still-proudly-waving Old Glory. It started to shape up soon after the last American refugee train out of Mexico City finally made it to Vera Cruz, the one safe town in the country for Americans. And there were about five hundred of our countrymen jammed into it, the most visible ones in the capital, the bankers and the major shopkeepers and most of the embassy people. The bankers who weren't on the train were in jail and the shops had been looted and the embassy had been stoned and torched, and all of Mexico was suddenly united in its hatred for America and Americans. Even our ambassador and his wife snuck into town and ended up comfy in Admiral Mayo's quarters on the *Minnesota*.

Not that any of that hatred dared to be openly shown around Vera Cruz. Nothing like an occupying army to straighten things out. Though the local Mexican government boys were lying low, after a couple more days people were free to come and go, and the shops and markets and *burdeles* reopened pretty quick. The band shell in the Plaza even got back to nightly business with a German band playing American tunes. The well-off Mexican couples returned to the ballrooms at the bigger hotels and they promenaded to the Cuban *danzon*. I thought about Luisa several more times, but what she taught me grew a little fuzzy. Not that any lesson you learn is simple. The first Mexican president of the revolution, the one before Huerta, a former big landowner, foresaw his revolutionary future in a Ouija board. And the peasants who rose up on his behalf did so because they were convinced Halley's Comet had been a sign from God to change their government.

And maybe Luisa did affect the idle track of my thoughts once more, near the end of that first week, as I sat at my table in the *portales* of the *Hotel Diligencias*. I was facing the *zócalo*, and I was in nodding distance of Richard Harding Davis, who was sipping a good wine in his evening clothes as the sun was bloodily vanishing beyond the mountains to the west. There was still a bouquet of death in the air from the unclaimed Mexican bodies. A Marine swaggered by with adobe dust on his clothes from pounding down the walls of people's houses in his search-and-clear frenzy. Though I admired the man,

I did find myself being a little critical, thinking that probably going through the doors would have worked for our boys just as well. And I realized that a good many of these leathernecks were hard-ass combat veterans from what William McKinley, Jr., had called our "benevolent assimilation" of the Philippines fifteen years ago. McKinley had the foresight to have no middle name at all, but it did him *nada* in the end.

Bunky abruptly appeared and he nodded his thickly-silvered head at me, once, emphatically, as economical and dramatic with his hellos as he was with his news leads in his heyday. He moved the second chair around to the side so he could watch the street, as I was doing. He laid his Kodak 3A folding camera in the center of the table and it was still unfolded, with its red bellows stretched out straight from the black case.

I said to Bunky, "You know that thing looks like a dog's dick when he's got your leg on his mind."

He was too much of a gentleman and too much in love with his Kodak to act as if he heard me.

"A *big* dog," I said.

He reached to the camera and collapsed the bellows into the case and snapped it shut. "Down, Rover," he said, but very quiet, almost to himself.

I've always liked Bunky. He was B. F. Millerman for nearly four decades, mostly when the *Post* was the *Post* and the *Express* was the *Express* and Bunky was the latter's man at the front lines in the Franco-Prussian War and in Cuba with Teddy and in South Africa when the Brits and the Boers went at it. He did good work. I read his every word in the *Express* in the spring of '98 when I was fifteen years old and Mama was dazzling Chicago as Cleopatra. B. F. Millerman was my Cap Anson, my Cy Young, and backstage at the Lyric Theater I charged up San Juan Hill with B. F. and Teddy. Bernard Francis. I finally wheedled the full moniker out of him a couple of years ago when he was drunk, and he was properly offended that I did so. Bunky took up the camera when he'd finally had a bellyfull of governments and their armies censoring and manipulating the news.

"What are we doing here, Kit?" Bunky said.

"You and me?" I said.

"You and me and all the rest of us red-white-and-blues."

"If we all head on up the road to Mexico City . . ."

"We won't."

The German musicians were tuning up across the street, in the band shell behind the almond trees at the center of the Plaza, and the tuba was struggling to find a B.

"I made up a postcard for you," Bunky said, and he took out the picture of me and Luisa and the dead locals.

I looked at it. "I should send this to Clyde," I said.

And we heard a gunshot off to the right, down *La Avenida de la Independencia.* The shot was nearby but oddly muffled, so I figured it was on the far side of *La Parroquía,* the great, gray, *el Norte*-blasted parish church, which also fronted the *zócalo* and took up the next block south along the *avenida.*

"Sniper?" I said.

A second shot. It sounded like a Mauser.

"Or a drunk," Bunky said.

"It's too early for the drunks to start shooting and there's barely enough light for a sniper."

Bunky shrugged.

"But still," I said, concluding the debate with myself, "it's enough." I listened for another shot. There was only silence.

I stood up. "I think I'll take a stroll to see if he got his man."

Bunky put his hand on his Kodak.

"This enough light for you?" I said.

He took his hand off the camera. "I'll hold the table," he said.

I headed south on *Independencia,* making it more than a stroll. I hustled along pretty quick, waiting for more gunfire, though there was still just silence. I was starting to doubt that it was a sniper. But the news had slowed down pretty dramatically in Vera Cruz and I could use a little exercise.

7

There was a high-voiced racket all around, the *zopilotes* in their twilight wrangling over their spots on the roof edges and on the bell tower and even on the high cross itself, where they would settle down to sleep. But when I turned the far corner, at *Calle de Vicario,* and faced along the street at the south side of the church, some different, agitated voices joined the din. Fifty yards ahead was a little gaggle of women hovering around something or someone on the pavement that I couldn't see. I strode on, expecting, briefly, to find a plugged fellow *gringo,* probably in uniform. But even before I arrived, I'd adjusted that expectation. The Veracruzanas wouldn't be making over an American like this.

I gently elbowed the women into opening a space for me, and I was right about the victim. It was not an American. It was a Mexican priest in a black cassock. He was lying flat on his back on the pavement, his right arm straight up in the air, and he was grasping his right wrist hard. The palm of his hand had a major bloody hole blown in it and it had already sent the priest into shock. Or, to take up the likely point of view of everyone on the street but me, it had sent him into a state of religious ecstasy: He was staring at the hole and talking to it, saying over and over, "I'm martyred. I'm martyred. By the wounds of Christ I'm martyred."

I almost pointed out the obvious to everyone assembled: His stigmata was actually from a rifle slug. But I figured most of these assembled señoras already knew that. I looked over my shoulder and up to the roof of the two-story row building across the street, where the sniper must have fired his two shots. If he was still up there, I figured I'd be next. But I didn't see anybody. Two shots to the priest and that was it, it seemed. I looked back at the *padre*. He was a slick-haired, corpulent, middle-aged man, and he was still clutching and waving his wounded hand and proclaiming his Christ-like suffering. The woman next to me said it was a miracle. I thought she was talking to herself and about the bleeding palm. But she was talking to me and she was about to answer the question that was now in my mind. She nudged me and bent to the priest and lifted the massive gold cross that hung on a chain around his neck, even as the priest yammered on, unaware of her.

The cross had been plugged right at the intersection of the upright and the crossbar. This was heavy gold plate. The Mauser slug had buried itself in the metal and it no doubt knocked him on his ass, probably right after the shot to his hand. Under his cassock he'd have another memento that I was sure he'd figure out how to exploit: the image of the crucifix imprinted on his chest in black and blue. The cross saved the priest's life, but it wasn't a miracle. The guy on the roof clearly knew what he was doing: sending a message. If this shooter wanted the priest dead, the priest would be dead.

I was taking all this in pretty quick, but meanwhile the priest was doing more than claiming martyrdom. He was bleeding. I knelt beside him. He had a hemp rope wrapped around his cassock as a belt. I undid it and pulled it off him. "Did someone go to find a doctor?" I asked the ladies.

"Yes. Yes, señor," a couple of them said.

"We need to stop the bleeding," I said, and I took hold of his lifted arm. He did not resist. He turned his face to me as I wrapped the rope around his forearm above the wrist.

"Did you see who shot you?" I asked him.

He just stared at me.

I cinched the rope tight and laid the arm across his chest. He kept it there and seemed ready just to pass out for a while.

I looked at the women gathered around me, seeing in their eyes that moment you learn to sense, the moment of the most trust you're going to get from people you want to get information out of. "Did any of you see the shooter?" I asked.

I got a little chorus of *No, señor* with a trailing *No vi nada* or two. They'd all seen nothing. As they spoke, I scanned the dark, round faces wrapped in their *rebozos,* and I noticed one woman, indeterminately old but older than the rest, who didn't say a word. As I looked her in her eyes, they shifted away. She was the one who knew something.

I needed to make another gesture. I looked at the priest, whose head had lolled to the side on the pavement. "We should make him comfortable," I said. "May I have something for his head?"

One of the women crossed herself and unwrapped her *rebozo* and rolled it and kneeled next to me. She lifted the priest's head very gently and slid the cloth beneath it. Though I was interested in the tenderness of her gesture and how she might have always longed to touch him like this, I put that aside, and instead, I looked up at the silent woman, who was watching. She felt my eyes on her and she looked at me.

"What did you see?" I asked her, with just a little bit of firmness, catching her by surprise.

"*No la vi,*" she said, and I could see in my periphery another woman's face turn sharply in the older woman's direction.

The older woman seemed to catch herself. "*No lo vi,*" she said. And then, "*No vi nada.*" "I did not see anything" is where she'd ended up. And just before: "I did not see him." But the first thing she said, the unedited thing, the true thing, was: "I did not see her." Her.

"The sniper was a woman?" I asked, looking hard at the older woman.

"No, señor," she said, lying in every little way a reporter is trained to see, by a blinking of the eyes and a slight fidgeting of the shoulders and a pinching of the voice. "I do not know who shot."

I looked at the other faces. "Was the sniper a woman?" I asked them all.

They weren't talking, even if they knew.

I'd done all I could do for the wounded man and this was all I was going to get from the women. I rose and said good night to them and they were polite and a couple of them were nervous, and I moved off.

And moving slowly back north on *La Avenida de la Independencia,* along the face of the church, I had the obvious crazy thought. She hated the Mexican priests. She had a thing to do before she got out of town. She was a pretty damn good shot, which wouldn't surprise me. It was Luisa. That was an intriguing little page-four-or-so story I didn't intend to file.

Overhead the great bronze bells in the *campanario* struck the half hour—six-thirty—and almost instantly up ahead, from the belfry of the *Palacio Municipal,* a tenor of bells echoed the church's bass. I could use a drink. I was trying to put Luisa out of my mind once again, but she was resisting. I tried harder: It might not even have been her; it probably wasn't her. Even if the sniper were a woman, an urban *soldadera,* Luisa was a washer girl. Where could she have learned to be a crack shot? But there was a simple answer to that: She could have learned the basics from a dad or a brother, and the rest you've either got or you don't. And I walked faster.

By the time I reached the edge of the *zócalo,* the band had started playing. I hesitated a moment under the coconut palms at the edge of the Plaza. My table in the *portales* was calling me, but I looked down the path to the band shell. Not only was a German ship sitting in the harbor with sixteen thousand cases of ammunition for Huerta or whoever else, there were upward of fifty thousand Germans in Mexico, many thousands fresh from the Fatherland and carrying the Kaiser's stamp on their passports and operating the banks that held a big chunk of Mexico's international debt, all this while Herr Wilhelm was clearly working himself up for some kind of war in Europe. So a German band playing "Give My Regards to Broadway" in a *kiosko* in Vera Cruz while under American occupation flared my journalist's nostrils.

8

The benches along the path were full of older locals, segregated by sex, some full of men with their sombreros in their laps, others full of women with their *rebozos* gathered no farther than their shoulders, their heads also bare to the cooling twilight. The local boys were mashing from the edges of the band shell as the local girls promenaded before them in their best skirts dyed in colors of the sunset that had just now faded or the Vera Cruz sky at noon, the girls in pairs with their arms around each other's waists, which was more than just girlfriendship. It was a taunting thing directed at the boys as well, which I knew from me looking at the prettiest of them and finding myself envying the arm of her friend.

And there were groups of strolling American Army boys in clean khakis, smart enough not to look at the local baby-dolls too close, briefed well by their officers to behave around the girls' Latin-tempered future husbands. The horny among our boys knew where to go later, a short ride along the trolley line for the professionals. So half a dozen of our boys were gathering as I approached and trying unsuccessfully but loudly to harmonize, "Give my regards to Broadway, remember me to Herald Square."

I moved around the shell a bit to watch the Germans making music. They all had Kaiser Wilhelm mustaches, thick over the lips with sharp upturns at each end. They all were dressed in white band uniforms with crimson trim and epaulets and brass buttons. The biggest of the musicians was pounding the upright bass drum. The cornets were carrying the tune and the trombones were sliding their sounds in and out, pointing up the melody, and I scanned the faces of these men who might otherwise have been training to fight the French or the Serbs or the Brits or whoever else. As I did, with the faces seeming as similar to each other as soldiers under their gold hat brims, a trim but solid-looking man sitting on the near end of the front row moved his eyes to me. He was blowing an alto horn, its bell bent to point upward. He didn't look away and I nodded at him and he looked forward again.

He seemed to have recognized me. My name was certainly familiar in the American press—and my stories were even syndicated occasionally into German and Spanish—but my face was not familiar. There'd been some magazine photos of me, but only a very few. I wasn't like the celebrity-seeking Davis. He could be recognized on any number of big-city street corners, or perhaps even from a band shell in a plaza in Vera Cruz, Mexico. But not me. Maybe I was wrong about the moment of recognition. Or maybe I just needed that drink. I looked close enough at the guy with the alto horn to find him later if I needed a German for a quote, and I headed back down the path. By the time I got to the *avenida,* the band had finished with George M. Cohan and had started up *La Cucaracha,* though more in the rhythm of a polka than a Mexican folk dance, the two pieces in sequence making up a lunatic music-hall overture for this night and for this half-assed invasion and for international politics in general.

I drifted away, back toward the hotel.

Working the city beat in Chicago as a cub reporter made me very familiar with the street lowlifes, all the grafters and prowlers, the hoisters and heavyweights, the crawlers and the gonifs. Made me never take a step in public without my full attention. So I usually knew when there was somebody else's hand in my pocket. And as soon as I passed out of the light from the bandstand and into a dark stretch of the path, I saw a small, deeply shadowed shape out of the corner of my eye. It slipped very neatly and quietly up to me—if I hadn't seen it, I wouldn't have known it was there—and suddenly a hand was in my right front pants pocket.

I clamped the wrist and twisted it out of my pocket and I dragged it and whatever was attached to it into the next splash of lamplight. It turned out to be a round-faced, splay-eared Mexican boy, maybe ten years old, and I was struck by the fact that he hadn't made a sound, though I was sure I'd been hurting his wrist since I grabbed him and he had to be scared about being caught. But his face was as placid as any old man's on a bench in the dark of this *zócalo*.

"What are you trying to do, kid?" I asked, addressing him as *niño*, which is actually closer to "baby" than "kid." This he winced at.

"Okay," I said. "Street punk." *Chulo callejero.*

He smiled broadly. "You can let my wrist go," he said. "You started off wrong, but now I can see you're okay."

"*I* started off wrong? You had your hand in my pocket."

"I was just introducing myself."

"I know a gonif when I meet one," I said, using the Chicago street word in the middle of the Spanish.

He cocked his head.

"Pickpocket," I said.

"Sure," he said. "But your wallet's in your other front pocket. If I wanted to steal from you, your wallet and I would be vanished already." He snapped the fingers on his free hand. "Like that," he said.

I touched my left front pocket and the wallet was there.

"If you let go, I won't run," he said.

I looked at this kid. He had something about him. I let him go.

He simply dropped his arm to his side, not rubbing the wrist even once, not showing any weakness. A tough kid.

"You're a big *gringo* newspaperman, yes?"

I gave him a frown.

He read me instantly. "*American* newspaperman." And he added in English, pointing to himself and then to me, "Even-steven. Because you call me *niño*."

"We're not even until I pick *your* pocket," I said, sticking with Spanish.

He laughed.

"You've got me pegged right, about the newspapers," I said.

"I see you writing cables." He stepped close to me and very briefly touched my writing hand, almost reverentially. "Page after page," he said, and he backed away again. "I don't write so much. Well, maybe not at all. Watching you makes me wish I can pick your pocket and steal that from you and run off with it. Knowing how to write."

"Don't you go to school?"

He laughed a razor-thin laugh and shrugged. "I am a poor boy. I work for a living."

"Picking pockets."

"I work for you. Yes? Honest work. I think a big American newspaperman needs some eyes and ears that can sneak around and find things out. I sneak very well."

"I bet you do."

As a matter of fact, we all paid locals now and then to find some things out that we couldn't as outsiders. Or to play courier. In the Balkans I had a good man, a Macedonian hardscrabble farmer, who would take my dispatches from the battlefields at Kilkos and Lachanos to the nearest accessible telegraph in Gallikos.

"So you're a good sneak," I said.

"The best." And he held up the wallet from my left front pocket. Which, of course, he'd lifted when he touched my writing hand with his pathetic little poor-boy-wanting-to-better-himself story.

I grabbed the wallet.

I did need him or someone like him, I realized. To try to track the one story that felt full of real potential.

"I want you to watch a ship," I said.

"Day and night," he said.

"That's what I need. You're free to do that?"

"Yes. Of course."

"Your family . . ."

"I am free," he said, his voice going hard in a don't-go-there kind of way.

"I'll pay you a silver Liberty Head half-dollar as soon as anything but slops goes over the side or she cranks up her engines or even anything unusual happens on deck."

"Each time?"

"Each time."

"Real silver?"

"Real silver."

"Shake," he said and he extended his hand.

I just looked at it and said, "If I take that, will you lift my wallet again?"

"I'm not that good. And I couldn't even begin to steal the money belt around your waist, under your shirt, just above your pants belt."

This kid continued to surprise me. And these were his credentials.

I took his hand and shook it. "I'm sneaky myself, street punk. You won't fool me again."

"I won't try."

"What's your name?"

"Diego. And you are Christopher Cobb."

"I thought you couldn't read or write."

"They talk about you in the *portales*. It's why I chose you."

"The *Ypiranga* is the ship."

"I figured," he said.

"I won't need your pickpocket skills," I said.

"Whatever you need, I can do it," he said. And I believed him.

And he made me sad. I've seen plenty of kids like this. This one seemed exceptional and we'd been talking light with each other, and I know how I am, moving through a world of war and human suffering with a kind of sport about it, and maybe you need to do that to keep sane. But a kid like this always brought me back to the tough truths. A kid like this—even an exceptional one with smarts and pluck and ambition and wit—hasn't got much of a chance in the end. He grows up a thief and dead or a hardscrabble peon and dead or he's just a kid who works for the outsiders, for the enemy, and ends up a dead kid.

9

When I got back to Bunky at our table in the *portales,* he had a *mezcal* before him and I wondered how many times he'd tapped his saucer already.

But he seemed perfectly clearheaded. "Sniper?" he said.

"Yeah. Plugged a priest."

"Dead?"

"Nope. Knocked on his ass and stigmatized."

Bunky nodded as if this were all clear to him, which it couldn't have been. He waited to see if I wanted to say more, and I knew he wouldn't ask if I didn't. He was a good man. Maybe he was picking up on my mood about this. I really just wanted to have a drink. I didn't want to think about a female sniper in Vera Cruz, even if she wasn't the girl who'd put a gun to my head a few nights ago.

But I said, "Bullet in the palm and one in the center of his crucifix that did nothing but topple him over."

"Quaint little story."

"Quaint little no-story."

Bunky nodded again. "Surprising lot of folks down here got a beef with the Church."

"It's about money."

There was a commotion off to our left. We looked.

A squat little Mexican man had entered the *portales* in a serge suit and a Panama hat, which was coming off in quick deference to a couple of American Army officers who rose from their table to greet him. All the Yanks nearby were murmuring their good-evenings.

"Who's the popular local?" I asked.

"Utility commissioner, I think," Bunky said. "I hear he's coming back to work."

"With us?"

"Yup."

"Do Davis and the boys know?"

"Don't think so."

And sure enough, I could see Davis a few tables down and his neck was coming up out of his stiff collar to crane in the direction of the low hubbub.

"Nice, Bunky. You want to write it?"

He looked at me. "We haven't talked about this."

"Now we are."

He shrugged.

I said, "How long do you want to stew about the censors? They'll let that story through for sure."

"The rest of my life, probably," he said. "And yes, they probably will."

"Listen, Pops," I said, and we both paused a moment, as this was the first time I'd called Bunky "Pops." "Listen, I learned this whole racket from reading you when I was a pup. You're swell with the Kodak, but I've filed today and I've got things on my mind and you'd be doing me a favor. And Clyde would love to see you writing again."

For a few quiet moments Bunky seemed to be looking at me closely, but I could tell he was really looking inward. "Okay," he finally said.

"Thanks," I said.

He stood up. "You've also got things to read," he said, putting a forefinger on a couple of cables I hadn't noticed lying by his camera. Bunky moved off toward the commissioner.

I ordered an *aguardiente*, a brandy they made down here out of sugar cane, which I found I was acquiring a taste for, and only after it came and I felt the sweet burn of my first sip did I draw the cables across the table and take them up.

The top one was from Clyde: *How is Ypiranga doing?*

It was the only story he'd asked specifically about. I'd wire him of my vigilance in the morning so as to calm his editorial ulcer.

I picked up the second cable.

It was from my mother.

I was used to her letters in perfumed envelopes and ornate hand finding me in Chicago or even out in the wider world, and I always clearly heard her speaking in my head, the nuance of every cadence, when she wrote. So it was odd to hear her voice recorded here in a strange, hasty hand, the local telegraph operator translating her words from the electrical dots and dashes. But it was her voice. No doubt.

My Christopher, she said. *My Chris my Kit my darling boy.* And all this excess of address—every variation of my name costing her real per-word cable money—all of it fell upon me like her leading-lady hugs, large-gestured enough to fill the Hippodrome, which was not to say they were for any audience but me. They were strictly for an audience of one, these embraces.

Accurst be he, she said, *that first invented war.*

This being from my namesake, who she was fond of quoting.

But war gives thee the work of words which is a good thing and it gives thee fame which wanes now in your mother's life as you know. Thus am I returned now to the city of thy birth to sing for rowdies and watch over those who can use watching over and you should not worry about me if I am silent for a time. Trust me in this. I know you think of me and sometimes seek me but for now I am playing a dark role in my own life so please do wait a while for my sake. You are always in my mind. Thou art thy mother's glass and she in thee calls back the lovely April of her prime.

She was also not averse to quoting my namesake's better, her last sentence being from one of his sonnets.

And she ended with *By heaven I do love thee. Your mother*

All of which worried me greatly.

I knew my mother well. I did not have a clue about her. And both these opposite but true things came together in her telegram. She'd been in a blue funk for a few years now about what she'd long called her "waning." When I was born in New Orleans—she'd gone back there now, it seemed—she was twenty-five and very much in the April of her prime, already one of the beautiful darlings of the American stage. Now it was thirty years later, and on a very hot day just last summer at the Lyceum Theatre in Memphis, Mother tried to play Kate in *Taming of the Shrew* under a thick white mask of makeup before a vocally skeptical crowd. She soldiered through to the final curtain but then refused to take a bow. Instead, she removed her makeup and walked out the stage door before anyone knew she was gone, and she vowed that was the end of her theater career. She would not be anyone other than who she had always been. She would not be anyone on a stage who was a secondary character. She would not be anyone on a stage who was not desirable and ripe for love. She would not be anyone on a stage who was fifty-five years old. She wrote all this to me in a letter that actually reached me in Sofia, with the Rumanian Army advancing and me getting a big beat on the other boys about King Ferdinand giving up. She said, *The waning, my darling, is now the having waned.*

And I have not been able to see her since. I have been on the road playing my own role as the crack war correspondent and unable to seek her out. Not that I even knew where she went. She wrote me but never let on what she planned to do or where she planned to go. And now I ran my forefinger over the words of the telegram. Fame, she said, "wanes now in your mother's life." She was precise with words. I learned much from Bunky and his ilk but more from her. The "having waned" had once again become an active "wanes." She played a dark role, she said. But it did not sound like theater. She sang. She does sing. She has a beautiful voice. One of her lovers when I was already grown and gone from her daily life was a songwriter of sorts, and she did an early, barely post-Kitty Hawk phonograph disc of one of his songs, "Kiss me, Orville, I Am Right for You." Not surprisingly, she passed

through that boyfriend quickly, and through her separate singing career too. But she can sing. "For rowdies" worried me. Much worried
me about this telegram, about her present life. Much that I could do
nothing about, at least for the moment, and so I tried to set it aside.

I folded her telegram and slipped it into a front pants pocket. I
took another bolt of *aguardiente*. Behind the trees the band was playing
"Waltz Me Around Again, Willie," and I had it in my head suddenly to
get up and go back into the *zócalo* and ask the prettiest Mexican girl's
girlfriend to let go of her so I could take the pretty one in my arms
and waltz her around the band shell, waltz her around and around and
around. But I didn't do that. For a couple of good reasons.

I tried to shoo the girl out of my head by making myself consider
the song: It was a big hit in the States a few years ago, but I wondered
if beneath their gold hat brims, the boys in the band weren't thinking
about their own Kaiser Willie and how he might waltz us all around
one of these days. If I were to write a piece on the German band in
the Vera Cruz *Plaza de Armas*—which was possible if Woody simply
were to have his Army settle down to cleaning up the filthy streets of
this town and faux-govern a few Mexicans—then I was glad to have
found this dandy little kicker for the end of the story. But given the
other things of the past half hour or so that were still rattling around in
my head, this was cold comfort and no permanent distraction for me.
I heard the clang of a bell float in over the music. An electric trolley
was coming up the *avenida* from the south, and now I was actually on
the verge of hopping on and heading up a few stops to the red-light
district and finding a professional girl.

There were very good reasons not to do this either. So I was glad
to have Bunky appear in the nick of time and sit heavily down.

"What's his story?" I asked.

Bunky shrugged. "Like we said. It's about money."

10

I'd had too much of the *aguardiente*, of course, and so it took the boy's actually coming into my room and shaking me by the shoulder to wake me, which I'd instructed him to do.

"Señor, señor," he was saying to me as I struggled up from a dream about Mother, who was kneeling on the pavement on the far side of *La Parroquía*, her head and shoulders shrouded in a *rebozo*, lifting her bloody hands before her, Señora Macbeth, claiming that it would take but a little water to clear her of this deed. But with the boy's shaking of my shoulder, she melted, thawed, and resolved herself into a dew, and I snapped fully awake. Even the hot bloat in my head dissipated as I threw on my clothes, and the boy said, "Some small boat is launching from the ship you have me watch." I grabbed my binoculars and I followed him out the door and into the street and we beat it east on *Calle de Benito Juárez*, along the northern edge of the *zócalo*, and we were approaching the docks pretty quick.

The harbor and the ship weren't visible yet as we came up on the wide, stone-columned Custom House and, beyond it, the back of the massive, monolithic row of pitch-roofed storehouses along the waterfront. I reached out and put a hand on the boy's shoulder and stopped him.

He turned to me. There was nearly a full moon, and he was a good boy, Diego, the eyes of his upturned face bright in the moonlight.

He was ready to do whatever I needed him for, and not, it seemed to me, just for the money, but for the boy's sport of it. A good boy, this one. I pulled out his silver half-dollar, and as I gave it to him, I put my forefinger to my lips. He nodded at me, my wee conspirator.

"Another time I'll have more for you," I whispered to him.

He gave me a second nod and vanished in a flash back up the *calle*. I turned toward the harbor.

I figured it was best to stay out of sight: In spite of our military trying hard now to make the city seem as normal as possible, whoever was coming in from the *Ypiranga* had decided to do it at the most inconspicuous time possible, and they would not give up their story just because a reporter had the enterprise to be waiting for them.

I circled the Custom House to the right and moved into the dark moon-shadow behind the storehouses. The air was full of their smells—coffee and ginger and the musky smell of uncured tobacco leaf—and I kept on heading south until I reached the building's edge, at the back end of the Customs Pier. If the party from the *Ypiranga* was heading north instead, to Pier Four at the train terminal, I'd have to hustle. I came around the corner of the building and moved up slow and easy into clear sight of the harbor and the pier, keeping close to the storehouse wall.

The Customs Pier stretched a good five hundred yards into the harbor. I lifted my binoculars, a swell pair of German Fernglas 08s I got in the Balkans last summer. It took me a few moments to locate the launch from the *Ypiranga,* and I was grateful for the moon or they would have gotten by me. Out beyond the pier and off to the left, crossing the broad white field of reflected moonlight, was the silhouette of a four-oar rowboat, sliding dark and quiet. I could barely make out the low hunkering of three figures. I'd seen enough and I stepped back away from view.

By their angle, they were not heading for the Customs Pier but not for Pier Four either. They were planning to put in at the more-likely-to-be-deserted Fiscal Pier, about a hundred and fifty yards to the north. Two storehouses up the way. I jogged back inland and turned and I made good time behind this storehouse and spanked across the opening and along the back of the second storehouse, and I pulled up at its northern edge. I moved slowly to the corner and looked toward the harbor. No sign of them yet.

I'd been winging it okay so far, but I needed to figure out my part from this point on. Given their obvious secrecy, if I was going to get a beat on what the boys from the *Ypiranga* were up to, I needed to do this indirectly, keep my distance and figure it out bit by bit. The shadows were deep between the two storehouses and I had a good view of the whole Fiscal Pier, so I crouched low and waited. Tonight I'd be content to follow them.

They took their time, but two figures finally appeared halfway down the pier and I put my binoculars on them. The sight of them startled me. Something seemed to glow there. I lowered my binoculars and cleared my sight and then raised them once more. One of the two figures was small and dark, blending into the night. The other was much taller and bright white. His size and his glow from the moon were still a little unnerving, out of proportion and startlingly visible, especially given this middle-of-the-night secrecy. But it was just a man, dressed in white. I watched as the small, dark one turned and motioned off the side of the pier to someone down below. I assumed one of the three men I first saw was left in the boat and he was returning to the ship.

These two headed this way, and I eased deeper into the shadows. I tracked their approach up the pier, and as they drew nearer, I could see that the shorter, stouter one was dressed in a pea coat and watch cap. He was probably part of the ship's crew, and he was hanging back half a step from the other man, in obvious deference. The bag the crewman was carrying no doubt belonged to the important man, who was quite tall and angular and whose suit should not have seemed so odd. He was a German of importance coming to tropical Mexico in a tailored white linen suit and a Panama hat. A German of arrogant importance, given his carriage, and given his white suit when he obviously intended to arrive without being observed. I couldn't see his face in the dark, but I wouldn't have been surprised if he had a monocle and a fencing scar on his cheek. In my 6-power binoculars, the two men were getting close and I suddenly had a little twist of panic. They were heading into the city and they might have been thinking to cut straight between these two storehouses.

I rose, repressing the impulse to leap and bolt. They were close enough now that quick movement might have been seen, even in the shadows. I backed up as slowly as I could make myself to begin with, and I increased the speed as I got deeper into the shadow. Now I was matching their speed and they were passing between a couple of processing sheds that flanked the back end of the pier, and when they came into the shadows of the storehouses themselves, which they would in just a matter of moments, and when their eyes adjusted to the shadows, they might see me. I looked over my shoulder and I had only a few paces to go, but smooth movement was even more important now and I looked at them again and they were veering off south.

Now it was a matter of my sprinting toward the south side of the customs building before the two men from the *Ypiranga* emerged from the far side of the storehouses. I took off. I made it to the Custom House and around to the southern edge facing the city, and I took up a spot behind the man-high plinth at the base of one of the front decorative columns. I had a good, mostly hidden view down *Avenida Zaragoza*, which they would have to cross.

And soon they emerged, less than a hundred yards from me. I picked them up in my binoculars. They didn't cross *Zaragoza;* instead they turned south on it. I came out of the shadows and followed well back. When they stopped up ahead, at the corner of *Esteban Morales,* I stopped too, and I was worried about them seeing me standing here, fifty yards back and all alone in the street, but they seemed sublimely, obliviously confident in their secretiveness. The talk was apparently about directions, because they pointed up *Esteban Morales* and conferred and pointed on down *Zaragoza* and talked some more, and then finally they headed up *Esteban.* As soon as they did, I figured I knew where they were heading.

This was confirmed a few blocks up when they vanished south on *Cinco de Mayo*. I came up quickly to that corner and I took the last step carefully to pause and watch. As I expected, halfway up the block the two men stopped in front of a wide, two-story brick-and-adobe house of the sort that had a deep back gallery of rooms around a courtyard. I'd noted the place on my basic lay-of-the-town reconnoiter on my second day. This was the German Consulate. The small man knocked, and when the door opened, he handed the bag inside and the tall man did a simple aristocratic bow of thanks—no handshake—and he went in and the door shut in the small man's face. Before he could even turn to head back to his ship, I was hustling down the street to get out of sight.

The tall man was clearly someone very important. Straight from the Fatherland and keeping a low profile. I could smell a story here as sure as I could smell the old-fish-and-salt-wind smell of the harbor before me. This wouldn't be an easy one, but I always had half a dozen tough stories kicking around in my head at any given time. This one sure couldn't be any tougher to deal with than an invasion that stopped a mile inland and promised to turn into civic planning and sanitation work. Not any tougher, either, than a girl sniper with a roughhouse sense of humor.

11

A very few hours later I was in the *portales* of the *Diligencias* having my morning coffee straight and sludge-thick to wake up from my little stroll in the middle of the night, thinking about how to get at the tall man sequestered in the German Consulate, when there was a lone gunshot straight across the *zócalo*. Somehow I knew it was her. The *Palacio Municipal*, City Hall, another symbol of corruption to the revolutionaries, sat massively over there beyond the trees and just the one shot was fired. And though I was sure of the direction, the shot sounded farther away than the edge of the Plaza. I gathered up the cable blanks I'd been filling with nothing-happening tripe and I put down some coins, and I saw Davis, a few tables to my left, standing too. He was ready for a new day as Richard Harding Davis, crack but elegant War Correspondent, in starched and pressed field togs and gray felt hat with a blue polka-dot puggaree, symbol of the Rough Riders, of which he was an honorary member for having turned them and their Hearstian war into romantic heroes to be heralded by every newsboy on every street corner in America. He was putting the proper tilt to the hat as I looked at him, and he picked up his riding crop, the final touch. He glanced my way. He nodded at me and I nodded at him, and by the time we hit the *avenida* we were shoulder to shoulder and moving briskly together, heading for City Hall.

"Cobb," he said.

"Davis," I said.

"You understand my usually keeping my distance?"

"Of course," I said.

"Out of respect," he said. "Your work in the Balkans—and in Nicaragua before that—was splendid. Did you get my notes?"

"I did," I said. And though Davis's style irritated me, I had his lengthy handwritten notes tucked in a drawer in my desk in Chicago. This was true of the man: He was famous for his frequent, generous, handwritten praise of his colleagues, be they newsmen or novelists. Though one of my criticisms of him was that he played a little too frequently at being the latter, the excesses of novels too often finding their way into his work as the former.

"Ironically," Davis said, "if I didn't have good reason to write those notes, I would be more inclined to dine with you. We do find ourselves working for the same beats."

"How sad," I said, "that we now find ourselves chasing single gunshots."

"Though at least it sounded like a Mauser," Davis said.

To an attentive ear, quite a different sound from our boys' Springfield 03s. A sniper, he was suggesting. I kept my mouth shut.

"No matter," Davis said. "We'll all be in Europe soon enough, I wager."

"I wouldn't wager against that," I said, and we both seemed to realize that we were losing our focus. If we didn't pick up the pace, we might as well go back to our coffee. So we fell silent and pressed on faster, around the band shell and through the trees and across the pavement before City Hall, an old Spanish building with its *portales* occupied now by cookstoves of the Second Infantry regiment.

"He's got guts, plugging away at our boys where they camp," Davis said.

Though most of the regiment at this hour was out patrolling at El Tejar, our western perimeter, what Davis said made me doubt for a moment that this was the woman sniper, a doubt that recurred when we came around the corner of the *palacio*. I saw a dozen or so of our boys on the case, a few in the street pointing toward the bell tower of *La Parroquía*, a few breaking off in both directions to circle the church and maybe catch the shooter coming out, a few others surrounding the victim. This was some local *hombre* gunning for an American soldier.

But when Davis and I arrived at the victim, I figured I better rethink things. It was the utility commissioner who'd decided to work with the Americans. He was sitting there on the pavement in his serge suit and with his Panama hat upturned a few feet away, and he and one of our boys were both pressing a wad of bloody cloth to the center of his face, the commissioner gasping his breaths through his mouth.

"What happened?" Davis said.

A sergeant standing next to us said, "Somebody shot the guy's nose off. Clean as a whistle."

Davis humphed. "You boys were hunting a man with a Mauser and a message." With the alliteration, he turned his face and looked me straight in the eyes. He was already shaping his lead and he had just staked his claim to the phrase.

I, however, was in the midst of realizing that I'd once again under-estimated our local *soldadera*. This clearly bore her signature. If Davis filed a piece on the guy with the Mauser and the message, I could beat him quite handily with my girl and a gun.

But I suddenly found myself concerned for her. I moved off quick to trail one of our little search parties around the church. By the time the two parties of infantrymen met up on the opposite side, on *Calle de Vicario*, almost in the exact same spot where the plugged priest lay yesterday, I was thinking these boys were wrong about where the shooter was. The angle from the bell tower was too difficult to shoot off a man's nose. And shooting off his nose was exactly what she'd in-tended to do. I didn't know where she was, but it wasn't the *campanario*.

Our boys were huddled to confer. They'd drawn a little crowd of locals across the street. At a quick glance, I saw them as basically the same neighborhood women who gathered around the priest yesterday. My glance was quick because I was intending to draw near the soldiers and listen in, get a quote or two just in case I did a little story, make an acquaintance or two I might glean a bit of information from someday. But I was suddenly having another one of those little afterimage experiences over a certain señorita: I thought I'd just seen her.

I looked back to the women. She was not there. I stepped into the center of the cobbled street. I could clearly see both ways, up and back down *Calle de Vicario,* and she was not walking off in either direction. I moved to the women. Some of the faces turned to me. Familiar from yesterday. Blank. They stayed shoulder to shoulder, though I was acting as if I intended to move past them. I kept coming, scanning the faces behind the ones in front and the faces behind those. She was not there. They knew I was coming through and finally, as if reluctantly, they parted.

To the left behind them was a door into a milliner's; to the right, another opening, a passageway leading between shops, no doubt to a back courtyard and beyond. I could have plunged into either one and gone after her. But the vision I had of Luisa could have been my imagination. And if she was real, she was fleeing me again. And if she was the shooter, she might just add a *gringo* journalist to her list of rapacious priest and collaborating local official. I shuddered to think what body part of mine she'd shoot off.

12

I walked away, telling myself to get my story priorities straight. The sardonic sniper was marginal as war news, even if I could figure out a way to identify her and even if it turned out to be Luisa Morales, which I remained unconvinced of. The mystery German had the whiff of something important. But at least the directness of the sniper's approach to collaborators led me now to a simple, similarly straight-forward plan.

So I found myself on the doorstep of the German Consulate on *Avenida Cinco de Mayo*. The door quickly opened to my knock and re-vealed a blond young man in a field-gray Uhlan uniform with captain pips on his tunic shoulder boards. A cavalryman on consular attaché duty. He had steely blue eyes and a Kaiser Wilhelm mustache so pale it felt as if I were looking at the ghostly specter of a dark mustache that had died and refused to move on along to its eternal fate.

Living the early life I did with my mother, traveling with her always as she toured not only the United States but South America and Europe and beyond, I eventually learned good Spanish, passable French, and workable parts of other Romance languages, but I also picked up strange rudimentary bits—more sounds than words—from the Germanic and Slovak linguistic cousins of those others. My Ger-man was more double-talk than anything, more an acting talent, ab-sorbed from all those years at the backs of theaters or in the wings and from hanging around dressing rooms and eating and drinking and sleeping in boardinghouses with actors and actresses and with the voices and dialects they put on. So I greeted this young man in Spanish, which I figured he would know, given his posting.

"*Bitte reinkommen,*" he said, stepping aside and motioning for me to come in even before I said what it was I wanted. I figured he hadn't had the time or the imperial inclination to learn the local language. My little bit of German would make me sound like a madman. I didn't know what our common ground might be, but I wasn't intending to pretend to be anyone other than who I was, so I said in English, slowly pronouncing each word, "I am a newspaperman."

"*Ach, so,*" he said, seeming to understand.

"I write for the *Chicago Post-Express,*" I said.

He nodded.

I offered my hand. "I am Christopher Marlowe Cobb," I said, the Germans I'd known in America loving the long elaborateness of names.

He took my hand and shook it, looking me steadily in the eyes.

Though he did not speak his own name in return, I continued to sense he knew what I was saying. Just in case, to establish German-friendly credentials, I said, "I also write for the *Post-Express* syndicate, which includes the Chicago *Abendpost.* They translate my . . ."

The young man cut me off by speaking pretty damn good English. "I have some family in Milwaukee Avenue, one uncle and three *Vetter* . . . Sorry. Cousins. I have three cousins also. They read the *Illinois Staats-Zeitung.* A more powerful newspaper."

I was not sure what unsettled me most: his nearly perfect English, his relatives in Chicago, or his tightly clenching his right fist as he stressed the word "powerful."

Perhaps the hand was the most unsettling, since as soon as it finished clenching, it shot out to me, demanding mine, which I offered and which he shook firmly with the announcement, "Captain Hans-Peter Krüger." He let go of my hand, clicked his heels, and bowed ever so slightly at the waist.

"*Kapitän* Krüger." I bowed as well.

"*Bitte,*" he said, motioning to a pair of armchairs facing a dark wood desk to my left. And then instantly, as if correcting himself: "Please."

I headed for a chair as he circled the desk. "Your uncle's also probably a Cubs fan," I said, the Cubs being the more powerful Chicago team. I didn't expect him to hear the little bit of a needle I was giving him, or even understand the reference. Indeed, *Herr Kapitän* Krüger simply ignored the comment. Meanwhile, I was taking in as much of the place as I could without seeming to.

This front room was large and sparsely furnished, with everything made of the same carved mahogany. Out the far door was a sun-filled courtyard, which was, at the moment, empty.

I sat, though I angled myself slightly to keep the courtyard in the periphery of my vision. Krüger was already stiffly upright in his chair.

Behind him hung a large, framed, color lithograph of the Kaiser, beribboned, bemedaled, and with a massive eagle sitting on his helmet.

"Have you spent time in Chicago?" I asked.

"Spent?" I could see his brain sorting through his American idioms. "Ah. Yes. I am in Chicago for one year when I am a boy."

"Good."

"It was not the Fatherland," he said. I got the feeling he had just clenched that right fist under the desk.

"Not yours," I said.

"Not the Fatherland for my uncle and my aunt."

"I understand," I said, filling a brief pause.

"Not for my three cousins," he said, not wanting to let any of his family escape his disapproval.

"They were your *drei Vetter,*" I said.

I was aware that sometimes my reflex, low-grade sarcasm undercut my full effectiveness as a newspaperman. I should have wanted to smooth this guy's Germanic feathers, not ruffle them. This remark could go either way. But almost at once he smiled. "Just so," he said. "Just so."

Captain Krüger was without irony.

We looked at each other a moment. I was still improvising here, as I often did when I was seeking a thing in someone's head and I wasn't quite sure even what category of thing it might be.

"How may I help you, Herr Cobb?" he asked.

"Your country is a good friend to Mexico. For my readers—Germans in America and all my other American readers as well—I would very much like to get the German point of view about my country's invasion of Mexico."

It is important to stress at this point that I am an American, through and through. I am a patriot. If I think Woodrow Wilson and William Jennings Bryan are a couple of ninnyhammers, they are our democratically elected and legally appointed ninnyhammers, respectively, and my right to think and say these things about them is part and parcel of my being a patriotic American. But I am also a reporter. I would not normally have been speaking loosely about the ninnyhammerness of my country's leaders to a foreigner, especially a German, but there was a journalistic goal here that could eventually better inform my fellow patriots, which is also part of being an American, having the right to be well and openly and vigorously informed.

So I leaned hard on the word "invasion" in spite of Woody's sudden disavowal of further hostile intentions, which, actually, was a worse sin in the opinion of a lot of patriotic Americans, which was, indeed, the reason he had every American military man—not to mention all us news boys—fidgeting and fretting and fuming in Vera Cruz. Wilson's public pose was that this was a simple operation to stop the German ship from unloading its munitions. But I figured every German official in Mexico thought otherwise. Krüger eyed me carefully for a moment. Finally he said, "You should be speaking to the embassy in Mexico City."

"No American can go farther than El Tejar without being arrested," I said.

"Or shot." Krüger surprised me with this addendum, delivered quickly and with a little too much intensity, accurate though it was. A very faint smile brisked across his lips and vanished. He may have had no irony, but he thought he had a sense of humor.

"You understand the problem," I said.

"I am not authorized to speak," he said.

"Forgive me, *Kapitän,* for not knowing your chain of command. Is there no one here to consult?"

I knew, in fact, that there was a civilian consular officer at the end of that chain.

Krüger looked me in the eyes for another long moment. I returned the gaze steadily. If I flinched, if I looked away, I suspected he would say no. He might have anyway. Our gaze went on for another beat and another.

Then he rose from his chair.

"Wait, please. I will inquire," he said.

He did a crisp left-face and moved across the room and through the open door into the courtyard, turning at once to the left and vanishing.

I waited a few moments and then rose from my chair, slowly, casually, as if I was being observed. I might have been. I looked at Wilhelm for a few moments. And I thought of Wilhelm and Wilson. Wilhelm and Wilson and Asquith and Poincaré. And Czar Nicholas. And Sultan Mehmed and Count Stürgkh. And, since I was standing where I was standing, I wouldn't let myself forget Willie's right-hand boy Theobald von Bethmann-Hollweg. Leaders of the world. What a bunch. A good war correspondent's ardent employers. And I thought they would soon figure out how to find us more work. Quite soon.

I'd stared at the lithograph long enough. I drifted, quite nonchalantly, to the doorway leading to the courtyard. The blue and white pavement tiles were faded from decades of sun. The rosebushes were severely pruned and the stone fountain in the center was dry. There were voices from one of the doorways along the upper-floor gallery. To my left. A distant churn of guttural German sounds. Krüger and his boss. I didn't expect anything from them. And then a door was opening on the right-hand upper gallery. I took a small step back, without losing my line of sight.

It was the tall man from the ship in the night. I could see his face for a brief moment, which moved me instantly farther backward, totally out of sight. I really didn't expect anyone to reveal himself here. Or speak to me. I just needed to get near all this, put details in my head that might be useful. I certainly didn't want to be seen by the tall man. If eventually I had to follow him, I did not want to be familiar to his eye. But I now had a clear image of his face, from the flash of it before me, and that much was valuable. Deep-set eyes. I did not catch their color, from this distance, but they certainly were not dark. Probably good, standard, Aryan aristocratic blue. And yes: His left cheek had the livid curve of an old fencing scar, his *Schmiss,* his smite, his medal of academic honor.

I sat down once more in my chair before the desk, and soon Captain Krüger returned. He did not sit. He stood behind the desk, his arms stiff at his sides. "I am sorry, Herr Cobb. We have nothing to say."

"I'm sorry to hear that, *Kapitän* Krüger," I said.

I rose. I added, "It was only from respect for your country's opinions that I have sought you out."

"We are aware of that," Krüger said. "And we offer to you our thanks."

He bowed at the waist. I bowed at the waist. I repressed the impulse to ask the reporter's classically abrupt, unexpectedly knowledgeable question, in this case something like: Oh, and one other small thing, *Kapitän,* what is the mission of the important German official who snuck in here in the middle of the night from the *Ypiranga?* But I could think of nothing Krüger might say in flustered response worth my revealing that I knew something was going on.

13

Almost as soon as I was on the street again, heading back toward my rooms and a siesta, which was a local custom I'd quickly taken to, I knew the story I'd file later today. West of the city, out in the Fourth District, a thick column of velvety black smoke was billowing up. I could feel the smoke in my nose, even from this distance, and in it, playing a feature duet downstage of the backup band of Vera Cruz street-carrion and sewage, were two distinct smells: crude oil and burning flesh. I'd known this moment was coming since after the first couple of days, so I'd already done the story's back-matter reporting in preparation. Most of the locals continued to refuse to step up and claim the dead bodies of their countrymen. So the time had come for the Marines to burn the corpses. A nasty little story with popular appeal that would glide through the censors pretty much untouched, given a developing theme of our boys doing the necessary dirty work of civilization for a semi-savage people. A theme that had its own smell, to tell the truth, but the Army had its message and we had our papers to sell.

It's funny how fast you can stop noticing a smell. Even a strong one. This is fortunate for a war correspondent. If you're in the right places most of the time, it's a foul-smelling job. There is always something dying or burning or exploding, and there are always newspaper-selling twists to put on stories. So by the time I got to my rooms and closed the door and found my clean laundry on my bed, my nose had calmed down, and I stepped away from my job and this town and the war, and the thought of Luisa came back to me, pretty much instantly, prompted by the American newspaper assumptions about Mexicans—how she'd hate that—but mostly prompted by my pants and shirts lying neatly folded there on my bed. It was like when I first saw her, sassing me in this room, and then a little later. I stepped to the doorway to the courtyard, half expecting to see her lounging once more under the banana tree, having reconsidered her new life, knowing I'd overlook the pistol to my head and welcome her back, even if she wouldn't jump into bed with me.

She wasn't there, of course. But the other two girls were. They were curled on pallets in the shade of the banana tree and they were fast asleep. Slim, sweet-faced girls, their arms bare in their work blouses, their knees tucked invisibly up under their skirts so only their bare feet showed. One of the girls arched her feet, flaring her toes from whatever it was that she was dreaming. I stepped quietly into the courtyard and took a few steps toward them, not wanting to disturb them, just being drawn in a tender way to their vulnerable obliviousness.

And now I was in a boardinghouse. Where? Providence maybe. Or Boston. It was noon and the sunlight was so bright outside that it illuminated the bed through the lowered, foxed window shade. Mother had a matinee in a couple of hours and she was taking her traditional fifteen-minute "goodly nap," and perhaps on this afternoon she was playing Kate in *Shrew*, where the "goodly nap" comes from. Whatever the play, whatever town this was, I watched her lying there on top of the covers, clutching the pillow to her bosom, as she always did, and I was not yet a teen, not yet able even to grow chin-whiskers, but I stood beside her bed on this day for every one of her fifteen minutes of sleep and I watched her dark-stockinged right foot tap briefly in her dream, tap upon the air, though in her dream upon some floor, I thought, and I watched her foot stop and she pressed the pillow tighter against her and her eyes moved beneath her closed lids. I watched her eyes move, as she saw someone or something that I could not. And I felt very close to my mother in that moment, and I felt very distant from her. I felt I could never really know her. Ever.

The washer girl who flared her toes suddenly opened her eyes. And they widened as she found me looking directly at her. She sat up abruptly, too quickly for having just awakened: Her eyes closed again and she tilted a little to the left, but then she straightened and opened her eyes once more and rubbed them briefly with the knuckles of her forefingers, and she looked at me steadily, clearly.

"I'm sorry, miss," I said, making my Spanish soft and precise. And I was aware now that I instinctively called these girls "señorita" and not "*muchacha*," which was the overtly patronizing mode of address that you were expected to use with a washer girl, and I thought how my doing this was something Luisa might have found to my credit.

"It's nothing," this girl before me said. Her eyes stayed fixed on mine and were softly inquiring in a way that told me something I was reluctant to hear, given my recent track record. Reluctant but also eager, I realized, my eagerness likely to quickly prevail.

"You need your sleep," I said.

"I have had enough," she said. "Are your clothes okay?"

"I haven't examined them yet."

"I am the one doing your clothes now," she said.

"I am glad it's you," I said. I almost asked her if she owned a pistol—in the spirit of flirting banter—I felt with some confidence now that we were flirting—but I was not sure she knew the whole story of Luisa's departure, and if she didn't, this would be the wrong approach altogether.

"I am glad you are glad," she said and her eyes had not moved from me for even a second, and now she smiled.

"I am glad that you are glad that I am glad," I said. It was not very original, but it survived the translation into Spanish quite well, it seemed to me.

"I am not like her," she said.

And she wasn't.

I offered my hand and she took it and she rose and we went to my bed.

I am aware that I am not a subtle man in these matters. I am far more subtle with words, though I am a man of almost no words in these matters. Something urgent and quickly commenced and not a little brutal-seeming comes over me with a woman who is willing to offer her body, and most of these bodies seem actually to appreciate the urgency and the simplicity and the ersatz violence. Not that I fail to be knocked out with a different sort of feeling by watching, from a few steps away, their eyes moving in sleep or their toes flaring. But to then get much closer to them brings on another, quite different, contradictory mood. And isn't the stuff of my career a darker variety of this human contradiction? The men across the field in battle were often men we could, in other circumstances, clap upon the shoulder and have a tankard of ale with and sing a drunken song with and in doing so become long-sought pals. But in this circumstance, across the field, all of us on both sides being patriots, we kill them. And they would kill us. Toward the very same people we can, at turns, feel tender and we can feel hurtful. Sometimes a little, sometimes a lot.

These are things I know about myself and sometimes think about and they were things I thought about even in the midst of what I was doing with this washer girl. When we were done, she and I, and when my thoughts ceased wandering, I did kiss her sweetly on the lips and I said I hoped she was all right, and she kissed me back and said she was fine. Then she rose and smoothed down her skirt and she went away.

I too rose, and I put my pants on, but I lay back down on the bed, and I clasped my hands behind my head, and I found myself worrying about my mother. She was singing for rowdies in New Orleans. I had not let myself think past that fact, and now I was wondering which rowdies they might be. She might have been singing in a nightspot in any of several parts of town where the crowd could get rough, in any number of saloons in the French Quarter, for example, but I was suddenly worried that she was singing in Storyville, that she had somehow been drawn into Storyville and her employers were playing on her stage fame, which lingered around her, of course, playing on that and her vanity, and on her liberal attitudes about women and their bodies. For going on two decades, prostitution had been legal from Basin Street to Robertson, from Iberville to St. Louis Street, twenty square blocks just north of the French Quarter, and this place called Storyville, or by the locals "The District," was packed not just with quick-time cribs but with fancy mansion bordellos and saloons and dance halls and cabarets, all of which featured the very best music, not only in New Orleans but pretty much in the world. They had ragtime, and even newer music than that, the new jazz, and there were singers, too, singing for the men packed in and drinking hard and getting rowdy, a few of them maybe there for the music but most of them just working up to sex. And not just in the bordellos but in the other places too; no matter if their front-of-the-house business was dancing or drinking or singing, they all had a covey of girls, upstairs or in the back rooms or in your lap ready to take you around the corner to their cribs.

And Mother had said in her telegram that she was watching over those who could use watching over, and my remembering that remark made me sit up quick here in my bed in Vera Cruz, where I'd just made it rough and good with a Mexican washer girl, and I knew what my mother was talking about. She was talking about the girls upstairs in some mansion in Storyville, and of course she had a soft spot for them. She was an actress, after all. My mother was the finest actress who ever trod the boards, but every church pastor in the country who wanted to mealymouth around the word "whore" declared that the dreaded white slavers were turning girls into "actresses." The country loved their actresses and in some intense ways admired their actresses, but at the same time most of the country had it in the back of their minds that these women were all, more or less, whores. And wasn't that contradiction, in its own way, like the contradiction shared by both sex and war?

And I was lying in my bed in Vera Cruz, but I was also out in the hallway where Mother had put me. I was a kid and she'd kissed me on the forehead and promised that it wouldn't be too long and this was in a rooming house somewhere near a good theater in a big city, and all through rehearsals she'd had the leading man wrapped around her finger and finally it was their opening night. They were thumping and shouting in there, and I worried now, in Vera Cruz, for her weakness and for how she was afraid of getting old and how she was fighting that. She walked off the stage and maybe she walked into a high-class whorehouse where she sang and she took care of the girls and she felt young. Trust her in this, she'd said in her telegram.

But I didn't. I could only think: *Sorry, mother of mine. You need to be helped, whether you are able to realize it or not.* But I was out doing my job, and so I had no choice but to trust her to get through whatever this was.

I did, however, rise from the bed in Vera Cruz and go to the rickety desk in the corner. I took Mother's cable from the drawer. Western Union via New Orleans Central. The main office on St. Charles and Gravier. I could write her a cable care of St. Charles and Gravier, and if I couldn't tell Western Union how to go find her, maybe she would at least think to come see if I'd sent a reply and she would find it.

My eyes fell now to the text of her cable, and her comment about playing a "dark role" leaped up at me. This was another of her weaknesses, though it went with her profession: She saw everything she did, even off the stage, as playing a role. Everything was always bigger than life, which made everything not quite real, made everything feel familiar in a professional way, in a way you'd spent your life masterfully controlling. You were just acting, grandly, for the back row of the balcony. Always. And that made most things feel safe. Which was fine if you were just unreasonably scared of the dark. But if there was a real danger, if someone bad had slipped into the darkness of your room and was just out of sight, this weakness of my mother's could be very dangerous indeed.

But I needed to make things a little safer for myself now. I always did that by writing words. So I rolled a cable blank into my Corona Portable Number 3, which sat in the center of the desk. I could dash off quick stories by hand in the *portales,* but my real writing was done with my friend, my pal, my typewriter. He went to the Balkans with me. Before that he went to Nicaragua with me, when he was brand-new, new to me and new to the world. The marvel of the age, the six-pound Corona 3. With his carriage folding forward over the keyboard, he fit into a case smaller than a bread box. But he took my words and made them real.

I put my fingertips upon his keys and I would write my mother a cable.

I didn't know what to say.

I knew many things that it would be useless to say. Advice and warnings and cajolings. Many things that she would sniff at or turn from or—if I were in her presence and said them—that would cause her to take a bit of my cheek between her thumb and forefinger and pinch it hard, very hard, even though I was thirty years old. "My Kit," she would say, "my silly sweet Kit Cobb, mind your own bloody business."

My fingertips sat on the keys for a long while until I thought to interpret for her a passage from my namesake. From his *Jew of Malta*. I wrote:

Dearest Mother. Though he freely admits to the friar that he hath committed fornication, Barabas, who if he were not a usurer would be a rowdy man, quite easily can say "But that was in another country, and besides, the wench is dead." Take care you understand your unconventional audience. Love from your Kit

14

Sundown this same day and I'd filed my corpse-burning story and I'd sent my cable to Mother and I was at my table in the *portales* taking my first *aguardiente* slow. I was also wondering if we'd hear from our girl sniper again before the day was done. Bunky showed up and sat. He and I and all the other veteran newsmen had our routines now. Your little routines are a hedge against the madness of the job. But when it's all routine and no madness, that's the worst for a war correspondent, when you're in a faux war and you end up trying to create stories out of something other than real battle that you're in the middle of, stories without real artillery and real gunfire and the movement of troops and without men dying for causes or for politicians or for both. And yes, without the possibility of your own death right there at your elbow all the while.

"Evening, Pops," I said.

"That going to become a habit?" he asked.

"The *aguardiente* at sundown?"

"Calling me 'Pops.'"

"That was just the second time, I think."

Bunky leaned toward me, which was his way of showing he was serious about something. "Twice in two days," he said. "Three time's a pattern. Four's a habit. I thought I'd intervene now, if we were heading there."

"'Bunky' then. Forever."

"Bunky's good."

I found myself with an odd little twist in the stomach. I told myself it was the *aguardiente*, not this thing about "Pops," but I took another drink to make sure the feeling went away, and it did.

"You find out about Davis and the sniper?" I said.

"He can be sly, but from all I can make out, he didn't file a story."

"He wouldn't be sly on this one," I said. "He probably just tucked it away as local color for a magazine feature."

So Bunky and I drank for a little while, and I only half listened to his familiar monologue about the way the censors have ruined war, from a newspaper's point of view, and if the government was going to lie, then the newspapers should also feel free to lie, though I knew Bunky didn't mean that, and then I wasn't listening to him at all so I could just drink *aguardiente* and not worry about a thing for an hour or two.

Before you knew it, the night had come upon us and the near-full moon was perched on the mountaintops, bloated and yellow, and the German band had been playing beyond the trees for quite a while already. Bunky had fallen silent, the effect of his own drinking. He'd gotten to his silent stage. And suddenly I was aware of the music in the air. I recognized Richard Wagner. Something from *Lohengrin*, I thought. Not that I'd been following their whole program carefully these past couple of nights, but this was the first German music I'd heard the German band play.

And then they played the *Kaisermarsch*, also Wagner. Mother had a fling in New York with a German orchestra conductor at some point when I was still around, and I got to know Wagner's music a little too well for my taste. This piece honored a Kaiser of about forty years ago and usually had a German men's chorus going *Heil! Heil! dem Kaiser!* The horns were doing that part from the band shell. And it struck me as odd, two German songs in a row all of a sudden, and I was on my feet and crossing the *avenida*.

I entered the *zócalo*. Up ahead, the band shell was lit by incandescent lamps. The rest of the Plaza was in darkness and the angle of the moon was still low, so we were all just dark shapes moving about or lined up on the benches. Only a few figures were standing in the light from the *kiosko*. Many of the moving figures were heading away from the music now. The concert was almost over, certainly, but these were not tunes for them.

That suspicion was what stood me up and brought me quickly here. And sure enough. Three figures were standing shoulder to shoulder in the light up ahead, apart from the locals, and as soon as I saw them I stopped, while I was still well-shrouded in the dark. I did not want to be seen by these three: Captain Krüger; a stout man in shirt-sleeves, unfamiliar to me but who I'd have been willing to bet was the head of the consulate; and my man from the *Ypiranga,* the tall man with the fencing scar, wearing his white linen suit. They were standing stiffly, facing the *Kaisermarsch* as if they were all about to salute in unison. I moved off the path and leaned against a tree, effectively hidden now, though still able to observe.

The *Kaisermarsch* ended, and the three men did indeed touch their right temples in precise military salutes, the two apparent civilians as meticulously correct in the execution of the gesture as *der Kapitän.* They released the salute, and they stepped forward as the musicians began to put aside their instruments. The bandmaster came to the edge of the stand to greet them, and more salutes were exchanged. Krüger hung back a little as the two civilians worked the front edge of the bandstand like politicians, shaking hands with the musicians for a time.

When the three were done with all this, they bowed and saluted and made a fine Germanic fuss of respect for the whole band, and they turned and started up the path. I slid a little farther behind the tree as they strolled past, talking low, moving casually. I considered following them, but I was certain they would simply lead me back to the consulate. I looked toward the band shell. The musicians had known from sight to crank up the Fatherland's Favorites. Krüger and the head of the consulate could easily have been familiar to them. But maybe the man with the scar was too.

They were all on their feet now, packing their instruments, at least some of them ready, I suspect, to head somewhere to drink. I figured I could do with a drink myself and maybe a little manly shoulder-clapping and drunken song-singing. I might even find a long-sought pal who knew something useful.

15

A few of the dozen or so band members headed off separately, and the rest stayed together till they got to *Independencia*. Then the group broke in two, with one part heading toward the *portales* and the other part, four of the musicians, including the bandleader and the alto horn player who seemed to recognize me, hopping a trolley south. It was an easy choice: I lagged behind the four, who boarded and moved to the front of the car, and I stepped up with the clang of the bell and I sat down at once on the right-hand, straw-seated, lateral bench. They were in twos now, facing each other on the opposing benches, talking volubly in German, their cased instruments standing on the floor between their feet. The alto man was pretty much out of sight, on my side of the car and beyond the trombonist. The bandmaster sat directly opposite him. I'd wait till we were all in the same place, drinking, to make a point of my presence.

Across from me at this end of the car were a couple of hayseed-blond Bluejackets, who could have been brothers, dressed in their tropical whites and looking antsy. I realized I'd been assuming the Germans were just going somewhere to drink together, but this was the route to the red-light district, and for a moment I was afraid I wouldn't have access to them. But the evening, though not quite young, wasn't yet middle-aged, so if they wanted girls—and even if they wanted to impress them with their uniforms—they probably would have at least unloaded their instruments before heading off. This still felt like some guys heading straight for a drink.

And I was right. They rose from their seats one stop short of the girls, and I followed them off the trolley, leaving my fellow Americans to go on along the line to a little Navy-sanctioned, country-boy sin. I hung back a bit and watched these four enter a *pulquería*, a one-story adobe house a bit larger than the usual, identifying itself by the bands of brightly colored tissue paper strung over its open doorway. They were four Germans with a taste for *pulque*. This was a quick-fermenting drink from the maguey plant, the Mexican national working-man's drink with about the same mild kick and certainly the same ubiquity as the band members' lager.

I gave them a few minutes to settle in, and then I entered the place, which stank sourly of the *pulque*. The boys from the band were at a back table with tankards of this stuff. The front tables were full of locals, mostly with dark, angular Aztec faces, the ones drinking *pulque* talking, the ones doing the distilled version, which was basically *mezcal,* looking glum. I went to the wooden counter that was not quite a bar but offered a place to stand if you were of a mind to, and I got my own tankard. I stared at it a little while before drinking, as if I could change how it would taste. I needed to drink some before looking at my Germans, just to make all this seem to have been casual when I started asking questions.

The *pulque* was just as I remembered from my days hanging around this country in '04, on my own, glad to be away from an endless succession of theaters, even Mother knowing it was time I went out and found a different kind of life, a life of my own. To her credit. You'd think with me being twenty years old, dreaming of becoming a newspaperman like B. F. Millerman, writing stories on cable blanks in Mexican cantinas with no one to send them to, and then finally writing a real story about the madman Nicolás Zúñiga in his third futile run against the tyrant Díaz and mailing it to the *Post-Express,* which started my career, you'd think whatever there was at that point in my life that served the function of beer, that stuff would strike me as swell. You'd think so, but that would be wrong. The *pulque* still looked like watered-down wallpaper paste and tasted like sour milk and yeast and faintly like something dead, just as it did a decade ago. But I kept a straight face.

I looked toward the Germans. And the alto horn man was looking toward me. He nodded very slightly. I nodded very slightly. The other three were in voluble conversation with each other, and this one guy seemed a little apart from them. The obvious thing would have been to use this as an invitation to go over and join the Germans. Buddy up with all of them at once and prep them for a few questions. But this one man, catching my eye on two different occasions: My instinct told me to deal with him individually first. Then if I decided I needed them all, he could be my way into the group.

There was a scraping of a chair nearby, and I turned to see one of the *mezcal* drinkers at this end of the room rise from a small table where he was alone. He wobbled there for a moment and then weaved his way to the door. I glanced at Alto Horn and he was still looking at me. I angled my head very slightly to the empty table and headed for it. I sat. He arrived and sat across from me. Nearly in unison, we set our tankards of *pulque* before us. He was older than his thinness made him seem from a distance. Beside his eyes were fine webs of lines and between his brows were two permanent furrows. He was probably pushing forty. Or, if he was younger, he was a serious worrier.

We offered our hands and shook. "Gerhard Vogel," he said.

"Christopher Cobb," I said, and then, in German: "I don't speak German."

He nodded at this and did not answer. He was looking at me closely. Very briefly I thought my German was even worse than I'd realized. But it was not incomprehension in Gerhard Vogel's face. There was something about the eyes that a reporter learns. But how do we read eyes? Part of this man was studying me closely and that should narrow his eyes. Part of him sought to open up to me and that should widen his eyes. These things canceled themselves out, and by rights, by an objective glance at him, his eyes should have seemed neutral. But you learn to feel this opposition of forces, and so his eyes were telling me: I want to reveal something but I don't know if I can trust you. If it was something critical for a story and he wanted me to forget it utterly after he said it, he couldn't trust me. As for some other conditions—keeping his name out of it, for instance—I was his man. I waited.

He made a decision. He lowered his voice and leaned a bit toward me. "I speak English," he said in English.

I glanced over his shoulder. The other three Germans were still involved in an animated conversation. They seemed not even to be aware that Gerhard was across the room.

"They don't know," he said.

Hell's bells was my first thought. If that made him nervous, I was unlikely to get anything important out of him. "That's a secret?" I said.

Gerhard shrugged. "It was a long time ago."

"That you were an American?"

"Yes."

"Then it's just between us," I said.

"I know who you are," Gerhard said.

"Don't worry," I said. "Your speaking English wouldn't exactly be a story for the *Post-Express.*"

"From your Balkans pieces in *Scribner's.*"

"Which you read in secret?"

"From a couple of pictures of you there, one with the Greek dead at Kilkis and one in Sofia," he said, finishing his thought. And then: "I play in the band. I live in Germany. But I do have a private life."

I heard myself, how I'd sounded with him for the past few moments: snide. I wasn't sure why I was disliking him.

"Your writing style is very clean," he said.

"Thank you," I said, trying to turn up the warmth in my voice.

"Very Tinker-to-Evers-to-Chance," he said.

And now I liked him. A lot. To compare my writing to those boys turning a slick double play? How could I not? "Man oh man," I said. "You a Cubs fan?"

"I hate the Cubs. But I appreciated the way they played."

"You do have secrets."

"The Pirates were my team," he said.

"Keep that one strictly to yourself."

He shrugged.

"You from Pittsburgh?" I asked.

"Eventually," he said.

"When did you leave the States?"

"'07."

"Couldn't handle the Cubs winning the Series?"

"My new wife hated being away from Germany. We went."

I was thinking more clearly now. Trying to figure this guy out. I flipped my chin to gesture over his shoulder. "They don't know about her?"

"She died the next year."

"I'm sorry."

He shrugged again. Indistinguishable from his shrug over my ragging him about being a Pirates fan. Maybe I was better at reading eyes than shrugs, but his voice carried a little tremor of actual feeling about that turn of events, so the sameness of the shrug seemed very sad.

"You stayed," I said.

He didn't seem to understand.

"In Germany after she died."

"I stayed," he said.

I watched him reading me the way I just did him: He thought I wasn't understanding. "By then," Gerhard said, "I was in the *Hüttner Kapelle.* A very good orchestra in Dortmund."

That was all he said. I didn't press him about the leap from a good orchestra in a concert hall in Dortmund to a brass band in a public park in Vera Cruz. With a potential source you have only a certain amount in your reporter's goodwill bank account. You can press him only a finite number of times. I'd keep something in my account for later, for more important questions.

But I did say, "That wasn't such a long time ago."

He didn't understand.

"Seven years. You said it was a long time ago that you were an American."

He gave me a faint, ironic smile. "It seems long."

I could have grilled him more. How if it seemed like a long time that he had not been an American and if he was no longer in the very good German orchestra and if the woman who caused him to leave America in the first place was dead, why the next move was Mexico with a German brass band and not back to the States. We've got plenty of band shells in plenty of parks in the U. S. of A. But it was not his story I was interested in.

As his odd little smile faded, he took a drink, his tankard rising high as he drained the last bit.

"Let me get you another of those," I said.

I didn't wait for an answer but grabbed his empty and headed for the wooden bar, where the tankards were topped off and lined up ready, and I brought a full one back to the table.

He took it with a nod as I sat. His "thanks" felt almost like an afterthought.

"You like this stuff?" I said.

"No."

"If you're going to hate the taste anyway, you can try the *mezcal*."

He shrugged again. All the shrugs were alike. "Wherever I want to end up by drinking," he said, "I need to get there slow."

"Or else you might start talking English."

He flipped his head in a little laugh that sounded more like a snort. He took a sip of the *pulque*.

"It's not just your style," he said. "You dig up the dope and you write it straight."

He caught me off guard with one of my own tricks. Get a thing halfway into the conversation and leave it, and then, when it is mostly forgotten, abruptly return to it. Not that it made me say anything, not that he was even trying to get me to, but I leaned back in my chair and he'd gotten me off my own tack.

Then his use of "dope" registered on me. "So you played the horses before you took off for the Fatherland," I said.

Now he was the one to sit back. After a few beats of silence, he said, "She saved me from that."

It was the right thing to say to shut me up for a while.

I lifted my tankard to him.

He lifted his, and we touched them.

We drank.

The tankards went down to the table.

The Germans at the back of the room brayed in sudden laughter. Anyone watching Gerhard and me would have thought we never even heard it.

We drank again and we both seemed to be waiting for something.

I said, "For a German band, you boys play a lot of American music."

"Ragtime and Broadway," he said. "That's our colonial empire. We'll rule the world."

"We?"

He looked at me like I was a damn fool. "Red, white, and blue," he said. "Why do you think I'm sitting at this table?"

"So what's what with the Wagner tonight?"

There was a stopping in him. But not like I'd caught him in something. He pulled in a breath and held it and nodded very faintly, like he'd been waiting for it to get around to this. But he said, "I don't know."

This guy was like reading a book in bed by candlelight and you're getting very sleepy. You run your eyes over words that seem familiar, but they're not sticking together to make sense.

"You figure it was for your visitors?" I said.

"Obviously," he said.

So I threw the fastball down the center of the plate. "Who's the tall man?" I asked.

You keep looking for little clues in the people you work on for the dope. He was giving me plenty of them, but I couldn't quite put them together. He'd suddenly gone very quiet. Whatever stopped in him when I asked about the Wagner was going again, but he was quiet. His hands were still. His eyes were steady. If anything, they were looking at me like he was disappointed. He just wanted an American drinking buddy, one who also happened to be in the magazines, and I was grilling him. After a few beats of silence that felt much longer, he said, "I don't know."

I wanted to ask him what took him so long to come around to saying that, if he didn't know. Normally I wouldn't have believed him. But I did, somehow.

Especially when he added, "He was striking. I wondered myself."

"'Striking' is a good word for him," I said.

"You have any ideas?" he said.

"He's your guy. Don't look at me." I realized I was sounding snide again. I thought to try to back out of it a bit. "I said he's yours since you're playing in a German band in Mexico instead of going back home to a band shell in Pittsburgh." Which maybe didn't quite sound snide but sure wasn't a backpedal.

In fact, he should have gotten wired up by that. But he didn't. He just seemed to get quieter.

So I said to him, "I'm sounding like a Cub fan ragging a Pirate fan. You and the boys make good music in a warm climate. It's not my place . . ."

He waved off the half-assed apology. "You're doing your job," he said.

I nodded at him. A thanks-for-understanding nod.

And he said, "I should get back to the boys." He dragged out "the boys" enough to let me know he was quoting me. He did it without cracking a smile. Okay. I deserved that.

"Maybe we'll have another drink sometime without all the racket," I said.

He said, "If I hear anything about the tall man I'll let you know."

"Good." And if he was serious about that offer, I had a thought that might help him get me what I wanted. Better him with this approach than me. I said, "Maybe your bandmaster knows something."

Gerhard gave me another thoughtful but unreadable look.

Then he said, "You mind doing the same? If you hear something? You've got me curious."

I didn't answer right away and he laughed the closest thing to a real laugh I'd heard from him, though it left a faint afterclap of irony.

"I promise I won't scoop you," he said.

I lifted my drink to him.

He lifted his and said, " I have a room at the *Hostal Buen Viaje.* On *Calle de Montesinos* near the station."

I nodded a thanks at this. "I'm beneath the *portales* of the *Diligencias* every morning," I said.

We touched tankards and they clanged like a distant fire bell.

16

When I stepped out of the *pulquería*, leaving Gerhard Vogel with his German buddies and his secret *Scribner's*, I was not aware that something had happened one stop up the trolley line, wouldn't learn about it till I was drinking my morning coffee in the *portales*. I took a few paces toward the center of the cobbled street, out almost to the trolley tracks, just to get away from the stink of the *pulque*, which was stronger now because I was carrying traces of it in my mouth. The more or less full moon was high, and spotted along this block of drinking joints were a few electric lamps, one of them across the street and thirty yards or so down to my right. I was lit up by the moon, with more light just down the street. And things were quiet. Even the *pulquería* behind me was keeping its sounds tight to itself now. Or maybe it had fallen silent in there. Maybe Gerhard chilled down his friends. I bet he had that effect.

The trolley lines suddenly sputtered and sparked above me. It happened, and it was over. Just a brief surge of electricity. The electric demons muttering in their sleep. There were no trolleys in sight. A dog barked somewhere. The night wasn't anything you'd call cool, but its mitigation of the heat felt good and I turned in the direction of the harbor and my bed, and I started to walk.

From the first step, my mind began working on the tall man with the fencing scar, and the thought I had was that I was a war correspondent without a real war who was trying to make something out of nothing just to keep himself from going crazy. But that guy had been sitting out there on the German ship for a few days, and then he came in like a sneak thief in the night. And yet, less than twenty-four hours later, he was willing to be seen in the center of town. All right. So he couldn't stay hidden forever. So maybe he promenaded in the *zócalo* so he wouldn't seem to be a suspicious figure. There he was in the open. He came in secretly simply to avoid an association with the *Ypiranga,* so nobody would have a reason to think he had a special mission of some sort. Without that association, he was just another German at the consulate. Overlooked heretofore, but nobody to lift an eyebrow about.

These were quick thoughts, and with another little crackle of electricity overhead I came up out of them. I was passing the streetlamp and maybe I saw a little something in my periphery. A little bit of movement. Not enough even to make me turn my head. I kept taking steps, that next one and the next and I passed from the piss-yellow lamplight and into the moonlight white as a corpse, and it was only now that my defenses started prickling up my skin. I'd been away from battle too long. But here I was with the instinct to duck.

I didn't. I stopped. I turned.

At first I saw no one. Because I was looking into the spill of light around the lamp. It was the area where I thought I saw movement a few moments ago, so it was where I was inclined now to look. Once again I was about to curse the jumpiness induced by inaction in Vera Cruz, but something registered on me. Beyond the far fringe of lamplight I dimly made out a figure. Facing this way. The figure moved toward me. The clothes were black: jacket and pants tucked into high, laced boots. A black sombrero. A slim young man, to my eye.

If I knew at that moment what I would know not very many hours later, that a Bluejacket in his tropical whites coming out of a bordello up the trolley line had only a short time ago been shot in his left buttock by a sniper with a Mauser, I would've figured out a few beats sooner who this was before me.

As it was, this slim young man reached up with his left hand to his sombrero, and the gesture made me notice that his right arm was pulled back behind him. And the sombrero came off and out tumbled lovely thick coils of a woman's hair, falling over her shoulders, and she lifted her face a little to the light, and it was Luisa. I took a step toward her and even as I began my next step she dropped the sombrero to the ground and brought that right arm out from behind her and her Mauser went up to her shoulder and she angled her head to put me in her sights.

Her rifle was not pointed at some darkly whimsical, nonlethal, but appropriately chosen part of my body, as had been her pattern, but rather it was pointed at the center of my chest. And I had no gold-plate crucifix to absorb the round and simply knock me on my ass. I did not take that second step but planted the foot and stood straight and still before her. She'd had this chance once before and she did not take it. Since then, however, she clearly had come up with some other agenda. I could dodge, I could run, but she was a crack shot and it would do no good. But it was not the futility of evasion that kept me standing there. I found myself still trying to impress Luisa Morales. I had a strong hunch that she respected courage, even in a masher of a *gringo* with imperialist politics and moral indifference.

She let me stand there for a long few moments with her rifle barrel dead-still in its aim, as befitted her expertise with that instrument. I wondered who taught her, and I wondered if that would be the last thing I ever wondered. Or rather—correcting myself—I wondered if wondering about whether that would be the last thing I wondered would be the last thing I wondered. Bravery affects me like this.

Then the rifle slowly came down.

"Luisa," I said and the rifle popped up again, right back into the killing zone, though I hadn't even taken another step. I slowly spread my arms, palms toward her, saying with the gesture: Okay, you're the boss. Whatever you want.

And still she did not move. The rifle was not coming down. I waited. And then, without lifting her head from her sights, she said, "Good-by, Mr. Christopher Cobb." *Adios. Adios, Señor Christopher Cobb,* she said to me with her eye still sighting along the rifle barrel, and I expected to die. I expected she was bidding me farewell as she would send me on my way to whatever was next. She was not yet pulling the trigger, and I wondered if she believed in hell, seeing as she did not believe in the priests. And I wondered if that would be the last thing I wondered. Or, rather—here I went again—I wondered if wondering about whether that would be the last thing I ever wondered would be . . . But I didn't get to finish that thought. Her rifle quickly came down and she faded straight backward into the dark and was gone.

I would come to understand in the next several days, as they passed without another sniper incident, that it was her own good-bye she was speaking to me. It would make me think—and I'd feel foolish even as I thought it—that she had an affinity for me after all.

17

But I've always been a fool about women. Made only more awkward by the fact that they seem, not infrequently, to be fools about me. I walked away from my encounter with Luisa and followed the trolley tracks back toward the *zócalo*, at one point stepping aside for, but otherwise ignoring, a trolley heading in my direction. I needed to walk.

When I reached the Plaza, the sound of a salon orchestra playing a *danzon* was wafting out of the *Diligencias*, but I did not go into the *portales* to continue drinking, even to get the taste of *pulque* out of my mouth. Instead, I went straight toward my rooms to work on my story—for it was time to write about the female sniper of Vera Cruz, *La Nueva Soldadera Vera Cruz*—and I found the washer girl of the afternoon dalliance curled asleep beside my courtyard door, in the midst of being a fool about me.

"What are you doing here?" I asked as she was knuckling the sleep out of her eyes.

She looked up, and those eyes were unreadable in the dark, though it was all too familiar to me. She did not reply.

"I'm very tired, young girl," I said, this time using *muchacha* instead of *señorita,* though gently.

"I wanted to make sure I did your laundry okay," she said.

"You did excellently," I said.

I gave her my hand and she rose.

"Go home to sleep now," I said.

"Yes," she said.

"You do have a place, don't you?"

"Yes." And her face was down, embarrassed. *I know how you're feeling,* muchacha. *This* muchacho *has to turn a girl with a gun into a headline for Chicago to be able to lift his own face.*

Then she was quickly gone, this washer girl whose name I should at least ask for the next time I saw her, and I thought how, in spite of the discomfort of being a unilateral fool about somebody, the real trouble came when you both were fools about each other.

I closed my door and I sat down at my desk and I rolled a piece of paper into my Corona Portable Number 3. I typed my byline. *Christopher Cobb.* And the lead came easily: *If you invade a country with a tyrant for a president, you make some new friends but you also make some enemies. The streets of Vera Cruz have felt the wrath of a lone sniper in the first week of the U.S. occupation, and she's angry at just about everyone. Yes, it's a woman. And she's a crack shot.*

And I did my eight hundred words and I told Luisa's story, though I didn't name her, and I was lucky the next morning over coffee, before I headed to the censor and the telegraph, to hear from Bunky about the shooting of the Navy man. The Bluejacket gave me three examples instead of two, which was a great deal better. And the victim broadened the targets of her anger to explicitly include Americans, which I was already suggesting in the lead. I realized I'd written that lead knowing more than I could say in the story. The pistol to my temple and the lecture by candlelight. The encounter beneath the streetlamp.

I finished the story at my table in the *portales,* writing it directly onto cable blanks, and it was a perfect ending, the Bluejacket's backside. I wrote it as it was, though I knew Clyde would euphemize the redlight district for our family readers, perhaps even so much that it would be unrecognizable to anyone other than a fellow newsman. No matter. The more immediate problem was the Army censor. But there was nothing about troops in the story, nothing strategic or even tactical revealed, and I figured the political subtleties hadn't made it onto the forbidden list yet. There was always a little time before those refinements occurred.

And I was right.

The next morning, it went through without a cut.

And I ended up, in exchange, with a telegram from New Orleans. That was quick. This is a wondrous electrical age we live in.

I didn't open it right away. I returned to the *portales,* as I'd promised Bunky, who was spending more and more time there. But the most pressing reason I headed back to the *Diligencias* was that I expected the enterprising young Diego to show up soon. I had an important job for him.

I sat down with Bunky, and he had already shifted from coffee to beer. He was starting light with *El Sol,* but there was still a long way to go, even till noon, and he'd be picking up the pace, moving on to serious drinking. I was about to call him "Pops" and tell him to slow down, but both those things were a mistake with him, so I kept my mouth shut for the moment, and I dropped into the flow of his talk when he turned his face to me and asked me a direct question. "You know who the first war correspondents were?"

"Russell and some of the others in the Crimea?" I said.

"Ancient," Bunky said. "Try the Peloponnesian War. Those boys that ran between the battlefield and the brass for the Greeks and the Spartans. They were really the first. And you know what happened when their audience didn't like the news? The real news, the real truth? They'd kill them. Kill the messenger. Kill the newsman. Same thing."

He looked sharply away from me.

"You okay, Bunk?" I asked.

He didn't answer.

If he went back to the beer and clammed up, I'd read what Mother had to say. He was keeping quiet and I was reaching into my pocket for the cable. But now I saw Diego coming up *Independencia* and I left the telegram where it was. Diego noticed me. He brightened and sped up.

"I'm okay," Bunky said.

I looked at him. He still had his face turned away from me, watching the street with a little slump to his shoulders.

"I don't want to have to worry about you, B. F.," I said. "If the snaps aren't holding your interest, let's get you back to reporting."

He acted like he didn't hear me. Maybe he didn't.

And Diego pulled up beaming in readiness before me.

"*Mijo*," I greeted him. *My son*. Casual. Like "sonny boy."

His head snapped a little in surprise and his smile flared even brighter.

"You been picking pockets this morning?" I said.

He put on a pout and shrugged his shoulders. "Only the Americans," he said.

"I'm an American."

"Only the Americans who deserve it," he said.

And he shocked the hell out of me by climbing up on my lap.

He was terribly thin. I realized this for the first time. A small bag of bones on my lap. He threw one arm around my neck like we were old pals drunk on a sidewalk somewhere.

"You in the process of picking my pocket?" I said.

"You don't deserve it."

"You'll get it from me anyway."

"I'd rather work for it," he said.

"Picking pockets is work."

He laughed. "I'd rather do secret stuff."

I glanced at Bunky and he'd turned his head to watch us. I couldn't figure out his expression. In all his writing and all his talk, he was a put-it-out-there-straight kind of guy, B. F. Millerman. I'd never sensed a shred of irony in him. But I'd swear this look was ironic. Maybe it was me without a father fussing after childless Bunky like he was my old man while this Mexican kid sat on my lap like he was mine and with Bunk the de facto grandfather forced to look on when he'd rather just drink beer at nine in the morning. Maybe that was enough to make a plain-facts newsman find his hidden sense of irony.

Diego still had his arm around my neck and was patiently waiting for an assignment.

And for all my reportorial thoroughness, I realized I was missing a piece of information. So this seemed like the time to ask for it. I looked at the boy in my lap. "What's your last name?" I said.

He had his own sense of irony, this kid. Irony and larceny. Before he could speak, I added, "Don't say 'Cobb.'"

"You don't love me anymore, *Papi*?" He said it with a straight face and then he laughed.

His calling me Spanish for *Pops* was one thing too much, after all this. I grabbed him up under the arms, though gently, and I lifted him off my lap and stood him before me. Even when I'd withdrawn them from him, my hands still felt the stark boniness of his ribs.

"Okay. Okay," he said in English.

"Time to get serious," I said in Spanish.

"You bet," he said in English.

"You're my employee, right?" I said.

"You bet." Again in English.

"So first, I want to know who you are."

"Your employee," he said, speaking Spanish now.

"Name."

"Diego. This you already know."

"Full name."

"I am Diego Cordero Medina Espinoza."

"You've got four names."

"You can call me that if you like."

"I don't think so."

"Hey," he said, imitating me, flapping his fingers at the street. "Diego Cordero Medina Espinoza, my employee, come here to me."

"Diego," I said. "Pay attention."

He turned to me. But he was not ready to let all this go. "And you," he said. "You are my employer. I want to know who you are."

"You know my name."

"Only two of them. Who are you?"

"Christopher Marlowe Cobb."

"Only three?"

"That's plenty."

"Christopher Marlowe Cobb," he said, grandly.

"Call me 'Kit,'" I said.

"Kit?"

"Kit."

"That's very small," he said.

"Like the point of a very sharp knife," I said.

Diego Cordero Medina Espinoza laughed.

"Serious now," I said. "Business."

He wound the laugh down and waited.

I looked around. The nearest reporter was Davis in his usual spot, out of earshot several tables away, writing furiously onto cable blanks.

I lowered my voice and said to Diego, "There's a U.S. silver dollar in it this time."

"All right, boss," he said, sounding like my employee, and since I considered myself as devoid of sentimentality as Bunky was of irony, I was surprised to feel a beat or two of regret at this.

But at least before I spoke to him, I flagged a waiter and ordered a couple of boiled eggs. Then I said, low, "The Germans have a special place on *Cinco de Mayo* just off *Esteban Morales*."

"I know this place," Diego said, in a near whisper. "I saw the flag there. Black stripe, white stripe, red stripe."

"Exactly. That's their consulate. Where the German government is represented."

"That man from the ship is there?"

I was about to confirm this—I even opened my mouth to speak—when it struck me that he had no way of knowing about the man if he had, in fact, beat it up the *calle* at the harbor, like he made a show of doing, and stayed there. He came back and shadowed all of us.

I closed my mouth without making a sound. Diego had been watching me closely. He knew what just dawned on me. Of course he did. I suddenly doubted if this kid made any slips. He'd deliberately let me know that he knew. And that he was good at all this.

"Yes," I said. "The tall man. He has a scar on his cheek."

"I should come get you when he goes out?"

"I bet you're good at following people as well."

He smiled.

"Follow him around and tell me where he goes, what he does. I don't want him to see me yet."

Diego gave a quick, deliberately sloppy salute. His body made the little flex and lift as if he was about to turn and dash off.

"Hang on," I said. I pulled out a handful of pesos. "I want you on the job, so if I give you these, do you promise to use them to eat?"

"Sure, boss," he said, grabbing the money.

"We'll start in a couple of minutes. Go on out there where I can see you till the waiter comes. Those eggs I ordered were for you."

He looked me in the eyes very steadily for a moment. And I didn't have a clue about what was going on in his head. Ten years old tops and he could make himself unreadable. I thought: *He'll be a dangerous adult, this kid. Or a great one. Or both.* Then he nodded and slipped out to the sidewalk.

Bunky had propped up his head with an elbow on the table and his palm to his cheek.

I pulled out Mother's telegram.

So I warned her in my last cable to be very careful about working in a Storyville brothel, no matter how swank. Even though I did it mostly in the subtext, quoting Marlowe, I was expecting a hard pinch on the cheek from her in one way or another. And Mother delivered.

She wrote: *Dearest Kit. Like untuned golden strings all women are, which long time lie untoucht will harshly jar. Vessels of brass oft handled brightly shine. You live your life and I'll live mine. Your loving mother*

This was also Christopher Marlowe, except for the salutation, complimentary close, and the line about minding my own business, which she'd even improvised into rhyme from her onstage talents. That was good advice, minding my own business. I did not want to ponder the subtext of this quote and what she might be doing in New Orleans. That was a story I would not cover.

18

The story I did cover the next day was for a whole pack of us to cover. A selective pack, however. The big dogs of the war correspondents. Davis and me and London. Arthur Ruhl from *Collier's* and Frederick Palmer from *Everybody's*. Lou Simonds from the *Atlantic*. A couple of the anonymous smaller dogs from the big-circulation outlets, the Associated Press, the United Press. We all ended up at the dinner table of General Frederick "Scrapping Fred" or "Fearless Freddie"—take your choice—Funston, lately installed as the man in charge of U.S.-occupied Mexico and lately installed in the house of General Maass near the Mexican barracks on the south end of town, with the Maass family stuff still around, from the piano to the matching pair of rocking chairs, from the couch-arm doilies to the white coral centerpiece on the dining table, from the bead curtains dividing the room to the dishes laid out for dinner to the parrot in the back room calling out drill orders in a man's voice that had to be an imitation of Maass himself.

Funston's first declaration when we all sat down was "I'm packing up General Maass's things at the first opportunity and sending them along to him." Like Funston needed to make it clear that our grabbing a Mexican city didn't mean we'd grab some Mexican general's dinner china as well. Funston paused for a moment to allow this declaration to register on us with all its ethical gravity, and in the silence, the parrot cried in Spanish, "About face. Forward march."

We didn't laugh. Funston was a little man, as small and thin as a teenage girl, and he was fidgety, with a little man's exaggerated derring-do, and famous for bragging, after he made his mark as a general in the Philippines, that he personally strung up three dozen Filipinos without a trial and he suggested we do the same with all the Americans who had petitioned Congress to sue for peace in the Far East.

He laughed, however, at the voice from the other room. And he said, "As for the general's parrot, he'll be dead before tomorrow's sunrise." And he laughed again. An I-really-mean-it sort of laugh.

Richard Harding Davis laughed too, that companionable manly-man's laugh of his. Most of the rest of us mustered an echo of it, from politeness, though Jack London just dropped his head and smirked at his dinner plate.

And we ate a meal from home—ham and cream gravy and boiled potatoes and macaroni and snap beans and pickles—and we were lectured by the general about our responsibilities to America and its righteous efforts here in Mexico. Knowing his reputation and hearing him lecture, I couldn't help but think that it was a good thing a certain sniper I knew wasn't aware of this man. Good for him, and good for her, too.

Later we sat on chairs in the courtyard and smoked cigarettes and drank coffee until we had the option of drinking a pretty swell Scotch, an option we all exercised, and Funston passed around editions of the big Mexico City newspapers from a few days ago. And in a collegial but grave tone he declared, "Read what your Mexican counterparts are saying, gentlemen."

Those of us who knew Spanish translated in low voices for those around us who didn't, creating an intense, low babble of vituperation in the room, which was no doubt part of Funston's rhetorical plan. The headline in *El Imparcial* was "The Soil of Our Homeland Is Defiled By Foreign Invasion!" with a sub-head of "We May Die, But Let Us Kill!" *El Independiente* assured its readers "While Mexicans Were Massacring *Gringo* Pigs, Church Bells Rang Out Their Glory!" *La Patria* took a cleaner, more Hearstian approach in its headline: "Vengeance! Vengeance! Vengeance!" And there were half a dozen more of this ilk.

After we finished with the newspapers, spending less time with each one, Funston said: "You see, boys, what you've got to counteract? And I have to admit, from all our own reports, these papers accurately reflect the attitude of the Mexican people as a whole. An attitude that's typical, in my experience, of uncivilized people. Our fellow Americans need to know what the reality is down here."

And the extra dose of reality that all us boys were hearing in these words was that our stories were now going to follow the Army's agenda, Funston's agenda, or they wouldn't be allowed out of this town. We passed the newspapers back to Funston and he accepted them in silence while the parrot screamed wordlessly in the background.

When he had all the papers again, Funston said, "Not from my mouth, boys, but you can find the President on the recent record saying how the Mexicans would certainly welcome us with open arms if we ever intervened. How they'd all understand that we were actually saving them from their latest tyrant. How in no time at all they'd create their own little old democracy down here and be grateful to us for giving them the chance."

The parrot began to sing "La Cucaracha," the stretch of lyric he'd learned coming from the pre-revolutionary version, which was still, in fact, about a cockroach. *La cucaracha, la cucaracha, ya no puede caminar.* The cockroach can't walk anymore.

Funston seemed to ignore this. "Not that these folks don't deserve a democracy," he said. "Everyone does. But they don't understand what we're offering. We learned in the Philippines that you can't create a democracy for savages unless you have complete control over them."

The bird started over and got farther into the lyric: *porque no tiene, porque le falta, las dos patitas de atrás.* Because he's lacking his two back legs.

Funston may have been ready to spell it all out: that we were expected to rally the United States to a major military action, total invasion. Maybe not. This may have been his intended stopping point anyway. The implication was inescapably clear as it was. But after his declaration about how to bring democracy to savages, he paused for a moment, and then he said, "Pardon me, gentlemen." He rose and vanished into the other room and very briefly the parrot fell silent. Then the parrot cried, "About face." Then there was only the faintest sound of a fluttering of feathers. And then silence.

We did not hear the bird again for all the rest of the time we lingered, milling about the courtyard with more Scotch and more cigarettes and a more relaxed General Funston. He made a point of working his way around the room to each of us.

When he got to me, he said, "Glad you've come down here, Cobb."

We were standing near a dry fountain in the center of the court-yard and the other reporters were out of earshot, talking and laughing among themselves, more than halfway vanished into a good-Scotch ground fog. I could have asked questions now, could have found out if Funston knew who the new German in town might be. But I felt certain this would be news to him. He just didn't seem useful to me at the moment. And till I had this story, whatever it was, I wanted to keep it to myself as much as possible.

"I'm not sure I'm glad," I said.

He cocked his head slightly at me. Why did it remind me of a parrot cocking its head? Hearing words and being interested in them but not understanding.

"Like you," I said, "I came for a war."

He cuffed me on the shoulder. "There you go," he said.

We each had a Scotch in our hand. We each took a sip.

"You know, I adore your mother," he said.

This happens to me quite often. I've generally gotten used to it. I learned long ago how to prevent even the first little sharp-toothed nibble of a troubling thought from getting at me, learned to assume that such declarations as this by a man are simply from an ardent fan on the other side of the proscenium. "Fearless Freddie" Funston, however, his face looking up into mine almost dreamily, his beard and mustache trimmed tightly close in what was neither a man's shaved face nor a man's proper beard, this man Funston troubled me. "Scrap-ping Fred" was an actor in his own way, and on a very big stage, and with an impressive costume. My mother could have fallen for him because of all of that.

"I saw her at the Morosco in San Francisco the year before the earthquake," he said.

I was gone from her daily life by then. I needed to stop this line of thought or it would drive me nuts.

"What was the play?" Funston was thinking aloud.

"Were you stationed there?" I asked him, trying to divert the conversation.

"'*The Eternal Feminine*,'" he said.

"The Presidio?" I asked.

"That was it," he said. "'*The Eternal Feminine*.' Your mother was splendid."

"You served there?"

"The Presidio," he said. "That's right. I was commander."

"This is good Scotch," I said, starting to lift my glass, intending to take the rest of whatever was in there as a quick bolt and excuse myself from him to get some more.

"My wife and I loved the theater in Frisco," he said.

I pulled my glass down for the moment.

"But your mother was the highlight. For both of us."

"Thank you," I said.

"So sad, the next year," he said. "The Morosco and all the rest were rubble."

Mother was long gone from Frisco by then. She was back in New York.

"I took over in the aftermath, you know," Funston said. "Ran the show."

I'd read about the downright admiration San Franciscans developed for Funston. With the water mains broken, he created a successful firebreak by dynamiting the homes of the city's elite. He fought the rats and disease. And he had looters shot dead on the spot.

"My task here is not dissimilar," he said. "The streets are open sewers. Insects and vermin live with these people unchecked. For every thousand Veracruzians, fifty die each month and more than half of those are infants. It breaks my heart. They're dying of dysentery, malaria, TB, meningitis, smallpox. I'm going to fix that. America is going to fix that."

And I knew we would. I took the bolt of Scotch. I let this complicated little man blur before me.

19

It was darkly shadowed at the doorway to my rooms and I'd had too much Scotch and too many cigarettes and too much war-correspondent gab and too much military point of view but especially too much Scotch and too much darkness and so Diego startled the bejesus out of me when he slipped from the shadows and slid something smoothly leathery into my hand and said, "He never felt a thing." He tried to vanish again but I recovered quick and though my reflexes may have been a little dulled by the Scotch I still caught him by his collar and hauled him back to me.

"Okay," he said. "Okay. Now you got me, you can give me that silver dollar. Scarface's wallet with his train ticket is worth a dollar."

"His wallet?"

"In your right hand."

My right hand was actually still holding Diego's collar. He realized that.

"Wait," he said. "Your left hand? Maybe your pocket? You're quick with your hands, Kit. You said I can call you 'Kit,' right? I remember my dad being quick with his hands."

His *papi*.

"How is it I've turned you into a little smart-ass, Diego Cordero Medina Espinoza?"

"You think it took America invading to make me a smart-ass? I am my own smart-ass, Kit."

"Don't call me that," I said.

"Mr. Cobb."

"Don't call me that."

"*Papi.*"

I still had him by the collar and I opened my door and pulled him inside and shoved him—though gently—in the direction of the desk chair.

"Don't call me that," I said.

I turned on the overhead electric light.

"Okay, boss," he said in English.

Now he was sitting in the chair like an obedient kid in the front row at school.

It was in my left hand, actually. "You nicked this from the man with the scar?" I used the English verb from the street in the midst of the Spanish question.

"'Nicked'?" he asked.

"A little American language lesson," I said. "Pickpockets," I said slowly, clearly, in English, "nick leather." And I held up the wallet with the last word.

"Diego Cordero Medina Espinoza nick leather on Scarface," Diego said in English.

"I think he's a dangerous man," I said, returning to Spanish. "I don't like you trying this."

"I am a sly one," Diego said.

"I don't want you dead."

Diego reared back a little. Like this was a surprising thought.

"I'd have to find a new boy." I added this in the offhand, tough-guy way we'd put up between us. But then, as gently as I'd shoved him to the chair, I said, "I don't want you to steal for me, either."

Diego shrugged. "Wallets are a good way to understand."

As far as he knew, I ignored this. I'd said the right thing to him. But damnation, I was glad to have this wallet. I sat on the side of the bed and looked at it.

It folded in thirds and was made of good oak-brown leather. Full grain from something young. He'd had it a long while, the patina of years upon it, including a rubbed wedge of darkness from the oil of his skin every time he grasped the wallet in the same place and pulled it from his pocket.

I looked at the wallet and then at Diego. Scarface was tall.

Diego looked at me looking at him. The boy was shrewd. He knew what I was thinking. "He put it here," he said, motioning with his hand to where the lower outer pocket of a suit coat would be. "For just a moment. When he changed some money at the post office window. I could not help but steal it."

"He was alone?"

"Yes."

"He didn't notice you?"

"No."

I opened the wallet.

"I nick very good," he added in English.

I reminded myself to remember where things were, to return them to their exact positions after I handled them. I was already thinking that some anonymous, honest Mexican needed to return this to the doorstep of the consulate pretty quickly, without it appearing to have been thoroughly searched.

The wallet was clearly on Scarface's person a great deal. But he used it simply for basic things. In one compartment was the ticket. A Pullman car reservation for day after tomorrow. For Friedrich Mensinger. The National Railroad via the capital to a city named La Mancha, *estado* Coahuila. Outside of Cervantes and Spain, the city name wasn't familiar to me.

"La Mancha?" I said, mostly to myself, but the kid was quick.

"What is the state?" Diego said.

"Coahuila."

"That's up north," Diego said.

"I wonder what he wants up there."

Diego shrugged. "I couldn't hear much of the talk with the ticket clerk. Do I get my dollar?"

"You'll get it."

"For this?"

"I'm still trying to see what we have."

"The trains aren't regular going up north these days," he said. "I think Scarface wanted to go sooner than three days."

Three days: Diego had already looked at the ticket. Of course he had.

I slipped the ticket back into the compartment. I put my fingertips inside the middle compartment and felt an envelope. I pulled it slowly from the wallet, noting its orientation, though Diego had already no doubt disarranged everything.

The address side up. Stamp lower right. It was out now, and I rotated it to look at the address, which was written in a tight, small, neat hand:

> *Herr Friedrich von Mensinger*
> *Deutsches Konsulat*
> *Vera Cruz, Mexico*

He had the "von" of nobility in his name. But Mensinger didn't use the "von" for his train ticket. The postmark was from Berlin. The writer knew he was coming to Mexico well before Mensinger boarded the *Ypiranga*. I turned the letter over. It was neatly knifed open at the top edge; the flap was still glued down. And Mensinger had used the back of the envelope to make what looked like random notes to himself, each item marked with an initial dash.

> *kein Einmarsch. Nicht nach T*
> *ENP ~ Dr.*
> *C u. W keine Eier*
> *Papiere*
> *entweder Hammer oder Amboß*

I could figure a little of this out. *Kein Einmarsch.* I wasn't entirely sure, but it had something to do with *not* something, and the cognate

would suggest marching. *Nicht nach T.* Not a T. On the next line I
didn't know what *ENP* represented. An acronym no doubt. The tilde
was from mathematics. Meaning the acronym was similar to the next
thing. *Doctor.* Between the two initials at the beginning of the third
line, the *u.* was an abbreviation for *und. And. Keine* is "*none.*" But I didn't
know *Eier. Papiere* is "*paper.*" The last phrase, I wasn't sure of either. I
thought the construction was "*either…or*" and one thing was obviously
a hammer. All five notes, separately and together, seemed meaningless. Certainly notes to himself. He knew what the blanks were, what
the context was.

I pulled the letter out of the envelope and unfolded it.

It began: *Mein Schatzi.* I knew this phrase. From a German girl
in Chicago. *My Treasure.* It went on for two pages in German and I
knew I would be at a loss. I needed some help with this, and I thought
of Gerhard. I slipped the letter back in the envelope and returned the
envelope to the center compartment. I found myself stuck on the writer,
a woman—the hand was clear to me now as a woman—a woman who
would call Scarface—Friedrich von Mensinger—her "treasure." He
was wealthy, of course. Maybe it wasn't tender at all. Maybe it was
"Dear Moneybags."

Which made me move on to the third compartment, where his
money would be. It was empty.

I lifted my eyes to Diego.

His own eyes were fixed on my hand, which still held open the
empty money compartment. He looked up at me.

"Give me the money," I said.

He said nothing.

"All of it. We have to get this back to Scarface."

Diego still wasn't talking.

"You've earned your silver dollar."

"Okay," he said, almost inaudibly.

I said, "I want to put him as little on alert as possible. We need
to get this back to him, like someone found it."

"Found it? He won't think he lost it. He is a careful man."

"Found it discarded after it was stolen."

"You want him to believe that?"

"Yes."

"Then the money will be gone."

Diego was right, of course.

"I'll split it with you," Diego said.

"Are you sure he didn't see you when you nicked it?"

"I'm sure," he said. "He never looks straight at any of us."

I believed this. Which made it even more striking that Mensinger dropped his nominal sign of nobility for his train ticket. Wherever he was going, whatever he was up to, he was taking care not to emphasize that.

I pulled Diego's silver Liberty Head dollar from my pocket and held it up in front of his face between my thumb and forefinger. I was unaware of how similar this gesture was to something else until he opened his mouth and stuck out his flattened tongue and he crossed himself. Like he was about to take Catholic Communion.

He had that narrow little look of Diego sass in his eyes, which had come to be familiar to me.

I thought of Luisa and her hatred of the priests.

I did not put the dollar on his tongue, as he no doubt expected me to do.

I lowered the coin. "I bet this attitude makes your mother sad," I said.

He withdrew his tongue and snapped his mouth shut. "I am a good Catholic son," he said.

"As far as she knows."

"I love my mother."

I reached out and took his right wrist and I lifted his arm and I put the coin in his palm. It disappeared into a tight fist. I let him go.

"How much money did Scarface have in his wallet?" I asked.

"Not nearly as much as he's got with him," Diego said.

"You didn't keep the ticket to sell."

"I thought you'd want to see that," he said, and paused so that, for at least a few moments, I'd think he sacrificed something for me.

But then he said, "Besides. You get arrested for using a ticket with someone else's name. No market for it."

"So you do still know how to confess."

"Never to a priest."

"Go home now," I said.

"What's next?"

"Find me in the *portales* later in the day. I need to hold on to the wallet for a little while. But continue to keep an eye on our man."

Diego saluted me and was up and across the room.

"Diego Cordero," I said, stopping him as he opened the door. He turned to face me.

"Good job," I said.

"I am a thief," he said.

"You are forgiven," I said.

He crossed himself and vanished into the night.

20

Early the next morning I sent a wire to Clyde asking him to find out anything he could about a German official or diplomat by the name of Friedrich von Mensinger. I also asked him to get someone to translate a few German words for me, putting only what I didn't know in the telegram, not the whole of Mensinger's personal notes. At the *portales* Bunky was nowhere to be seen. I should have gone immediately to find him. But no. He was almost certainly sleeping one off. It was best for him simply to sleep. I could talk to him later about what was going on with him. I had another guy to see.

The *Hostal Buen Viaje* was up *Montesinos,* just across from a loudly clanking, brake-grinding, engine-huffing switching section of the railroad tracks a quarter mile or so from the main terminal. It was a run-down one-story courtyard building made to work as a cheap by-the-week-or-month hotel. Gerhard's name and room number were chalked with all the other lodgers' on a board behind the front desk, where an old man sat deeply asleep in an upright position.

I knocked on Gerhard's door, which faced a courtyard whose cracked and shattered tiles were overgrown with ankle-high grassy weeds. It was shortly after nine o'clock.

There was a stirring inside the room. Gerhard called out something huskily in German. I figured he was asking who the hell it was. "It's Christopher Cobb," I said.

"Cobb," Gerhard said, and though it was still husky, his voice had a tone of recognition.

More stirring, and the door opened.

Gerhard was mostly dressed, wearing dark gray outing pants but also a sleeveless, button-front undershirt. The man's arms were thickly muscled. He had the build of an athlete, which had escaped my notice when he wore his band uniform.

"The room is small," he said, stepping out and closing the door behind him. He led me to a far corner of the courtyard and we sat at a metal table.

I've not spoken much of the filth of Vera Cruz. Just as the background of things, which it certainly always was. I've not mentioned the flies. A reporter focuses on events and strips away the incidental details that don't come directly to bear on the events he's interested in, and that's a strong writerly habit and one that I think makes for a better story of any kind. But Funston was right about how the Veracruzanos lived. And how they died prematurely as a result. And a big part of that was the flies. The flies of Vera Cruz were everywhere. You walked through a curtain of them most of the time. And the *zopilotes,* as useful as they were, could not do a fully effective job. Or even a halfway effective job. Dead things were always around, and usually, in the heat, they pretty quickly became totally unidentifiable dead things. It was true of the streets, the plazas, the markets, the yards, the shops, the houses of the poor, and even, to some considerable extent, the houses of the wealthy. And it was certainly true of cheap hotels near the train station.

So Gerhard and I sat in the overgrown courtyard of this particular cheap hotel near the train station and our heads were surrounded by a swirl of flies and we waved at them now and then but we mostly lived the way the locals lived and let them come and go, and we were surrounded by a smell of dead things, no doubt some of them nearby in the courtyard, hidden in the weeds, being eaten bit by bit by the insects and an occasional rat, and all of this moved me to ask Gerhard Vogel of Pittsburgh, Pennsylvania, the obvious question: "What the hell are you doing here?"

"It's cheap. It's out of the way."

"So you can read your *Scribner's.*"

He smiled faintly at this. "Sure."

"But I mostly meant Vera Cruz."

He shrugged. But he shrugged with his eyes fixed closely on mine. Usually a guy who you're asking questions, when he shrugs, he looks away. At least briefly.

So I took the initiative. "You hear anything about our scar-faced friend?"

He didn't blink. After a few moments, as if this answer actually took some thought, he said, "No."

I wanted him to translate Mensinger's letter for me. Still, I found myself hesitating. I wondered what was going on here that I wasn't understanding.

"But you have something?" he said.

I shrugged, keeping my eyes fixed on his. It wasn't a natural gesture for me, and I didn't mean it sarcastically. I just wanted to try to keep my leverage with him.

"Are you under censorship now?" he asked. Full of surprises. "All you war reporters?"

"Looks like it," I said.

"What do you think about that?"

"What do you think I think?"

"Sorry," he said, and this time he did look away when he shrugged.

"No, it's okay. I don't mind saying the obvious when it's what somebody really wants to know. But you're a smart guy. You can ask me straight."

He looked back to me and smiled. "We're both smart guys," he said.

"So what do you want to know?"

"Are you a patriot, Christopher Cobb?"

"I'm such a patriot," I said, "I believe the press has to be free."

"What if your country is fighting a war and your being totally free to write everything harms that effort?"

"If anything needs to be understood totally and freely, it's a war," I said. "Especially by a public whose sons are being asked to fight it."

"And what about all the lying, sensational papers?"

"Who's going to be the omniscient and impartial über-authority to read everything beforehand and say what's lies and what's not? The American way is where everything is freely expressed. Then the free man gets to sort things out for himself."

Gerhard acted as if he was about to say more, but he stopped himself with a little shake of the head. Like he didn't mean to get off on this anyway.

I had a quick bloom of newsman's intuition. Something seemed suddenly clear about this man before me. I would find it out now. I began by asking, "You want to know if you can trust me?"

"Why'd you come here today?" he said.

"To ask you a favor."

"And you trust me?"

"Didn't *I* just ask that of *you?*"

"Yes."

A couple of beats of silence passed between us. I had to answer first. Okay.

"I don't see the risk," I said.

"What's the favor?"

"I have a letter. In German. Can you translate it for me?"

He looked at me for a long moment without saying anything.

"Go ahead and ask," I said.

"From him?"

"To him."

I felt sure now.

Gerhard extended his hand, palm up.

I didn't give it to him right away. Instead, I said, "Gerhard Vogel, around me at least, you don't sound or act like a horn player in a small-time German band. Even if you're from Pittsburgh."

He slowly turned his hand and put it palm down, on the table between us. He said, "I understand why you reject censorship. But it's my understanding that among the best of you, there is a code of some sort. When someone tells you something, you can come to a gentleman's agreement beforehand."

"Of course," I said. "We can negotiate the restrictions about how I use what you want to say, and we either come to a binding agreement or I'll tell you to keep your mouth shut."

He showed the palm of his hand again.

"Let me ask you a question first," I said. "And I give you my word the answer will never leave my mouth, much less my fingertips."

"Yes?"

"Are you a spy?"

"I am." He hesitated only briefly to give me this answer. He had been thinking about this all along, bringing me into this secret.

"For the red, white, and what?" I asked.

"Blue," he said. "Not black."

"That was my own question about the obvious," I said.

"You had to ask it."

"You didn't have to answer it."

"I trust you."

"And you think we can help each other."

"Of course."

I pulled the letter from my shirt pocket and put it in Gerhard's hand. I'd brought only the letter, not the envelope. Now that I knew who Gerhard was, I regretted not getting his immediate help on Mensinger's cryptic notes. But that could wait for another meeting. Soon. I said, "Scarface is a man named Friedrich von Mensinger. He was carrying this letter."

Gerhard drew it to him but kept his eyes on me.

"Don't ask how I got it," I said.

He nodded in assent. He unfolded the letter, very gently. He read, translating with only an occasional pause to parse the German and to say it right:

My Treasure,

You have only now gone from our rooms. On my fingertips I still feel the rough badge of your manhood that you wear upon your face. I remember when that was an open wound and I saw it for the first time. I waited for you at our table in the Stadtgarten, hoping you would come in time for the music. You came at last. I know why you were late. The blood had barely stopped flowing. I wept at the sight of it. You had to strike me then to make me strong. Twice. I know you must be strong now, as you always must, as you always are, though I do not know why it should take you to such a savage and distant place. My heart breaks already, though your footsteps down the hall have barely ceased to echo about me. We belong in Madrid, together, my darling. Or Buenos Aires. Together. Do what you must quickly and come back to me or send for me if you can. I give you my heart and mind to carry with you.

Your loving and obedient and patient wife, Anna

Gerhard folded the letter as carefully as he unfolded it and he was not looking at me and I was looking at him only long enough to see that he was not looking at me and I looked away as well. I was happy to do so. A woman in love had just sat down at this table beside us in the midst of the cheap raggedness and the stench, and with the clank and huff of track-switching, and she had spoken things that we were not meant to hear, things that would profoundly embarrass her if she knew we'd heard them, tender things intended for a man I now both envied and despised.

Gerhard and I sat like this for a long few moments. In my periphery I saw his hand come across the table and place the letter gently before me. I turned. I picked up the letter and placed it in my shirt pocket, keenly aware now that it was pressed there against my heart.

Gerhard and I looked at each other and I figured he was feeling roughly the same things I was about Anna Mensinger. We looked away again. Halfway across the courtyard, near a broken and tumbled fountain, I saw a stirring in the grass. Something moving there.

I said, "So he's a Spanish-speaking diplomat."

Gerhard did not respond.

"Without portfolio," I said.

"But with a mission," Gerhard said.

I turned to him. He seemed to be watching the same spot in the grass that I was.

"He bought a train ticket," I said.

Gerhard slowly brought his face back to me.

We looked at each other for a moment. I asked Frau Mensinger politely to leave. I apologized to her. But I insisted.

After a moment of silence, as Anna gradually complied, Gerhard asked, "To where?"

I looked him fixedly in the eyes. "Before you answered me a few minutes ago, when I asked if you'd heard anything about the scar-faced man, you hesitated ever so slightly before saying no. If we're trusting each other, you need to tell me about that pause."

Gerhard said, "I was thinking about the whole issue of trust. I had no answer on Mensinger, but I was taking the question seriously. You and I were about to start something."

I let this sit with me for a moment. It made sense. And this time he answered me at once, though he must have been surprised at my challenge, at what I'd observed of him to make the challenge. But.

I said, "You're a spy for our country. You're now in the middle of things. But you're a horn player, not the booking agent for the band. And even if the President was looking for an excuse to invade Mexico, it can't be for more than a couple of weeks that he'd think it would focus on Vera Cruz."

"I understand your suspicion," he said. "Some bad luck turned into good luck. We were playing in Mexico City. That's where I was supposed to be."

I kept my own silence now.

He said, "I was looking for a way back to the capital without causing suspicion. Then this happened."

"To La Mancha," I said, offering more to him now.

"La Mancha?"

"The train ticket."

"Yes," he said. "I understand."

"It's a National Railway whistle-stop in *estado* Coahuila."

"On the way to Torreón?"

"Yes," I said. "Carranza's home state."

"But Pancho Villa country now. He took Torreón only a few weeks ago. He might still be there."

"Or in La Mancha?"

"I can't imagine why."

"Would Villa go there for the secrecy of it?"

"It's not in his nature," Gerhard said. "He doesn't sneak around. And why should he do that for a lone German emissary? But this has to be about Villa. The Germans are making an overture."

My sense of the alto horn player from the Vera Cruz *zócalo* continued rapidly to change. He was not just a street-level spy from a band shell. He seemed to have a grasp of the bigger picture. You play the reporting game long enough, you learn to make yourself dumb with each new source. You ask questions you think you've already gotten the answers for. Then you weigh the discrepancies. So I said, "Why Villa?"

"I bet you already have an idea," Gerhard said.

Of course. His line of work required the same willingness to play dumb. He was telling me he knew that. I would have expected him to shoot me a little smile, to keep it friendly, since he was the one challenging my intentions. He didn't. He was acting vaguely offended. I leaned forward. I said, "I'm just putting the obvious question in the center of the table for us both to chip in. We may see things a little differently."

He didn't miss a beat now. He acted as if we hadn't just puffed our chests a bit. "All right," he said. "Let's say Huerta's days are numbered. The Kaiser might try to pick a winner in the civil war."

"Pick him when it still counts," I said. "Before he's truly got the upper hand."

"Precisely," Gerhard said. "So we have three major revolutionaries— or four or five, depending on how you sort them. Forget Gonzalez, though. He's incompetent on the battlefield. Orozco beat him again and again when he was fighting to keep Madero in power. The three then. Villa, Carranza, Obregón."

"You wouldn't put Zapata ahead of Obregón?" I asked.

"We need to talk from the German point of view, yes?"

"Yes."

"Zapata is a fool and a primitive Bolshevik. He just wants to make all the land communal for all the peasants, and once that's done, he'd be happy simply to play the bespangled *charro* in the mountains of Morelos."

"And Obregón is probably the smartest military man," I said.

"He probably is. But not in a way that would register in Berlin. At least at this point."

"Carranza then. Isn't he the ostensible leader of the rebels now? The *Primer Jefe*, even for Villa?" I was ready for Gerhard to throw all these questions back on me. But he seemed only to have wanted to make it clear he knew my tricks. When it came down to it, he apparently liked playing the authority and wasn't really inclined to listen to a possible different opinion. He wouldn't make a good reporter in that way. Maybe not even a good spy. But he did know some things.

He was talking Carranza now. "That First Chief title won't last long. He doesn't seem a natural leader for the radical change the others are after," Gerhard said. "He came from a landowner family, like Madero. He went to the National Preparatory School in Mexico City and wanted to be a scholar, but he had to go home to play the son of a wealthy cattle owner instead. Nevertheless, the scholarly world was the natural one for him, and it shows."

"The Kaiser's not looking for an intellectual."

"What do you think?" He made a faint snort and a snappish little furrowing of the brow.

I meant it as a statement between us of the obvious thing, a step-by-step articulation of our reasoning, and he acted as if it were a naïve question. I was remembering that I didn't like Gerhard when I first met him. He won me over with baseball, but he was a damn Pirates fan, after all.

"What do I think?" I repeated, as if that were the naïve question. "I think the *Escuela Nacional Preparatoria* hardly makes you an intellectual," I said, converting his translated "National Preparatory School" back into its real name. All of this suddenly felt like a low-level game of one-upmanship that I shouldn't be playing.

"Even worse," he said. "The most blindly insistent intellectual is the intellectual who got stunted in his growth."

And that was true enough. I needed to get rid of this odd sense of rivalry and just let him tell me what he thought he knew. And I realized the attitude that irritated me a few moments ago could have been directed at the Kaiser, not me. I was breaking my own rules. I was jumping to conclusions too easily. In this case about Gerhard. "So not Carranza," I said. "Which leaves us with Villa."

"Which leaves us with Villa. And the case for him is strong, if you think like the Kaiser. He's got by far the largest army, the best-trained army, and the most aggressive, straightforward combat style."

"Which is why Obregón's virtues as a general are still not registering in Berlin."

"That's right. And Villa's got a string of victories that would impress the Germans. Ciudad Juárez, Tierra Blanca, Chihuahua, Ojinaga. And now he's beaten Huerta head-on at Gómez Palacio and Torreón. And Carranza's getting very nervous. He thinks Villa's in the process of clearing the way to Mexico City for himself. Something's going to happen over all that. They will break, the two of them, they'll turn into enemies and I think they both know it."

"And that means renewed general chaos for all the rebel leaders, everyone fighting everyone," I said.

"Villa's shrewd," Gerhard said. "As strong, comparatively, as he is, he still knows he can't prevail in chaos. The great mass of Mexicans are just keeping their heads down. Villa needs something."

"So the time is right for Germany to approach him."

"*Jawohl, mein Herr,*" Gerhard said with that little snort of a laugh. I was finally realizing his attitude I'd been picking up on was actually directed at the country that was not his country but that was in his blood.

I said, "So the question is: What's the 'something' Mensinger is going to offer? And what do the Germans get in return?"

We both took a deep breath and sat back in our chairs. There was a glib answer to this. Arms. But there were six hundred tons of arms sitting in a German ship out in the harbor right now. Was the simple offer of more arms enough to prompt a Friedrich von Mensinger and all the secrecy? Gerhard and I both understood that there was something else going on.

"Are you going to follow him?" Gerhard asked.

"You're not?"

He shook his head very slowly no.

I said, "It's the next move if I want this story."

"Can we talk before you file it?"

"I'll file."

"Of course you will. You work for a good newspaper. I work for the United States of America."

He didn't need to say the next thing. "If it's feasible," I said.

"If it's feasible."

"I'm an American too."

"I know you are. Baseball."

"Baseball."

Either of us could have said this now, but Gerhard did: "We both have some work to do."

21

At the *portales*, pretty far advanced in the morning now, there was still no sign of Bunky. The waiter gave me the telegram Bunk would normally be holding for me.

It was from Clyde. This was a quick turnaround and he was only starting to inquire about Mensinger. But Hans, the tenth-floor janitor, was apparently still puttering around when Clyde got my cable, and so Clyde had sent me quick answers about the German words I was unsure of in Mensinger's notes. *Einmarsch* was literally "marching in." *Kein Einmarsch*, then: "not a marching in." Not an invasion. The other phrase where there was *not* something: *keine Eier*. I'd given Clyde both words, for what I presumed was a phrase. Clyde said Hans had a good laugh. *Eier* was "eggs." *Keine Eier* was the German way of saying somebody has "no balls." *Ningunos cojones*.

Which gave me a good, though quiet, laugh. With all their posturing and militarism and Prussian blood, the German men thought of their balls, their nuts, their stones, as eggs. As fragile, easily cracked eggs. Maybe that actually explained all the posturing and militarism.

And *Amboß*. Anvil. *Entweder Hammer oder Amboß*. Either a hammer or an anvil.

So as it turned out, I didn't need Gerhard to translate the notes. But I wondered what he'd make of them. I decided to drop back in on him at the first opportunity. But Bunky first. He was always ambulatory

by now. He was on my mind. I was hoping perhaps that his writing
that story about the utility commissioner deciding to work with the
Americans—but with a B. F. Millerman cynical twist about the financial
motives—had warmed up his reporter's blood and he'd been working
on a new lead.

However, this wasn't the case. When I arrived at his *casa de huéspedes* on a side street near the docks, where Bunky'd taken a furnished
room, I was met at the door by the manager, a Colombian woman
with her hair so tightly knotted at the top of her head she seemed
perpetually wide-eyed in surprise. When I asked for Señor Millerman, she shrugged and then pantomimed the knocking back of what
surely was meant to be a stiff drink. She gave me his room number
and stood aside to let me in.

I went one flight up the carpeted steps—it was one of the better
boardinghouses in town—and I stood before Bunky's door. I knocked.
No response. I knocked again and called his name and he was still not
making a sound and I tried the handle. It turned.

As the door moved, the smells came out first, of *mezcal* and of
potassium bromide—from his Kodak developer—and faintly of vomit.
And the door was open: the room was large and in the center was a
round table with a nearly empty *mezcal* bottle and Bunky's face beside
it, turned toward me, his eyes closed, his mouth open.

I stepped quickly to him and my passage was buoyed by panic,
but as I drew near, I heard an upsurge of scrabbly, heavy breathing,
and his mouth closed and opened and closed and then opened and
stayed open as the sound of his stupor receded for a time.

I found myself glad he was drunk. Simply drunk. I did not like
that first impression I'd had of him, though there was no reason for it.
There was no reason for Bunky Millerman—even B. F. Millerman—
to fear for his life in his rented room in Vera Cruz, Mexico. He was
simply knocked-out drunk. This had to have started this morning.
Maybe before dawn but not long before. Bunky was too experienced
not to have slept it off by now if this was from last night. But he clearly
still had some gutter-time left in him. His head and his arms lay flat

against the table and a beer mug's width of his butt clung to the edge of his chair and the rest of his torso stretched between, over empty air, all in perfect balance. Perfect for the moment. But it was clear what I should do.

"Come on, Pops," I said, and I dragged him upright. He was almost no help, barely shuffling his legs, but I got him to the narrow bed in the corner and I laid him out there on his side. I got his shoes off and his tie off and he instantly rolled onto his back to mutter and gag a few more breaths until his breathing dissolved into a rattling snore.

I took the chair he'd been clinging to and dragged it to a spot beside his bed. I sat. If there was food in his stomach, there was a chance he'd throw up. If he did that on his back—and it seemed to be his oblivious preference—he could choke to death. I was not going anywhere for a while.

It was okay. I could think some things out. But the first thing I thought about was Mother teaching me how this could happen, this thing that would keep me at Bunky's bedside for the next few hours, though this had been an unspoken corollary lesson, not the one she was actually intending. She sat me down the night I had my first taste of beer, from an obliging rummy on the back alley steps of the Nathan Hale when I was maybe thirteen, while she was somewhere in the third act of *Macbeth* at the Bowdoin Square a couple of blocks away. She smelled it on my breath that night, and with all the Isabel Cobb theatrical flair she told me the harrowing tale of how a splendidly handsome leading man, whose name she withheld, died just like that in his prime, in a bed, on his back, choked to death on his own vomit, and how that man had begun with a beer in an alley as a boy. She wept what seemed to be undramatized tears.

My mother was my teacher in most things. I spent some time in formal schools as I grew up, when she did a stint of repertory now and then or took a few months off between seasons, but mostly I read my way through a thousand books. Indeed, over those learning years, it was probably closer to three thousand, from Aristotle to Shakespeare to Henry James, most of which she chose. And she sat up late with me, still smelling faintly of greasepaint, making me write and talk and write and write, and she got various actors and actresses with various bodies of knowledge or flairs or actors' skills—Medieval history or plane geometry or bare-knuckle Queensbury fighting or fencing or whatever else—to teach me what they knew. And as the occasions arose, she would perform these intense dramatic monologues of life's hardest-won lessons, performances for an audience of one, usually at the end of a night, by candlelight or by gaslight, or sometimes whispered in the dark.

So this little harrowing tale of the death of a leading man was not unusual. But there were certain gaps in my mother's education of me. And this tale was harrowing in a way she did not intend. I said, almost at once, "Was that my father?"

The question surprised me as much as it did her.

Not that I hadn't asked it in one way or another before. But over the years she worked her way from my being brought by the stork to being found in the bulrushes of a Louisiana swamp to being conceived like Perseus from a shower of gold until she simply put me off with its being a sad story that she'd tell someday and wasn't she plenty of parent on her own. But it always seemed to take us both by surprise when it came to my mind and out of my mouth.

And this time she did what she did the last time I asked. After a moment of silence, when I presumed she was forced to think of things that to this day I know not of, she clapped a hand onto her chest and did a stagy pre-swoon.

And this time I wasn't having any of that.

"If you don't want to drive me to drink," I said, "you need to tell me the truth."

The hand unclapped from her chest and the imminent swoon evaporated and she looked at me. "What have you been reading?" she demanded.

It was true that among the near three thousand books of my life with Mother, there were some contraband titles, and I'd just challenged her from the plot in a penny romance I'd recently found abandoned in a dressing room. But I wasn't letting her divert me.

"The book of life," I said to her.

"Oh, balderdash," she said. "That's bad melodrama."

"Our life together is bad melodrama," I said, learning the lesson, on this very same evening, that a couple of drinks can enhance one's argumentative powers.

The hand clapped back onto her bosom.

"You're not going to swoon, Mother," I said.

The hand fell once more and her face collapsed into sincere concern. "Have I lost my credibility?"

"If I were beyond the footlights, not at all," I said. "But I am here before you in our rooms."

"And you are drunk," she said.

"In vino veritas," I said.

"Vino, my dearest, not beer."

I recognized her tricks. I had to focus. "Was that my father?"

"No."

"Who is my father?"

"Dead," she said, swiftly, firmly. She hesitated and I knew what her mind was searching for.

"Quote me no Shakespeare or Marlowe or anyone now," I said. "Just tell me his name."

"Cobb."

"What Cobb? Who was he?"

"He is a dead Cobb. A Cobb whose kernels have been gnawed away utterly. My darling, he had some good things about him that are showing up in you and some bad things that you show not even the merest trace of, for which I am profoundly grateful and largely responsible."

"What good traits?"

"Your devastating good looks. Some aspects of them." And she put her two hands on my two shoulders and she is a splendid actress, but not, I think, from less than twelve inches, which is how closely she had brought her face before mine. And even from this distance she seemed to be on the verge of real tears, and she said, quite low, quite unaffectedly, "Can we please leave it at that, my darling? This is very painful to your mother and there is no reason for me to live all that over in telling you and no reason for you to carry these same painful memories for the rest of your life in that lovely brain of yours. For both our sakes, would you please trust me and leave it at that?"

I could say nothing but yes.

And Bunky began to mutter in his sleep.

Just sounds. Nonsense words.

I put a hand on his shoulder. I rustled him a little. "It's okay, old man," I said. "Sleep it off."

And he grew quiet.

But he had me thinking now about Mensinger's cryptic words, which was what I should have been focused on anyway. I could see the list clearly in my head and I started with the first words.

kein Einmarsch.

No invasion. Well, that was certainly in the minds of all us news boys down here. We invaded Mexico but it wasn't an "invasion" and likely not to become one. As obvious as this was to all of us Americans, it may have been literally notable to a German musing on the back of an envelope. His assumption would have been the Germanic one. The logical one, in this case. Once you marched your army into a country and routed your opponent's army locally, you did what comes naturally to armies. You continued the invasion. What seemed frustrating to those of us who understood a man—an American type—like Woodrow Wilson would have seemed baffling to our German aristocrat.

But this brief notation. Was it a "musing"? I needed to consider the purpose of the list. "Musing" had to be wrong. If he had to write to think, he'd write in a journal or some such and he'd be writing it out in full, detailing his line of thought. No. These items on the envelope were more likely a listing of things he'd already thought out. He was about to go off to *estado* Coahuila, almost certainly to meet up with Pancho Villa one way or another. He'd had an impulse to start organizing his thoughts; he made a list of the things he wanted to say. Talking points.

It had to be about Villa. Friedrich von Mensinger didn't sneak into Mexico on the *Ypiranga* to confer with Huerta. That would have been done with an open approach. If this was a secret diplomatic mission, it had to be with a rebel. And the Germans are precise. Scrupulously so. He must have known the tactical situation, known who it was now in charge of that part of Coahuila. I assumed, for the moment, that he wanted to stress to Villa that there would be no American invasion. But wasn't that an odd thing for a German to emphasize to a man who might someday rule Mexico? Mensinger was not here as a neutral mediator to ease the Mexican rebels' minds about U.S. intentions. Of course not. Mensinger had the same scorn for Wilson's timidity that the rest of us down here did. And as Gerhard pointed out, Villa had an aggressive, straightforward combat style. However outraged he might have been about the U.S. seizing a Mexican port, he'd have been temperamentally scornful about our not straightforwardly einmarsching on along to Mexico City. Mensinger expected to have a nice little bonding moment with Villa as they snorted at the American president.

Nicht nach T.

Not T. Linked to "no invasion." If this were *Nicht nach MC*—or however the Germans would initialize "Mexico City"—I'd have understood. But no. After saying there'd be no invasion, singling out the capital would have been redundant. If the "T" was something specific not being invaded, there would have to be an implied "not even." And I had that little newsman's rush of fitting things together. Tampico. Of course. The U.S. wasn't going ahead with the invasion. We weren't even going to march three hundred miles up the coast to the town that had actually set the invasion in motion in the first place, the town with all the oil fields. A town presently in the hands of the *Federales* but that any of the competing rebels would love to control.

"Toads," Bunky said.

I turned to him. He was still on his back, his eyes closed, still unconscious. His mouth, though, was working. Soundlessly, now that I was looking at him.

"Toads, Bunk?" I said.

"Toad shit," he said, though there wasn't a clue that he was aware of me other than that his words followed mine. He'd said this rather emphatically, in spite of the present impediments to his voice. And again: "Toad shit." This time almost sadly.

I waited. Whatever he was dreaming went on, his mouth still trying to put it into words.

I said to him, just as sadly, because I wanted to be having this exchange with him sober, at our table in the *portales:* "So, Bunky, would that be a larger or a smaller lie than the bull variety?"

His mouth stopped working.

I patted him on the shoulder.

I turned away from him.

ENP ~ Dr.

Doctor on one side. The abbreviation was the same in German as in English. That much I got. Similar to "ENP." I tried to run through all the figures of the Mexican revolution and then the prominent men in Germany, and I could think of no one with those initials. If these letters referred to something other than a man, with no context I didn't even know how to start my brain to figure out what it might be. Obviously he or it was not clearly associated with doctors or Mensinger wouldn't have to be making a note of it. So that was no help.

C u. W keine Eier.

C and W. No balls. I had a context for one of these initials. No invasion. No balls. W is Wilson. Any little zip I might have gotten from figuring this out was instantly squelched by a surge of anger. Who the hell was Herr Friedrich von Mensinger to say the President of the United States of America had no balls? It was okay for me to say something critical of Wilson. I got to vote. But to hear this Hun sneer at him made Wilson my well-meaning but pathetic Uncle Woody. The family thinks he's off base much of the time but he's ours. He's family. Mensinger abruptly had another strike against him.

And who else was he talking about? I ran William Jennings Bryan through my head for obvious reasons. No C there. Secretary of War Lindley Garrison. L. G.

There was a rustling beside me. I wasn't ready to give up on this one yet.

More rustling and I turned to Bunky.

He was trying to sit up.

"Whoa," I said. "Take it easy."

His head was down and I didn't see his eyes. He braced himself with one hand as he tried to put his legs on the floor. I grabbed him by the shoulder on his unbraced side and helped him get upright. He lifted his face to me. His eyes were open but I couldn't tell if he was seeing me or if he was seeing a dream he was in the middle of.

He had his feet on the floor now and he looked down, as if to check that out. I let go of him.

"Take it easy, Pops," I said.

"Don't call me that," he said. He looked at me again and he was clearly seeing me.

"Yeah, right," I said. "Just checking to see if you're really here." And now I found myself pissed at Bunky. Not Pops. Okay. My savvy but pathetically self-destructing Uncle Bunk.

"I'm here," he said.

"I'm surprised."

"What about?"

"You were talking about toad shit just a few minutes ago."

"Toad shit?"

"Yep."

"Not surprising at all."

"You remember what that was about?"

"Hell no," Bunky said. "But that's how my benders go. I'm way out of it, and then after a while…What time is it?"

"About one."

"In the afternoon?"

"That's sunlight you're seeing at the window."

He turned his face in that direction. "So it is. Anyway, I'm out and then abruptly I'm not."

I found myself impatient with him. *B. F. M. keine Eier.* But I had no reason to feel superior. I could hit the *mezcal* myself sometimes, once a month or so, to the point of a heavy, oblivious sleep. But I kept writing. Bunky needed to keep writing. That took balls. What a damn waste.

I needed to go back to Gerhard. Show him Mensinger's notes.

"You okay on your own now?" I asked.

"Always am."

"Now *that's* toad shit," I said.

Bunky shrugged. I cuffed him on the shoulder to make it right.

22

I headed straight for my rooms, and my clean clothes were laid out on the bed in my own shape: shirt, pants, socks, as if I were lying there on my back. I still didn't know her name,

I heard the low voices of the girls out in the courtyard, about to have their siesta. I almost stepped to the door, and I knew all I had to do was appear there and she would rise and come in to me. She had already laid me out on the bed.

But I went to the desk and pulled the one drawer completely from its enclosure and removed Mensinger's wallet and I laid it on the desktop. I put the letter back in its envelope. I removed the train ticket and made sure I had its departure day and time right. Tomorrow. Early. I slid it back into its compartment. I put the wallet in my pocket, replaced the desk drawer, hesitated one moment more at the voices of the girls outside, and then I went to the front door and through.

Diego was sitting on the stoop.

He jumped up as I stepped out. "Boss," he said. "You wanted me to come by the *portales*. You were gone."

"Do you know how to write?"

He popped his head back a little at the question. It surprised him. Then his lower lip pooched up slightly and he shrugged. He didn't. He regretted it. He was a good boy. I wondered where he lived, who was there.

"I've got it covered," I said. I looked carefully around the street and no one was near, no one was watching from afar.

"Come close," I said, and Diego and I huddled in the doorway. From my pockets I pulled the wallet and a note I'd written on a scrap of paper in a crude, childlike hand. *objeto perdido.* Lost object. I slipped it into the fold of the wallet with an end sticking out prominently and handed it to him.

I said, "I want you to wait hidden till you are very sure no one is going in or out of the German Consulate. Then I want you to put this in front of the door and run away quickly. Don't knock. Just run. They'll find it. Do you understand?"

Diego gave me his narrow-eyed, independent-thinking look.

"This is what I'm telling you to do," I said.

"You want to get this back to Scarface with him thinking somebody just found it lying around. Is that right?"

"Yes."

"He didn't lose it. He knows that."

"Lying around because the thief took the money and ditched the wallet with the worthless stuff still in it. Somebody found it and wanted to give it back."

"Why would he run away?"

"He's afraid if he shows himself, the Germans will think he was the one who stole it."

"No poor *Mexicano* will think like that. He could get a reward. I'll knock on the door and I'll ask . . ."

"No," I said. And I snatched the wallet from him.

"Wait," he said.

"You do it exactly my way or the boss fires you."

Diego grabbed at the wallet but I pulled my hand back and straightened up to keep it away.

He continued to grab in vain, as I kept it just barely out of his reach to make him understand he could have it back only if he behaved. I did this even as I simultaneously tried to reason with him, an impulse he oddly seemed to provoke in me. "I don't need this to be perfect. If they wonder, let them wonder. I want them to get it back with at least the possibility it was just locals. And I want you safe."

This last assertion made him stop grabbing at the wallet. His hand fell. He looked at me closely. I didn't know what was going through his head now, but he'd gone very still. Then Diego said, "So maybe the thief's *papi* makes him do it. But he's a poor man, the *papi,* so he keeps the money and he makes his son give back the rest."

My first thought was that I doubted the Germans would look at it that way. Not that I'd say it, because it would just cause him to sass and defy me some more. But my second thought made *me* go very still: He'd cast me in the role of *papi* again. And now I found myself thinking: He's not just sassing and defying; he's trying to reason with me.

I put my hand on his shoulder. "Sure," I said. "They may think that."

He lifted his hand and I put the wallet in it.

And he was quick: He was under my arm and took one step into a run. But I was quick too: I grabbed him by the collar on his shirt. "Slow down, Diego Cordero. If you want to do this cleverly, you do it slow. Watch the consulate for a while. Out of sight. Make sure no one is moving in there, no one is coming along the street."

He looked up at me. And he gave me one firm little nod. I let him go. He slipped the wallet inside his shirt and he stepped away, started to move off down the street at a stroll. He was still in earshot and I was about to call him *un niño bueno,* a good boy. But I'd learned my lesson about Diego Cordero. "*Un chulo callejero,*" I said. A good street punk. He rolled his shoulders but did not look back. I knew he was pleased.

And I stepped off the other way. I headed for the *Hostal Buen Viaje.*

23

The old man who'd been sleeping this morning at the desk had now vanished altogether. In the lobby there was only fly buzz and the distant huffing of a train engine and Gerhard's name still chalked on the lodgers board. Most of the other rooms were empty.

I stepped into the ragged courtyard. The loopy drone of the flies increased, but behind that was only silence. In my normal operating area—on or around or approaching or retreating from a place of battle, be it the volcanic mountaintops of Nicaragua or the streets of Sofia—I had a pretty acute sense of the wrongness about a situation. But my first thought now was simply that I'd missed him, he'd gone out already.

This thought did not last for long. I took a step into the courtyard and another and the silence was starting to thicken into aftermath, into a thing that made me move more quickly to Gerhard's door and I found that with my first knock it yielded a little bit, unlatched, and I pushed it open and he was lying in the center of the floor, filling the tiny room with his sprawled body, his head surrounded by the wide penumbra of his blood, his throat slashed, his eyes open sightless to the ceiling. I leaned back into the door, clicking it shut, steeling myself in the way of the battlefield. I'd seen a thousand men dead, a hundred alive in this moment and dead in the next, but this one was personal, this one was very personal. And I thought perhaps my own visit to him this morning contributed to this. And I thought this was all getting

very big, whatever I was after here. And I thought I was thinking just
to keep myself from letting go to the urge to run.

I breathed deep and let it out, once, twice. I became the war
correspondent, the reporter. The blood looked fresh. This was recent.
He was still wearing his outing pants and he'd put on a plaited dress
shirt but didn't get to the collar. The shirtfront's whiteness was sprayed
with red. There were relatively few flies, no vermin. Recent. I looked
around the room. His open music case lay on the narrow bed, the
horn removed and dropped beside it. The bed was angled away from
the wall. There wasn't much to search, but the killer did it thoroughly.
Gerhard's clothes were scattered at the foot of the bed, his leather
suitcase gaping open, mouth down, against the floor. On this side of
the room, a small chair was leaning on two legs against the wall. On
the floor, near the chair, was Gerhard's wallet, open. I stepped to it,
bent to it, touched it lightly with my fingertips to see that the money
compartment was empty. But I did not think for a moment that this
was a robbery.

I straightened and I looked back to Gerhard. His body had preoc-
cupied my first glance at him. Now I could see two things beside him.
On the floor to his right, near his slack hand: a folded white paper.
On his other side, isolated on the floor, a pale-blue-covered booklet.
REISE-PASS. The German Imperial Eagle. Gerhard's passport.

I bent to the folded paper and picked it up. I opened it. And the
eagle was American here, an olive branch in one talon and a bundle of
arrows in the other. This was the certificate of naturalization making
Gerhard Zimmerman an American citizen in 1896, at age twenty. I
folded the certificate and placed it back on the floor. I moved to the
passport and picked it up. Gerhard Vogel. His assumed name. The first
page had his photo. This man was the man from across the courtyard
table a few hours ago: dark, wide-set eyes, his curled Kaiser Wilhelm
mustaches framing the center of his face like quotation marks. The
Kaiser perceiving his false identity and calling out the irony.

I closed the passport.

I had some quick and complicated decisions to make.

Mensinger and his mission were involved in this one way or another. That seemed intuitively clear to me.

There was nothing I could do for Gerhard.

I could only bulldog this story now. Tomorrow morning I would follow Mensinger north.

And that would be the best I could do for Gerhard. To figure out what was going on and to expose it.

I couldn't travel as myself. Mensinger had not seen me yet, as far as I knew. But I couldn't travel as an American. I'd never even make it to Mexico City.

I put Gerhard's passport in my pocket. I looked to his naturalization papers on the floor. Both these things were left in the room, in the open, to tell the Americans that the killers—the Germans—knew who this man was and what he was doing.

I could get Bunky to put my photo in the passport. For the *Federales* along the route and for any possible bandit ambushes, this would help. I needed to keep away from Mensinger, but he'd be in a Pullman, reclusive, I was sure. I'd be several cars behind. I did worry about an entourage. But I had to risk this.

I'd leave Gerhard's other papers on the floor. I couldn't afford to get involved in an investigation, but he needed to be identified.

I took another deep breath. I looked at Gerhard. I nodded him a respectful good-bye. I turned and eased open the door, peeked out. The courtyard was still empty.

I stepped from the room. I approached the front of the hotel carefully. The old man had returned, but he was back on his chair behind the front desk and snoring heavily. I moved quietly past him and I stopped a few steps from the door and watched the street. I waited for a passerby to cross in front of the hotel, heading away from the train station. And I slipped out of the *Hostal Buen Viaje,* unnoticed. I turned toward the station and moved quickly off, leaving the murder behind but carrying it with me very closely now indeed.

24

The train station was ahead but I needed to transform the passport in my pocket into my own passport before I could put a name on a ticket. I needed Bunky first. I needed to turn into Gerhard Vogel. I headed for the *Diligencias,* where Bunk was no doubt by now seeking a remedy with the hair of the mangy Mexican street dog that bit him. I put my head down and walked fast and expected to think about Mensinger's talking points; the time had come to focus on this story as if I were with the Greeks again at Kilkis and I was ready to go on ahead to Sofia if they beat the Bulgars as badly as I expected. All of which clear, professional thinking was impossible in the present moment. It was not every day you saw the throat slashed of a guy who could admire the way the Cubs turned a double play even though he was a Pirates fan. Or who played a minor horn in a brass band like he actually enjoyed making music. If he was such a bully American spy and he had a build on him, how did he let some Hun feed him to the worms?

I stewed about this till I was coming up on the *portales,* and the place was not even a quarter full, with the siesta in full snore and the newsmen either adopting that particular local custom or off trying to invent stories. Davis, I'd learn later, was at this very moment with Fred Palmer and Medill McCormick getting themselves arrested up the train line toward Mexico City, asserting their rights as journalists and giving Davis one of his meaningless, self-instigated, derring-do magazine stories out of it. I knew better than that.

And there was Bunky, as I expected, sitting alone at our table nursing a *mezcal* to ease the pain in his head. As I sat down with him, he was full of avid assertions that it was only one drink so he could actually focus his eyes.

"I know, I know," I said, and I wasn't sounding sarcastic. He wasn't totally out of control yet, old Bunk. He did still know how to arrange for a fairly sober week after a really bad night.

And the bit of *mezcal* had already done its work sufficiently to let him notice my face.

"What's happened?" he said.

I told him the whole story.

He listened in focused silence, and then, when I finished, he looked off to the street and whistled, low.

I slid the passport across the table to him. He took it and glanced at the picture page and slipped it into his pocket. "I've got a couple of shots of you that'll work," he said.

"I need it right away," I said.

"No problem," he said.

"You think you can face the smell of the chemicals right now?"

"Two more sips and I can sniff Satan's butt," he said.

"Looks like that's going to be *my* job," I said.

"You be careful," he said. "These guys seem to know what they're doing."

I gave him a single nod, like my catcher had just asked for a fastball that I was ready to throw.

Bunky lifted his glass of *mezcal* to me and took the first of his two-more sips. He said, "You want to try some of those things on me that Mensinger wrote down?"

"Sure," I said.

I looked away to bring them to mind and I found myself staring into Diego's face. But from across the street, and he was passing by quickly.

He was cutting across the *zócalo* at a medium trot, as if he was being chased but didn't quite want to show it. And he was giving me a look as if he had a little bit of a problem and he was checking to see if there was anything the boss could do. Then he was looking forward again and he vanished behind the trees up the path toward the band shell. I didn't have time to think about this: Walking briskly across my sight now, unaware of me, seeming to match Diego's pace for the moment but apparently not ready to catch him, was *Kapitän Krüger*. For a brief moment I didn't recognize him. No Uhlan uniform. His outing pants were dark and so was his shirt and he had on what looked like a very dark railroad workman's jacket, but also vaguely military, with unadorned epaulets, and his head was bare. The clothes, in being so at odds with Vera Cruz weather in their darkness, seemed consciously chosen for some specific purpose; the bareheadedness seemed as if he had gone out in haste. And he was clearly following Diego, who had probably tried to embellish his orders from me about the wallet and of course it had gone wrong.

All this ran through my mind even as I was jumping to my feet and crossing the street as soon as Krüger was past easy head-turning range. I jogged into the path and Krüger was thirty yards or so ahead of me. I reckoned Diego was about that far ahead of the German, so I slowed to their pace and followed. We circled the band shell to the left and headed back toward *Independencia.* I caught a quick sight of Diego far up ahead. He had come this way to get my attention and to show me, even now, that Krüger was definitely following him.

I did nothing to hide my presence, other than keeping my distance. I was not afraid of Krüger seeing me. If he did and it made him break off, then all the better. But he was not focusing on anything except the boy. This wasn't going to end well.

We crossed the *avenida* now and we were heading south on *Calle de Miguel Lerdo.* The streets were nearly deserted with everyone sleeping. The sun was high and Krüger was badly dressed for this heat, overlayered and dark. I would have liked to wear him down a little if he and I were going to tangle, but this was a Prussian-blooded officer.

He was used to much worse. And I started thinking about what I'd learned from stage fisticuffs, especially in the character of ruffians. The dirty fighters from melodramas. *The Trail of the Serpent.* Or *The Black Swine Gang.* Not that I hadn't done enough pretty serious fistfighting just from being a theater kid dropping into real schools now and then. I did plenty. And I was doing too much thinking, I realized. I needed to focus my body now. I was in the wings, ready to go on.

And we crossed *Avenida Cinco de Mayo* and *Cortes* and *Hidalgo* and we were keeping this same pace. We'd been bounded by runs of shops and stucco houses with courtyards and then adobe houses and then there were open stretches of rubbled lots and we crossed the tram tracks at *Avenida Bravo.* And suddenly Krüger was moving faster. But still at a brisk walk. If he were really making a move on Diego, he'd be running. Diego himself must have picked things up. If I couldn't see him because of Krüger, maybe he couldn't see me. Maybe he looked quickly back over his shoulder and all he could see was the Hun in pursuit, and Diego was truly scared now. But I just kept up. And still Krüger failed to look over his own shoulder, which was arrogance, one way or another: that Diego had no one to defend him and Krüger could easily have his way, or that somebody was following and Krüger could deal with him in due time without even checking out who it might be.

We crossed *Avenida Guerrero* and ahead was a set of train tracks that had curved out of the great tangle of switching tracks south of the terminal, the main branch bearing the National Railway to Orizaba and on to Mexico City. There was a run of warehouses just ahead, dead quiet in the afternoon siesta and lightly populated anyway and with corridors between that were out of public sight. I figured if Krüger was going to make a move, this would be the place. There was one thing for me to try to make this go relatively easy. With no fight at all maybe; maybe with just some hard looks and bad words.

"Captain Krüger," I called out.

He glanced over his shoulder at me without breaking his stride and then he turned back toward Diego ahead of him. And now Krüger started to sprint.

"Watch out!" I cried and I ran hard to follow the two of them.

Ahead I saw Diego dart off the street to the right and between two warehouses.

Krüger angled toward the corridor and I followed, pressing hard, sprinting too, and the Hun was fast and he vanished between the warehouses, and this was a bad moment, every stride I took too slow, too slow, and rocks were underfoot, a scattering of trash, I had to watch where I put my foot with this step and this one so as not to stumble and I was into the dimness of the corridor and Krüger was twenty yards ahead, and by his ignoring me I figured he was thinking I'd still be around after Diego was dead, but if he turned to take me out first, Diego would vanish, so he would deal with the boy quickly before he dealt with me, and all that was bad, that was very bad, I strode hard and Krüger was lunging now as he ran and I couldn't see Diego but Krüger must have been knife-slashing at him as he ran, he was close, he was close and all Diego needed to do was stumble once, I had to get Krüger to deal with me, and a stone was ahead on the ground a smooth rounded stone and one stride more and I bent and strode and grabbed and strode and rose and slick as Joe Tinker charging a slow roller toward short I was up throwing and I put something on the throw and the stone flew straight and Krüger was just coming up from a lunge and the stone caught him hard in the center of his back and he broke his stride but it was not enough to make him fall, his torso dipped forward a bit and twisted at the pain and I saw a flash of Diego just ahead still okay and running and Krüger straightened and he was running but I was suddenly gaining on him and he slowed and I strode and I would fall on him from behind but I needed to grab his knife arm, needed to grab it, but Krüger was quick and he was in full control of his body now and he knew I was coming and he lunged a little to the left and he was doing a spin flashing around to face me and I stepped hard and pressed at my legs to stop, I could no longer tackle him from behind, and I saw the blade of his knife now coming around and I stopped, I was stopped, but he was barely ten feet before me and he was squared around and he crouched a little and spread his feet, spread his arms like he was relaxing in a reading chair, and his knife was ready to do its work.

And beyond Krüger I could see Diego. He had stopped and was coming back our way.

"Keep running," I called to him, having the presence of mind not to use his name. If we all three came out of this alive and Krüger had a tale to tell, I didn't want it to be clear that Diego and I knew each other. I could just be a guy poking his nose into somebody else's nasty business.

The profoundly stubborn and undisciplined Diego Cordero Medina Espinoza was not minding me.

"Run away, boy," I shouted.

He took another step in our direction.

I had not let Krüger leave my vision, but now I looked fully at him again. He hadn't attacked yet because he knew what was going on beyond him. I could see him thinking: *Perfect. The boy refuses to go. I can still kill you both.*

He smiled.

I looked at his knife and I took a step back, and it occurred to me that this was the knife. This was the knife that killed Gerhard. This very morning. And Krüger started forward now. He was thinking he could toy with me. Maybe he could. I took another step back.

He took another step forward, still in his crouch. He had returned to my line of sight toward Diego. The boy had vanished. It was just Krüger and me. This was probably better. I had to focus totally on the Hun and his knife or I was a dead man. I figured I might be anyway.

Fencing, fine. Bare-knuckle brawling, fine. Pistols even. Fine. But my stage training had nothing in it to prepare me to defend myself with my bare hands against a German soldier and a knife. I took another step back.

Krüger was enjoying this. "Will you run now, girlie?" he said in English. "Why don't you try to die like a man."

And as I realized it was time to take a stand and I formed the intention to move my eyes to the knife hand, the world slowed way

down, and Krüger straightened a little to come at me and he lifted
from the shoulders just a bit and started to move his leg and suddenly
his right shoulder flinched forward and a gray chunk of stone popped
up off him from behind and I started to move my leg to close on him
as the stone veered and glanced off his right ear and his head jerked
a little to the left and my eyes fell now to the knife hand and it was
moving but not toward me it was moving in an angle off to the right
as he jolted a little forward from the stone's blow and I stepped again
and my hands were coming up and opening wide and his knife hand
had stopped its unintended push forward and his arm had opened up
enough that I had a clear shot at his wrist and my hands lunged and
his arm was starting to move back to me but my hands clamped now
on his wrist, clamped hard, and I'd been in enough schoolyard brawls
to know to fight dirty and for now I held on to the wrist even as I felt
his arm tense and I would deal with this arm but first I turned my face
toward him and down and I shifted in my footing, rotated slightly,
and I planted my left leg and I was lifting my right leg and my hands
resisted his straining arm which was struggling without the leverage
of a body behind it and my right foot rose and my eyes now were on
my target, which was his right knee, and I kicked, I thrust my leg hard
I thrust as if my foot would break straight through and the bottom
of my boot cracked heavily at his knee joint from above and across
and the knee jerked downward and inward and I heard his scream as
a distant thing, a very distant thing, and now I turned and it was time
for the arm even as it had gone slack, I brought my right foot back and
planted it and I jerked his knife arm high and I ducked and twisted my
body downward and under the arm and around, all the way around,
holding the arm tight where it was and I was facing him again and he
was wrenched down on the ground, legs folded beneath him, and his
arm was twisted up and far behind him.

The knife fell from his hand. But my hands, my whole body,
roared on. I twisted hard at the arm, twisted it even farther across his
back, I put my foot against his right shoulder blade and I wrenched at
the arm and felt it give way at the socket.

I heard screaming. Distant screaming.

I stopped. I was on both my feet. He was down against the ground.

I heard screaming. Nearby now. Very loud. Krüger was screaming.

I looked at his arm. I'd let it go. It was lying nearly flat across his back.

I looked down along his body and I saw his right leg splayed out from under him, the angle all wrong at the knee.

I was breathing fast and heavy and it was like I wasn't breathing at all, my lungs felt utterly empty, and I slowed it down, slowed it all down. I thought about what this all was. I started to actually feel the air I was drawing into me. I was breathing. I was slowing down.

I could hear Krüger struggling to control the screaming, struggling to be a man, though the low sobbing moan that abruptly took over for the scream must have embarrassed him just as much.

I turned to Diego, who was pressed back against the warehouse wall. His eyes were wide.

"Are you okay?" I managed to say, though my voice was thin and soft.

He nodded yes.

Krüger had gone quiet. I looked down at him. He was lying face forward, his head turned to the side, his face pressed against the dirt, his mouth gaping. I thought he'd passed out from the pain. But his lips seemed to be trying to move and he was starting to moan again.

He'd chosen this.

Diego and I had to go.

But before we did, I had to understand for certain what my instincts had told me a short time ago.

I leaned down and grabbed Krüger's torso and I tried to turn him over onto his back. He moaned loud as he turned, and his arm stayed twisted and vanished beneath him, keeping him from going flat, but I could see his dark shirtfront. I clearly made out a darker, faintly glistening stain there, a great dark stain splashed upon his chest. Krüger had known that he would be covered in Gerhard's blood and that his dark clothes would hide the stains for his return to the consulate.

I looked back to Diego. He had not moved. His eyes were not quite so wide now, but he was still frozen there.

I took a step toward him. My legs were unsteady. But I focused. I took another step.

And for a moment Diego pulled away from me. Ever so slightly. But I could see his shoulders go back, his face tighten, his eyes freeze.

It made no difference that my violence was in his defense. For one terrible moment—as terrible for me as for him—I was his *papi* coming for him.

I stopped. And the moment flickered and passed. The moment passed. He was looking at *me* again, not at his father. He knew it was me again.

"You sure you're all right?" I said.

"Yes," he said.

"You caught him outside, coming back to the consulate," I said, more a statement than a question, though Diego understood that I was asking.

He nodded yes.

"You tried to hit him up for a reward for finding the wallet."

He nodded yes.

"Will you ever learn to do what I say?"

He nodded yes.

We just looked at each other. For one breath, and another.

Then I said, "Thanks for the stone." He'd probably saved my life. And he could not have known that I'd thrown one only a few moments before.

Diego said, "David and Goliath. I am a good Catholic son."

I turned back to Krüger. He murdered Gerhard. I had no doubt. I thought to kill him. Right now. Take his own knife, which was lying a few feet away, and do the justice that, in this time and place and circumstance and considering the victim's secrets and the killer's diplomatic status, I knew would not be done.

The part of me that sounded so reasonable making this case but raged wildly beneath, that part wanted to do this thing, wanted to kill this son of a Prussian whore. But the other part of me that trembled now in muscle and nerve from what I'd done so far and yet was calm beneath, that part wanted me to live my life the way I'd always lived it, at observant peace amid war, watching, writing, taking care. Gerhard and Krüger could eventually come to justice through my printed words. Let God be God; I'd be Christopher Marlowe Cobb.

I knew I was being watched. Not from heaven. From a few feet away.

I turned again to Diego. My high-energy little street punk was still pressed against the warehouse wall, had still barely moved a muscle. His eyes had grown wide again, as if he knew what I was considering.

Krüger was beginning to moan once more. I turned back to him. I took a step. Diego gasped a little. I did not stop. I would not kill Krüger, but if he was going to live, then he had to understand.

I stood over him. He was still partly on his back. His eyes fluttered open now. I bent near his face. His eyes closed and then opened, not in a flutter but in a single, waking gesture. I waited. I waited for his eyes to fix on me.

I watched something surge silently in him. He cut off a moan. He was fully conscious. He knew who was before him.

I said, "The next time I see you." And I paused to let it sink in. His eyes focused, flared. "The next time," I said, "I will kill you." And I meant it.

I straightened up. I turned to Diego. I gave him a snap of the head toward the light at the far end of the corridor between the warehouses and he was off at once, at a run, and I was following him.

25

Diego led me to a tiny, cobbled-together hovel—once fully adobe but now *el Norte*-ravaged and patched with smears of cement, a panel of scrounged wood, a rusted sheet of tin. I could hear a woman's voice—a sweetly wavery woman's voice—singing within. I looked at Diego, who heard this too, and he shot me a brow-furrowed glance. His mother. He was embarrassed.

"It's good," I said, meaning something that Diego surely didn't get. This neighborhood of hovels was piled everywhere with great heaps of long-rotting garbage. The smell was a different kind of putrid but just about as intense as the next-afternoon smell of untouched carnage on a Nicaraguan battlefield, and the slop beneath our feet had run straight from the waste buckets of these households. But she sang. I was instantly sure that some of the good I saw in Diego was due to his mother singing in the midst of all this, and my little *chulo callejero* didn't get it. Maybe he would someday.

She sang that her lover should not give the mole next to his lip to anyone's mouth but hers and she moved into the refrain: *Ay, ay, ay, ay, Canta y no llores, Porque cantando se alegran, Cielito lindo, los corazónes.* Sing and don't cry, was the message. Singing gladdens the heart.

Diego flung up the palm of his hand at me and darted ahead through his door and out of sight. I stopped and waited. All right. Not quite the verse of the song he might have liked me to hear from his mother. There was singing and there was singing. And I thought of my mother singing in Storyville, and I preferred to just take a deep breath of this neighborhood and clear my head of that.

The singing stopped. The hut was quiet. Diego appeared in the doorway and motioned for me to enter. It struck me now: He never questioned that he would bring me along to where he lived. We didn't say a word about it, but after he and I, together, lived through the moment when he was to be knifed to death as a child, after we caught that particle of time and deflected it elsewhere, this was where we needed to go. Together.

I moved to the door and I stepped in. His mother was sitting cross-legged on a rush mat in the center of the floor, a dark shirt I recognized as Diego's crumpled in her lap, a needle and thread placed upon it so she could receive me. The walls of the one room were bare and there were half a dozen sleeping mats around the edges of the floor, one with about a six-year-old girl, cornstalk-thin, asleep on her side, one with a half-naked toddler boy who looked like he was on the verge of tears but did not make a sound, one with a chicken picking at it, having wandered in through the open back door, where I could see other dwellings like this one arranged around a common ground with a stone washtub and pump in the middle.

Diego wasn't clean. Never had been. He was smudged and he was ragged around the edges, but he always looked better than this place. He hadn't prepared me for this.

His mother was probably not much past thirty but looked to be fifty. She was mixed dark, Aztec but with some evident Spanish blood in her from randy hacienda owners having their way with various generations of her grandmothers. She wore a faded green sleeveless dress. A brown scapular on a cord hung around her neck.

She lifted her round face to me—I could see Diego there—and she smiled. "You are good to my boy," she said.

"He is a good boy," I said.

And she straightened at this, lifted her eyebrows.

I felt Diego rustling next to me. I wondered if it was at my praise or at his mother's resistance to it.

"He is a thief," she said.

"He does what he needs to do," I said.

And now she sank a little into herself, her eyebrows fell, her eyes went dark. *Yes*, she was thinking. *And is that not my fault?*

"He would have it another way," I said. I looked at Diego, who startled me slightly in his face already being lifted to mine, as if it had been there all along, and he had that intense attention of his focused on me. I said, "Isn't that right, Diego Cordero Medina y Espinoza?"

"Yes sir," he said.

"I was married to his father," his mother said.

I knew that from Diego's two last names. Most couples among the urban poor of Mexico did not formally marry. The State required both civil and religious ceremonies, and the custom when they went through these formalities was for the children to take the surnames of both parents. But the formal marriages were too expensive for the poor. And when the man and woman didn't marry, their children could take only the father's name. Diego's parents somehow managed to have the ceremony. If they had not, he would simply have been Diego Cordero Espinoza.

"I understand," I said. "You both have done what you need to do."

She smiled at me. "You will drink with us? Some *pulque?* And there is some fruit."

"Yes," I said, "thank you." And I sat on the floor before her, and Diego sat beside me, and we ate figs and bananas, and the mother looked at her son when she served the figs and she said "These are stolen," and I said nothing, but Diego stirred beside me and I knew he was looking at me and I thanked his mother for the fruit and then we drank *pulque* together, Diego and his mother and I. And though I knew I hated the stuff and though the air around me stank from the way of life in this place, I touched her tin cup and Diego's and I drank, and the *pulque* tasted okay. The *pulque* tasted pretty damn good.

26

Diego's mother rose when I rose to go and she held my offered hand with both of hers. I put my other hand on top and squeezed very gently. Though I expected him to get pissed at me for doing it, I said again to her, "You have a good boy. He will make you proud."

I was happy to see not a single flicker of surprise in her face.

"Thank you," she said.

Diego walked with me away from his house, and we stopped and faced each other. We both knew that tomorrow I would slip onto the train to follow Mensinger far up-country, and it was unclear where I would end up and when I might see Diego again. I put my hand inside my shirt, opened a flap of the money belt and I found a certain sort of coin by shape and heft. I pulled it out and bent down so I was eye-to-eye with Diego. I held up the coin between us.

His eyes went wide and I was feeling bad—more than bad, very uneasy—about maybe not seeing him again. I was glad to be doing this for him and for his brothers and sisters and for his singing mother, and I was very glad to see his eyes widen over a good thing on this day, for I wouldn't soon forget the wideness of his eyes after he was nearly killed and after I ripped Krüger's arm out of its socket. In my hand was an Indian Head Gold Eagle coin. I was looking at the Indian himself, in profile with war bonnet. I wanted Diego to see the Indian. I turned the coin, and the standing eagle on the other side, also in profile, made me think of the thing I told Gerhard and he told me. We are Americans. Together. But go far enough back and Americans have all come from somewhere else. And this kid before me had the heart of an American. The coin was 90 percent gold, worth ten bucks. Which would go a long way in Vera Cruz, Mexico.

"This is to stay away from the Germans while I'm gone," I said.

He nodded, without ever letting his eyes shift from mine.

I offered him the coin.

He struggled a little with his face now, trying to keep his eyes dry and his mouth firm, but I had to look very closely to see it. He was a good kid. He put his two fingers on the top of the coin and we both held it for a very brief moment. Then he gently extracted the coin from my hand. "Thanks, boss," he said.

And he turned and he was gone.

I knew what he meant. Just as briskly, and with just as much control of my feelings, I stood and I turned and I walked away.

It was mid-afternoon and there was much to do.

Bunky first and it was not till I was up the steps of his *casa de huéspedes* and heading for his door that I realized how I'd been trusting him till this moment. I did glance as I trotted past the *Diligencias* and I noticed he wasn't there, but the alternative didn't really register on me. Only now did I wonder if he was drunk again and I'd be in Dutch on the train tomorrow, trying to travel as myself or with no documentation. I knocked.

Bunky answered at once. "Enter."

I went in. The room was heavy with the smell of sulphur and bromine. Bunky sat at his table. The tan, wooden Kodak developer box with the roller handles had been pushed away from him and he was hunched over the open passport, smoothing a page with his thumbs. He was coming through for me. He knew what was at stake now and he could do this.

"Just in time," he said.

"Bunk, would you do me a favor?"

He looked up at me.

I said, "Keep a chair wedged under your doorknob when you're in here."

He straightened up, sat back.

"Are they after us too?" he asked.

"I wouldn't be surprised."

He nodded.

"And keep an eye on the kid," I said. "Give him some things to do but keep him away from the Huns."

"I'll do the best I can."

We looked at each other for a long moment. He knew and I knew, but I needed to say it. "You need to keep off the juice," I said. "At least while I'm gone."

The nod of assent he gave me was so minute I could barely see it from across the room. But it was more believable because of that.

He looked back down to the passport and took a cloth from beside him on the table, put his forefinger in it and began to wipe. I crossed the room and stood beside him. He was tracing the pasted outer edge of a photo of my face. Gerhard had vanished beneath me. I'd taken his place. I put a hand on the old man's shoulder. "Thanks, Bunk."

He nodded. "And what about you? Do you have a plan?"

"Follow him."

"And?"

I shrugged. He waited. "Get the story," I finally said.

"At least I know to put a chair against the door."

"At least you know there is a door."

He nodded. We both understood. Even covering a real war, everything is always new. But you know to find the high ground or the top of a building or a place beside the artillery unit or along the lines or with a certain officer at general headquarters. You have people to walk up to and ask how it is and what's next. You can simply go out and dodge bullets and say how that felt. It's a drama and each set is a little different, but you know the theater. You know your way around. Everything before me now was improvisation. And this had better be the last I thought about that. I had to anticipate some things, but only my next move or two. There were too many unknowns, and as for any good reporter on any story, you keep your mind wide open for surprises.

Bunky handed me Gerhard's passport. My passport. "Take care of yourself," he said.

"You too," I said. "And the boy."

We shook on that.

And I found a clothes store around the corner from the *Diligencias*. The fawning shop owner made suits to order but he also had racks of rentals for occasions and he was only too happy to sell me a used one. I passed over a linen suit that looked too much like Mensinger and I ended up with a light gray mohair that more or less fit me. I added a gray felt fedora and I was ready to be Gerhard Vogel. I paid, and as I put the brown-paper parcel under my arm, I thought of packing and I thought of my rooms and I thought of Gerhard dead in his and of my warning to Bunky.

Krüger might have somehow made it back to the consulate by now, though given the shape he was in, maybe not yet. He was going to need some help. But it was quite possible they would come to find me. I needed to pack my things and vacate my rooms and I needed to stay public for a while, act normal, and then lie low till the train left in the morning.

I beat it back to my room and found the lock secure and the room untouched. I followed my own advice and pulled the wooden chair from the small desk and wedged it under the knob of the outer door. I packed my valise. And as I did, I heard a woman's voice, reedy and light, singing in the courtyard. I went to my courtyard door and opened it quietly.

She was unaware of me, my laundry girl. She stood beside a low, rickety wooden table with a man's shirt spread out on it. She was bending to a tin of hot coals beside her, pulling the iron from the handle, straining hard to lift it. Her arms were bare. Her throat was bare. She turned to the table and began to press the iron onto the shirt.

I crossed the courtyard and she didn't hear me till I was very near. The song was familiar. Very popular, but still odd on this day: from Diego's mother's voice to this señorita's. She sang from a later verse: *De tu casa a la mía, Cielito lindo, no hay más que un paso.* From your house to mine, darling one, there is no more than a step.

The señorita sensed me and stopped singing and she turned her face to me. Her forehead and the bridge of her nose and her upper lip were beaded with sweat. I was close to her now and she smelled of musk and starch and I passed the palm of my hand over her forehead, my hand going moist and cool and I grabbed her by the ear and I pulled her and she dropped the iron in the coals and I dragged her by her ear, though not hurting her, quite, and she yielded enough, as I knew she would, and she moaned a little at the pressure on her ear, but it was a familiar moan, something like the moan we both now sought, and by the time we were in my room we were fierce—she as much as me this time—and it was over, and we disentangled and we lay beside each other for one moment, and another, and I had to leave this place, and I said to her, "I am going away now."

She said nothing.

"I'm not sure when I will return," I said.

Still not a sound from her.

"I will leave you a little something in the desk drawer," I said. "Not for this. For my clothes, how nicely you did them."

She touched my hand.

"I'm sorry," I said. "For not asking sooner. What's your name?"

She took her hand off mine and she rose and she drew her underthings up upon her and she smoothed down her skirt, and she was another one, on this day, who was not going to show feelings. She moved past me toward the courtyard door. I even thought she had somehow not heard my question. But as she put her hand on the doorknob, she paused, and she said, in a barely audible voice, "It is not important," and she was gone.

27

I slipped into the *Diligencias* through the back veranda door. The first wave of American refugees had recently shipped off to New Orleans and I was able, without drawing any attention, to get a room for the night. A good one, on the upper floor looking over the *zócalo*. I dropped my bag on the bed and went out and hustled to the train station, watching my back carefully. And I had to think the next step through. I was going to end up on the train with Mensinger. His ticket terminated at a strikingly obscure destination. Even if I followed him off the train in La Mancha, I didn't want my own ticket to make anyone suspicious. An inquisitive and talkative conductor, for instance. I'd buy my ticket for a stop somewhere up the line. Torreón. One of the ironies of the civil war was that the trains did run from one rebel's jurisdiction to another's. From the *Federales'* jurisdiction to a rebel's and out again. The rebels allowed it for the sake of occasionally waylaying a train and robbing it, certainly. But also to avoid simply shutting the country down. The rebellion had gone on for more than three years already and showed no signs of stopping.

And so, a short time later, a certain Herr Gerhard Vogel pointed at Torreón on the train schedule, fifty miles north of La Mancha, and he asked to buy a "*Zugkarte der ersten Klasse für Morgen*," which was about as much as I could expect to effectively say in this situation without resorting to double-talk faux-German. But the Mexican

clerk had plenty of German travelers pass through, so in a mixture
of Spanish and hand signals he verified if it was a first-class ticket I
wanted, for tomorrow, and I was able simply to nod. And Bunky had
done swell. The passport itself would work at customs in Hamburg. I
gestured effectively enough to get the first-class car as far back of the
Pullman as possible.

And it was not long before I was sitting at my table in the *portales,*
breathing a little easier as the end-of-the-afternoon sunlight stretched
out across the rooftops of Vera Cruz. The waiter, who knew me by now,
immediately delivered two telegrams. There were only two people
wiring me in Vera Cruz. I put the one aside with an unpleasant fizzle
in my head. I opened the Chicago wire. Clyde wrote: *Girl sniper great.*
Sold out Bulldog in half an hour, boosted Daybreak 30 percent, Morning simi-
lar. Too bad she didn't nick you. Dope on your man FVM vague. Some sort of
government banking official. You got a whiff?

I was glad his Bulldog edition sold out quick and carried into
the next day. Our big bosses loved that. And as for Scarface officially
being an economics guy, Clyde might as well have wired that he'd
confirmed Friedrich von Mensinger as a high-ranking German Secret
Service officer.

I signaled the waiter and he brought me cable blanks. I checked
my pocket Elgin, which I was back to carrying, now that I expected
to avoid trouble, at least for tonight, and I had a little time to get to
the telegraph office. So I also ordered an *aguardiente.* I wrote to Clyde:
Got a big whiff. Will be out of touch for a while. Bunky will handle VC inertia.

I figured that would boost Clyde's coffee intake 30 percent, his
sleeplessness a similar amount. But I laid the cable blank before me
on the tabletop with a tiny nod to Clyde Fetter. Clyde did not doubt
that I knew what I was doing, and he let me do it.

As did my mother. I wished I knew what it was *she* was doing and
could happily let her do it. Not that I had any choice but to let her,
whatever it was. I picked up her wire and put it down and picked it up
and put it down and drank some of the *aguardiente* that had just arrived
and then I picked the wire up and held it. She was capable of hinting

further about her "golden strings" being tuned or her "brass" being handled. I don't think she even understood how I didn't really want to hear about that. To be fair to her, as I grew up with my mother, when she was being a woman, she rarely could do anything but simply put me in the hotel hallway and regretfully expect me to now and then put my ear to the door. For her to have had no passion or, worse, for her to have it and never act upon it were her only realistic alternatives. And her genius as an actress meant she must, by her very essence, live her life openly, always upon a stage, even if it was in a play called *Life*.

I didn't respond to her last wire. And though it'd been but a relatively short time since she sent this one, it likely had already registered upon her that I was not giving her my blessing for whatever golden-string-tuning she'd decided to do. I was providing her with no end-of-the-act curtain. So the play had to go on. She felt she had to further explain. I opened the telegram.

We have always quoted the Elizabethans to each other, out of context, for our own purposes. And in her new message, after her *Dearest Christopher Marlowe Cobb*—her use of my name in its fullness reflecting her irritation—I recognized a tiny pastiche of *The Winter's Tale*: *'Tis hoped his sickness is discharged. To see his nobleness conceiving the dishonour of his mother! Go play, boy, play. Thy mother plays.*

And her closing words worked roughly upon me: *Love et cetera et cetera, Thy mother.* She could do better than that, I felt, in emoting her annoyance, but her uncharacteristic lapse made it all the worse, for the realness of feeling behind it. Though she could feign realness as well, I realized.

I put a cable blank on the table before me, took a bolt of *aguardiente*, and I wrote: *Discharged it is. Play on, Mother. My own play enters a new act. Love et non cetera. Kit*

The first sentence was a lie. And so was the attitude of the second. But I could not board the train in the morning and ride it wherever it would lead me without making this thing right between us.

28

I woke before dawn. The red-crowned parrots had started to chatter in the treetops of the *zócalo* outside my open windows, harsh, grating voices, speaking the German of bird languages. I was definitely awake— and even thinking already about Germans on this day of the pursuit of Mensinger—but now, abruptly, before I could rise, a memory began without an antecedent I could identify. But this was memory, certainly.

I was a boy. Seven years old. Maybe eight, tops. I'd come upon some local boys in a vacant lot, and they had a pocketknife. They were older than me—maybe ten or twelve—and they were playing mumblety-peg, going through the progression of trick throws. Spank the baby. Tony Chestnut. They didn't like me watching and they tried to chase me away and I challenged the boy doing the best, who happened also to be the biggest boy, to a game of Flinch. Or so I called it. Simple. We faced each other and we threw the knife as hard as we could toward our own foot, trying to miss but progressively throwing the knife closer and closer to our foot, and we kept doing it till one of us flinched, backed off, quit, or one of us buried the knife in the ground flush against our skin without drawing blood. It was summer. We were all barefoot. I was little, he was big, and he couldn't back down.

We started. I'm good with a knife. I was good as a kid. I put one about three inches from my foot. Suckered him in. He was a little hesitant at the start of this, but he suddenly smiled and figured he could show off and beat me easy. So I walked him in closer on our next two throws, but still not severely, and then on my third throw, I put one a thumb-width from the outer edge of my foot. He was scared now.

I took him off the hook. I uprooted my knife immediately and I threw it again, with all my might, and I felt it pop coolly against my skin and nuzzle there. I didn't even have to look down. The big boy's eyes went wide and they all took off, thinking me a dangerous boy.

But I realized now, remembering this, that the game itself wasn't about these other boys. Not them at all. It was about my mother. And though she was offstage in the memory, as she was in the game, it was about Mother in my room at the *Diligencias:* I went out into that vacant lot because I chose not to linger beside her door in the hotel hallway.

And realizing this, I could push it away. I rose from my hotel bed and I changed into the mohair suit and the fedora. I became Gerhard Vogel. I closed my bag and lifted it off the bed. The heft of it reminded me that I was bringing my Corona Portable Number 3. It was only a little over six pounds, but the bag was heavy already, and I hesitated. I could have left it with the waitstaff for Bunky to take care of. But no. When a story is big and complex and has life and death and much in between brimming out of it, I need my Corona to think straight. I need to see the words before me shaping themselves not in the personal quirks of my hand but in the uniform surety and clarity of actual type.

I went out. And from the south, coming up *Independencia,* was a heavy, cobbled rumble, the sound of what I took to be caissons. I paused, I moved a few steps down the *avenida,* wondering if Woody was going to make a move at last, a predawn deployment of cannon to begin an offensive. A foolish, wishful thought. What I saw coming up the street was a caravan of horse-drawn supply carts stacked high with nested, silver-metal, corrugated 42-gallon garbage cans. Today was the day the city of Vera Cruz, the United States of America's little piece of Mexico, would begin its struggle against street trash, the day the U.S. Army turned into garbagemen.

I backed away from the onslaught. I did a sharp about-face and retreated from the advancing regiment of garbage cans. I headed for the train station with an odd little ripple of something akin to respect for Friedrich von Mensinger and the men who had dispatched him. They seemed to have a much clearer grasp than my own president on what was at stake here.

As I anticipated, at the station, though it was still a couple of hours before departure, the Mexican travelers were already gathering and flowing down the platform to clamber on board to claim seats, dragging bags and baskets and birdcages and bundles of pots and pans and bedding, some traveling with the intention of returning and some taking whatever they could carry as they abandoned an occupied city. I followed them. Up ahead, all along the platform, in the wide cones of piss-colored electric light, the Mexican travelers were pressing into passenger cars. I strode on more quickly, past second class, where all of the early seat-grabbing hubbub was going on. I arrived at the rearmost of the two first-class coaches and there were only a few figures in the windows. I moved along nearly a car's-length farther and stepped away from the train to view the Pullman up ahead. The windows were dark. No one was near the car but a sentinel conductor smoking a cigarette.

I went up the forward steps into my coach and headed for the rear. The last row was empty. I sat at the train's left-hand window, where, just outside, a wide, jaundiced beam of electric light illuminated the platform like an upper-balcony death-scene spotlight. From here I would be able to see Mensinger pass by for his car. There was a possibility he had changed his plans, particularly after his train ticket disappeared for twenty-four hours. Though I had to admit that Diego was right: The risk he took to extort money from the Germans could help to ease their suspicions. My showing up to defend the kid would itself be suspicious, certainly. But that could well have been unrelated. Krüger surely sensed I didn't like him, and so if I happened to notice him ominously following a boy, I might well have meddled. Would the Germans accept it as a coincidence, my noticing the situation? It was, after all, unfolding in plain view in the *zócalo*. Was I more likely to have a Mexican kid steal the wallet and then give it back to him to extort a few pesos for the thing, private letter and train ticket and all? Mensinger would arrive, I told myself. They would stick to their well-made plans.

I settled in, but I kept my hat on for now to minimize the view of my face. Krüger was the only one of the Germans who could directly recognize me, and he was in no shape to go anywhere. He likely had already spoken of me as his assailant. I had to hope they didn't have one of a few specific old issues of *Scribner's* or *Pearson's* or *The Century* around the embassy to show Mensinger my mug. Which was a reasonable hope. And perhaps it was not so likely that Krüger told the truth about what happened to him. I took him for an arrogant man, a man proud of all his manly skills as a soldier. That he could have been physically overwhelmed by a mere journalist, an American journalist at that, would be humiliating. What was, in fact, likely was that he made up some other explanation for his injuries. Still, I needed to be cautious. And my main challenge now was to stay awake before dawn, on short sleep, till I verified Mensinger's arrival.

And it was not long before he arrived, briskly moving past, dressed in high boots and puttees, khaki pants and shirt, and wearing a slouch hat. A pistol sat on his right hip. And over his shoulder he carried a pair of outsized saddlebags. He passed quickly out of sight.

I tried to hold the image of him in my head. To figure this out. Dressed for the field as he was, he looked incongruously clean and pressed and crisp. But certainly ready to ride. His clothes and their pristine condition seemed familiar to me: He was in costume. It was theater. It was pure theater. I thought of La Mancha as his destination. And I understood. Mensinger didn't have a rendezvous there with Villa. He had a rendezvous with a horse. It made sense if he wanted to impress the *bandito*-turned-rebel leader. Villa was where everyone thought he was, in Torreón. But Mensinger would get off at La Mancha to ride those last fifty miles on horseback, far enough to break a real sweat and gather some trail dust. He was a German aristocrat. He'd gotten his combat scar within the stone walls of an ancient university from another aristocrat with whom he then went out drinking. Mensinger was approaching a volatile, emotional, suspicious, uneducated, thieving, cavalry-charging, war-seasoned Mexican, and he had to convince this man of his own credibility.

29

I hooked my feet in the handles of my bag, pulled my hat down farther over my eyes, and I slept. Dreamlessly, I thought, for I woke with a start with nothing in my head but a feeling of movement and then I thought I was wrong, that *this* was a dream, for I lifted my head and turned to the window and in the pale first light of the day, across a ragged verge of grass and stones, across a wide, dark *calle,* was the low adobe sprawl of the *Hostal Buen Viaje* and I thought perhaps the other Gerhard—for I was Gerhard now to protect my own life—I thought perhaps the *other* Gerhard was still lying in a room off a courtyard behind that hotel facade, he lay there dreaming his own dream from which he would not wake, and then this vision was gone, it floated past and we were curving, curving, and now before my eyes—or perhaps before only my unconscious mind—was *Avenida Guerrero* and a familiar row of warehouse buildings, and flashing past was the very one in whose shadow, just out of sight, a knife was lifted to kill a boy and I fought for him. But these vanished now too. I blinked hard, and still the streets passed by, with the tile-roofed houses and the gray scattered tombs of the *Cementerio General* and the wide *alameda* at the south end of *Independencia* and the great wooden bowl of the bullfighting ring. These were recognizable but irrelevant to me, and I realized that I was not dreaming, that this was Vera Cruz flowing past me, and I settled back again, closed my eyes. But I was awake.

I opened my eyes. I removed my hat. We were running out of the trees of Vera Cruz and the city vanished, replaced by a stretch of marsh, the thin veneer of water among the rushes starting to lighten as the sun cracked the horizon behind us, with a scattering of slow-stalking blue herons looking black in this early light. And now the water vanished too and the sands took up, lifting into minor dunes, and our train slowed abruptly. I pressed the side of my face against the window to look forward. I saw branch tracks heading off south and switching tracks and now a siding and boxcars with uniformed men—*Federales*—sitting in the doors. Our own train was crying out beneath us, as we ground hard to a stop. The engine pitched low. I understood what would happen now. My hand went to Gerhard's German passport, just to touch it, and I recognized the danger of that thought. I rethought it: I touched my *own* German passport, just to reassure myself it was there. Mine. *I* was Gerhard Vogel.

A low Spanish murmuring ruffled through the car and I looked at my nearby fellow first-class travelers. They all seemed to be Mexicans, well-dressed ones. Sitting next to me was an old man in a cream suit, a *mestizo* with a massive gray Porfirio Díaz mustache. In the seats in front of me were a middle-aged couple, he also in a suit, American-style serge, she wearing a bright blue *rebozo* draped over her head and shoulders. No possible Germans were nearby to find my speech suspicious. In spite of my taste for irony and the impulse to indulge in German double-talk, I decided my best course was to inject a clear undercurrent of an admittedly stage-German accent into a simplified Spanish and fake a lapse into the language of the Fatherland only if absolutely necessary.

Two *Federales* in proper regimental uniforms were beginning to work their way down the aisle, a conductor trailing them. The *Federales* were looking at each passenger intently, asking for papers from some, passing others by with only a single lingering glance, the conductor checking tickets of everyone in their wake. I couldn't clearly see if there were other non-Mexicans farther up, but the two government soldiers did pause, once, and then again, and then once again, to check documents closely, and I turned my face to the window as if unconcerned. But as their voices came near, stopping a few rows in front of me to ask for a *pasaporte,* I thought now it would seem evasive to be looking away from them when they arrived. And if I could, I wanted to see who it was they would expect to be carrying an actual passport.

The *Federales* were several rows down and focused on the seats on the other side of the aisle. I moved my head very slightly to the right, not wanting to seem anxious, and I could see between the couple in front of me and barely through the two people in front of them and then my sight was mostly blocked by a black sombrero with silver trim. The soldiers were soon satisfied, and they moved this way. One was lagging behind a little, deferentially, and the senior man turned to this side of the aisle. He had a dark face, carefully twirled black mustaches, a sharp-scanning eye. I knew I shouldn't be looking out the window but I shouldn't be staring at him either. So I eased back in my seat, waited with a vaguely sleepy stare in front of me, as the soldiers moved closer.

Now I saw them in my periphery as they approached my row, and I looked up, slowly, as if this was all quite routine. And I knew I was thinking too much. What I'd learned about actors—even the hammiest of them—was that they worked out their self-consciousness in rehearsals. In performance, even the broadest, phoniest gestures were actually executed straight from the body. I was thinking too much, and now I was thinking too much about thinking too much, as I stared up at the officer who was clearly in charge. His mustaches were so black and the confluence of lines converging on the outer corners of his eyes were so deep that I wondered if he rinsed indigo and henna into his *bigote grande* like a fading leading man.

"Good morning," he said to me in English, going straight to the top of his list of targets.

My head cocked slightly in brief incomprehension—which I was pleased to note had occurred by an actor's reflex—though I also needed to stop noting my own performance, even when good, as that was the time when actors tended to muff their lines.

"*Guten Morgen*," I said, not really capable of going very far past that if this man happened to know any German. His uniform was far too correct for the conscript *Federales* Maass had been able to gather to fight for him. He even had pips on his shoulder that I could read: a captain. A real soldier. Not an inflated *rurale*. Not a field captain elevated in battle from corporal with all the officers around him shredded by bullets and shrapnel. These onyx-stone black eyes had a legitimate *Kapitän* behind them, lately arrived from the capital and tasked with finding guys like me. He could even have known some real German. That was the great risk of this moment.

A beat of silence passed between us. Even a German would have reasonably understood the words "Good morning" in English. "*Buenos días*," I replied, offering this to the officer as our common language, but pushing the pronunciation to the back of my throat, tightening my cheeks, applying my mimic's mouth for German to my fluency in Spanish.

He looked at me for another silent moment, and I could feel him hanging on the edge of belief, still not convinced, but not unconvinced either, as he did not move his eyes from mine for even the briefest moment. I waited, fearing actual, knowledgeable German from him. The Germans had a major presence in Mexico City. This was a smart man. But instead, he said, "*Pasaporte.*"

I pulled my new self from my inner coat pocket without even glancing at it, and I handed it to him, holding my eyes steadily on his. He broke off. He opened my passport to the picture page, as I put my ticket in the conductor's outstretched hand without a word, without shifting my gaze from the captain, who looked at my image. He lifted his eyes to me directly and then lowered them back to the page. He looked at me in the flesh once again. I very casually took off my hat to reproduce the picture.

I saw his eyes move to the facing page, which had some descriptive information. "You've lost some weight," he said, without looking up. We were speaking Spanish now. That much, at least, seemed to have been established.

I said, "If you would control the rats and the flies and . . ." I paused as if looking for a word. And then, quite heavily guttural and loud, I finished my thought: ". . . *die Scheisse* in your streets, I would not catch the dysentery and lose my weight."

The captain lifted his eyes to me. Slowly. It was meant to be faintly ominous. But the look was also clearly defensive, prideful, a challenge to my criticism of Mexican sanitation. A rebuke. Good.

I rubbed it in. "We are meticulous about these things in my country," I said.

He took my ticket from the conductor and gave it a very quick glance. "And why are you going to Mexico City?" he said. This was a cheap little trick, and he no doubt knew it, because the smolder in his eyes was no longer suspicion. It had become a look that said: You arrogant German jackass.

"I am not going to Mexico City," I said. "I am going on to Torreón."

"And what takes you to Torreón?"

"I am going to wait there with my uncle the banker," I said, starting to raise my voice, "until fine Mexican soldiers like you, *Kapitän*, can figure out how to throw the invading American *Schweinehunde* out of your country." I was nearly shouting now.

And the captain's eyes shifted away. He conceded the skirmish, as the train car filled with the responsive cries of "*Viva Mexico!*" and "*Mueran los gringos!*" and even a soft "*Olé!*" from the man with the Díaz mustache sitting next to me.

The captain shut my passport and handed it back to me with my ticket. "Our country has many enemies to fight," he said.

"None of them are German," I said. I regretted it at once. I was afraid I was pushing my fake attitudes too far when I'd already said enough. But the bigger regret was still brewing in me, as the captain managed an almost respectful nod of the head. He turned away and led his subordinate and the conductor out of first class and into the second-class car behind us.

When he was gone, the real regret played like a brass band inside my head, made even worse by the admiring looks I was still getting from a dozen Mexican faces wrenched around in my direction. The faces turned away one by one and I was left with that band doing a rendition of "It's a Grand Old Flag" with all the trumpets and trombones and tubas and one sad alto horn variously playing flats and sharps. A cacophony of Cohan mocking my betrayal of my country in a sordid little play in a first-class car outside Vera Cruz, Mexico. Those Americans I'd publicly called invading *Schweinehunde* were my pals and drinking buddies and fellow baseball fans and hot dog lovers, and they were lovers of free speech and the free press and freedom of religion, and for them and for me, everybody was welcome and nobody was turned away and anyone had the chance to make himself a millionaire or a doctor or a general or even maybe President of the United States, and anyone could be my pal and my drinking buddy and a Cubs fan no matter where he came from, and damn if I don't know we fail at all that now and then, and sometimes we fail badly and maybe way too often, but that's what we believe, and no man has walked the face of the earth who didn't sometimes fail to live up to what he believes, but we do believe it, we do really believe all that, and now I'd cried out insults to my country in a foreign public place and inflamed hatred for my country in a train car full of people who didn't truly understand us.

I turned my face to the upswoop of a sand dune out toward the horizon, and right in front of me a wide-winged, ugly-mugged, shit-eating *zopilote* floated past, and as far as I was concerned at the moment, he could come land on my chest and eat out my traitorous heart if he wanted to, and I wouldn't even push him away.

But this passed. Pretty quick, though that didn't mean I was insincere in my guilt. But I figured I'd just played Iago for one performance to a small house in Vera Cruz. And for bigger stakes than applause. I saved my own life, or at least my freedom. And I saved my chance to figure out where this German agent a couple of cars up ahead might be going and what he might be doing that could pose a possible danger to the country I love.

30

Before we left the federal checkpoint, the captain and his aide stepped back into our car and stopped at the doorway, just beyond arm's length to my right. I found I was confident now in my role. I looked up at him easily, without any thought that he was here having been nagged by a suspicion about me. He didn't even glance my way. He said in a loud voice, "Attention. Attention, travelers."

All the faces in the car turned in his direction.

"For your safety from the foreign invaders and from the bandits who masquerade as so-called Constitutionalists, we will be adding a car of federal soldiers to the back of the train. Please accept our apologies for the brief delay."

He paused, turning his head slowly, with a faint bounce, to each part of the car, seeming to study every face. He ended by looking across his shoulder and down at me. I gave him an approving nod, which he acknowledged by making no apparent acknowledgment at all. He returned his attention to the car in general.

"*Viva Mexico*," he said, without raising his voice but with a firmness that filled the place. And like a church congregation, the Mexican travelers answered as one: "*Viva Mexico*."

Then he strode up the aisle.

I was placid through all of this. But I was glad when, after a few clanking and jostling minutes, the train was moving again and I was officially just one passenger among many, checked and authorized, on his way toward the city of Torreón in the state of Coahuila.

And we began to climb. I leaned my head back against the seat and turned my face to the treetops and the bright morning sky, and I was suddenly alone. I was a man inside a man, Christopher Marlowe Cobb inside Gerhard Vogel, and I was rising high into the air and there was a landscape around me through which I moved and it was real to me but if I put out my hand to actually touch it, I would have been blocked by an invisible barrier. I was contained. I thought this was what the actors felt, all the actors I'd known—the good ones—from before I could remember, this was what they felt inhabiting a role on a stage. This. And it felt safe inside here. And since what my role involved for now was to be silent, I simply watched and waited and prepared for the scenes to come. I drifted inside this space. I prepared.

We crossed the *Río Jamapa* on a narrow steel-girdered bridge four hundred feet above the ruins of a Spanish causeway, and on we continued to climb, more steeply, ever more steeply, the forested ground tumbling away beside us. And the experienced travelers of this route opened the windows from the top to let the cool of the air and the first scent of pine into the car. We were nearly two thousand feet above Vera Cruz and the sea, with another mile to climb to Mexico City. Up here, the decorative birds and the exotic birds, the fragile birds and the peasant-fishermen birds—the heron and the egret, the grebe and the kingfisher—these had all vanished. Now the eagles and the hawks and the ospreys had taken over the sky, and I thought on this. I thought, but not thoughts exactly. I looked at the birds circling inside my head the way I read faces and gestures and tones of voice when I am working a new source for what he knows about a story I want to write. And sometimes the source doesn't even know that he knows this thing. The birds circled in my head above Vera Cruz, above all that had happened these past few days.

I thought about the birds even as the locomotive, which was made for climbing mountains, pitched its voice from its huffing on the flatland into something deep and strong and tremulous, like an operatic bass who was finished with his warm-up humming and lip-trilling and now at last was singing his aria, fully, opening his lowest register, unloosing his vibrato. Even the great-taloned birds outside veered away from this voice. This was an oil-burning engine, this mountain locomotive, so as it labored, there was little smoke and no grit, there was a taint of the smell of oil exhaust but mostly there was the smell of pine forest filling the car and a smell that seemed to be the chilled sunlight itself. Many of the hot-country trees had fallen away—the palms and the palmettos and the Spanish bayonets—but the banana trees were still here even as the pines densely mounted the peaks above us, the broad banana leaves dipping by the tracks at our passing, flashing glimpses of the glossy-green leaves of the coffee trees they shaded.

And we turned. And through a cut in the mountain, I had a sudden view of tableland covered with cane fields. And above these, the hawks and the ospreys and the eagles were circling. And they kept circling in my head as well. I thought of the aggressor birds with talons for grabbing and beaks for tearing flesh, and I thought of the long-legged, long-billed birds wading in the marshes of Vera Cruz, who would not dare go near these birds of the high mountains. I thought of the birds. How the birds of the marshes would themselves dip those flat bills into the water and they would grab a passing fish and swallow it and dissolve it inside them. These birds who would be snatched by the talons and torn apart and eaten by the great circling raptors: They found their own place to hunt and kill. You were a bird of prey or you were its food. And I thought: *Entweder Hammer oder Amboß*. Either a hammer or an anvil.

The German agent, mounted on an exhausted horse and soaked in his own sweat and covered in Mexican dust—as if he were an intrepid man of hot-country action—would ride into Pancho Villa's camp near Torreón and he would sit with the rebel he wished to make into an ally and he would remind him that Germans have long believed—they even had an old saying for it—that you have to be either a hammer or an anvil. And Mensinger intended to tell Villa—having noted to himself: *Kein Einmarsch. Nicht nach T*—that Woodrow

Wilson would not invade any farther than Vera Cruz, would not even go to Tampico to grab the oil fields. Because Wilson had no eggs. No balls. *Keine Eier. Ningunos cojones.* And Villa would laugh with this man at the American President. And Villa would feel close to this man who said these things. He would understand from his German friend that Woodrow Wilson and the United States were not a hammer. They were an anvil. Waiting to be struck by a hammer. Germany would encourage Pancho Villa to launch an offensive against the Americans.

I remained sitting very still, though I had a strong urge to leap to my feet. Indeed, I was rendered near perfectly still by that very urge, which was the way any good reporter has learned to respond when someone has just said a thing that suddenly opens a view into your story as if into a deep mountain gorge. I was keenly aware now of the man who sat in his Pullman suite, just two cars forward, looking at these same circling birds of prey.

And the question I had to ask myself was this: Did I have enough —right now—to step off this train in Córdoba or Orizaba and write this story and telegraph it to Clyde? Every enterprising, competitive, big-city newspaper in the United States of America had gone with big-splash front-page stories on fewer actual confirmed facts and more speculation than this. And this would be a pretty big one. Headlines and subheads and bits of story started gabbling at me. *German secret agent makes covert trip to rebel enclave, urges Pancho Villa to launch counterattack against American forces. Agent tells Villa: "You're either the hammer or the anvil." Brave American secret agent murdered trying to foil German plan.* And so forth. As I was imagining the way this story would play in print if I were to file it now, one thing did establish itself as part of my still totally speculative but instinctively probable assessment: Mensinger would not be going to Villa empty-handed. *Envoy promises German support, German arms.* I was sure the offer of arms was part of his message. Maybe that was the *Papiere.* Maybe the "paper" on the list of Mensinger's talking points was some official document pledging arms to Villa. Maybe even a pledge of support for him as the future president of Mexico. He was the odds-on favorite at this point. All of which, however, was just seductively plausible speculation in my own head. As for dispatching my speculations as reportorial truth, by the second day either Nash or Svoboda, without even leaving his desk, could write a "sources say" story about the *Ypiranga* itself and its cargo being part of this whole plot. Those arms were poised to go to Villa for his commitment to push Funston and our boys into the Gulf of Mexico. Nash, of course, would be Svoboda's unnamed source, or vice versa. And who knew where they would go on the third day.

And all of that stank. Sure the free press of my beloved country felt so fully and comfortably free that it routinely ran unverified stories, half-assed stories, or even outright lies to sell their goods. But that had never been done under my byline. All I had for sure was a secretive German official in a riding outfit on the way to a nothing town in a rebel province, a dead German-American who played a minor horn in a minor brass band who made some pretty extravagant claims about himself, a few cryptic words on an envelope and my own puzzle-page answers for a few of them. There could be less to this story. There could be more. But the only thing for sure was that I could not be legitimately sure about anything yet. The movements of armies, dead men in a field, advance and retreat and surrender. These were the sure things. These were facts. That's the reporter I had been. As for the reporter I'd suddenly become, the man I'd become, in a suit I'd never wear, with a phony passport in my pocket, tempted to write a newspaper story that had not been confirmed to be true: I didn't like any of this.

31

I did not get off in Córdoba. Even to stretch my legs for the half hour of our passenger stop. Clyde and the whole system were breathing heavily in my ear and I didn't want to let myself be tempted. I blocked them out in the clamor of the Aztec-blooded women below my window hawking their mangoes and *Dominico* bananas and diced sugarcane, their sweetmeats and white cheese and bunches of high-mountain lilies.

And then we were moving through the valley of the *Río Seco*, with its fields of cane and its banana farms and its plantations of pineapple and tobacco and coffee. And we began to climb once more. We took a long, rising, easy-gradient curve up a mountain, slow enough for everyone on my side of the car to notice something in a verge of flatland beside the track. They all turned their faces to it: a run of blackened, gutted railway passenger cars, some upright but most of them on their sides, their axles and their undercarriages exposed, like naked corpses laid out on the road after a battle. These had been here a while, judging by the jungle growth snaking into and over them, but they stirred an immediate murmur among the first-class passengers about the bandits and how they were capable of doing any number of terrible things to any of us but how at least we had a car full of soldiers at the rear of our train and how things were in a unique uproar now, so the rebels were preoccupied with figuring out what to do about the *gringos* and so maybe we'd slip through, and the word was that since the invasion, trains to Mexico City had been experiencing no trouble at all. So we were all going to be okay. Maybe.

Nor did I get off when the train stopped in Orizaba, though Clyde was whispering to me pretty intensely now that it was my duty to send this story to him right away, right here in this town, so it would not be lost forever when the rebels burned my train and stole my money belt and cracked my head open because I tried to get rough with them, and even if I woke up from that, I would at least have forgotten everything I knew, including both names in my byline and even the name in between. I didn't listen to Clyde. We sat in the station at Orizaba, halfway between the *tierra caliente* and the *tierra fría,* the tropical zone and the temperate zone, and it was raining. Hard. The passengers in the car were heartened by the rain. If it could just rain like this all the way to Mexico City, maybe the rebels wouldn't bother.

But Orizaba was known for its rain. The passengers all knew that. The train started to roll again, and soon the rain ceased and the clouds dispersed and the high-mountain sunshine returned, insistent in light but meek in heat. If the passengers' confidence waned, they made no remarks about it, and soon we'd pulled into Esperanza, with forty minutes for lunch, and I stepped from the car, hoping to have a chance to observe Mensinger.

I found myself briefly breathless. Not from Scarface. We were nearly eight thousand feet above Vera Cruz and the sea now. Just the exertion of stepping off the train and moving along the platform informed my body in no uncertain terms of how thin the air was, and it took a little time for me to adjust. I slowed. I tried to breathe deeply. A strong smell of coffee filled the air, but I got no caffeine kick from it. I had to work hard at filling my lungs. Some of the Mexicans coming out of second class up ahead were slowing as well. Veracruzanos. Others, from the high country no doubt, strode on. This was their element. They were happy to be free of the thick sludge of sea-level air. I was walking slowly. The Pullman was behind me and I was hoping Mensinger would pass me so that I could follow him without a chance of his realizing. But he was not yet among those slipping by.

The station platform was wide. I was drawing near its center, from which a broad fieldstone path led to the pine-log facade of the simply named *Restaurante El Ferrocarril,* the Railway Restaurant. All the morning trains from Vera Cruz stopped here for lunch. Along the path were Indian women wrapped in their serapes selling peaches and pomegranates, tortillas and tamales for those eating cheap and quick. Most of the Indian women, the young as well as the old, had the bulge of a goiter on their necks, a high-mountain affliction I recognized from the mountains of Nicaragua as well.

I paused at the steps from the platform to the path, and I didn't descend. I casually turned around, pulling my Elgin out of my pocket as if I were checking the time, weighing lunch options. I glanced at the faces heading this way. No Mensinger. I looked beyond them to the Pullman. I lit a cigarette and waited, keeping tabs on the car as I seemed to smoke and look at the scenery. The smell of coffee was still strong. Beyond the restaurant to the west were a dozen hip-roofed warehouses, full of the dried coffee beans I'd been smelling, not grown this high but stored up here to keep them from spoiling before they were sold and exported. And beyond the warehouses, far beyond them, looming over us all, was the *Pico de Orizaba,* the great, snowcapped volcano that rose from the high plain we sat on. It startled me. It had been there all this time and I'd been too preoccupied to actually see it. I lifted my eyes to *Orizaba* now and it straightened me up, sucked the thin mountain air out of me, as if Mensinger had just appeared.

And he had. When I lowered my eyes from the mountain, I saw him stepping down from the Pullman's back vestibule, still done up in riding clothes, carrying his crop. Director's note to Fritz Mensinger: Get rid of the riding crop if you want your performance to win the trust of a *bandito.* Mensinger, though, seemed, even from this distance, serenely confident, unthreatened. Good. All the Krüger stuff—if Mensinger was ever aware of it—had been left behind. I took a drag on my cigarette, lifted my eyes again to the volcano but didn't see it. I could see at the lower edge of my vision Mensinger pause, adjust to the thin air, turn this way, take a step and another.

And a voice beside me said, "*Guten Tag.*"

Mensinger would be within listening distance in moments.

I turned to the voice. It was the elderly man with the Porfirio Díaz mustache who had been sitting for hours beside me on the train utterly silent but for his one, almost whispered *Olé*.

I looked into his rheumy dark eyes and I could sense that this reserved man had been working up the initiative all morning to speak. I could not be faking German when Mensinger passed by. I said to him in Spanish, "Good afternoon." I cut back on the preciseness of my natural Spanish pronunciation but I skipped the German accent. It was better the old man be confused than Mensinger pick up on anything familiar or odd when he passed by. I said, "Would you mind that I speak Spanish with you? I must practice."

"Not at all," he said. "You're doing very well. Much better than before." He was looking surprised but not disbelieving.

"When I am angry," I said, "I have trouble speaking properly."

He nodded. "Of course. The captain was an ass."

"He was doing his duty," I said.

"I don't really speak much . . ."

"Sorry," I said, cutting him off, as I was afraid he was about to say "German" and I sensed Mensinger drawing near. I put my cigarette in my mouth and reached for the pack inside my jacket. "I am very rude. Would you like to smoke?"

Mensinger passed us, moving briskly now.

"No," the old man said. "Thank you." He continued to say words but I was not hearing them, even though he would have sworn I was looking him full in the face with great attention.

Mensinger turned, quite near us. He smelled of starch and gun oil. Then he was out of my sight and I heard him going down the steps.

". . . only a few words," the old man was saying.

"I understand," I said.

"Yes," he said. "I once had a reading knowledge was all. In the university."

"I see."

I turned my head briefly away, looked at Mensinger's receding figure, passing by the women vendors, heading for the restaurant.

"I am Doctor Manuel Agusto Tejeda Llosa."

I looked back to him as he began giving his name, "Doctor Tejeda Llosa," I said, shaking his offered hand. "I am Gerhard Vogel."

"Herr Vogel."

"Do you have a practice in Vera Cruz?" I asked.

"Ah, no," he said. "I am not a medical doctor. I am a doctor of philosophy. From the University of . . . from abroad." His eyes shifted away.

It was easy to read him: His degree was from an American university. Which meant he probably spoke excellent English. And he knew America and Americans. Which meant sitting next to me all the way to Mexico City wanting to talk, this man would be an ongoing danger. At least he would exhaust me from the effort to keep up my role. And he could easily get around to grilling me about my life in Germany, my job in Mexico. He seemed a nice old man and I regretted it, but as soon as his eyes returned to mine, I narrowed my own. He knew why.

I let the German accent slide lightly back into my Spanish. I was only a little angry at him. But it would be enough to make the rest of the trip silent. "I suspect your American English is much better than your German," I said. I clicked my heels and said, "It was a pleasure to meet you, Doctor." And I walked away.

I headed down the platform, toward the rear of the train.

There was nothing to be gained from following Mensinger into the restaurant. And this walking away was just the gesture of a German ass. The logical move. I had to protect my Gerhard from exposure. I finished my cigarette and paused and stubbed it out on the platform. I half turned. I pulled out my Elgin. I glanced back up the platform. The old man was gone.

I thought now to go to the Pullman car and find Mensinger's berth and his bag and go through them. If I could look at the "*Papiere*" he was bringing to Pancho Villa, I might find enough confirmation to file a legitimate story.

And I had sense enough to stop myself. It was Gerhard who was making me consider this. I was too much Gerhard Vogel now, American secret agent. But I was not Gerhard Vogel. I was Christopher Cobb playing the part of Gerhard Vogel in a melodrama entitled *Christopher Cobb, War Correspondent*. No. That was wrong. In that melodrama I was Christopher Cobb playing the part of Christopher Cobb faking the surface identity of Gerhard Vogel. I would not do what Vogel did. In life and in any little drama I played inside it, I was still who I was behind the mask. I was a war correspondent. A newspaper reporter. A real one. Not a yellow-journalist hack who'd buy or steal or invent whatever he needed. Nor was I a spy. Neither in my life nor in the snatches of theater in my life was felonious breaking and entering a legitimate action of a newspaper reporter. I was a reporter. Not a spy. Even though it was true that something larger seemed to be at stake here. Something that had to do with my country.

I wavered again. Wars always had something larger at stake. I hadn't faced this dilemma before because the major wars I'd covered had never directly involved my own country. In Nicaragua, faction against faction. In the Balkans, Bulgarians against Servians and Greeks and Rumanians. I am an American, but I am an American reporter, a war correspondent, standing apart, telling things as they are. And an American does his job with the integrity the job calls for. Other Americans do their own American jobs. Soldiers. Secret agents. I am not those other Americans. This is what I told myself.

Besides. There had to be a train guard to keep the second-class hoi polloi out of the Pullman. The chances of getting into Mensinger's berth unobserved and finding his documents and discovering the Germans' ultimate goal with Villa were a good deal less than the chances of queering the whole story by getting caught.

I turned my back on the Pullman, the volcano, the restaurant where Mensinger was eating a meaningless lunch, and I strolled along the platform, keeping tightly bound inside my head for a time, thinking there was a very long way to go before La Mancha. I needed to stay patient.

And now I was nearing the boxcar at the back of the train. The dozen or so *Federales* who were supposed to protect us had emerged. Boys mostly, a few men, a motley group of *rurales* and impressed farm boys with a couple of weathered noncoms to lead them, the ragged, unmotivated loose ends of Huerta's army on dangerous, thankless duty. And they were watching the women. Half a dozen women, the wives— official or unofficial—of the half dozen actual men among the soldiers. Women typically traveled with Mexican armies—governmental and rebel alike—to forage for their men and cook for them and service their bodies and tend their wounds and hold their hands as they died and even bury them. *Soldaderas.* Along the platform these women were crouched over an improvised fire, cooking some unidentifiable meat for their men's tortillas.

I turned away from them. Faced the volcano. Began to walk back toward it. When Bunky asked me what my plan was, I gave him the only answer I knew. Which was vague to say the least. I had this role, for now, of Gerhard Vogel, but I was wrong a few minutes ago thinking of this as a play with fixed personalities in a structured melodrama. This was all new. It was all improvised. I didn't know what my lines were, what my future actions were. La Mancha was a very small place. How did I follow Mensinger unobserved? And then what? But I couldn't think about any of that yet. To improvise, you must stay in this moment and then the next and the next.

And in this particular next moment, a small thing in the landscape presented itself to me. A wooden shack a hundred yards up the train track. The telegraph office. Once again I was tempted to tell this story as I now had it. But I'd been so absorbed by my journalistic scruples, I'd overlooked a far more immediate problem, which trumped all the rest: If I tried to file the story from any of these public railway tele-graph stations, there was a serious chance it would never even arrive in America. A telegraph operator who knew enough English to get a sense of what he was sending—and the operators tended to know pretty good chunks of the languages they frequently worked with—such a man would tell the authorities and then I'd be grabbed off the train and not only would the story die but the event itself might then be drastically altered in ways I would never be privy to. Hell. Forget the translation. Given the Mexicans' feelings for Americans right now, a telegraph about anything that was written in English and bound for the United States would go nowhere except into my arrest file.

I had no choice. I had to follow this thing all the way to Villa. And then somehow improvise myself across the border.

32

When the train was moving again and I turned my face to the long, flat run of the Central Plateau that would take us to Mexico City, I found the women in the car at the back of the train lingering in my head. And I thought of Luisa. If she had gone off to do what I suspected she had, she was a *soldadera* of quite a different sort. I wondered who she actually went to. Zapata in the south? He just didn't seem much motivated to campaign outside his own state. Or Carranza the alleged thinker? Obregón the tactician? Most likely Pancho Villa. She would be drawn to him for the same reasons I suspected Mensinger and the Germans were drawn to him. He was the boldest rebel of them all, clearly the strongest of them at this point, the one most likely to make a radical change in favor of the vast majority of Mexicans, the poor and disenfranchised. She would go to him.

I realized I was in danger of violating what I'd resolved about staying in the moment, about not looking ahead. Even though this matter of Luisa Morales was simple curiosity; even though I had objectively, analytically assessed *her* next moves, not mine; even though I had not, in that analysis, ever actually summoned up a full-fledged image of her in my mind; even though I was convinced all of this about what I'd been doing was true, now that I'd come to a conclusion and was ready to set her aside, Luisa Morales slipped quietly into me in quite a different way, as if from the shadows beyond the lamplight in a dark street. She appeared vividly, in the flesh, and she was unarmed and her hair was tumbled about on her shoulders, and she looked me in the eyes, and her eyes were as dark as the barrel of a gun. And then she vanished. And so I found myself refusing to operate in this present moment, on this train between Vera Cruz and Mexico City, and instead I was looking far ahead, to the possibility that Luisa, as well, might be waiting at the end of this trail with Mensinger. And the consequent hot twist in my chest made me feel like an incurable damn fool.

I needed to rid myself of all this. Right now. When Dr. Tejeda Llosa sat down beside me after the lunch stop in Esperanza, he rolled his shoulders a little to silently declare that there was nothing more to be said between us. Which was what I'd hoped to accomplish with my bit of willful rudeness. But at the moment I even considered turning to him and engaging him in conversation. Tell me about your time in America. I am a German with a banker uncle in Torreón and I do something or other and I am from somewhere or other.

I glanced in the old man's direction. He was dozing, his head nodding forward and then jerking up and then nodding forward again. Dr. Tejeda Llosa. Doctor. *Dr.* The last little bit of the puzzle of Mensinger's notes. I'd been assuming that *ENP ~ Dr.* involved a medical doctor. Of course not. If it was Wilson who had no balls in the notes, then this might be Wilson as well. The first President of the United States with a PhD. From Johns Hopkins University, in history and political science. Dr. Woodrow Wilson. And it was the PhD part of him that Mensinger wanted to stress to Villa. Villa who was utterly uneducated but was known both to deeply regret the fact and to dream of teaching every Mexican child to read.

So what was Mensinger's point with the tilde? What was similar to Wilson's PhD? What was *ENP*? And a phrase returned to my mind that slipped through a short time ago, in connection with Luisa's choice of rebels: Carranza, the alleged thinker. And I remembered talking with Gerhard about him. And I was pissed at Gerhard for treating me like a naïf. So when he cited, in English, the "National Preparatory School" as part of Carranza's intellectual resume, I tweaked him by repeating the name of the school in the correct Spanish: *Escuela Nacional Preparatoria.* ENP.

Mensinger couldn't be sincerely suggesting that the two things were, in fact, similar. The ENP was a high school. The most exclusive in the country, but a high school. He could, however, expect it to represent, in Villa's mind, all that he was not. The antithesis of Villa's upbringing. Mensinger wouldn't be rubbing Villa's face in that. But if he was trying to induce an attack on American forces, he'd want to convince Villa that Wilson would never support his larger ambitions. *ENP ~ Dr.* Villa might believe that Woodrow Wilson feels an intellectual affinity with Carranza. That Wilson would be scornful of Villa's lack of education. The note Mensinger made was to indicate Wilson's point of view, the ultimate message being that the United States would never back Pancho Villa as leader of Mexico. Carranza was Wilson's man. So there was nothing to lose for Villa to stand up to America by attacking Wilson's invading army. Though he could be self-deprecating about his lack of education, Pancho Villa was a vain and self-aggrandizing man. The thought of Wilson's scorn would infuriate him. And with the present Mexican outpouring of hatred for the United States, Villa could become an even greater hero. He could unify the rebellion behind him.

And I was simply getting angry. Angry at Mensinger and the Germans, angry at Villa and the Mexicans. I was angry at Wilson already, but once again I was struck by how my anger at him was of a completely different sort, like being angry at a smart but goofy uncle from Virginia, or at your mother, or at the Cubs. Family anger.

I took my hat off the hook by the window and put it on and pulled it down over my eyes and I settled back to make myself sleep. I was still weary enough from the short night. I could sleep if I just put my mind to it. No. I could sleep if I turned my mind off.

And I slept. I knew I'd slept because I pushed the hat up off my eyes and the sun was low, and passing outside was the *pulque* district just east of the capital, vast fields of maguey in dense, even rows of spiky, gray-green leaves as tall as a man with a tip that could cut deep as the bone and sap that could blister the skin, a plant that could produce the wretched *pulque* and the estimable *blue agave* with the effective *mezcal* in between. A complex thing indeed.

We were not far from the city now. Those of us going north would change trains in Mexico City. So I needed to avoid sitting next to him again and he was likely to disembark at the capital anyway, but even if I knew I'd be sitting beside him for another long trip, I would do this anyway: I turned to Dr. Tejeda Llosa. He was reading a book. The *Meditaciones* of Marcus Aurelius. I knew a few words from Aurelius. I remembered my mother quoting him to me when I'd finally calmed down after an early-teenage raging tantrum over something or other. She quietly let the fit run its course. And though *in medias res* I scornfully recognized her portrayal of suffering patience from her role of Marguerite Gautier in *The Lady of the Camellias*, I eventually calmed down and awaited her rebuke. But putting her hand gently and sadly on my shoulder and acting as if I would instantly understand his authority, she said, "The great emperor and philosopher Marcus Aurelius once wrote, 'Anger is always honest.'" And that was that. She patiently turned my fault into a kind of virtue, thus letting me fill in for myself the fault of it, and I think, as a result, I never overtly lost my temper with her again.

Dr. Tejeda Llosa read on, as I was stuck—though sweetly—on my mother. But now in my head I prepared a Spanish translation of the Aurelius quotation and I said to him, "Forgive me, Doctor Tejeda Llosa."

He lifted his face from his book and turned to me. He had a look of suffering patience on his face.

I said, "I am sorry to interrupt and sorry for much more than that."

He closed his book.

Putting just a trace of German into my Spanish pronunciation, I gave him a shot of his Marcus Aurelius. I said, "*El enojo es siempre honesto.*"

He smiled faintly and nodded. "Quite all right," he said.

"That's from Aurelius," I said.

He lifted his eyebrows.

"But anger isn't always smart," I said.

"No offense was taken," he said.

I said, "The place where you earned your doctorate degree..."
But I interrupted myself. I glanced quickly around the car, making
sure no one was paying attention to us.

He nodded again, pushing up his lower lip and wrinkling his
brow at me as if to say, "You were right to be discreet, señor; at this
moment in history, they would not understand either." Before I could
continue, he finished my sentence in a very low voice, barely able to
reach me over the clack of the wheels beneath us. "The University of
Pennsylvania."

I spoke low as well. "Ah," I said. "So. Good. That country you
studied in, that is a good country, an admirable country."

"In spite of this terrible thing they are doing, yes. It is," he said.

"Created from the wish to be free," I said. "We Germans are a
nation with roots in a barbaric race. I regret my treatment of you on
the platform in Esperanza."

"I understand," he said.

"I wish I were more like an American," I said.

"Not at all," he said. "You Germans are a fine race. But may I
offer a respectful correction?"

"Of course," I said.

"I seek his meditations on every trip and holding the book in my
hands is a good thing, but I could probably recite all of Aurelius to
you from memory. As I am an Aurelius scholar, he is my passion. The
quotation you cite cannot be his. It is very much unlike him."

"Thank you," I said, and I knew the sudden stiffness of my voice
sounded like my German arrogance reasserting itself, refusing to be
corrected.

I turned my face to the window. It was best for the conversation
to end anyway.

Of course she made it up. Improvised. Like the patience. Like
the gentle hand on my shoulder. But it was the right line and the right
gesture at the right moment in the little drama I'd cast her in. I could
not be angry with her for that.

33

And Herr Friedrich von Mensinger sat down next to me.

In Mexico City I'd followed him into the waiting room of the National Railway's *Estación de Buena Vista*. I was careful not to be noticed. I found a place at the very end of one of the long wooden benches otherwise packed tight with Mexicans in serapes and *rebozos,* a class of Mexicans I figured would be invisible to Mensinger, as Diego had once observed about him. Being among them, I thought he might not notice me either. I watched him when I could, but there was no pressure to do so. He floated past and out of sight and then floated back again, his head and shoulders sticking high out of the middle of the dense Mexican crowd where he seemed trapped. And he began to float away again. But as he passed this time, he surprised me. I had been imagining him as implacably, aristocratically impervious to anything that did not fit his purposes. But the face that was passing now was pinched in intense discomfort. And for a moment he turned his face in my direction, found me instantly, focused on me as intently as if he were about to thrust with his fencing saber. In the next moment, he was borne away, but I knew he would be back, and when the young man sitting to my right suddenly stood up and moved off, Mensinger was beside me, arriving so quickly and unobserved that I imagined he had somehow scaled the wall and clung to an electric light fixture in the ceiling and had thus dropped down beside me in the instant the space was vacated.

And so here we now were. Shoulder to shoulder. This must have been as discomforting for him as it was surprising for me. That he should have lost his composure in the press of a crowd of heathens. That he felt the compulsion to seek refuge next to the only non-Mexican he could find. And now, to regain his composure, he was not speaking. He was sitting here beside me as if it were simply the only available empty space on the bench. Which gave me time to decide a couple of crucial things.

I found myself calm, though I also found that the impulse to make a wise and prompt retreat was stronger in me right now than on any hot-lead-filled field of combat I'd ever covered.

But I was calm, and it was time to improvise.

I could not be Gerhard Vogel. That much was abundantly clear.

Outside of the occupied zone, it was less likely I'd have to show my passport. And if I did, such a moment would not be in Mensinger's presence. For documents and tickets, he would be in the Pullman drawing room and I would be in a first-class car.

I could be anyone I wanted.

Except German. Except American.

We could speak Spanish. But since I didn't know what else he might speak, I figured I better be English-speaking in my assumed identity.

Mensinger cleared his throat.

I was not ready yet.

I held very still, letting him have no cue to speak.

Could I be English? They were high on the list of Germany's imminent enemies. If I wanted to actually make this a fruitful exchange, I should not be English.

South African. English but not quite English. But possibly a sore point for Mensinger, since the Germans strongly sympathized with the Boers against the Brits, and not so very long ago. Not South African.

Canadian.

Mensinger shifted a little beside me. I could see him enough in my periphery to watch him fake a cough into his fist.

I remained absolutely motionless.

Canadian. The Germans, as far as I knew, never had a thing to do with what was now Canada. The only question was Quebec or Ontario. I could pull off the French. But it was a different French and another layer of complexity. Simple. This needed to be simple. Toronto.

I was ready, and suddenly I was keenly aware of the way things had abruptly changed. The man I'd been observing from afar and delicately following for some days now was pressed hard against my right shoulder and arm and thigh.

I ever so slightly flexed my right shoulder, and with a little head-flip to the left I popped my neck. I glanced for a brief beat in Mensinger's direction. He sensed it and was turning his face toward mine as I looked back to the front again. The afterimage of Friedrich Mensinger was almost entirely his scar, a fibrous white scimitar running along his left cheek from ear to lip, as wide as a pipe stem. Wider than any dueling sword would leave under normal circumstances. He was one of those who packed his wound with horsehair to keep it agape while it healed. A further assertion of Germanic manliness.

I blinked the image away. I waited. I could sense him pondering how to speak, not knowing my language.

After a moment, he said, in a slightly pinched, slightly nasal voice, aristocratic to my ear, "*Sprechen Sie Deutsch?*"

I looked at him. His eyes were shockingly pale, the gray-green of a scummy pond on a cloudless afternoon. His mustache was his own, not Wilhelm's; it was full and dust-colored but with no uptwirls, no points at all. He was his own man.

"Deutsch?" I said. "No. *Nein.* Sorry. Do you sprechen English?"

He narrowed those eyes at me a little.

"I'm Simon," I said, thinking Legree, in the spur of the melodramatic moment, staring into this face. Now I needed a last name. Canadian-sounding. "Chance," I said, drawing on the Cubs of my youth, their peerless leader. "From Toronto." Simon Chance would do.

He was still not unnarrowing his eyes.

"Canada," I said.

I lifted my right hand from between us and angled it toward him, inviting a shake of sorts in the tight quarters.

"*Nein* English," he managed to say. And then, remembering, "No. No English."

"Do you speak Spanish?" I said in that language.

He nodded.

"No problem then," I said. And this became our common tongue.

"I am Friedrich Mensinger," he said, taking my hand and shaking it firmly enough that I was glad I got the crotch of my thumb into his or this would have been painful.

"We are conspicuous here, aren't we, you and I," I said, nodding my head toward the crowd of Mexicans from whose currents he had just washed ashore.

"Yes we are," he said, letting go of my hand. "We are different."

"What part of Germany are you from?"

He hesitated for one brief beat. "The north," he said.

Though he was vague, he did not look away from me. His pond-eyes showed nothing. They were still. He needed to be sitting here next to me, in our little Aryan corner of this world. So he was more comfortable now. Which meant, ironically, he'd recovered his reserve. He was fundamentally a man of secrets, after all.

I had to be careful if I wanted to work even a little something out of him.

Ask nothing. Give something. It didn't have to be meaningful. "I came up from Vera Cruz this morning," I said.

He didn't give a damn, of course.

So I matched his mood. And I showed him I expected nothing. I broke off our eye contact and looked out at the crowd.

Mensinger was feeling like himself again, extracted from this mass of his inferiors. What did Richard Harding Davis call these people a few days ago? He was, in effect, talking of their ingratitude for our occupation of a piece of their country. Spigotties and squaws. There was no German translation for that, but I suspected Mensinger had his equivalents.

I needed to make it clear to Mensinger that I was not going to small-talk him. But before I fell silent, I regretted that I needed to play my gambit once again, to set the political mood. "Couldn't be witness to that any longer. *Schweinehund* Americans," I said. And without looking at him, I added, "I think that's the appropriate German."

"It is," he said.

And I said no more. He said no more.

If he was watching the crowd too—which he must have been; he was certainly not staring at me—then eventually he'd want to keep the connection going. Even if just a little bit.

It took a while. But finally he said, "They will not go forward, these Americans, do you think?"

"Their president has no balls," I said. I did not look at him, but I felt him—what? hard to describe—do something like a faint expansion of his chest to hear his own thought confirmed in the very terms he'd thought it. But I had to be careful. No more allusions to his envelope.

"You are right," he said. "We have a way of saying that in German."

He was about to try out his line for Villa. I still wouldn't look at him, though I thought he had turned to me now. I would have trouble keeping the eagerness out of my face.

"*Dieser Nation hat doch keine Eier,*" he said

I clenched the fist that was sitting on my thigh. I'd picked up the critical, unexpected word. The whole *nation* has no balls. The United States of America. Not just Woodrow Wilson. Or *eggs*, actually. The U.S.A. has no German balls, which are rather like eggs. I was tempted to ask him if that was chicken eggs that Germans were proud of having. Goose eggs? Quail eggs?

I bucked up my reportorial objectivity.

I looked at him.

He winked at me. He offered no full translation.

I smiled and nodded and hoped it didn't look forced.

We stayed silent. He looked away. I looked away.

The crowd jostled very near us and a woman's *rebozo* loosened from her chest and an infant's head and shoulders emerged and swayed close to Mensinger, nearly into his face. He recoiled and his hands moved out of sight and I wondered if he still had his pistol on his far hip, if his hand had gone there by reflex. The woman caught up her child and the crowd flowed on, and the space before us, though slight, was clear again. It was enough. Mensinger's hands reappeared and stretched to his knees and settled there, his arms straight and stiff. He was resolved not to be provoked by these people.

But he was. They deeply unsettled him. He needed to talk, to escape inward. "They are full of guile, however, these Americans," Mensinger said. "We can say they have no manhood and it is true, but they still can cause trouble."

I turned my face to him. He was not looking at me. He had once again, to my eye, become his scar, upward-bent, like a musing frown. It was all I saw for the moment. He was going on: "They can meddle in things that are not their affair. This much is clear from Vera Cruz."

He paused. He seemed to be watching the crowd, but he'd retreated into his mind. His scar pivoted away. He fixed his eyes intently on mine. "Is this not so?" he said.

I had an abrupt stopping in me, a hot flush in the face from being caught. I heard this as a direct challenge, as if he knew I was an American. But he said, "I ask for your opinion as one who shares a long and vulnerable border."

I shrugged, glanced away for a second to recover my composure.

I said, "Their President seems timid." I believed it. I hated to admit it to this Hun. But I needed to draw him out.

"They are not so far removed from Theodore Roosevelt," Mensinger said. "He was more like a German. So there is that element in the Americans. This is the trouble with a mongrel country. They are inconsistent. And I do not expect even this man Wilson to be timid forever."

Mensinger was sounding a little heated now. He seemed to realize it. He stopped abruptly. "*So*," he said. And he shut up again.

But quotes. Quotes. I already had some very fine quotes for my story, straight from a German secret agent.

"What is your work?" Mensinger suddenly asked. He realized he'd been talking too much, even with an apparently meaningless Canadian. He wanted to know if he'd made a mistake.

"Coffee," I said. "Mexican coffee. High-mountain, shade-grown, cheap-and-getting-cheaper coffee. Wonderful beans. Did you smell the coffee in the warehouses of Esperanza? Great bouquet. Half those beans will end up in Canadian cups. It's cold and it's dark in Canada. We need to get our blood going and we do it with Mexican coffee, which I export to great profit for the everlasting benefit of my countrymen."

I had no idea where all that came from. Unpremeditated. Improvised. To be honest, actors—who were, collectively, my aunts and uncles, my older sisters and brothers, my trainers and my professors, my fathers—through all my formative years—actors, I say—including the actor I myself often am—sometimes scare the hell out me.

But Mensinger, who I'd been playing to as if he were the Mayor of New York in a loge box with his party at the Belasco, seemed convinced. He very slightly tilted his head and nodded. "I like a good cup of coffee," he said. "But strong. Very strong. Your Mexican coffee is not strong."

"It can be made strong."

"Very strong," he said. "Strong in the bean."

"Strong in the bean," I said. "Right. Of course. I don't think Mexican coffee is strong in the bean."

"No."

"No."

"Some people cannot take it strong in the bean," he said. And by "people" I gather he meant "nations."

"In your country you make sure you buy it strong," I said.

"In the bean. Yes. Very."

"And what do you do for a living, Herr Mensinger?"

He did not miss a beat. "I also am a businessman."

He offered no more.

"What sort of product?" I said.

"Money," he said. "Money is the product. I advise banks. There are some very powerful German banks in Mexico."

I was not interested in having him elaborate on his cover identity. So I took the opportunity to chip away at any suspicion he might have had about me. I said, "Can I ask you a question about your German bankers in Mexico?"

He did not answer. His lower lip pushed up into the same curve as his scar.

I said, "What do they do for strong coffee?"

It was not what he expected, of course. The face froze for a moment, and then he actually smiled and chuckled. A creepy smile. His mouth undid its curve, flattened, then spread wide and puckered a little at the corners and opened in a quarter smile with gray teeth. The chuckle was a slow turn of a Gatling gun. None of this, of course, prompted by a sense of humor. I didn't think he was capable of perceiving irony, much less attributing it to a Canadian stranger, much less appreciating it as a subtle joke. This was a smile and chuckle of cultural and intellectual superiority. Prompted by my continuing to think and talk and ask such questions as this about coffee after he had already made the international politics of that subject clear to anyone who had ears to listen.

"They suffer," he said.

I put on a sympathetically constricted face. I nodded.

I looked out to the crowd for a moment, to let Mensinger assume a drift in my shallow Canadian mind. Without looking at him I said, "Will these Mexicans ever have a viable government again?"

Mensinger snorted. "They need another Díaz."

"Perhaps Carranza. He seems keen on taking over."

Mensinger snorted again. "A weak man. He is no Díaz."

"Not strong in the bean," I said. Now I looked at Mensinger, ready to put on a vapid face for him, to keep him off guard.

"Not strong in the bean," he said. I had him, for the moment at least. He'd bought into the metaphor and was watching the crowd. He was thinking—and not about me. This was good.

"Pancho Villa, then?" I asked.

"He is very strong in the bean," he said.

"But he seems regional. All the rebels seem regional."

"It doesn't have to be that way," Mensinger said.

"What could Villa possibly do to put the whole country behind him." I didn't ask it, I said it. And I said it with a scornful, dismissive tone. The dumb Canadian coffee merchant. I wobbled my head and smirked, hoping he would see it.

Mensinger looked at me.

I wobbled my head and smirked some more.

He was thinking whether I was worth instructing.

Wobbled and smirked. Though I knew I'd better stop that. I was overacting.

He was thinking I'd never understand. But part of him liked instructing the ignorant in things they could never understand. How superior he was.

I'd stopped wobbling and smirking. "Permanent chaos," I said.

"Something bold," Mensinger said.

I held still. I said nothing.

"He is a very good military man," Mensinger said. "He can do something bold."

I shrugged. Very very slightly. "They all just fight each other, the rebels."

Mensinger hesitated again. Those eyes. Pale though they were, beneath their scummy surface, things rose near and then swam deep again. I tried to read those eyes. I was afraid I'd done all I could do. What I had going now in order to induce him to let down his guard: I could see all that dissipating. He had no reason to feel anxious surrounded by mongrel Mexicans. They were beneath him. He had nothing more to say to this idiot merchant from a marginal country. I was beneath him. But his eyes now gathered a focus that you sometimes see in pedants and preachers and the supremely powerful.

He said, "You bring a country together by finding someone you can all agree to hate."

34

I knew this was the last thing he intended to say to me. And it was. We'd been hat brim to hat brim all this time, me in my gray felt fedora and him in his slouch hat, and now he took his hat off and laid it in his lap and he ran a hand through his hair, as if he'd just wiped me from the surface of his brain like a trivial thought. And he closed his eyes. Ramrod-straight upright he sat, and he slept.

And later we nodded a good-bye as our new train was called and Mensinger headed for the track and his Pullman. But I lingered a few steps behind and then I stopped. I had such fine quotes. I had a mind for remembering quotes—it was like a facility for memorizing lines in a play—and I would shortly write them all down to preserve them, all the things he said for my exclusive interview with a named German secret agent. In spite of its being largely speculative, I longed to file the story now. But I knew it would never get out of the telegraph office. This was becoming a personal thing. Between me and this man. I had to be careful. A good reporter can never let it get personal.

So I took my place in a window seat at the rear of a first-class car. I let myself think of the next major challenge: The character I created for Mensinger in the station was just the right character for the moment, but now that he knew me as Simon Chance, the Canadian coffee seller, how could I get off the train in the tiny La Mancha and follow him without being instantly noticed? This too had to be improvised.

I put it out of my mind. The night train began to move. I slid down a little, resettled my feet on my bag, pulled my hat over my eyes, and I slept, fitfully, awaking to undifferentiated blackness out the window and to the sound of snoring and dream murmurings in Spanish and to the smell of cigarette smoke and *pulque* and to the smell of old sweat and the Mexicans' heavy cover-up of soap and perfume, manufactured smells of lilac and rose and jasmine, and I woke to an ache in the side of my neck from the sleeping angle of my head and the ache in my butt and in my back from the rush-work seat.

I stirred. I gently nudged my head upright against the neck pain. I found myself thinking in a new way about how to get this story, in a way that stretched my principles. Why? Mensinger's mission against my country, of course; the nasty smile and the laugh he gave Simon Chance; those eyes; the deception I'd already played on this man I profoundly disliked, and the remarkable de facto interview it yielded; the darkness outside and the sleeping forms all around me. Even his wife's letter, that he struck her twice for weeping over his saber wound. All this made me rise and step over the legs of the man sleeping in the seat next to me and into the aisle. I stood straight, stretched my spine, and shook the last remnants of sleep from my head. I saw my job differently now. This was an important story. Important for my country in a world of countries who would despise us. A timely warning needed to be sounded. I would not fabricate my story. I would not casually speculate on it when there were alternative viable speculations. But if I somehow could break-and-enter, with a reasonable chance of not getting caught, and gain access to his saddlebags, I would see what facts I could find, no matter how I did it.

I moved forward along the center aisle of the car.

As gently as I could, I opened the passage door and stepped out, the train-rush of air whipping through the join of the cars and billowing coldly into my shirt, my jacket. I closed the door behind me. The next car was the Pullman. I pressed through the swirls of air and I crossed the shifting steel plates between the vestibules and I approached the Pullman's door. I put my hand to its handle. I was Simon Chance. I just had to see the Pullman for myself. Perhaps I'd travel that way myself next time. Coffee did well by me, so I should do well for myself. I turned the handle and slowly dragged the door open, but only to the width of my body. I squeezed through sideways and pressed the door quietly shut again. I turned.

A dim, amber-shaded electric light burned to my left, at the beginning of a carpeted passageway along the windows. I stepped beneath the light. The passageway was empty, lined at this end of the car with half a dozen curtained sleeping compartments. Beyond them, the car opened up to its drawing room. I could see only the left half of the room, the ambered electric glow bright upon a setting of overstuffed burgundy wingback chairs. They were empty. The background clack of the rails was the only sound. The Pullman travelers seemed to be sleeping soundly in their affluence.

I moved along the corridor. I paused at each curtain as I passed, listening intently. I could hear a heavy shifting in one. A fleeting basso moan in another. I didn't think it was him. I could lift a hand, pull back a few inches of the curtain, answer the question. But it made no difference which berth held him. I would run too big a risk of getting caught if I entered his compartment and searched his bags with him sleeping at arm's length. I moved on and emerged from the passageway into the fullness of the drawing room.

And there, on one of the wingback chairs on the other side of the car, sat Friedrich Mensinger.

He was asleep.

He was not ramrod upright this time. He had sagged deep into the chair, his head angled against one of the wings. His slouch hat hung on a hook next to the window. A whiskey glass, with most of a double left in it, sat on the arm of the chair, which was just wide enough, flat enough for it to maintain a tenuous balance in a sometimes swaying train car. This was not his first tonight. His hand was vaguely surrounding his unfinished drink, but his fingers were slack. The car swayed slightly and the glass trembled. His hand did not move. Perhaps he'd only recently fallen asleep. His mouth was open slightly, though he was making no sounds. His sleep was not heavy enough for him to be snoring.

Most important, however, beneath his feet were his saddlebags.

I sat down in a chair, facing him from across the width of the car. Did he know this of himself, that he was apt to pass out from weariness and drink? Was that why he'd taken the precaution of having his bags beneath his feet even when he was sitting in an overstuffed chair in the drawing room of a Pullman car? Something important, of course, was inside the bags. The *Papiere*.

I looked at his high-laced boots, his spiral tan puttees lapped over their tops. The boots sat on the flaps of the bags, which were folded tightly together. I looked at his slack-jawed face. His eyes were moving beneath the lids. He was dreaming, Friedrich Mensinger. Of what? The touch of a fencing saber to his face? Himself slicing the mark of manhood into another young man? And another? And another? Each night perhaps he dreamed of a different face, a different stroke of his saber. Or perhaps he dreamed of his wife. His own hand like the sword. He struck her. If he struck her twice for her sympathetic tears, how often had he struck her for other things? Or he dreamed of Pancho Villa. Dreamed of mounting a horse and riding hard across the plateau to his bandit.

The train swayed left, smoothly but clearly, and it held this angle for a time. We were taking a mountain curve. I looked at the glass of whiskey. Mensinger's fingers had closed against it. I looked instantly to his face. I expected the eyes to be open, seeing me. But his head had not moved. His mouth was still slightly agape. The hand had its own reflex, to close on the glass, to keep it from spilling. The autonomics of a lifelong drinker.

The car righted itself.

I rose.

Mensinger's mouth shut. His lips grew restless, pressing ever so slightly and letting go and pressing again. Perhaps he was speaking in his dream. Attack, he was saying to Villa. Take your men and ride to Vera Cruz. Ride hard. Ride through the night and the Americans will not see you and attack them as they are collecting garbage and trapping rats and swatting flies.

I moved to Mensinger. I stepped to his side, careful not to touch the chair, the saddlebags. Nothing to wake him. But I leaned to him, brought my face close to his. His eyes had stopped moving beneath the lids. The scummy pond was still. I could hear him breathing. Steady. Complacent. Arrogant.

And I whispered to him. So softly I could not even hear it myself except in my head. "I will find a way."

35

I returned to my dark window and I tried to sleep—I needed to sleep—but I could not, and the dawn came and we were in a level run on a wide landscape of wind-whipped young barley, like a vast uncut yard of grass, and then we arrived in Aguascalientes, a major stop under the vaulted glass roof of the station's multitrack shed, and I lingered on the platform, ready to become Simon Chance even if just to nod my head to Mensinger and watch him snub me and pass. I suspected Mensinger would have those saddlebags over his shoulder, though I would wait for him so that I could be sure. But after a few minutes it became clear that he would not even emerge. He was probably back in his compartment sleeping off the whiskey.

So I went into the station, to the communal tables of the restaurant, and I ate eggs and mashed red beans and bits of something that once was an animal, all wrapped in a tortilla, and I drank coffee, and we were on the train again and we were running on the great Central Plateau and I was tired of looking at the Mexican landscape. Nothing was there to keep my mind from teeming with the man in the car ahead of me, and I knew that there was nothing my mind could do with him for now, that my mind could only be a hindrance.

I was glad that I'd packed a book. My typewriter and a book or two: These I have always carried, no matter the weight and no matter where I've gone in the world. A Standard Folding Number 1 in

Nicaragua, my Corona Number 3 ever since, and always a new book, but one that would bear several rereadings. Always these things in my life: to write, to read, to be near the clash of arms, near the life and death of men striving for something and prepared to give everything for it. In some ways this man I was following was not so different from these other men I'd written about. But he was drastically different as well. The world that he and I and our countries inhabited was changing.

I opened my book. A collection of stories by Henry James. I once read him for Mother and I have continued to read him for myself. I was drawn to his voice, though it was far from the voice I must take upon myself to write the things I write. But he was a voice inside me as well, a character inside me. And I opened straight to a passage I'd already marked in a story about a writer that I would reread now as I crossed the Mexican plateau. "We work in the dark—we do what we can—we give what we have. Our doubt is our passion and our passion is our task. The rest is the madness of art."

I was not creating art. I was simply writing what was happening in the world for men to read over their eggs and their coffee. But my passion was my task. And now my eyes grew heavy and I slept. And I only briefly awoke when we stopped in Zacatecas, and I hardly woke at all through a subsequent flag stop or two, and I only began to struggle into enough consciousness to decide if it was worth it after the conductor's voice floated into my head with the word "dinner," and after my brief, veiled glimpse out the window was of cacti and mellowing late-afternoon light and some horsemen standing in the long shadows of the approaching station, I closed my eyes again and I thought I heard the conductor from somewhere forward in the car announce the name of a town called Carlos, and I thought there was nothing that could possibly be cooked in Carlos appealing enough to prevent me from going back to sleep instead.

And then I was surrounded by gunfire and I was fully awake.

36

Ah, this was a familiar sound, for it to be this close. Not since that first hour or two of our boys coming into Vera Cruz did my heart and blood and head and limbs spring to the life of nearby gunfire. But my mind caught up now. This was not a battlefield. I was not doing my classic job. I was sneaking around as a German and these were rebel bandits stopping a train to rob and to kill and I had nowhere to stand apart and I had no weapon of my own and I had only everything to lose and the doors to my right flew open and men stinking of horses and cordite and sweat rushed in and my ears pounded and rang with more shots and my skin pinged with splinters of the ceiling scattering down upon us, and the men, wearing unpinned sombreros and khaki and ammo belts crossed on their chests, were crying out orders for us all to rise and bring any bags we could carry and line up outside and we all were obeying and you could feel the wave of unvoiced fear gather and rush from the passengers' awkward risings and bendings and bumpings and stumblings. This was a moment like moments from the Balkans and from Nicaragua that I'd been part of, civilians caught in the clash, but never in a tightly closed space, never with the civilians being the sole and focused targets, and I tucked away the feeling of this collective terror—tucked it away so I could put it into words if I got through this and wrote again—this collective terror that you could feel roll over you, like an onrushing pressure on your skin—the sense of a wave was more than a metaphor—these people were putting out a unified, undulant something, a palpable something—and I was indeed standing apart now, even as I moved, I felt very calm pulling my bag up from between the seats to cries of *Andale! Andale!* and more cracking in my head from the pistols—I was calm but uneasy, too, with not very many options. I was uneasy for my typewriter and I was uneasy for my Henry James—but these were things of no use to the rebels—no use to Pancho Villa—I realized now that these must be Villa's men—we were in his range of command now surely—and I was in line going into the vestibule bumping a man before me in a spangled sombrero and being bumped from behind by someone else. And I was uneasy about the money belt of gold coins around my waist, hidden beneath my clothes, and I was uneasy that I was calm enough to be thinking of Henry James before the money, uneasy because I might be so calm as to be dangerous to myself.

And now we were all lined up along the length of our cars while sombreros and *bandoleros* and Mausers and brown faces were ranging up and down the long row of us, and more of the same sat mounted on horses beyond them. I knew it was very chancy to be overtly looking around, but I did let myself take one clear glance to my right, toward the Pullman, and I could see, over the heads and sombreros and *rebozos,* Mensinger standing tall, a horseman before him, bending to him. I did not look closely at the horseman, except to notice he was dressed in black, a *Villista* officer no doubt. I simply took a single snapshot in my head of the German and looked back to the front again.

I kept my face mostly forward, angled only very slightly, unnoticeably, to the right, where I let myself glance briefly with just my eyes and strained to focus on my peripheral vision. I did not want to draw any more attention to myself than I already inevitably would. The man I followed from the train was an arm's length to my right. His *mestizo* face was chamois tan, light, a dangerous thing for him now, as he showed his preponderance of ancestors from the much-hated Spanish. When Villa took over the state of Chihuahua he executed key Spaniards and drove the rest of them out. One of the dark *Villistas* stood before the man who had Spain lingering on his skin and the rebel ripped the spangled sombrero from the man's head and ran his fingers in the sweatband. He pulled out half a dozen large-denomination greenbacks. American money. Spain and America and wealth, a *hacendado*. I gently but as quickly as possible turned my face straightforward—so as not to be seen as a witness—even as the *Villista* drew a Colt revolver and the gun cracked loud and I heard the passenger fall heavily down.

"For holding out," the rebel announced loudly, a lesson for all of us, and though that was no doubt part of it, I knew much more was behind that bullet. America, for one thing.

And now he stepped to me. The darkly chiseled Aztec face drew itself very near mine and his mustache was covered in dust, and he said, "Where are you from?"

"I am German," I said.

"You are a *gringo*," he said. "I will shoot you now."

"I am a German," I said. "Let me show you my passport and you can save your bullet for the *Federales*."

This gave him a moment's pause.

"For the next *colorado*," I said. He grunted in affirmation. The *colorados* were the *Federales* who once were the private army of Pascual Orozco when he was just another rebel opposing President Madero, an army of bandits and murderers recruited from the jails, the most indiscriminately murderous of all the many rebel forces, fighting now as equally murderous irregular *Federales* since Orozco became Huerta's commanding general. Villa and his men never took a *colorado* prisoner. They killed the killers summarily. My invocation of them made my *Villista* receptive to the notion that perhaps I was not a *gringo*. I did not take time to count, but I was keenly aware that I had denied my country more than the Biblical limit of three times now, in various ways. God forgive me.

"Inside my coat," I said. "The passport." I motioned and moved my hand slowly.

He let me.

I took hold of the passport, and as I was pulling it out, the man before me said, "This will only perhaps save your life. You will still owe us all your money and valuables as a railway tax for the revolution."

"Of course," I said.

I handed him my passport, and he looked at it.

I had plenty to give him from the usual pockets. But I was heading for a crisis with the money belt. Not only was the money absolutely essential to my ability to follow Mensinger and get the story and find my way to an American telegraph to file it, but all of my American credentials were in that money belt as well. That was the real danger, and it was severe.

I thought: I am a dead man, so I might as well go down fighting.

The *Villista* before me checked my face against the picture, which I knew was fine, and as for the rest, I didn't think he was actually reading. He thumbed the passport looking for flags or symbols or perhaps a few words he recognized. I hoped Vogel had no American visits stamped in the back pages of his passport. He probably didn't, given what he was doing. And the German Imperial Eagle grandly spread its wings on the front cover of the document. But the passport wasn't the real problem.

This might be the end of things now, I thought. Even if I could overpower the man in front of me, there were horsemen right behind him. So I lifted my eyes away from the *Villista,* away from the sombreros on the horses, I turned my eyes to the distant jagged line of mountains, their flanks going buttery in the long-angled late-afternoon light. I thought of my mother. I wished I could think of her now on the stage. Think of her accepting her age. Playing Gertrude or Volumina or even Lady Bracknell—my mother could play with the lightest of touches as well. Storyville fell like cloud-shadow upon my mind, wiping away that lovely afternoon sunlight before me. But last mortal thoughts could rightly focus on any moments of the life that was passing away, and so I would think of her—as I could, for there were many such moments even well into my teens—I would think of her when she was still convincingly Juliet or Antigone or Kate. She played Kate ever so lightly.

My *Villista* was pushing my passport back into my hand. "Your valuables now," he said. "Do not hold out. You saw what happened."

He motioned my attention to a mere boy of a *Villista,* sombreroed and bandoleraed but no older than I was when I watched from the backs of theaters as the great Isabel Cobb brought sobs from the audiences as she nightly died as Juliet Capulet. This boy held an open canvas bag.

I took my Elgin from my pocket and dropped it showily into the bag.

I pulled a wallet—with money only—from my other inside coat pocket and I opened it for the bandit before me, to reveal all the pesos inside. A great thick wad. And I dropped it into the bag.

I was going too slow for my *Villista.* His Mauser was slung over his shoulder and both his hands leaped into my coat pockets now, outside pockets, inside pockets, ambidextrously working through my coat, finding my passport again and replacing it, finding my Waterman fountain pen—chased black rubber with a sweet extra-fine, flexible nib—no worry about my holding out a utilitarian thing like that—but he tossed it into the bag anyway, which got my goat—and his hands were arrogantly assuming I would stand here and do nothing till he was finished with me, which, of course, would normally be a safe bet, given the firepower backing him up, but he would frisk me next and that would be that.

His hands moved under my arms and started to pound their way down my sides, my money belt awaiting about three more strikes. Strike one—the center of my rib cage—and I could hear a horse directly behind him nickering, its rider perhaps noticing this special, aggressive treatment and shifting in his saddle, lifting his rifle a bit, ready to back up his comrade. Strike two—below my rib cage and taking my breath away for a brief moment—and now there was the dust-muted lollop of hooves from off to my right, another horseman coming up, and I knew my *Villista*'s next strike would be in the center of the plate and I had to at least swing the bat.

He pounded his hands down at my hips, right on the money belt, and his eyes flared wide and his pistol hand started to pull away from me and now his eyes flared wide again as I leaned into him and kicked hard, straight up and centered, and I crushed his balls with my

shinbone. He crumpled onto his knees and I could hear rifles clatter-
ing up, bolts being thrown, and I cried out as loud as I could, "This
man is ill!" and I was about to fall to my own knees and grab his pistol
and use him for cover and take out a few of these sons of whores and
donkeys but another voice bellowed, "Hold your fire!" and the lollop of
hooves I'd heard a moment ago scuffled loudly to a stop, the shadow of
the horse and rider falling over me and over the gasping *Villista* whose
pistol I was, nevertheless, still grasping for.

And the bellowing voice bellowed some more. In English. "Jesus
H. Christ! I know you!"

And leaping off his horse in black shirt and black sombrero and
bandolera and striding toward me was Tallahassee Slim.

37

I stood up straight and stepped away from my crumpled *Villista* and squared around to face Slim.

If his brown eyes seemed, upon my first meeting in Corpus Christi, to be the color of mountain-lion shit, they were now the eyes of the critter itself. Cool and ravenous. And he gave off not even a first-glance impression of gaunt anymore, unless you'd call a steel cable on the Brooklyn Bridge gaunt.

We clearly both had the notion to shake hands, but given the context, we also both thought the better of it for the time being.

"What the hell are you doing out here?" he said, lowering his voice, acknowledging our little bond, but speaking Spanish. There was no doubt that everyone knew he was an American, but soldiers of fortune had no fixed nationality. Slim was smart. He was doing this for me. He knew I couldn't have gotten this far on a train as an American.

"I'm after a story," I said.

"What the hell have you done to my man?" he said.

My *Villista* was now on all fours, making vaguely sexual-sounding, feminine sounds.

"Kicked him in the nuts. He was about to shoot me."

Which reminded Slim of the body he had just ridden past. He glanced at it. "What the hell has my man done to this one?"

Slim and I both knew that was a rhetorical question.

I said nothing.

Slim shrugged. "I'm sure he deserved it."

"Who am I to judge?" I said.

"Are you trying to get to my boss?"

"Villa?" I asked, also rhetorically.

"Villa," he said anyway.

"Yes."

Slim nodded. "Wait here. I've got something to deal with."

Slim jumped back up on his horse and shot his Mauser twice in the air, paused for a beat, and then shot once more. All the *Villistas* stopped what they were doing and turned his way. He clearly was, as I'd assumed, in charge. "*Compañeros!*" he cried. He had the pipes-power of Caruso. "Work quickly now and do not damage the train!"

And he nudged his horse forward. I thought he was going to say something to me, but he looked past my shoulder, at the ground. I turned to see. The man I'd put down was sitting now, clutching his crotch, looking very unhappy.

"Hernando," Slim said sharply. My *Villista* looked up. Slim said, "Do nothing to this man. Is that clear?"

Hernando lowered his head and cursed softly.

Slim spurred his horse along.

I looked to the right, past the first-class passengers, who were still in the process of being robbed, and I did not see Mensinger. I was daring to hope Slim would take me with him. If I could get to Villa without trying to follow Mensinger out of La Mancha, that would be very good. But it took a moment to absorb Mensinger's absence and I thought: This was why Slim had hurried his boys along and wouldn't burn the train. He knew who the German was, knew he was expected. I'm sure Slim offered Mensinger what I thought he would offer me, to ride with the train-tax company to Villa's camp. Would Mensinger take him up on it? Would he let himself become a protectorate of a gang of bandits, even if they were under Villa's command? Or if I was right about his reasons for getting off in La Mancha, would he excuse himself with Slim—whom he did not expect and may not trust—and stick to his own plan? Would he insist on making his entrance on his own terms?

And who was I, either way?

Soon Slim rode back to me, leading a chestnut stallion saddled up with an empty rifle holster and bags. He motioned me over and I knew we needed to say more private words. I moved to him and I stood in his shadow and looked up.

He was still speaking Spanish, but low. "Who were you pretending to be in order to get here?"

"A German."

Slim nodded very faintly. "Interesting. Got another German on board."

"To him I was a Canadian."

Slim laughed. "Canadian newsman?"

"Coffee merchant."

"You ready to go back to what you really are?"

I didn't answer instantly, but I didn't hesitate more than one slow blink of the eye, and Slim jumped in: "If you want some kind of story, you pretty much have to."

"Will that work?"

And Slim was speaking English now, though still low enough for just the two of us. "Don't know. He likes his publicity. No doubt about that. But he blows hot and cold. And I'm the only American fighting for him that he hasn't sent packing. If I bring you in, I'll know as soon as I look in his eyes. If he's in the wrong mood, I'll have to make like you're my prisoner. Which, I have to tell you, is what you'll be."

"Fair enough," I said.

"Mount up," he said. "Courtesy of one of the last stubborn *hacendados* around these parts. Put your stuff in the saddlebags."

He handed me the reins. "I'll be back for you as soon as we finish with our tax collection." And he rode off.

I moved to the chestnut, who shook his head at me but let me stroke his muzzle. I leaned near him and exhaled heavily into his nostrils, just to introduce myself. He dipped his head and muttered a little and I knew we'd be all right.

Repacking was tough. Fortunately, the saddlebags were big, and though I had to lose its nifty carrying case, I was able to squeeze in my Corona. Sadly, though, volume XVI of the Scribner's monogrammed New York Edition of Henry James simply could not fit and would have to be abandoned a long, long way from Washington Square. About as far away as I was feeling at the moment from Michigan Avenue.

38

We rode hard into the plateau, into the mesquite and the greasewood, racing against the fading of the daylight into twilight, the mountains going black against the sky. We were trying, it seemed, to get somewhere specific, and to keep up I was soon riding like the Mexicans, with stiff legs and constantly flapping them to urge my horse on. There were no sounds but our hooves and all of us panting, horses and men alike. The night threatened—the moon had not yet risen—and though we still could see around us, it was clear that we soon would be blind.

So we rode even harder and then someone yipped. Perhaps a mile ahead we could see the yellow smoke of evening fires and now we were on a dusty road, and a stone fence was running with us. We were in the lands of a sizeable *hacienda*, the *dueño* long since fled or dead. Slim and his boys all seemed not to be seriously wary here. I took the place to be their staging area for raids on the trains.

At a half mile from the fires, someone among us shot two quick rifle rounds. Shortly, from up ahead, came one Mauser reply, a beat, and then a second. And soon we all arrived through a man-high stretch of the stone wall, a wide, iron-gated portal guarded by half a dozen more *Villistas,* and we slowed for another few hundred yards up a desert rise to the *casa grande.*

It was dark now, but as I climbed down from my horse, a little shaky and aching from the ride, I sensed off to the west and below us the vastness of the plateau. And the *casa* was *grande* indeed, porticoed like the city hotels, one-storied but high-roofed, built around a court-yard large enough to set a wealthy *Veracruzano*'s house fully inside.

We ate in one of the *casa*'s lofty *salas*, stripped of its furnishings, only a tattered brocade on one wall—custom-made with cattle and mountain peaks, images of this very ranch no doubt—and an empty mahogany sideboard on another. There were women shuttling in and out to serve Slim and me and his core group lounging on the floor and other women serving the rest of the men in the courtyard. I didn't know if these were peon women left to make a life in their adobe huts on the ranch after the owner had gone or if they were the mated women of the *Villistas*, though from what I saw of this culture, from the perspective of any low-bred and poor Mexican woman, there was little difference: She existed to do this, to cook and feed and give sex and whatever comfort she could to whatever men claimed her.

We ate goat meat and corn and tortillas, and Slim and I ate with-out speaking much at all while the men around us laughed and pro-gressively elaborated on the tales of their day's exploits and got drunk on *pulque* and on *sotol,* a local drink made from wild-growing Desert Spoon, closer to beer than to *pulque,* which made the stuff okay for me while I was eating, but I knew Slim had a bottle of looted anisette, and as soon as we finished our food, he gave me a little head-nod toward a door into the far wing of the house.

We wound up in the kitchen. At one end were the large adobe stoves and ovens and a vast fireplace with a spit and the goat carcass picked almost clean. Several women—older ones, stouter ones—were still working there, cleaning up. Slim told them all to *vamoose* and they did, quickly. Smoke still hovered around the high ceiling, adding to its greasy dark layer from years of meals, and we pulled a couple of stools over to the doorway that led outside. Slim opened the door, and we sat in the place between the stars and the sharp chill of the high-country night on our one hand and the goat-flesh and tortilla-saturated warmth of the kitchen on our other.

"We doing this straight?" I asked, nodding at the bottle of anisette he was opening.

"Sure. We've ridden fast enough already."

The times I'd had anisette, it was mixed with cold water and it turned milky and sweet. *Palomita*. But even if we had the water, Slim was right. We'd take it straight and strong and slow tonight.

"Glasses," he said. He stood up and moved past me into the kitchen. Under the circumstances, the glasses were a nicety that surprised me in him. I'd have been happy to pass a bottle with any *insurrecto* who earned the name of "Slim."

I looked out at the stars. I was content for the moment. I was on my way to Villa. I would make my own kind of entrance. When we both got to where we wanted to go, Mensinger was going to end up learning who I really was anyway. I still had to finesse the story out of someone, but sitting in the doorway of this *hacienda* kitchen with a profusion of stars before me that were progressively invisible now in any big American city in this still young but electrified twentieth century, and with a bottle of good liquor on its way across the room to me, I would not try to plan my next move.

But I did have things to learn. And the man who might know some of them was back on his stool beside me. He handed me a tin cup. He had one of his own. "Sorry for these things," he said. "All I could find. But if we don't want to burn the shit out of our gullets, we each need to bridle our own pace."

I nodded at his reasoning. He poured me half a cup of anisette, which I figured would last me most of the night. He poured himself likewise and put the bottle on the floor beside us. He lifted his tin cup and offered it toward me. I touched it with mine.

I brought my cup to my mouth, and I paused to take in the anisette smell that was already grabbing at me. It was the smell of licorice. A half-eaten stick of licorice going soft in the Chicago summer heat and draping over my knuckles and stuck in my teeth and I wished I could find a mirror to see my tongue gone black and I was straight off the Van Buren Street steamer and walking by the lagoon of the Great

White City of the Columbian Exposition, and I was lately nine years old, and I was surrounded by the immensity of the domes and columns and vaulting roofs, and my mother was on one side of me and there was a hand on my shoulder from the other side. Even with the smell of anisette in me, I couldn't remember which actor he was, some leading man or other. He was a good man, was all I remembered, one I was still young enough at the time to hope would stick around, to hope would find roles to play with my mother forever. But of course he didn't. Of course we were off to New York, just my mother and me, by the end of the summer and he was off to tour the Midwest, and all that remained of him now was the smell of licorice, and that was a hell of a thing to suddenly get stuck on in the presence of a hired gun called "Slim." I took a quick bolt of my drink and it was like sunburn going down my throat, and for the moment that was okay.

Slim took what looked like too big a hit of the anisette as well, and he squared his stool around so he was at a right angle to me and to the night both, and he and I watched the sky while our throats cooked for a while.

"This is better than the stuff we drank together in Corpus," I said.

He nodded. "That wasn't the best whiskey I ever had."

"What was?"

Slim laughed softly. "We ain't even drunk yet and we hankering for the past, are we?"

"About your best whiskey ever? You can hanker sober."

"You're probably right."

"So?"

"Well, like with a woman, there's something about your first one."

He paused. I didn't know if he was still on my question or thinking about his first woman.

"But it's not usually the best," he said.

"So, the best," I said.

Slim didn't look at me but back at the sky. I'd been mostly joking. But from his present manner, I believed him about this being a serious matter of hankering for something passed. He said, "A sixteen-year-old

Green River, which I had down in Panama where my dad was causing some trouble more or less on his own and I got him out of a scrape and we sat down together in a bar where you wouldn't expect to find anything but rotgut. They had that nice old Green River. Mr. J. W. McCulloch of Owensboro, Kentucky, do certainly know how to make him some sweet-oaked whiskey."

I let Slim sit with his memory for a bit.

I didn't begrudge him his whiskey with his badass *insurrecto* daddy, but I was sorry I brought it up.

Finally he turned his face away from the sky and sipped minutely at his anisette.

"I've never had a Green River," I said.

"Pity."

"You were right in Corpus," I said.

"I been right in everything I said in every bar I ever sat in," he said, straight-faced, though I heard the elbow-nudge in his voice. "But what thing in particular?"

"About Woody going to war over a chaw of tobacco."

"If war you want to call it."

"Well, didn't we pretty much figure that too?"

"If we didn't, we could've."

"So," I said. "Knowing what would transpire ahead of time, what brought you back to fight for the Mexicans?"

"Not for the Mexicans," Slim said. "For Villa."

I heard a thing in Slim's voice like respect. "Why him?" I asked.

Slim took another bolt of anisette, since I was apparently asking him to loosen his tongue some more. He rested his tin cup on his thigh. "What if a guy in my line of work had a chance to sign on with Napoleon? Villa fights like him. He takes advantage of his opponents fighting stiffly, by the book. He's relentless and fast-moving and secretive. He'll come at you at night and he won't stop coming at you. He's always changing what he does to fit the terrain and his men. And he's very close to those men. No saluting. No nonsense. They know in their bones he's the *jefe*, but they also feel like he's one of them. And he knows how to make his legend and get it out to the people he'll come up against. You news boys help him there. You let the world believe he's living by some lucky star. That nobody can kill him. That his army can't be beat. You boys treat that like truth and then it's as good as being true. And it all comes natural to Pancho Villa. He didn't even know how to read till a couple of years ago, which he insisted on learning even though he was already the commander of ten thousand troops. That's the guy you sign up with."

"How'd you find him?"

"He found me. During his exile in El Paso early last year. Big guy—a real big guy—is pounding on me in a bar for some little old thing I said to him, a thing which was right, incidentally. I try my fists and my legs and I got *nada* working for me and he has me up against the rail and the bartender is just letting it go on. So I find a heavy glass beer mug with my right hand and I crack this Johnny in the left temple and he goes down like he took a Mauser bullet to the brain. Villa and a couple of his pals was there watching. I think he liked my tactics."

"Can Villa be the next president of Mexico?"

"Some think. He talks like he don't care about that. But he's the only leader out there who'll do the thing that he wants the most. Which is give all the land to the peons. So he'll be president if he has a chance."

"You think he'll ever come after us?"

"Us?"

"The U. S. of A."

Slim didn't give this a moment's thought. "Much as I think he's a hell of a military man, I'll retire from his service if he does." Slim didn't sound defensive. He was just objectively pointing out the terms of his employment.

"I don't doubt it," I said.

"He'd fight us in ways we're not used to."

"I was just wondering if he's capable of attacking us."

"Pancho Villa is capable of anything," Slim said.

I nodded. I waited. Sometimes you simply wait long enough and somebody thinks he's got to say some more and then he says more than he should.

But Slim didn't seem to have any news in him to spill. He said, "You know he's pledged to do Carranza's work. Villa never calls him anything other than his *jefe*."

"Pledged, is he?"

"Like I say, he's capable of anything."

I humphed a little.

"Including unpledging," Slim said.

"That going to happen soon?"

"Any old day. Our Pancho's an emotional man. A very warm man. Warm either way. He'll hug you and kiss you on the cheek if he's got his feelings for you right. But if he gets some reason in his head otherwise, he'll turn around and shoot you dead."

At this I took a sip of anisette.

So did Slim. Then he said, "He let himself be Carranza's general before he actually met the man. He laid eyes on him and he hated him instantly. Carranza's a sharp-gilled, dead-in-the-eyes, coldwater catfish."

I sipped again, too soon, at the anisette. I let it burn. Mensinger was smart about hitching Wilson to Carranza. And he was even probably right.

Slim said, "Carranza's afraid of Villa. Always has been. Really is now. Afraid we'll head south from Torreón and keep on going to Mexico City. So the *Primer Jefe's* insisting we campaign pretty near two hundred miles due east and take Saltillo."

"That so?"

"Yup. Probably Monterey after that. Probably run us on over to the border and set us there."

"Will Villa do it?"

"Take Saltillo? He's gone partway already. Slow going, having to re-lay track torn up by the *Federales*."

I nodded. The trains carrying his cavalry to targets were crucial to Villa's tactics. For him this was a war fought within twenty miles of railroad tracks. I said, "Well, he's got time to think."

Slim laughed. "Plenty. Thinking and cockfighting and cock-dipping while he's creeping east with his track layers. That's his life right now."

The cock-dipping twisted hotly in me, much to my surprise. Up popped Luisa running off to her goddam bandit rebel leader. It made me irritable. I blamed Slim for even mentioning it. I said, "And train robbing."

Slim looked away. I hit the nerve in him I expected to hit. I was still trying to get Luisa out of my head, and all I could think to do was needle Slim, like punching a pal in a bar for telling me my girl was opening up for some other guy. "Was there bullion on the train today?" I said. It didn't come out sounding like a question. I was challenging him over his previous excuse.

Slim didn't say anything.

This wasn't his fault. I tried to clear my head by making it up to him, giving him new excuses. "It's the nature of a revolution," I said. "He's got to find a way to pay for it."

Slim still didn't speak, but I could sense a little letting-go in him. That was how he'd already rationalized it for himself.

Not that this stopped the squirming in me. I heard myself say, "Plenty of women always around for the cock-dipping."

"It's the damnedest thing," Slim said, happy to change the subject. "Every army in every war has got their camp girls, but down here they got that beat. You can bring your own woman or grab one along the way and they're like your own personal cook, nurse, and whore."

"Does Villa have women fighting for him?"

"Not really. Not like I hear Zapata does."

Okay. Maybe Luisa wasn't even with Villa. Maybe she'd heard this about Zapata and went south.

"But Zapata's meaningless in this whole thing," Slim said.

Which put an angry big-dreamer like Luisa right back here. I really needed to get away from this line of thought. I needed to focus on what I was doing here, who I was. The story.

I didn't know how to play this one, whether or not to bring Slim in on the essentials of what I knew and what I was after. For now I simply asked, "So who was the German in the Pullman?"

"I been thinking about that too."

"And?"

Slim looked at me and I bet he was making the same decision I was, about confiding. Him first. Maybe only him.

Slim shrugged. "I was told there might be somebody on one of the trains we hit. A German official. His name would be Mensinger."

"Somebody you'd make sure the train keeps running for?"

Slim looked at me like how the hell did I know. But I'd heard him revise his orders to his boys in the middle of a pillage, and I thought he suddenly remembered this. "Right," he said. "He was cleared all the way to Villa himself."

"So why isn't he sitting here with us, having some anisette?"

Slim shrugged again. "Arrogant prick of a Hun, I guess."

"You offered to bring him?"

"Yup. Was told to. He declined. Said he had some things to do. Said he'd ride in on his own. I just told him where."

I needed to be quick about suppressing it but I managed to keep the smile off my face. I figured it was like I'd figured. I said, "Any idea what his business is with Villa?"

Slim took a pull at his tin cup, let the anisette slide down, relaxed with the burn, looked out at the night beyond the door, and without looking back to me, he said, "Don't know."

All that preamble. A real "Don't know" would've come quick, it seemed to me. "What is it, Slim?"

"I don't like the Huns," he said.

"What do they want with Villa?"

"Don't know."

I believed him this time. I said, "But you worry."

"You see those boys in Europe and the guy they got rattling their sabers?"

"Not a Woody Wilson," I said.

"The Kaiser could even provoke Woody Wilson into being somebody he ain't. Not sure how good Wilson would do at that." Slim was still talking into the night.

"If Vera Cruz is any indication…" I let Slim finish the thought in his own head.

"Like I say."

We drank. We burned. We watched the stars. I finally decided I might need some help in Villa's camp.

So I said, "I talked to Mensinger along the way up here."

Slim turned to me.

He waited. I let it rest for a moment.

"About coffee?" Slim said.

It took me a moment to remember I'd told him about the Canadian. "Sure. I sold him a bag of beans."

"What's with him?"

"I got no proof but a bunch of little things that makes for pretty good guesses."

"Which are?"

"I think the Germans will bankroll Villa if he goes after Funston and the boys. Make a big show of kicking the *gringos* out of his country."

"Why would the Germans get involved?"

"To put their chips on the next *presidente*. They see a move like that uniting the country behind Villa. All these divided loyalties in Mexico have one thing in common, thanks to our man Wilson: Everybody hates the United States. The rebel leader who can grab that issue, make it his own, defeat *El Diablo del Norte*, that guy can finally get some traction in the civil war. Then he can throw out Huerta on Mexican terms and rule the country."

"Is this what he said?"

"Enough that these are good guesses. But they're guesses. If I had more I'd be at a telegraph office across the border about now."

Slim nodded.

"Does this make sense to you, though?" I asked.

"Might could," Slim said.

"So we'd end up with Mexico and Germany latched together," I said. "And there are lots of good guesses about bad things from that."

We drank some more and then some more, and we stayed silent for a long while.

The stars started to jitter around in the sky. I was watching this phenomenon pretty closely when Slim flopped his head in my direction.

He looked me in the eyes as best he could. I focused my eyes on him as best I could. And he said, "Me, I'm just a goddam train robber."

39

Anisette or *pulque* or *sotol,* it made no difference. There was plenty of it in the *casa* and in its courtyard and out on the perimeter, and at the main gate and in the corrals. There was plenty and there was a hard day's ride to Carlos yesterday for most everybody in Slim's gang and the stress and strain of a lot of robbing and a little killing and then an even harder ride back to the *hacienda* on the plateau at night and there was plenty of food and there was the anisette and the *pulque* and the *sotol.* And so, as I have reconstructed it, when the sun came up, there was clearly no one to notice the cloud of dust out on the plain and no one to notice the front-gate guards having their sleeping heads beat in with rifle butts and no one to notice the nickering of horses and the metal slip of gun bolts and the creaking of saddle leather coming up the high ground toward the *casa* and it wasn't till some *Villista* had the good but bad fortune—bad for him, good for the rest of us—to step out in front to take a bleary-eyed, *pulque*-stinking piss that any of us knew there was a band of *colorados* about to lay siege on all of us.

The pisser only barely got his dick out when he knew something was up and, being a shrewd bandit, did not take the time even to put his dick away before drawing the pistol from his belt, which his shrewdness always had him carry around no matter how focused he was on mundane matters, and he shot once—probably to warn us all just before the *colorados* breached the top of our high ground—and

we were most of us rushing awake while two or three of the bad boys
under their red flag and with red bandanas around their necks were
plugging the pisser in several places about his body.

I was fully awake very quickly after that first shot and I found
myself on the kitchen floor, curled over in the shadows beneath the
fireplace where I guess I came to draw a little heat for sleeping, and
there was shouting now and scuffling feet from the front of the house
and gunfire and I was on my feet looking for Slim and he burst in
through the kitchen door and found me and he threw me a pistol belt
pretty near across the whole length of the kitchen and I caught it and
he motioned me to follow as he headed for the back door and I did,
strapping the belt around me as I went, not even thinking yet what
it was I was putting on exactly, and I was behind him and he had his
Mauser in one hand and his *bandolera* draped over his other arm and
we cut along the back of the *casa* with serious gunfire going on inside.

Slim stopped just this side of another rear entrance to the house
and he looked in quickly and drew back. He put on his *bandolera* and
began strapping it and he was saying, "*Colorados.* Don't know how many,
but we'll try to flank them. Sorry for the pistol. Just kill one of them and
grab his rifle." He winked. From covering a couple of wars, I knew two
things about a guy who winks when the shooting starts: You're glad to
have him on your side, and you don't want to be following him around.

"Good plan," I said.

"But it's an excellent pistol," he said and he was cinching up and
almost ready to go.

I looked down to see what I had to work with.

I was wearing a beat-up belt, but in the holster and now in my
hand was a very up-to-date Browning-designed Colt Model 1911.

"One in the chamber already, seven in the clip," Slim said.

This was the standard issue for all of Funston's troops in Vera
Cruz. I was glad to have it. On my other hip was a magazine pouch.
I had no time to do anything but pat it once and feel something in
there. Slim said, "Let's go," and we were slipping past the doorway and
I gave a quick glance through an empty room and an open door onto

the inner galleria and the courtyard beyond where I saw a couple of bodies but at least some live *Villistas* were crouched behind a fountain and a couple of overturned tables returning fire toward the front of the house.

We made the edge of the *casa* and Slim held up a hand. I stopped beside him, pressed back against the wall. He set himself, and then, as he looked quickly around the corner, my thumb made sure the safety was off on my pistol. I'd handled these. Fired one that was the proud possession of a Greek officer at Kilkis. It had a sweet little punch and a nice flat trajectory from about home plate to the center fielder. I just wished I was a better shot with a handgun.

Slim flipped his head and we went around the corner. But we angled off away from the house, sprinting for a big side-yard garden that was no doubt the prize of the *hacendado*'s wife, with pomegranate trees and pepper trees and Mexican fig and with the roses and asters and calla gone wild now. And most important, the woman had a pretentiousness very useful to Slim and me as we heard the gunfire clustering from the front of the house and we sought cover: Running parallel to the house was a long row of fake Greek fluted columns holding up nothing.

And we were behind these and we were crashing through the flower beds to get to the front end of the garden where we could have an angle of fire on the *colorados* on the attack. Slim went to the farthest column and set himself. I stopped at the column next to his and crouched and looked.

Eight or ten untethered but well-trained saddle horses were calmly backing off in a loose pack to wait as their riders banged away inside the house. But half a dozen *colorados* in front-pinned sombreros and red neck-scarves were in the next wave pounding up and they stayed mounted and they split up and spurred their horses, obviously to circle around back, and of the three who turned in our direction, the center guy, a big guy, a fat guy with a major mustache, this fat guy lifted up from both shoulders and he went wide-eyed and the center of his chest bloomed red and he lifted up from his horse and I'd just

heard the crack of Slim's Mauser and the fat guy was flying back
and the other two *colorados* were pulling up on their reins and Slim's
Mauser popped again and the fat guy's boot-bottoms were flashing
in my sight and the *colorado* on the left jerked his left shoulder but
just a simple jerk-back and the third guy's rifle was coming up from
pointing toward the ground to passing the horse's shoulder, and all of
this was going way too slow and I was going too slow, I realized I was
just watching, and I had to move, I had to act, I raised my pistol and
I pulled the trigger and the pop recoiled into my arm and shoulder
and I didn't know where that bullet went but certainly not anywhere
useful, though the guy on the right started to shift his face toward me
as his rifle was up where he wanted it now and though he was glancing at me I thought his rifle had a bead on Slim and I was telling my
hand to hold still and to pull off another round and I did and I realized
what I'd done, pulled the trigger of my Browning twice now when
pull was the wrong thing for me to do and that was where I'd always
gone wrong in the times I'd shot a handgun, not doing the same as I
did more easily with a rifle because I could lay the rifle against me
and hold it with both hands and the pistol was all in my one hand and
stretched outward and it was not so easy but I needed to *squeeze* the
trigger not pull it, and things were still going as slow as a bad dream,
and I was bringing my other hand up to my pistol hand to steady it
and the muzzle of the rifle of the guy on the right flared even as his
horse was rearing a little and he missed Slim I was sure he had to have
missed with his horse moving like that and I was trying just to focus on
what I had to do, focus on the chest of the guy on the right as his horse
settled and I pulled the trigger again and my Browning popped and
nothing happened to my target because I'd pulled again and another
pulse-beat of nothing and then the man's throat exploded as if it was
his red bandana that was full of blood and had suddenly popped, and
this was not from me it was from Slim's Mauser and the *colorado* was
flying back and I looked to the guy on the left and he was bringing
his winged shoulder around bringing the shoulder with a jagged red
chunk out of it back around so he could shoot but it was his bad arm

that he was using to hold on to the reins and he lost his grip and the horse was spooked anyway so it veered right even as the man tried with his other arm to aim his rifle and I swung my pistol in his direction but Slim shot again and this one caught the wounded *colorado* in the side of the chest and he was going down and Slim cried "Now!" and I looked and he was motioning toward the front door of the *casa* and I rose and I was running forward and Slim was beside me and I angled toward a lever-action Winchester on the ground near a dead *colorado* as a riderless horse flashed past nearly running over me and I reared back and I needed to watch these other things going on, I felt myself too single-minded and that was okay when I shot but not when I ran, and Slim was angling the other way.

I slowed myself. I turned my head. Slim was twenty yards off, bending to another rifle, probably for me, and I knew what was next, we would storm through the front door and catch the *colorados* in there from behind, and I shifted my eyes away from the bending Slim who was focusing on the rifle he was reaching for, and coming up the rise from farther off to my left, from behind Slim but heading straight for him, was a horseman, was a *colorado* riding hard, late to the party and ready to kill and he was unslinging his rifle from his shoulder and it was starting to come down from aiming at the sky and he was going to shoot Slim in the back and ride him down and I cried out "Slim! Behind!" and my own pistol was already coming up and Slim heard me and he was straightening and was turning and I needed to get off a round just to draw the *colorado*'s attention to me, make myself the bigger threat and I tried to squeeze the trigger, squeeze it not pull it, and I did and I missed the horseman but I could see him flinch his head back, I'd gotten his attention and his face was turning to me as Slim was turning to me also and I knew I was not going to hit this guy from the forty yards that separated us now and I knew I needed to be a threat to him and I squared around and I took one long quick stride in the *colorado*'s direction and he was still spooked from the zip of my bullet past him and I saw his muzzle turn to me and I strode toward it and it flared even as he was jerking his bridle in my direction and I was taking another stride as I realized a razor cut of pain had slipped across my left arm at the lower edge of my deltoid, which was okay, the round came and went and was gone, and it was not my shooting arm and I took another stride and I was lifting my left arm and it seemed to be working fine and I braced my left hand under my right and the horse was scrambling to finish its turn and it brought the *colorado* a little off my direct line but full square in my sights and I stopped and the *colorado's* muzzle flailed a moment as the horse finished veering into its new direction and I squared myself up and the horse took a gallop at me and I clasped my hands together to steady the Browning and the rifle muzzle was adjusting onto me again and another gallop and I squeezed the trigger quick and gentle I squeezed and felt the recoil roll through me firm and sweet and the horse galloped and its nostrils flared and hissed before me and I tried to move my feet and I tried and I moved and the horse flashed past spraying sweat and dust and I stumbled back and the saddle was empty and I planted my rear stumbling foot and I strained to stay upright and I caught myself and squared my feet underneath me and I was standing and the horse was gone and I was facing Slim from twenty yards away and he was looking at me. He'd been watching me. And now, as one, we both turned our heads. And we saw the *colorado* on his back, absolutely still and his chest agape in crimson.

40

Slim gave me one sharp little nod and he lifted the extra rifle in his hand, also a Winchester, and he pushed it slightly in my direction. I lifted my pistol in response: The Browning and I had an understanding now. Slim kept the extra rifle and I knew we were about to head for the house, but Slim's eyes moved to my wounded arm and it was like the cue for the pain to enter stage left. A thin strip of flame. I looked. The bullet had ripped about four inches of the sleeve of my mohair suit coat and, of course, out of sight, ripped the layers of shirt and flesh beneath, and all around the rip the light gray of the coat had gone dark, was even tingeing red, and now, come to think of it, I could feel the warm wet imprint on my arm and even a single far-falling rivulet of my blood down my forearm to my wrist.

I holstered my pistol and removed my passport from my inner coat pocket. I put it in my pants pocket, took off my coat and tossed it away, and the sleeve of my white shirt was crimson and Slim was moving toward me and I turned to the *colorado* I'd killed and I stepped to him and bent to him and I unknotted the red bandana on his throat and pulled it free and I straightened and Slim was beside me now and he knew what I was intending. He took the bandana from me and he wrapped it tight around my wound. "Nice and neat," he said. "A graze." And he was cinching it and knotting it and it was done, and without another word we beat it across the yard and I looked for and counted the *colorados'* empty dismounts as we went—ten—and I glanced at Slim and he'd been counting too and we plunged through the front door.

The great, empty, looted receiving room had seven men, all dead, one of them right before us and we vaulted it, one more near the door—these two with red bandanas—and then four of Slim's boys scattered about, a cluster by the fireplace, another in the middle of the room where he'd stood to shoot. And across the broad tile floor was the doorway to the inner galleria with the courtyard beyond, and that was the area where the now-deafening ruckus was happening. Eight more *colorados* somewhere in there, though maybe not all still alive, and I didn't know how many of Slim's boys were left.

He and I headed for the windows flanking the doors, him left and me right. I was on my own now and I hit the wall at the far side of the window and pressed back against it and I went low, just my arms and shoulders and head ready to show themselves, and then I looked out the window, ready quickly to withdraw, and I had two *colorados* right before me in the galleria, shooting into the courtyard from behind posts.

They were close enough that I didn't have to hang out the window. I pulled back to the wall, stood up and squared around to the room, took two paces in, turned and sidestepped to frame these two *colorados* in the window. I extended my arms—the left hurting like a son of a bitch now, but workable still—and I steadied my hands and I started to draw a bead on the middle of the back of the guy on the right and Slim opened up with his Mauser from the other window on somebody else and my two guys were jerking around.

I squeezed off a round and the *colorado* I was shooting for spun and I wasn't sure I got him but his chest was before me now and I put one in the center to make sure and he flew back and the other one had located me and his rifle was swinging my way and he'd have me in his sights before I could have him in mine so I squeezed off another round as I threw myself to the right and his shot traveled through the space I was in.

I scrambled up and back to the wall beside the window. I didn't know if there was another round left in my pistol. I popped the magazine just in case and grabbed one from the pouch on my hip and punched it in, hoping while I was working at it that the other *colorado* wouldn't lean in at the window, gunning for me. But Slim continued to fire. He'd take care of my unfinished business.

Shooting the bad guys from behind suddenly registered in me: Besides the three that Slim and I took care of, three other *colorado* horsemen went around to the back of the house. If there were no targets out there and no one was trying to escape through the rear, the *colorados* would go inside to pick off our courtyard *Villistas* from behind.

I turned to Slim. He'd pulled out of the window and pushed up against the wall and was stripper-clip filling his Mauser's magazine. I lifted my pistol and set myself to cover him, just in case someone burst in.

"Slim!" I called while he finished loading. "The horsemen heading for the back."

He chambered a round and was ready and he'd heard me, he knew my concern: He waved his arm to me, a swooping angle out the front door and around the house.

I started to move. He held up his hand to stop me. He reached for the Winchester leaning against the wall next to him.

This was prudent. I holstered my Browning, took a step toward him, and he tossed the Winchester to me clean and slick, vertical all the way, and I caught it and he lifted his Mauser and pointed it out the window. I broke for the front door, giving a quick look over my shoulder to the door behind me as I came into its line of view. It was empty.

I pulled up at the front and checked outside and I was clear here too and I stepped through and beat it along the front of the *casa*. I stopped at the corner, checked again, and then sprinted the length of the house, pumping the lever on the Winchester, ready for my first shot. There still was steady gunfire inside and I arrived at the crucial back corner. I crouched low.

I had to make sure I drew a good bead on the first one I tried to take out.

I slowly opened my line of sight beyond the corner, and long before I could look down the house toward the door, I saw the stables a hundred yards off, and about halfway between, cantering this way on a chestnut, was one of the three *colorados*. I pulled back out of his view and I stood and backed away from the corner a couple of steps, a bit more than the length of my raised barrel, and I took two steps to my right, pulling the Winchester up to my shoulder, hoping it was sighted properly, and I went quickly to my set position and found him along my barrel and he still didn't notice me and I had him and I tracked with him and I squeezed the trigger and absorbed the kick and even from where I was I could hear him go "Ooff," which may have meant he was only winged, but he was falling backward anyway, he was off his horse and going down.

I'd have a few seconds of confusion from the other two if they were closer to the house. They probably heard the man's sound but they had to turn and find him and I was still not showing to them and they wouldn't have a fix on the direction of the shot and maybe it even got lost in the other gunfire going on from inside, and I strode forward past the corner into full view and spun left and crouched flat-footed as low as I could get and I set myself for a shot even before I took in the targets and the nearest *colorado* had just come down off his horse and the other was vanishing into the rear door of the *casa*—he was about to do some damage in there—but I wouldn't let him have any back-up in the meantime: the guy just off his horse was snapping his head toward me, having just looked in the direction of the man I shot and the spooked chestnut that was rushing his way, and he saw me now and my initial set was off and I was swinging my rifle toward him and he happened already to be holding his rifle pretty much directly at me, for all the rotten luck, and I squeezed off a shot a little bit quick and I winged him in the side, and his horse—a nice-looking pinto— reared and whinnied in pain, my bullet having grazed the *colorado* and entered his horse's side, and it bolted away and I centered the man before he could get back to me and I plugged him in the gut, which I didn't mean to do either. He went down and he wouldn't be killing me, but he wouldn't be dying really promptly either, and I regretted both horse and man, and I knew that taking time to regret was the biggest danger to my own life at the moment and I put all this away, put it all out of my head because this was a goddam war that I was in the middle of and I wanted to survive it and I was upright once more and I sprinted to the doorway and stopped. The empty room was around the corner of this doorway and the courtyard action was beyond, but the guy who went in may have known something was wrong behind him, though he couldn't have seen the fall of his fellow *colorado* who was supposed to be at his side by now—that one was moaning behind me, away from the door—but the guy inside maybe saw the pinto bolt. This was a corner I was not wanting to peek around. But it had to be done. I did it quick. And what I saw made me look again.

The man who went in was lying dead on his back in the center of the floor, halfway to the doorway to the inner galleria. Standing in that doorway was the mustachioed *Villista* I kicked in the balls yesterday. He was surprised to see me. I stepped full into the doorway and raised my Winchester into a vertical position. I gave the rifle a little lift and I said to him, "I took care of the other two."

The *Villista* was holding a Colt revolver in each hand and I was sure something in him wanted to use one of them on me. But I'd made it clear that I was on his side and had even been useful, and his eyes moved to my left arm, which reminded me that it was hurting like hell. He nodded minutely, but he crossed to me and I stepped aside, thinking he wanted to pass. He did, but he stopped first and looked at the wound again. Then he looked me grimly in the eyes. "I'm good with the needle and the thread," he said, and he cracked me a grin.

"No goddam way," I said, and his grin turned into a laugh, like we'd been spending the last hour getting chummy-drunk together. He stepped past me and looked out to the first *colorado* I hit, who was lying real still and was probably dead. And then the *Villista* and I both heard the other guy start a new round of moaning from his gut shot. We turned to him. Before I could say a word, the *Villista* stepped to the man on the ground, lifted his pistol, and shot him in the head.

41

It took much of the morning to prepare to decamp. We buried the dead. Eight of ours. Sixteen of theirs, four of whom were wounded and were still alive and were summarily dispatched where they lay. Slim made it clear that we were burying the *colorados* only because we might want to use this *hacienda* again and it was easier to deal with their bodies now. Our men went into individual graves, the *colorados* went into one, and six of their heads went up on the spikes of the front gate with their identifying red bandanas tied on them like they were peasant girls.

We tended to our own half dozen wounded. Two were in bad shape, but we dug out their slugs and cleaned and bound their wounds and filled them with whiskey and strapped them to their horses, and a couple of the religious among us said a prayer for them.

My new-buddy *Villista* did indeed get a shot at sewing up the arm of the guy who kicked him in the balls. Hernando Soto. He told me his name and I told him mine and he did not even smile as he doused me with the fire from a phial of iodine and then he focused on my wound with absolute concentration, protruding and gently biting his tongue through the whole process. He sewed me up with a meticulous delicacy that I could only describe as feminine.

And when he was done, I said, "*Gracias, mi amigo.*"

And he said, very softly, "*Viva Mexico.*"

"*Viva Mexico,*" I said.

And we rounded up the riderless horses and packed them with loot from the train and the canteens of the dead for the dry and sun-emblazoned ride before us, and we gathered in front of the *hacienda,* many of us still on foot, and we were ready to ride. But suddenly all the men of Pancho Villa's train-robbing gang gathered around me, including those already on their horses, who came down to stand with the others.

Slim stepped forward. In his hand he held a sombrero the gray-green color of maguey leaves, the base of the crown rimmed in darker green from sweat, the front of the brim pinned up. He unclasped the pin and threw it aside, straightened the brim. He held the hat out to me.

I hesitated for a moment, and he identified the hat. "The *colorado* you killed for me," he said.

I looked at all the faces arrayed before me, dark in the shadows of their sombreros. They had that placid inertness which was a fighting man's stare of respect.

I reached up and stripped the fedora from my head and tossed it aside. I took the sombrero from Slim and lifted it and put it on my head. It fit me as if I'd carefully chosen it at a hatter on Michigan Avenue. There was now a moment and then another in which these faces before me did not change but held their expression and in which no one spoke a word, and another moment, and then, as one, we all broke and mounted our horses and we headed north.

Had I killed a man before? For all the men I'd watched die in battle, for all the scrapes I'd gotten into so I could write stories about men dying in battle, until this morning I had never killed a man. But for a long while on the day when I'd done this thing for the first time, as I rode with the *Villistas,* wearing that man's hat, which fit my own head precisely, I could only think about the pinto I'd inadvertently shot in the side. I could only hear the pinto neighing in pain and galloping off as if it could outrun this burning in its side. Before we'd left the *hacienda* I'd mounted my horse and ridden around for a while in the land behind the *casa* to see if I could find the pinto to at least put him out of his pain. But I couldn't find him. And on the ride north I thought and thought and I couldn't stop thinking about where he was right now, how hard it surely was for even an animal to die alone. I worried about the horse and not the men I'd killed. Horses are innocent. We men kill each other in wars because men are guilty. We are all guilty.

And eventually Slim made a point of dropping back and riding by my side. Slim and I rode together through the high-plateau desert of *estado* Coahuila, and we didn't say a word to each other. We rode together because I saved his life and he saved mine.

42

On the second day, we passed through the *laguna* country, the bed of a vast, ancient lake, vanished eons ago into the air, and we turned east and began to climb the ascending peaks curling through Coahuila, a stray plume of the long tail of mountains that started as the Rockies and ended as the Sierra Madre, and as the sun verged low behind us we came over a rise and found, half a mile off, the small town of Hipolito. Stretching out from its center were a dozen trains with hundreds of cars, most of them strung farther than we could see back along the single eastward-bound track, and eight thousand cavalry troops and four thousand infantry were living in the boxcars or camped now for the coming night without shelter in the chaparral.

We'd been pushing hard since the *hacienda*, at first even more intensively because of the two men who needed serious medical attention. We buried them both along the way but we kept pushing, and now we paused, strung along the rise, and we rested for a long moment, leaning on our saddle horns, and there were no yelps of joy, no words at all, but we were glad to be at the end of our journey.

And I became acutely aware of how I was thinking. We buried our dead. *We* buried. *Our* dead. This was the end of *our* journey. The past forty-eight hours had lifted me from the life I was leading into quite a different life, a life that was familiar in many ways but one that I'd always viewed from the outside. I was inside the war now. I'd become part of it. Who was I as I sat here on this horse? Was I a *Villista* now? The *Villista* Hernando Soto, who barely more than two days ago was robbing me and then was about to draw his pistol and shoot me dead, shared his canteen with me an hour ago, wordlessly, riding up as I drained the last bit of mine and he offered me his and I drank and I nodded at him and he nodded at me. And the men who lately would have killed him—technically soldiers of the Federal Government of Mexico—would also have killed me, and these men he had lately killed, I had killed as well.

And now, without any one of our band of *Villistas* giving a command or seeming even to be the first one to take up his reins, we all moved forward together as one and descended into the mountain valley and we rode toward Pancho Villa's army. Our army. And only now was my other self reawakening. Christopher Marlowe Cobb. Kit Cobb. Byline, Christopher Cobb. He thought of Friedrich von Mensinger. *I* thought of Friedrich von Mensinger. I wondered if the German agent had arrived. I assumed he had. I felt confident I'd correctly figured out his plan of arrival, and he had time to execute it. But perhaps only barely. He went up the train line ahead of us and he no doubt quickly secured his horse and he rode hard to cover himself with trail dust and sweat. This man carried some serious promises that could well shape the decisions of the man that I, too, must now impress. Impress enough so that I could discover and confirm what was going on so that I could then vanish from the camp and find a telegraph and write a story so that my readers—and the country they were part of—knew what was happening. *That is who I am,* I reminded myself. *I am a reporter.*

And we were moving among the soldiers, a thousand small fires beginning, their horses nibbling whatever was near, some of the lucky men camped next to mesquite, where they could hang their serapes and dry their meat. Some were even luckier to have women, who were beginning to cook the tortillas and the jerked beef. And they all watched us, and many of the men nodded at us as we passed, and some of the men stood as we passed, and many were confused at first glance to see me, but I rode at the front beside Slim, and I had a serape thrown around me now and I wore a sombrero and my bandaged left arm was exposed and the upper remnant of the sleeve of my white shirt was red with my blood and I had a place at the head of our band, and all these things made the first confusion vanish quickly and I received special nods and one man took off his sombrero to me and another reached out and patted my boot as I passed.

And we neared the trains and we moved along them, some of our men splitting off now to take care of the riderless horses and the spoils from the train, to find a place among the other fighters preparing for the night, to find their way to their women. The flatcars and the roofs of many of the boxcars were full of the *soldaderas*—the name seeming entirely ironic in this camp, the women shouldering children and not arms, cooking on small fires, waiting to service the men. I could not keep from looking at the faces of the younger women, the women of the right size, to see if one of them was Luisa. None was.

We approached a box car painted with a white cross, one of forty such that Villa brought with him to the areas of engagement. They were enameled inside and outfitted for medical care and he had doctors and he had nurses, a thing this untutored man had decided for himself to make part of his army, with no other army in Mexico, including that of the *Federales,* having anything like it.

Slim broke off from me and rode back to the four wounded men who had survived our journey and he made sure they went in now for treatment, and he returned to me and he said, "They should look at your arm."

I said, "Hernando the tailor has done a good job."

I said it loud enough for Hernando, who was nearby, to hear me. He turned his head away and flipped his chin.

"They should see it," Slim said.

"Are you going to Villa now?"

"Yes."

"I'll do it after."

"All right," Slim said. "No use wasting the medicine if he's going to shoot you for a *gringo* at first sight." And he said this without a wink, without a flicker of anything on his face.

"That'll be my final little contribution to the cause," I said as gravely as I could.

Now the wink. But he did that going into battle as well. I was starting to grind in the chest a bit as we rode on forward along the tracks. Not from fear of Pancho Villa shooting me. That was the least suitable, certainly, of a range of things that he could do that would make it impossible for me to get the story I came here to get. But I was happy to find that it was the story which was my main concern.

By the time we neared the engine of the penultimate train, there were only three of us left. Hernando, it seemed, was Slim's lieutenant. I was glad to have him able to vouch for me now. We passed the engine. And before us, at the end of the lead train, was a classic red caboose, the paint faded and peeling, all but one of the windows of the crow's nest shot out. This was where Slim and Hernando pulled up and so, then, did I. We dismounted.

The windows of the main cabin were hung with chintz curtains, the flowers faded almost beyond recognition, and behind them the place was full of male laughter, the voices of many men. Slim and Hernando looked at each other and then Slim turned his face to the west, noting, I think, the time of the day. Then he said to me, "Wait a moment."

I did. Hernando appeared beside me and waited also as Slim went up the back steps and stood in the open doorway. He did not go in but almost instantly the laughter stopped. From the abrupt silence I heard a single voice, a faintly nasal voice at once commanding and barroom-friendly, speaking loud enough for me to clearly hear it but giving the impression of casual conversation. The voice told his *muchachos* to get the hell out now. And there was a scrambling sound full of the ringing of spurs and the clacking of boots on the wooden floor. Slim stepped out of the doorway and to the side and a dozen *muchachos* streamed out and they were not, as I imagined, a group of Slims and Hernandos, veterans, officers, but rather a group of young men, *muchachos* indeed, awkward in their flight, pretty clearly privates and corporals of Villa's army.

When the stampede was over, Slim motioned us to come up, and Hernando and I climbed the stairs and I took off my sombrero and I stepped through the door and into Pancho Villa's field office. On the left-hand wall was a rough-hewn wood desk, and beyond was a long, built-in bench seat with stuffed green leather cushions. On the right-hand wall was another, even longer bench, and at the far end, a potbellied stove. The walls were hung with magazine-page chorus girls. What were those chintz curtains doing there? Patterned with what I could make out now as trellised roses.

And in the center of the room, sitting near the desk in a wooden swivel chair, clad in a shiny-cheap, frayed brown suit and a buttoned-up gray cardigan, was Pancho Villa. He was facing us. He abruptly leaned back in his chair at the sight of me. His eyes were wide-set—but not separated widely, just wide, their inner edges normal in their nearness to the bridge of his nose but the outer edges extending even beyond his thick, matinee-villain mustache—and they were dark, his eyes—and they were, for all their width, rather narrow, as if in a perpetual squint, with an almost Oriental feel to them—and they were *very* dark—and they were restless even as they were commanding you, jittering ever so slightly and you got the feeling that if no one was in the room they'd be paranoid in their restlessness, checking the door and the windows constantly. A Smith & Wesson .32-caliber top-break revolver lay within Villa's easy reach on his desk. Farther back on the desk lay a British thrust-optimized cavalry sword with a honeysuckle hilt.

Instantly, Villa said, "Put that back on." His voice was soft-edged, almost diffident in tone. Which somehow made it all the more commanding.

I began to lift the hat and he said, "No clicking your heels either."

I settled the sombrero on my head once more and I was beginning to figure out what the last remark was all about.

"Who do you think I am?" he said. "President of Mexico?" He threw back his head and laughed.

And we all laughed. Just enough.

He thought I was Friedrich Mensinger. Of course he did. I was the man he expected to arrive with Slim and the boys. Which meant Mensinger had not yet arrived.

Villa stopped laughing. We all stopped.

His restless gaze fell on my bandaged arm and bloody sleeve.

"Did they drag you here?" Villa asked with a smile.

"*Jefe*," Slim said. "This isn't the German."

Villa looked at Slim and his dark eyes grew even darker.

Slim said, "The German did not expect us. He had some business to do at his destination. He will ride in."

At mention of the riding-in, I saw the slight nod and pinch of the mouth in Villa that said Mensinger knew his man. Villa liked that the German was riding in on his own. He looked back at my wound. Then searingly into my eyes.

"Who are you?" Villa said.

"I am Christopher Cobb," I said.

"A *gringo?*"

"Yes."

"A hostage then?" Villa said to Slim.

There was a beat of silence. I was standing between Slim and Hernando, but half a step behind, and in my periphery I could see the two exchange a quick glance. They did not want to anticipate Villa's attitude toward me, but any answer to this question would carry an implication. They both looked back to Villa and this had all been done in only a tick or two of a watch but I could see that Villa's eyes did not miss a thing and he had taken it all in and those eyes of his suddenly had the narrow alertness of a predatory animal deciding whether to pounce.

Slim said, "The hat he wears belonged to the *colorado* he killed."

Villa's eyes moved instantly to me. The flexing to pounce vanished. He looked back to Slim.

Slim said, "We were quartered at the Guerrero *hacienda*, after the train, and a band of *colorados* came in while we slept. They killed our guards quietly. We fought. Their company is dead. To a man. We lost ten."

Villa rose from his chair.

His mouth was set in rage. His eyes were filling with tears.

He looked at me.

"The *colorado* he killed would have killed me," Slim said.

Villa's eyes slid on past me to Hernando. I had a sudden sense— though I could've been wrong—that in spite of Slim being in charge of the company of train bandits, in spite of Slim having a second tour of duty with the *Villistas* and the Army of the North, Villa still was quite aware that it was Tallahassee Slim, not Chihuahua Slim. And the two Mexicans in the room looked at each other and, to my surprise, Hernando said, "He killed two more *colorados* who would have come through a door when I was facing still another one of them. He saved my life as well."

I did not look at Hernando. He did not look at me.

Villa turned his face to mine. "Are you a soldier?"

"I am a newspaper reporter."

Villa's eyes widened, and then he laughed. He laughed and he strode across the floor and he threw his arms around me and clasped me to him and hugged me, his right arm squeezing tight on my wound and sending a shock of pain running up my shoulder and down my arm. But I bit off any sound and put my arms around Pancho Villa in return and we pounded each other on the back and he reared away abruptly and then he lunged to kiss me on the cheek, and I thought of Slim's observation about this very thing, that it did not exempt me from later being shot dead by Pancho Villa.

He let me go and he took a step backward and he seemed to re-member something and he looked at my arm and at my blood, which had soaked through the bandage that he'd just pressed to his arm, and he looked at my blood on his own sleeve and he laughed again. And the laughter stopped and he looked at my sombrero. And his face seemed to collapse toward the center in thought for a moment, and then it opened again in a smile and a nod and I was having trouble keeping up with this man and the flow of his feelings. He was living very fast. But he was still looking at my sombrero.

And I said, "*Jefe*, may I take this off once again? I would like to give you the sombrero of your dead enemy."

He straightened sharply. His face went blank. I was afraid I'd made some sort of mysterious, terrible mistake. But his eyes filled with tears yet again. He was waiting.

I lifted my hands and removed the sombrero and I held it between us.

He took it and he turned it and he lifted it to his head, quite slowly—given the speed at which he was living, quite slowly—as an improvised ritual between us. And he put it on. "*Viva Mexico*," I said.

"*Viva Mexico*," he said.

43

Pancho Villa sat us down on the horsehair cushions and he went to the far end of the caboose and returned with four unlabeled bottles. We each took one and he sat in his swivel chair. "One plant," he said, "grows fifteen years to make one bottle." He did not say its name but it was *sotol* in our hands, nearly clear, perhaps with a little tinge of yellow. Neither did he draw, from his observation, any lessons about lives or wars or revolutions or governments. We simply lifted our bottles to each other and we drank and it went down smooth and dangerous and it tasted like a field of something green that had been burned to the ground but still tasted green and also tasted like smoke.

And Villa listened intently to the details of the train raid and the fight at the *hacienda*. He wore the sombrero I gave him. The German on the train, the man Villa expected me to be, wasn't mentioned again. And when Slim and Hernando finished speaking, Villa did not comment on any of this, but his eyes, which had grown still and grave, suddenly became animated again and he spoke of the afternoon cockfight and how he lost much money on his best bird, who, bespurred and seasoned though he was, showing the scars of a dozen other successful fights, suddenly spread his wings and managed to fly over the heads of the tight ring of spectators and make a break for freedom in the desert. Villa, though he was tempted to wring the bird's neck for betraying him, took compassion on him and let him go.

Just as I'd been told that Pancho Villa drew on no book knowledge whatsoever, no theory, that his military and political acumen was totally based on instinct, I sensed, in his conversation, that there was no metaphor in him either. All that he said simply was what it was. He moved from one moment of the body to another. One intense engagement to another. One fight, one death, one drink at a time.

He looked at me now and said, "Though you are a brave man who has done me good and who has made my enemies your enemies, I do not think this is why you are sitting here now. You have not enlisted to be a *Villista,* I do not think. And you were not kidnapped by Tallahassee Slim and Hernando Soto."

"I want to write a story," I said.

I waited.

He waited. Then he prompted. "About Pancho Villa?" he asked.

"About what is happening now in your country," I said.

He smiled. This was the right answer. Then the smile was gone. "About what is happening in your country, as well," he said.

"Yes. That's why I have traveled here at great risk from the *Federales* and why, along the way, I have come to fight at the side of these two good men."

"I have often taken a train car of newspapermen to my battles," he said.

I found myself about to say that the people of the United States knew him well for that, even about to say how they admired him. I sensed he could be flattered. I sensed he'd be happy for a sympathetic ear. But I also sensed he was attuned to bunk, and I was feeling also that I was full of that, that I was becoming a goddam bunco artist. Killing some enemies of Pancho Villa in such a way as to win his trust, making a sentimental show of giving him the *colorado's* sombrero: All this, too, felt like consummate bunk. It would have been better just to walk out in the middle of a field of fire in a pitched battle and put my Corona Model 3 on a tripod and write the feel of the bullets zinging past my ears. That would have been better than this. But this was what the world had come to. This was the role I was cast in. There was another kind of story in another kind of time that I needed to write. Nevertheless, I bit my tongue about all the admiration people would have if he talked to me. I just nodded at his invoking the train cars full of newsmen.

I lifted my bottle of *sotol* to him. He lifted his. Slim and Hernando lifted theirs. We drank.

"So," I said to Villa, "I'm just curious. Who is this German I'm supposed to be?"

"A formidable man," Villa said. "Like yourself."

"A formidable journalist?"

Villa laughed. "I forgive that in you, because of your skills as a fighter."

"He is a military man?"

"I am to learn more about him when he arrives. But I understand he is a fighter. It is on his face, I am told."

"He is a man who joins you to fight, like Tallahassee Slim," I said, as if I understood.

"No. He is a man officially representing his government," Villa said.

I had the feeling that a good reporter cultivates: You've pushed as far as you can for now.

I drank my *sotol,* making a show of being content with his answer. But my keeping silent did prompt Villa to say one more thing: "Germany is a good friend to the Mexican people."

As there was no metaphor in Villa, neither did I detect irony or indirection. I didn't feel as if he'd said this in order to say an unspoken thing. In this case: a friend, unlike the United States of America, who has invaded Mexico. But even if he was not trying to say this, even if he was simply speaking his feelings and thoughts of this very moment, that conclusion—not only was Germany his friend, but America was his enemy—was one he could readily come to in a future present moment.

Neither did I break my silence to say: I would not like to share a border with Germany.

I realized I knew nothing of actual military importance to Pancho Villa, so I could make an engaging offer now without worrying about consequences. I said, "I was in Vera Cruz to cover the events. I left only a few days ago. Is there anything you'd like to know about the situation there?"

There was a slight recoil of surprise in Villa. He smiled. He had bad teeth, small and separated and the color of old coffee on a porcelain cup. "I can ask a question of a man whose job it is to ask questions?"

"I've killed for you," I said, ready once more to dole out bunk. It would be useful for me to know what questions this man had on his mind. "The least I can do is answer some questions," I said.

Without a hesitation Villa asked, "Where will your army attack next?"

"Rats and garbage in the streets," I said.

That sense of his face collapsing toward the center happened again. His thoughtful mood. Or confused. I explained: "I'm saying they're going nowhere and are happy now simply to bring their ideas about sanitation to Vera Cruz. Our President is staying put and trying to look humane."

Villa's face relaxed. "What wars is he fighting inside the country?"

"The country?" I asked. I assumed he meant Mexico, but I thought I just answered that.

"America," Villa said. "Which are his rebel states?"

He was serious.

"None," I said, trying hard to keep any tone out of my voice that smacked of astonishment, as if he was somehow ignorant.

"None?" Villa asked in exactly the tone I just suppressed.

"We've not had rebel states for nearly fifty years."

Villa shook his head in wonder. "How do you pass the time?" he asked. And I was almost certain he was still serious.

I lifted the bottle of *sotol,* as if that was my answer. He lifted his and laughed. "You can do both," he said. "Drink and fight."

We drank.

"And your women," he said. "They are good?"

"Good," I said. And then, on impulse: "But not as good as yours at fighting."

Villa laughed again.

"There was a woman in Vera Cruz," I said.

"You cross them . . ." Villa said.

But the momentum of my impulse cut through his thought. "A true *soldadera*," I said.

". . . our women will scratch your eyes out," he said.

"A crack shot," I said.

"Like a fighting cock," he said.

"She turned into a sniper in the first week of the invasion," I said.

He heard me now, and his look changed to something complicated. As if I were a subordinate speaking out of turn. But I didn't get the feeling it was about my interrupting him.

I kept going, however, thinking the rest of it would intrigue him. I said, "She shot a stigmata into the palm of a priest, the nose off a collaborating city official, and she plugged a U.S. Marine in the butt while he was cruising for a whore."

And all this did seem to intrigue him. He wrinkled his brow and narrowed his eyes and he nodded, as if impressed.

"She's a hell of a shot," I said. "Then she vanished from Vera Cruz."

I let a couple of moments of silence pass, and I knew that Villa was engaged, as he did not leap in to speak.

"I thought she might have come to join you," I said.

"If she came to me she would find that Pancho Villa is a hell of a shot," he said and he grabbed his crotch.

He laughed and the other boys laughed and I managed a laugh as well, realizing that I'd flown over the heads of the spectators and out toward the desert. I was not doing what I was supposed to do. And I was jeopardizing the real story, the one I had to write. So I laughed.

When the laughter faded a bit, Villa said, "And then I would give her a woman's work to do. She would be happy."

I took a drink of the *sotol* just to keep quiet and let this all pass.

"Did you have this woman in Vera Cruz?" Villa asked. From his tone and look, the "having" clearly meant the sexual taking.

"No."

"Well, maybe she did come here. I have had some of the new women these past weeks. Do you know her name?"

"No," I said, without the slightest hesitation.

Villa drank, and he wouldn't get off the subject.

"If she wants to act like a man, she would be better off if she had gone to Zapata," he said. "He does not know the difference."

More laughter.

I was thinking of Luisa and of Villa taking her and then handing her off to the tortilla brigade on the top of a box car, and I knew I had to stop this conversation.

From the end of the caboose, in the open doorway, came a shuffling of feet.

We all turned our heads.

A finely mustachioed man with a sombrero but a vaguely military jacket, without pips or ribbons but clearly official, was standing in the doorway. "*Jefe*," he said. "The man you were expecting has arrived."

"My German?"

"He has the letter of passage."

Villa rose.

We all of us rose.

"Where is he?" Villa said.

"Just outside," the man said.

"Give me a few moments," Villa said.

"Yes, *Jefe*," he said, and I thought I even saw him repress a salute. This one had been trained under someone else. He did an about-face and went out the door.

Villa turned to us, raised his bottle. We each touched it with ours, Slim first and then Hernando and then me.

We drank and we broke from each other and we put our bottles on the table.

Villa took off the sombrero. He held it out to me with both hands. He said, "I thank you, *compañero*. But you were the one who earned this. And you will need it in the sun."

"Thank you," I said. I took the hat from him and I put it on.

Then Villa said, in the same tone he'd just used to give me back the sombrero, "You should look around for your *soldadera*. One of them I recently had may have claimed she could shoot straight, and she may be a *Veracruzana*. But I warn you she is a sour one."

I nodded at him and I made my mind go blank at what he'd just said and I moved away, Slim and Hernando following me.

Not that it was easy.

But what was most important, I reminded myself, was the man just outside.

I feared we were about to confront each other face-to-face. But I knew that Mensinger would be thinking about making his first impression on Villa. And with my sombrero and my bloody arm and my serape and the absolute unexpectedness of the context, if I could avoid his direct look, perhaps I would not be recognizable to him. I stepped through the door onto the back platform, my face lowered. He wasn't there. All the better.

I let myself look up briefly.

Mensinger was standing on the ground, several paces away, wearing his costume of sweat and dust and scar. He did look the part. He'd already removed his slouch hat. He was ready to click his heels. Villa would have little to bond with in this man. But Germany was a friend to Mexico, and America was Mexico's enemy. That was this man's message, and there would be much apparent proof of that. And Germany could help Pancho Villa fight and win and unite his country behind him. I was afraid that, for all his manly, comradely tears no German would understand, Villa would be persuaded by this.

I lowered my head, letting the dead *colorado*'s sombrero utterly disguise me before Friedrich von Mensinger, and I descended the steps, and Slim and Hernando and I mounted our horses and moved away down the line of trains.

44

We rode only one train back and pulled up at a postal car.

Slim said, "Our boys are quartered here." He said no more about that but he swung a leg off his horse. "Our boys" included me.

We all dismounted and a kid not much older than Diego suddenly appeared. He was wearing an overlarge sombrero and a single *bandolera* over one shoulder, mostly empty but with a few rounds of what looked like shotgun cartridges. He was not carrying the weapon itself. He took Slim's reins and Hernando's, and Slim nodded him toward my horse as well. We went up the end steps and into the postal car.

Inside, it smelled of mildew and old wood and of the complex body-and-equipment stink of fighting men in the field. At the far end were bag racks stuffed with gear and weapons. Stretching this way below the windows along one wall were sorting tables, which functioned like low-slung bunk beds—one man to sleep on the tabletop, one below. Along the other wall were a couple of little clusters of spindle-back chairs.

Slim and Hernando stepped ahead of me and started clearing bunks. Our losses from the *hacienda*. They were finishing up and Slim said, "We most of us sleep out in the open if the night's good. Old habits."

"Thanks," I said to him, putting my saddlebags on one of the cleared doubles. Even as I ostensibly settled in with our boys, I was starting to get restless as Christopher Cobb. I could see using one of the chairs with my sorting-table bunk to break out the Corona and start serious work on writing the back end of the story.

I'd had no way to act upon this till Slim got me quartered, but I realized the story needed me to take a specific, immediate action. Villa seemed to understand the press and he used us for his own ends. He also seemed impulsive in his speech and a little naïve about international politics. But in this case, whatever would happen between Mensinger and Pancho Villa was likely to stay strictly between them until it was too late. I had to get ahead of this story. And the only way I could see to do that was to look at Mensinger's papers.

And the image of him standing near Villa's car snapped clearly into focus in my head. His horse and saddlebags were elsewhere. He had nothing in his hands, nothing under his arm. Okay. He was not going to play all his cards straight off his horse with the night coming on. This was the time just to register his horsemanship with Villa and have a drink. He would keep the papers to himself overnight. He would make that presentation formally. Probably tomorrow. The papers weren't left on the horse. They were in his quarters. And this might be the only shot I had at them.

"I need to step out for a while," I said, my first impulse being to head up to Villa's car and wait for Mensinger to come out and then follow him. I needed to know where he was staying, but this plan would simply leave me waiting for him to go out again. Which he might not do.

Slim and Hernando shot each other a sly look. Slim said, "Next train back, the first boxcar behind the tender. Ask for Señora Toba-Rojas. She keeps track of the unattached women. She'll know about your girl if she came to us."

"Use my name with the señora," Hernando said, and he flipped his chin at Slim. "Not the *gringo*'s."

The two shared a laugh, about Slim's problems with Toba-Rojas, not about me supposedly looking for Luisa. I was content to let them think that was why I was going out. And I was glad to know how to look for Luisa, if it came to that.

I took my first step away from them and my hand fell to my side. I touched my holster. I paused. Do I want my pistol with me? Yes. And then another thought: Before I dashed off to find out something the hard way, I should see if there was an easier way. I turned back to the two men. They knew I was a reporter. They would assume I'd consider anyone fair game for my questions. And this guy was obviously interesting.

So I asked, "Do either of you know where the German will be quartered?"

Hernando and Slim looked at each other, thinking together in silence about this.

After a moment, Slim nodded, and then Hernando. As if the one made a suggestion and the other agreed, though neither of them said a word. These were two men who had fought beside each other for a long while.

"Well, not your journalist car," Slim said.

Hernando said, "No. The journalist car is full of whores now."

Slim shot me a glance. "Always has been," he said.

The two laughed loud, this time at me.

I made myself laugh too.

Slim said, "There's another caboose a couple of trains back."

"Right."

"They'd put him there."

"Any important visitors go there when we're on the move," Hernando said.

I had to lead up to a suspicious question now, but I didn't know any other way.

I asked, "Does everybody in camp realize the important visitors stay there?"

Slim and Hernando were still giving my questions thoughtful consideration. They looked at each other and nodded. "Pretty much," Slim said.

"Do the big boys get a guard?"

"Sometimes," Slim said. "If they bring one."

"And when they go out? What about theft?"

Slim shrugged. "If there ain't exactly honor among all the thieves here—and there is actually some of that, believe it or not—there is at least fear. Everyone knows not to mess with whoever's in there. The man who does has nowhere to run and he'd end up shot if he tried to."

"The guy who brought him to Villa. Would he be able to ease the German's mind on that?" I asked this of Slim, in English.

Slim gave me a quick now-I-know-what-you're-up-to look, but he said, also in English, "Major Ostos. Yeah. He'd put your man's mind at ease."

"Thanks," I said and I took a step toward the door.

"Hey," Slim said. I stopped and turned. "Chicago Slim," he said. Meaning me.

I was surprised at how this filled me up like a racing tire on a Stutz. But all I could do was nod very slightly. Which was enough for Tallahassee Slim, I knew.

He said, in Spanish again, "When you're done mashing, if you want to do some drinking, we're fifty yards due south." And he pointed very deliberately out the window of the car to show me where he meant.

I nodded again and turned and I went out the door and down the steps. I thought: Mensinger wants to keep it personal with Villa tonight. Ostos assured him of the safety of his quarters. Mensinger took the papers inside and put them somewhere out of sight. They are waiting for me. For a little while, at least.

And though I was focusing on the story now, as I headed in the direction of Mensinger's car, my thoughts of the saddlebags carried me to an image of Mensinger taking them from his horse and hiding them away, but my mind ebbed back to the horse being led off and then on to the boy who took our own horses. I thought of his *bandolera*, and then I thought of Diego, and I thought of all the children I'd seen out of the corner of my eye in the past hour or two. It was not just the women of Mexico who went off to live inside the war as it was being fought; it was the children. And my mind flowed back again to Diego.

And to Bunky. I reassured myself that when I finished this story and got to the nearest safe telegraph office—and given the story's contents, that would mean a telegraph office across the border—and as soon as Clyde cleared the story and was ready to run it, I would head back to Vera Cruz.

I was passing the first boxcar after the tender on the next train. The door was open. And I thought of Luisa too. But I didn't know how long Mensinger would linger with Villa tonight. Every moment was crucial. I put aside all the peripheral people in my life. I walked faster, as fast as I could without drawing attention to myself.

45

I removed my sombrero and sloughed off my serape and held them low beside me on the side nearest the train as I approached Mensinger's caboose. Anyone observing me was more likely to wonder at one of their own entering the car reserved for special guests than at a seeming *gringo*. Still, I drifted a little beyond the car and hesitated and looked around, and for all the potential observers arrayed widely before me, camped in the open and lounging by their campfires, and for all the irregular flow of people along the track, no one seemed to be paying any attention to me whatsoever.

I went up the back steps of the caboose and entered. I put my serape and sombrero on. There was still a bit of post-sunset lightness in the sky and I could see well enough inside to find a kerosene lamp on the desk and a box of matches beside it. I removed the chimney. The wick was new and trimmed and I struck a match and replaced the chimney. I turned the wick knob so the lamp would burn as low as possible but still provide reading light.

I looked around. The car was similar to Villa's, though the benches on both sides were made up like bunks. Except for the lamp, the desktop was empty. The bunks had only bedding. The chair before the desk, the chair farther along, next to the potbellied stove, were empty. No saddlebags. I moved farther into the car, passing the stove, and I saw something out of the corner of my eye, a shape in the deep shadows behind the stove. I stopped. I bent near.

Mensinger's saddlebags.

I took note of exactly how they were folded there.

I pulled them out and carried them to the desk.

I laid them flat and opened one side and began to put my hand in to feel around. But I hesitated. Mensinger could have set a little trap. I ran one hand inside, palm upward, very slowly, keeping the hand absolutely flat and with the back of it pressed against the inner wall of the bag, my hand and forearm sliding into the bag till my fingertips touched the bottom, feeling cloth on my palm the whole way. I imagined a stacking of folded clothes. I spread my hand and hooked my fingers upward at the bottom edge of as much of everything above it that I could, and I carefully began to draw out the contents in a single, preserved stack.

I felt a few small items slough away and remain inside. It couldn't be helped. I had to deal with them later. The stack was free and I set it down on the desktop. This packing job was the work of a meticulous man, a careful and suspicious man. That was my fear. That it would be impossible to prevent such a man from knowing someone had gone through his things. Perhaps it wouldn't matter. If I found out what I needed and did it before he returned, perhaps it would be all right. He didn't know me and I'd stay out of his way and I'd do what I needed to do here and slip away. But I at least had to try to conceal what I was doing. If I concentrated, perhaps I could replace these things so he'd never know. Unless he was meticulous to the point of obsession.

I realized sweat was dripping from my forehead, and my heart was pounding in my throat. I'd ignored my body's awareness of the time slipping onward and of the possibility he could walk through the door at any moment. I would have to ignore it again.

I began to lay his things aside so that I could relayer them when I put them back, as if they'd not been touched. His shirts. His woolen socks. His underdrawers, which were made of silk. Which I handled as if they were rotten fruit. His handkerchiefs. Another pair of riding breeches. And in the center of all this, a six-inch, no doubt keenly sharpened knife, pointed in the direction of the top opening of the bag. The little surprise for the prowler, as I suspected. And on and on. The usual stuff. A small rubber bag with medicines: quinine, calomel, Sun Cholera Mixture in tablets. His toothbrush. A union suit. And I went back into the bag and withdrew the sloughed-off items.

Three bars of soap. In delicate wrappers. Smelling strongly of lilac. Were these soaps his choice? Was this a side of Friedrich von Mensinger that he'd better keep hidden from Villa? Or were they specially given him by Anna, his Anna who loved him in spite of his striking her in public, twice at the Stadtgarten for her sympathetic tears, which meant he struck her often, in public and in private. She gave him these soaps and he still had them. If he scorned them when she gave them, he would have no doubt told her so and struck her again or at least thrown the soaps at her feet. If he scorned them but while he was in a placid mood, which even a man who beat a wife could find himself in now and then, if he scorned them but took the soaps, he would have disposed of them long before this. But he took them and he kept them and he waited, perhaps, for a chance to use them. Would he feel close to his wife when he did? Men who beat their wives could embody this paradox also. To wish to hurt them and yet, at times, to feel sentimentally nostalgic over them. I'd seen men do this to women. To my mother. She'd spoken of this paradox. She spoke of it and found nothing in Marlowe or Shakespeare or Sophocles or anyone else to quote so that she could express this paradox, and she thus spoke of it to me strictly in her own words, with no quotations to help distance her from whatever complex feelings she was having and I clenched at Friedrich von Mensinger's briarwood pipe, which I now found in my hand and which I would snap in two if I didn't control myself and stay focused on what I was here for. So I controlled myself. And I focused. And I was keenly conscious that time was slipping away and I was not finding any papers.

There was another side to the bag.

But first I carefully restacked the items I'd already withdrawn, leaving everything restored on the desktop, ready to be inserted later. All but the soaps. I didn't know how they'd been arranged on top. But he couldn't possibly read anything from them. They would have shifted from the jostling of the ride. If there were clues for Mensinger, they were in the arrangements of these other items. I'd done the best I could.

And now the other side of the bag. I opened it. I withdrew the items as a single unit. I once again peeled back and set aside layer after layer of Friedrich Mensinger's quotidian life. His carefully folded white linen suit. His shoes wrapped in a towel. His clothes brush. And more. And more. And there was no *Papiere*. There were no documents. No papers.

I restacked this final collection of Mensinger's meaningless stuff.

Everything from the saddlebags sat upon the desk in two piles. I took a deep breath. And I heard a thump. A sound from outside. I straightened. I stopped breathing. I could simply bolt in the other direction, to the joined end of the car. There was another door, another platform, a way out. Unless it was locked. But now I heard laughter beneath the windows. Passing. Two male voices now. Speaking Spanish. Two drunken *Villistas*.

He could have taken the papers out. He could have hidden them separately. I turned around. I looked to the bunks. To the bedding. To the stove. Perhaps inside the burner of the stove. I was about to move to these places but I thought of Mensinger's saddlebags once more. One more possibility.

I picked up the bags, one compartment in each hand.

One side was heavier than the other. The first side I searched.

I laid the bags down. I opened the heavier side and looked at the top stitching. Nothing unusual. I ran my hand to the bottom. I pressed my fingertips as far in as possible and then bent them downward. The inner wall was one large flap. I ran my hand along the bottom of it and at the far left I found a heavy button. I undid it. I moved my hand

along the bottom edge to the far right and I found another button. I
undid it. I pulled the flap out of the bag. I reached back inside and I
found an inner compartment, shallow but sufficient to hold the thing
I drew out. A thin, leather document portfolio.

I had him. I cleared the space beneath the lamp. But time was the
thing. I had to keep that in mind, but I had to slow down now. I slipped
the leather flap of the portfolio out of its loop and I opened the cover.

I ran the fingertips of both my hands in the leather margins surrounding this little pile of documents. There were several things here.
Heavy paper. I lifted them out. I had to be obsessively meticulous now
myself. If I'd inadvertently, inevitably left him some little clue in his
personal items that someone had been here, I could at least make him
think the intruder did not find the papers. But I was suddenly keenly
aware once more of the beating of my heart, each beat marking time,
like the ticking of a clock in a world sped up. These seconds were
rushing now, these minutes. I thought: I should just take the papers.
Take them and get on my horse and ride away. I could not only write
a story but produce the documents themselves, could give them to
the U.S. government.

And now I felt the sudden demand to define myself. Or to rede-
fine myself. I was a reporter. I'd already stretched the boundaries for
a reporter. But not by the standards of most of my colleagues in the
business. The Hearst men. The Pulitzer men. They would do anything
for a story. I'd already done more than I'd expected. Here I stood in
this man's quarters, rifling through his private things. Intervening was
another matter. Richard Harding Davis would intervene. They all did
in Cuba. They all worked up a dandy little war of their own, all at Mr.
Hearst's bidding. And taking the papers wouldn't change Mensinger's
intentions. It would come out that the American stole these things
and perhaps simply give weight to his arguments. And the story itself,
without my actually stealing the documents, would be just as good. A
story about what Germany was trying to do. What Mexico might do.
Bring it into the public light in a newspaper.

I kept the documents in my hand but I centered them in the bright, immediate arc of the kerosene lamp. Voices. I straightened up again. Spanish. Mensinger spoke Spanish. But I knew his voice now. Pinched. Sucked through his nose. The superior man speaking the inferior language. These voices passed. They were not him. I bent to the documents. I needed to read them quickly, get their gist, a flavor of their phrasing. Needed to apply my best quote-gathering frame of mind.

The first was a letter in German. The Imperial Eagle sat spreading his wings at the top. At the bottom was a signature. Clearly Wilhelm's, with wide slurs of ink at the peaks of the "W" and the "l's" and the "h," the man pushing heavily, grossly at a flexible nib. My German wasn't good enough to waste time trying to read it. I moved this document to the bottom of the stack. And I found a letter in Spanish on the same paper, with the same eagle. I pulled the bottom letter up again and I matched a few words, and the two documents were the same. This was a translation for Villa. Full of warm, fellow-warrior backslapping. And a promise of general financial support and the immediate gifts of arms if they were used to advance their "appropriate, immediate common goals," as would be explained in person by the Kaiser's special emissary, Friedrich von Mensinger. A further promise was made of unwavering support in whatever form was necessary in the event of "longer-term engagements with common enemies."

All of this was consistent with the suspicions I'd already formed. The Germans wanted Villa to take on the Americans. And they would be very happy, I was sure, if it became a longer-term engagement.

Both letters went to the bottom of the stack. And now I was looking at another eagle. The American eagle. The appropriate common goal. I was holding heavier paper, curled at the edges, a photograph that was not quite the size of a letter. The image was somewhat blurred, rather dim, as if the original item was photographed covertly in low light and was enlarged beyond its negative's natural capacity. And what I was looking at was a typewritten memo on the apparent letterhead of the President of the United States. It read:

19 February 1914

To Secretary of State Bryan,

I think our conversation clarified our thoughts. Under no circumstances can the United States of America allow the bandit Pancho Villa to gain control of Mexico. He is an illiterate man who can not think rationally. Venustiano Carranza is a man of breeding, education, rational good sense. Our total support of him would allow to control the Mexican government for our business and political interests. We shall speak soon about ways for implementing this.

And it was signed "Wilson" in a clearly legible, pretty straightforward hand, sharp-edged and forward-slanting, with the "n" extended outward and then slashed downward and slightly to the rear, a flourish, but a stiff one. It struck me—though without an authentic one to compare it to—as reminiscent of the President's actual signature, which I'd seen a few times. But it had always struck me that his signature was simple enough and legible enough that someone with any such skill at all could easily create a forgery of it.

And certainly the memo was a forgery. I doubted the form of the dateline. It was the Europeans who put the day before the month. The phrasing sounded off. From its stiffness to the odd "allow to control." The word "us" might have simply been omitted by accident in that phrase, but I thought I'd heard Germans make this mistake in English. There must be a phrase in German they were trying to reproduce.

Not that Wilson and Bryan were incapable of coming to the conclusion expressed here. It might even be likely. I just didn't believe the proof was authentic.

But Villa would have no way to doubt this memo. The next sheet under the photograph was the Spanish translation, which was all he'd care about. And even that, he wouldn't be able to read very effectively. The irony was that this element of the Mensinger mission was based on the very assessment of Villa they were ascribing to Wilson. The forged memo exploited the man's near illiteracy and emotionalism.

And maps were next. The first was large and folded. I laid the papers on the desktop and unfolded it. A Rand McNally map of Texas, only two years old, specially featuring the railroads and military forts of the state.

I refolded the map.

I was aware again of the shortness of my breath.

I opened the next map. It was a U.S. Department of the Interior topographical map of San Antonio and its surrounding area, detailing the streets and the railroads and highlighting the military posts in red.

I'd been making a major incorrect assumption all along.

And there was one more map. An original. Hand-drawn. But professionally so. By some German-American. No. Gerhard Vogel, the real one, was a German-American, and he gave his life for his country. This was a German *in* America. Seeming to be an aspiring artist. Visiting this tourist site. Making sketches. Chatting with the guards. A charming man. A talented man. And he'd made a detailed map showing entrances, guard stations, communication lines, the parts of the walls that were in disrepair, the places of weakness. He'd drawn a map of the Alamo.

The immediate goal.

Ignore the Americans in Vera Cruz. Raid America itself. Destroy the Alamo and cause whatever damage you could along the way. And even maybe try to hold on to southwest Texas. Hold on till the rest of Mexico stopped fighting itself and united behind Villa and, as one, undertook a glorious campaign to avenge their loss in 1848. Between all the rebel factions and the *Federales,* the Mexicans had significantly more men in arms than the whole of the U.S. Army. And they were battle-seasoned. And they could even dream of getting it all back, all the way to California.

And even if Villa and his country would be crazy to do it, even if they were doomed to fail, with the Kaiser working up his own conflict in Europe, German interests would be well-served if they could arrange a major, protracted war between America and Mexico. And the war would cut off Mexican oil, which the U.S. and Britain both greatly relied on, with Mexico's prime ally, Germany, reaping the supply

What a hell of a front-page story.

And my hands were already working quickly. Quickly but carefully. I was bent very near to the portfolio to put these things back in, just as they were when I found them. They were inside now. Right order. Squared up. The portfolio was closed. I pulled the inner flap out of the saddlebag. I laid the portfolio in its space. I pushed the flap back in. I reached deep inside the saddlebag and found the first of the two buttons on the flap down there.

Too much of a hell of a story. I was racing too fast inside. My hands weren't working like they should. The goddam button wouldn't go. Wouldn't go. Were my hands trembling? Hell no. Maybe.

Voices. I clenched in the chest. I unbent a little, though my hand stayed where it was, still struggling with the button. The voices passed. He wouldn't come with a heralding of voices. He would be alone. He would appear suddenly at the door. He could appear at any moment.

I didn't like this. It felt like goddam stage fright. Which I had once, as a very young man going on the stage for the first time. To carry a spear. To open a carriage door. Something. I felt like that. I'd rather face machine gun fire than this.

I put both hands inside the portfolio. One to hold the button hole open. They fumbled in there, my hands. I couldn't even find the buttonhole now. This was not who I was. This was not. I took my hands out of the portfolio. I pressed them against the tabletop, braced myself there. I worked to control my breath.

And a sound from the door.

And I found my body upright, my head turned toward the back end of the car, my right arm extended, my Browning pistol pointed at the door. All this happened just now by reflex, I realized. And I held my breath. Held it. My breath was not clenched. I was holding it. And my hand was steady. The barrel of the pistol was utterly motionless. I could squeeze the trigger as softly as I needed so as to put a bullet in the center of his forehead. I was who I was again.

But the door was not opening.

The sound once more: a scuttling along the floor, and then silence. A rat. A different rat from the one I was expecting.

I lowered my arm.

I put my pistol in its holster.

I bent once again to the portfolio and thrust my right hand deep inside and I buttoned first the one side of the inner flap and then the other.

I picked up the stack of objects from that side of the bag. I slipped them in as I'd found them. The shirts and the socks and the riding breeches and the silk drawers and the knife in their midst. The soaps. And then the other side. The linen suit. The shoes. The clothes brush. All the rest. All of it went in as it had come out and I secured the outer flaps of the saddlebags.

I turned down the wick on the lamp, angled a hand over the top of the chimney, and I blew out the light. I picked up the saddlebags.

I turned toward the front of the caboose and walked into the darkness there. The glow of a hundred campfires outside showed me the shape of the stove, and I returned the saddlebags to the space behind exactly as I'd found them. I stepped farther on to the door that adjoined the next car, a boxcar. The door was, as I suspected, locked. I was quite calm. I turned and I walked to the rear door and I opened it.

The back platform was empty. I stepped out, closed the door. Mensinger likely would approach from the same side of the train I'd earlier walked along, the side where he'd dismounted from his horse. I could go down the steps to the other side of the train. But I knew where I wanted to go next. And I was not afraid of Mensinger. I wouldn't be in Villa's camp for long. I had what I needed for the story.

But I did take off my sombrero so I could peek around the corner of the car. There would still be some inconvenience in running into him in the next few moments.

I looked. It was dark but I could see from the desert glow of campfires that he was not in the immediate vicinity. I went down the steps, put my sombrero on, and strode off toward the forward trains.

254 ROBERT OLEN BUTLER

I walked perhaps a dozen boxcars along and I saw him approaching on foot. He was still fifty yards away and he was looking at me, I thought, but I simply let my head fall slightly forward. The brim of the sombrero made him vanish, made my face disappear from his sight. It was dark. I could not see any details of his face. So he could not clearly identify mine, especially when he knew my face only as a Canadian coffee salesman and the rest of what he saw was so wildly out of context with that.

I made myself stumble a bit, stagger a bit, and I cursed in Spanish, pitching my voice high, putting on just enough of a tinge of the melodrama-Mexican to still stay real but to make my voice unrecognizable as the voice from the station in Mexico City. I sang a little: "*Ay, ay, ay, ay, Canta y no llores . . .*" Enough for him to hear, and I broke off, as if I could not remember the words. And I saw his high-booted legs, his puttees, and though he slowed—he did slow down—nevertheless he was passing. And I saw the British cavalry sword that had been on Villa's desk. It was hanging now at Mensinger's side. A gift for the German government representative. And Mensinger passed, and I kept going, staggering ever so slightly once more. "*Ay, ay, ay, ay,*" I sang.

46

I reached the postal car and I stopped. I walked this far expecting to walk on past. To find Señora Toba-Rojas. To find Luisa. But things had changed. I had my story. I could saddle up right now. I had a map. I had a compass. It would take me five minutes to figure out what the smart destination would be. An American border town, certainly. Just which one? Somehow I got the inkling it'd be good to get on the road as soon as possible. But I had some long riding ahead of me and some serious times just behind. I was weary. I wanted to spend a night on bedding, even in a postal car like a bag of mail. And there was Luisa. This would likely be my last chance to speak to her. If she was here at all. And after what Villa said, part of me hoped she wasn't here and never was. I walked on.

The wide, center door of the boxcar was open. Against the left-hand jamb sat two heavyset women, side by side, quietly watching the night, gently swinging their legs. They turned their faces to me.

"Are either of you Señora Toba-Rojas?" I asked.

They said no.

"Is she here?" I asked.

One of them angled her head toward the darkness inside the car.

The two resumed their quiet watching.

I stepped to the empty part of the open doorway. Dimly I was aware of faces inside. And in a far corner, a low-burning lamp with shapes beside it. And I was filled with the smell of straw and of borax and a mix of flowery cheap perfumes and, underneath it all, the smell of bodies, but with that special musky undercurrent of women's bodies. Even without the added scent of greasepaint and cold cream, the women's bodies carried me out of the dark of a Mexican night and into the doorways of countless actresses' dressing rooms in the countless theaters of my boyhood and young adulthood and young manhood.

But I returned from there quickly and I was standing before the boxcar door and I called out, "Señora Toba-Rojas."

Nothing.

As softly as I could and yet be heard, I said, "May I speak with you, Señora Toba-Rojas? I am just arrived with Hernando Soto and we have been with our *jefe* and he said I might inquire with you after a woman."

And I drew back. In absolute silence she appeared massively before me, emerging from the dark but with no sound at all that I'd heard, no scuffling, no rustling.

"Señora," I said. "Thank you."

Now I could hear that she was real, as she scraped and sighed a bit in bringing her heavy body down to sit at the edge of the doorway, letting her legs dangle like the other two women. She smoothed her skirts. She looked at my face, though my back was to the fires and I was sure my sombrero cast an even deeper shadow.

I lifted my hand and removed my sombrero.

She straightened a bit, unaware until now, I thought, that I was not Mexican.

I said, "I'm looking for a woman who has arrived within the last week or so. She was known in Vera Cruz as Luisa Morales."

The señora did not answer. Perhaps she was considering if there was such a woman.

"She is a wonderful shot with a rifle," I said.

The señora said, "*Jefe* sent you to me?"

"Do I look like I could find you on my own?"

She smiled at this.

She said, "You spoke Hernando Soto's name."

"I have ridden with him," I said. I lifted my left shoulder a bit to draw her eyes to my bandaged arm.

She nodded.

Between the postal car and this place where I was standing, I'd removed a gold quarter-eagle coin from my money belt. It was in my pocket. It might be time.

She said, "Would you want this girl as Hernando Soto would?"

"I only ask to speak with her," I said.

She considered this, looking at me carefully.

I said, "If I were to offer you some token for your trouble, you must understand it is not an attempt to buy Luisa Morales. It is simply a gift to you. I will treat her with respect."

At this, the señora slowly lowered her face, keeping her eyes fixed on mine as she did, stopping only when she would have had to let go of our gaze. Perhaps there was, in this gesture, a sense of disbelief. But it felt like more than that. It felt as if she was also saying: It is too late for respect. She has lost that in a terrible way already. No woman here has this thing.

I withdrew the gold coin from my pocket and I brought my hand discreetly near hers, which lay on her leg just above the knee.

"Señora," I said.

She lifted her face. She looked toward our hands. She turned hers and I placed the gold piece in her palm. Her eyes widened a little when she recognized it.

"I ask only to speak," I said.

She closed her hand on the coin, put it in a pocket in her skirt, pulled her *rebozo* over her head, and offered me her other hand.

I took it and helped her down from the boxcar door.

She led me forward. We passed Villa's caboose, quiet but lit brightly. We passed a flatcar with *Villistas* lounging and smoking, though fundamentally alert, manning three tripod-mounted Maxim guns. We passed a boxcar of soldiers, also apparently on-duty, the half dozen standing and sitting in the doorway bandoliered and holding rifles. I nodded as I passed. They nodded. And at the next boxcar, the señora stopped. The door was only partway open. I could see the car forward had soldiers as well. Given its placement, if this was the car where they were keeping Luisa, I had a sudden worry that I knew I better put into a question. It might even explain the look Señora Toba-Rojas gave me when I spoke of respect.

She was about to reach up to the door, but I touched her shoulder and she turned to me. "Señora," I said. "Is this the car . . ." I hesitated, trying to say this without saying it. I thought of a phrase and began to speak it.

"No, señor," she said.

Even as I said, ". . . of the public women."

"No," she said again, emphatically. "They are the newly arrived women who do not have a man. They are not for sale."

I nodded. They were only three cars away from Villa's quarters.

"But available," I said, low, as if it was an understood secret between the señora and me.

We looked each other steadily in the eyes for a moment.

"Only in a very limited way," she said, just as low.

They were Villa's alone for now.

We looked at each other for a moment more. Then Señora Toba-Rojas bent near to me. She said very softly, "Do you love her, señor?"

I hadn't a clue as to how to answer this question, even simply to say no.

She seemed to think she understood my silence. She touched my arm and turned to the door. She fisted two echoing knocks there.

"No," I finally answered, though the señora acted as if she did not hear.

She called inside. "Luisa Morales."

We waited.

I thought: *I should walk away. I should ride away.* She'd been disarmed and sexually taken—probably raped—by Pancho Villa. It would be all I could do to walk past his little red caboose and not go in and try to kill him.

"Luisa," the señora called again.

"It's all right," I said.

And then she was standing in the door of the boxcar.

All the private fires burning in the desert behind me lit Luisa only dimly. But what I saw of her face I'd seen in women's faces in Macedonia and in Nicaragua. And seen in other women's faces, away from wars. And it was not necessarily specific to rape, I was sure. I'd seen some form of this in my own mother's face late on certain nights, just a few times, but it was a similar thing, and she'd offered no words to explain. Something happened to women, I knew, and in some ways I didn't know anything else but that. Except it was clearer for me with Luisa Morales. What she had lately been through.

She did not seem to recognize me. Or did not care.

I took off my hat.

I was aware of Señora Toba-Rojas passing behind me. Discreetly leaving us.

Luisa's face did not change. I assumed she recognized me. Of course she recognized me. I wished now she'd yell at me. Call me a *gringo* bastard invading her country. Pull a pistol from beneath her *rebozo* and start shooting. Do something. But her face did not change. And after a moment she vanished back into the darkness, a move so quick and smooth that she seemed to have dissolved into the air. The grace of her vanishing encouraged me. It felt like *her*.

I should have let that be. I should have turned and gone and let myself keep this final sense of her still being who she was in Vera Cruz. But I would have been lying to myself.

I stepped to the door. I spoke into the darkness. "Luisa."

I didn't know what else to say.

"*Viva Mexico,*" I said.

I waited.

After a long moment she was suddenly standing above me. I looked up. Her face remained a mask. A woman of the chorus of some Greek tragedy.

And now she was beginning to kneel.

I took a step back from the car, gave her some space.

She folded herself down at the knees, sat on her lower legs, so I only had to lift my face a little to look into her eyes. And I was close enough that I could see the campfires reflected there.

And she lifted her right hand and she slapped me across the left cheek.

Hard.

My head flipped to the right. My cheek burned.

Somehow I understood.

I straightened my face to her once more.

She lifted her left hand and slapped me across the right cheek. Just as hard.

I kept my head where she'd put it, almost against my shoulder, my eyes forced back to look the way I'd come. I kept my head there for a clear and thoughtful moment so that when I presented it to her again, it would not seem an act of defiance. It would be an offering.

I gave her my face once more.

She looked for a long while at me.

The fires of the desert wavered now in her gathering tears.

She lifted her right hand. As if to strike. But it paused there between us.

Very softly I said, "Once more, Luisa Morales."

And she slapped me. Not quite as hard, but hard enough. I braced myself and I did not let my head turn.

Both my cheeks were aflame.

Luisa and I looked at each other.

The light of the desert was tracking thinly down her cheeks.

"As many times as you need," I said.

She bowed her face and put both her hands there and she wept. Quietly. But wept.

I waited.

She wept. I would have expected, when these tears began to prevail, that she would have retreated back into the darkness. But she did not. She let me watch. And this made me inordinately happy.

I wanted to take her in my arms.

But sometimes I was not stupid with women. I waited and I let her continue to weep, even as I was ready to let her continue to strike me.

Finally, though she made no sound through all this and though she did not withdraw her hands, I sensed that she had stopped. And now she put her hands on her legs, though she kept her face bowed.

I should have waited some more, but I felt I needed to say something. I didn't know what. Something. And I said, "Thank you for not killing me in the street in Vera Cruz."

She did not seem to hear at first.

But then, without lifting her face, she said, "I would not have killed you."

I said, "Thank you for not shooting off the part of me you probably wished to."

I could see enough of her face to perceive a kind of stopping in it, and she even shook her head minutely, just to one side and back, just once, but then abruptly her hands returned and so did the tears. She wept again, and I could hear it now.

I blundered on. As impulsive as these words were, I did at least quickly look around to make sure no one could hear. "Kill him then," I said. "I'll help you."

This brought her hands down and her face up. Her torso straightened and we were silent for a time: She looked at me and saw me, and she looked beyond me and saw nothing, and then she looked at me and did not see me. And now her legs were moving and she was standing up and she vanished into the dark.

Okay.

I once more thought to go. And I would have. I even turned and took a step away from the boxcar. But I stopped. I stood very still, facing down the track, immobilized now by the ways I'd said the wrong things to her yet again. I understood them all as abruptly as a slap across the face.

And behind me I heard sounds: a rustle and then a foot-thump. She had jumped to the ground from the boxcar.

I turned.

Luisa was before me. Barely an arm's length away. She unsheathed a small hunting knife with a four-inch blade.

Something in me went: To hell with it. Let her at least make the gesture to kill me.

And Luisa lifted the knife straight up, the blade vertical, and there was a very brief moment, at the apogee of the lifting, where I expected it now to come at me, a straight thrust forward toward my chest, and I was very conscious of the blade tip, so I recognized at once—at its tiniest first impulse—that it was not meant for me. She moved the blade not slowly, not slowly, but quickly and the blade fell to the horizontal and went flat and pointed inward and I knew it was her throat she wanted to cut and already my left hand was in motion—my baseball-glove hand, which was a good reflex, I was racing her knife hand from behind—and the knife started its plunge to her throat and she was quick but I was quick too and my hand was open wide and our hands flashed and I caught her at the wrist and I had her.

And the strength of her arm vanished at once. Her arm yielded to me and my other hand came up and touched hers and I was working my fingers into her palm and under the knife handle and I was pulling and she let it go. She let me take the knife from her. I dropped it at our feet, and I let go of her wrist and I stretched out my arms and put my hands behind her shoulders and I pulled her gently toward me, in small incremental tugs, and her hands fell to her sides. She did not lift her arms to go around me in return, but she did not struggle, she did not pull away, she let me enfold her, let me hold her close.

47

And after a time, yes. She put her arms around me. And I was smart enough to keep my mouth shut. I was smart enough not to try to explain what I realized about how I'd said the wrong things to her. And now with the knife at our feet, I understood even more. That her country was more important to her than her own life. It was why she wanted to come and fight. That her country needed Pancho Villa. And so if he raped her, the answer was not to kill him. It was to kill herself. And for an American of all people to offer to help her kill him? That kind of obliviousness was why she put a pistol to my head in the candlelight. I was surprised she had her arms around me now, though perhaps she realized that in my offering to help her kill the man who raped her, to kill Pancho Villa, I was offering up my own life alongside hers in the act of revenge. And I was inviting her to take up a weapon again. *She* would kill him. I would simply help. I understood that perhaps even worse for Luisa than Villa violating her was Villa taking away her rifle and forcing her back to a woman's work. The man she so admired turned her back into a powerless washerwoman. All this I now knew. And I said none of it to her. Her arms were around me.

We were, in the embrace, entirely motionless for a long while. Then, as if we both knew the precise moment when it was time, we let go of each other. She looked at her left hand as if it were not hers. She was still holding the scabbard of the knife. She looked at me. I gently took the scabbard. I located the knife on the ground near us and I picked it up, sheathed it. Luisa and I both looked at the thing, and I supposed I should simply throw it as far as I could into the night. Certainly I should not give it back to her. But something made me slip the scabbard onto my belt. She watched me do this and then she turned and I stepped up beside her and we began to walk together.

We walked along the track, going forward, past the engine of Villa's personal train, past the farthest fringes of the encamping *Villistas*. We walked toward the isolated mountain peaks to the east, visible only as a vast, dark absence against the starry sky. We walked side by side but we did not touch. I did not take her hand. I did not slip my arm around her. I was determined to make no more mistakes with Luisa Morales, and though I thought I understood certain things about her and about how I'd done badly by her, I realized there were many other things about which I was ignorant. Like exactly why she had forgiven me. This was something women could do about which I was utterly ignorant. Especially this woman, in this circumstance. And I was ignorant of how a woman felt in the aftermath of what had been done to her. How she might feel about the act my body wanted very badly now. I did understand this: The way I was inclined to do that act would likely be entirely wrong for her at the moment. But I was not sure I could change.

And at last the campfires seemed as distant as the stars. The moon was rising and our night shadows stretched long before us. And somehow we silently decided to move away from the railroad track. Not far. Fifty yards or so into the desert, we found an outcropping of large, humpbacked boulders but with a broad, table-flat stretch of rock at their base. Perfect for us. We sat. We were silent for a while.

Finally Luisa said, "Why did you come here?"

"I'm following a story."

She did not ask. And I realized I should not say. Should not raise the politics of Mexico with her. But if this had to end badly again because of who I was, then it was better for it to just end now. I said,

"A German has come here trying to persuade Mexico to invade the United States."

She did not reply for a long while.

I watched my hands lying motionless on my knees. They were white as a dead man's.

And then she said, "How were you hurt?"

She'd noticed my wound, though when she asked the question, she was looking back toward the camp. Or at the moon.

I said, "I ended up riding with some of the *Villistas*. A man I know is an officer. We had to fight a gang of *colorados*."

She turned to me.

I realized I'd surprised her.

She said, "You fought?"

"Yes."

"Did you kill some *colorados?*"

She trapped me before with a question. I thought it was happening again. I didn't know if she would feel better about me for killing the worst of the *Federales*. Or feel worse about me for killing Mexicans. But I answered her. "Yes."

I'd made a mistake in sitting to her east. My face was lit by moonlight. Her face was in deep shadow. I knew she was looking intently at me, but I could not read her. Still, I kept my gaze steady on the darkest parts of her shadowed self, which were her eyes. This would have been easier if I'd not grown up in theaters. Aware of what she might be seeing in my face, I was inclined now to try to play myself. But I understood the paradox. The more I tried consciously to portray me, the less I actually was me. It was too late. I gave her my profile.

She said, "Why did you find me?"

I didn't answer for a moment. I didn't even fully know what the answer was.

She made a little sound. A quick letting go of a breath. I turned to her and she was looking away, back west.

"Not what you think," I said.

She gave her face to me again. But she did not speak.

And what I said was true. In spite of my desire, it was not why.

I said, "I wrote a story about you."

She cocked her head slightly.

"About a woman who fights for her country, one bullet at a time. There are many people now in America who know what you tried to say with your Mauser."

"I don't understand you," she said.

And for a moment I badly misunderstood her. "I write for a newspaper . . ."

"Not that," she said, but with a gentleness that surprised the hell out of me, given the assumption I'd just made.

She waited.

I felt I was in the same position I was a few moments ago. Having to portray myself. In words this time, which shouldn't have been as intimidating, as inevitably distorted. But this was not how a reporter used words. I was stuck. But I needed to speak.

"I report," I said. "I ask questions. I know more now than I did when you put a pistol to my head. A lot more."

"Not that," she said, even more gently. I didn't have a clue what she wanted. Perhaps a clue, but I dared not be wrong. So I said nothing. I looked beyond her to the waning gibbous moon. I looked away from her altogether. I stared into the night in front of me, seeing nothing. Thinking now: *I have my story.* I dared not rush with her but I had no time. I had to go. I had to write. I had to telegraph. And whatever else might follow that, one thing was certain: I could not return to a Pancho Villa camp.

And I had to go very soon.

So this was when I would, under other circumstances, take a woman.

I heard myself.

I thought it in just such terms.

And though the woman would have to be willing or readily persuadable, I suddenly could not ignore the frame of mind.

I knew more now than I did yesterday riding into Villa's camp.

I knew much more than I did three days ago sitting next to Mensinger on a bench in the train station in Mexico City. About so many things. And some of them had to be told to the people of Chicago and the people of the world. Urgently.

Without looking at Luisa I said, "I have to ride away from here. Soon."

She did not answer.

"I won't be able to return," I said.

Still there was only silence beside me.

I moved my face, but just barely enough so that I could see her. She was looking forward into the night as well.

I said, "Forgive me if this is the wrong thing to ask. And please understand that it is not a way to suggest what I suggested in Vera Cruz. But do you want to ride away with me?"

I was still watching her. She did not react. She did not even seem to hear me. But of course she did. The stillness in her went on. And it began to feel like its opposite. The stillness was, in fact, intense and complex activity. And this was how she was showing it. I stopped watching her.

Before my eyes and hers were the same stretch of moonlit mesquite and high-plains desert floor and train bed and darkness and stars, but we were seeing quite different things, I was sure.

I laid my hands on the tops of my legs, halfway to my knees. I scattered all the matters of my life out before me, turned them into the stars, simply watched them burn, coolly and distantly, indistinguishable one of them from another.

And I waited. I waited. And then I felt her hand fall lightly on top of mine.

I turned my face to hers.

I did not understand her. I did not understand why she might want to do this now. But I did know that I could not let myself behave as I usually did.

She was waiting and I was waiting, her hand on top of mine. And we understood each other.

She lifted her body and swung her leg over my lap and she pushed me down and I lay back upon our bed of stone and we each exposed the parts we needed for this and then we did this act in a way I could never have imagined: She rose above me against the stars and I could see her face, half lit bright in the moonlight and half dark in shadow, and I let her move for us and I let her do for us and I did not know, exactly, who I was with her, but I did know I was with her now, this Luisa Morales.

And when we finished, and she slowly let her body sink down upon mine from above, and she kissed me on the lips and I kissed her, and she moved a little downward and turned her head and laid it on my chest, when we were quite still and we were quite happy in our bodies, I said to her, "So does that mean you will ride with me?"

And she said, quite gently, with a soft quaking of regret in her voice, "It means I will not."

48

And once again I knew nothing.

Except, with Luisa's head on my chest and me watching the night sky, the time that followed felt as if it was not time at all but a kind of death.

And then we knew we must return.

We rose and we covered the uncovered parts of us and we walked west along the train tracks. When we neared the first fringe of the thousands of soldiers billeted in the desert, we began to hear singing from the campfires, from many campfires, each group hearing only itself, but Luisa and I heard them all in soft cacophony.

And we stopped beside the boxcar where she slept with the other women who had lately arrived.

We stood before each other, searched each other's face. "Why?" I asked.

"I must do it my own way," she said.

And she stepped into me and we kissed for what surely was the last time.

"Go," she said. "Quickly."

I did.

I was passing Villa's car and I was suddenly aware of something I'd not thought of since I left Mensinger's quarters: A pistol was strapped to my hip. I stopped. I looked at the lights in Villa's windows. I turned and looked back along the track. Luisa was gone.

And inside my head, maps were unfolding: Texas, San Antonio, a hand-drawn layout of the Alamo. It was time to report. I hustled along the tracks.

In the postal car I took off my sombrero and my serape. I lit a kerosene lamp and carried it to the sorting table which was soon to be my bunk but now would be my desk. I set the lamp off center to the left. I unbuckled my pistol belt and removed it. Luisa's knife hung there next to the holster. I felt a surge of fear for her. Would this be her own way? But no. I didn't think that was in her anymore.

I rolled the belt around the holster and the scabbard. I didn't know where to put the objects in my hand. They did not feel as if they were mine. Finally I just laid them at my feet, next to my saddlebags. I moved to the nearest cluster of spindle-back chairs and I carried one to my desk and carefully positioned it.

I had not opened my saddlebags since we arrived. But for now I needed only two things. I bent to them. I removed my Corona and a packet of foolscap. I placed the typewriter before me and unfolded the carriage. I rolled a piece of paper into the machine. I sat down before it. I was happy to be in front of this machine once again. My fingertips knew me. They wired me like a telegraph to the place in my head where my reporter's voice was ready to speak what it had heard, what it had learned.

I'd type the contents of Mensinger's document portfolio straight into mid-story form. When I crossed the border I would have a large enough writing task ahead of me as it was.

I focused. I pictured the first document. Kaiser Willie's letter to Villa. I saw the Imperial Eagle spreading its wings. It would turn into words. I lifted my hands. They hung, fingers curled, over the keyboard.

And my hands snapped back as a voice suddenly filled the room. "Do you find rebellions fueled by strong coffee, Mister Chance?"

I let my hands fall to the tabletop, one on each side of my typewriter. I did not look at him.

He said, "Or is it Herr Cobb? Yes, I think it is Herr Cobb."

I turned my face. My concentration was keen and he was quiet. Mensinger was standing barely ten feet away. His hands hung at his side, palms inward, like a gunfighter. He was not wearing his pistol, however. He was wearing his British cavalry sword. If he was planning to kill me—and he probably was—then he'd rather do it his own way, and silently.

"I think it is Herr Cobb," he said, "the journalist turned bandit. You seem to have impressed *Jefe* Villa."

And I considered my pistol somewhere nearby on the floor. But to bend, to unwrap the belt, to draw the pistol, to straighten up, to turn, to find him, to shoot him: He would have easily drawn his sword and run me through long before I could do all that. He no doubt knew this. He'd been quietly watching me for some minutes, I realized.

"You apparently tried to hide your tracks, but you are a sloppy man, Herr Cobb, and I have a keen eye."

"Your clothes were quite dull, as it turned out," I said.

I saw a flicker in him: He was not sure I'd found the documents.

"And a clothes brush?" I said. "Do you understand the scorn Pancho Villa will have for you if he finds out?"

"So will that be your big story, Herr Cobb? You will expose the Germans for keeping their clothes brushed?"

"I would only care about the one reader," I said. A mistake, however. There was another flicker in him at what I'd just admitted: I understood he had intentions with Villa that I needed to somehow thwart.

"It is a shame he cannot read," Mensinger said.

"He'll get the message," I said.

"But he will forgive me, Herr Cobb, when he knows that you were a sneak thief, and an incompetent one. And when he knows I have bravely faced your pistol with a sword and defended myself."

I understood at once: He would put my pistol in my hand and discharge it after I was dead.

But he still had not drawn. Arrogant ass.

I slowly rose, pushing the chair out from behind me with my foot. I turned to face him. It was how he wanted me. It was how I wanted to be, given Desperate Plan Number Two.

I had not moved away from the desk to face him. My right hand remained at the side of the typewriter, hidden from his sight. I worked my fingertips underneath the base of its frame. Desperate Plan Number Two featured Corona Portable Number Three.

He smiled. And he drew. He was fast and the blade was coming out quick and I grasped the Corona tight from the base and it was coming up quick too and his sword was out and angling back and he was committed to a thrust and he did not imagine anything could intervene and the Corona was heavy, very heavy, slower than I expected, and I strained hard and it rose faster and the sword started forward and Corona was up and it was before me perpendicular to the floor showing its bottom to Mensinger and I grabbed its left side and braced my arms straight out even as the sword clanged in and sword and typewriter together jumped toward me and I tensed my arms and they flexed as Corona came at me but I steeled my arms and the typewriter slowed even as the sword flashed through the type bars and my arms braced and the sword emerged and the tip plunged toward me, a foot away, nearer, and my arms strained harder against the thrust and they held now, my arms held against the push and the tip of the sword stopped not six inches from me.

And we were suspended, Mensinger and I, we were a tableau for the briefest of moments and I pushed back, with arms and legs I pushed him back, the sword wedged still in my dear Corona, whose life I feared for even as I drove Mensinger back and I had to hold fast at the base of Corona because Mensinger was pulling that way now, trying to get his sword out and he did. The tip vanished from between the key bars and I knew his jerking momentum gave me just a moment, I could see his arm flying back even as he stopped and braced to begin another thrust but I continued toward him a strong step as I flipped Corona from its exposed bottom to its strong wide back and I was inside his striking distance and he started to step back too but I strode and I raised Corona to Mensinger's face level to his forehead level and I thrust it hard forward. We were moving together in the same direction and I was not as close as I wished but the thump in the center of his forehead was loud.

And Corona went "ding."

And I found Corona in empty air and my feet were tangling and I stumbled and he was beneath me and I sidestepped and stumbled again and I made a conscious step away, into empty floor, I planted one foot hard and firm and then the other, and I stopped.

I breathed. I thought I had not been breathing much. I turned.

Mensinger was on his back. Out cold. John L. Sullivaned. His arms sprawled wide, his sword still in his hand, though the fingers had gone slack. He would have a serious headache for his big meeting with Pancho Villa.

And I knew it was time to leave.

Now.

49

"Walk with me," I said to Slim. He knew from my voice that he shouldn't ask why. It felt good to say three words in English at the moment.

He took a last pull from a bottle of *pulque,* which had to be about eighty degrees at the coolest. I couldn't imagine drinking the stuff in the desert. But Slim also fought wars for money. And it also struck me about this moment that I was having thoughts like these. Which led me to think: *part of me has already gotten on a horse and ridden far away and written a news story and found a telegraph operator and has left my participatory days far behind me.*

Slim rose and we both nodded to Hernando and the rest of the boys, and Slim fell in beside me as I headed back to the postal car.

"I need your help," I said.

"You know you got it," he said.

"I have to ride out of here tonight."

"That was fast. Your story done?"

"I had a breakthrough."

"What do you need from me?"

"Help me retrieve my horse."

"I'll find the boy."

"I've got a map and compass," I said. "It looks like Laredo."

"Okay. Probably best, if the U. S. of A. is your intention. Take you three days if you don't want to kill your animal."

"Much trouble along the way, you figure?"

"I'll get you a Mauser just in case. But no. Not if you stay at least twenty miles away from the railway till you get to the Salado River. You could lead your horse over the train bridge there, and you're good the rest of the way to the border."

We were approaching the postal car.

"I'll get my saddlebags," I said.

"Horse and rifle," he said. And as an afterthought: "And a phial of iodine and clean bandages." He headed off up the tracks.

I stepped into the car and Mensinger was still out cold. I'd checked his pulse after quickly pulling my things together and before I'd gone after Slim. The pulse had seemed fine.

He was drooling a bit now. His fingers were starting to twitch. There was some incipient movement under and around the closed eyelids. He had a knot in the center of his forehead, as if all his secret plans were being drawn into the open.

I put the bags over my shoulder and sat for a moment on the chair. I needed to wait. I was ready to give Mensinger another tap if he suddenly popped back awake. But before I had to do that, I heard Slim on the steps. I rose and I moved toward the door and I stopped when Slim stopped, framed in the door, a Mauser in his hand and a *bandolera* draped over his arm, and his face had an expression as close to true wondering surprise as Tallahassee Slim's face had probably ever come. He was staring at Mensinger.

"My breakthrough," I said.

Slim looked at me with every bit as much admiration as he'd showed when I saved his life.

I said, "If he has his way, you'll need to leave Pancho's employ. He'd like you all to take back the Alamo."

Slim shook his head, once, like didn't that beat all. And he thrust the Mauser straight out into the air between us. "Go tell 'em," he said.

50

I woke as if I'd just fallen asleep and begun to dream. I floated on a felt-stuffed mattress, and above me a four-blade ceiling fan spun like the sleep-slowed propeller of an aeroplane approaching me, but I just drifted before it, unfazed, serene, and since I was softly held now, I was free to lie once again on a bed of stone and it was soft there too, and this dream veered, as dreams sometimes do, into a thing so deeply wished for that only in this way can it happen and it feels real but you know even as you go through the motions of it that it is impossible. Luisa returned to me now like this. She fit herself upon me and rose above me, and beyond her the aeroplane slowly rushed at us both, but we were safe, joined like this we were safe, and then she was gone and I was in the Hamilton Hotel on the corner of Convent and Matamoros in Laredo, Texas, but as in a dream you can know where you really are and still dream on, I saw my mother and she was singing in a brothel in New Orleans and I sat up in the bed and put my feet on the floor.

I was in Laredo, Texas, in the United States of America. Last night I sat beside a telegraph operator whom I paid handsomely to stay late and I wired the scoop of a lifetime, the king beat of king beats, to Clyde Fetter in Chicago, and now I waited. I waited for Clyde and I also waited for Bunky Millerman and the great Isabel Cobb, both of whom I also wired as soon as I got to town and located the telegraph office, even before I started writing the story. To Bunky I said: *Got him. In Laredo writing stories. How are you? How is the boy? Wire care of Hamilton Hotel. Kit*

To Mother I began: *The third act is full of sound and fury and signifying something.* I spent more time struggling with the next sentence, what to say and how to say it, than I later would in the whole of the massive news story about an active and advanced German plan to instigate a Mexican invasion of the U.S.A. starting with San Antonio and the Alamo. Finally I set aside Shakespeare and Marlowe and Ben Jonson and Sophocles and Homer and Henry James and Montaigne and all the rest and just said straight out what I wanted from her.

Where are you? I wrote. I almost asked, as well, *What are you doing?* but I did not. One thing at a time.

And I drank my coffee black in the hotel restaurant, which was on the corner and looking into the *zócalo*. Ah, I was in the United States now. The *plaza*. Jarvis Plaza. But I was looking through glass and sitting with a tablecloth under my hands and this was the United States now. I found myself missing the *portales*. Even if the open air was to stink, it would be the open air. But I always had odd feelings of displacement after returning from assignments. I was known to get nostalgic over the smell of cordite.

And the only news of Mexico in the Laredo newspaper was an Associated Press scoop that an American private who went missing in Vera Cruz and was thought to be insane was in fact captured by the Mexicans and was now thought to have been executed but, if true, the event was "unlikely" to provoke a larger military encounter between the Americans and Mexicans. Of course, the private could have been both insane and executed, a possibility I was surprised the AP reporter didn't explore since he obviously had too much time on his hands and not enough news.

Today I would write about Gerhard Vogel, his service to his country and his murder by a German military officer from the Vera Cruz consulate, to run as a stunning background revelation for the big story of the day before. And then I would write the story of a *Post-Express* reporter who found himself riding with the *Villistas*. I would not tell all of the details of that story, however. The men I killed. They would not be part of the public record.

And my coffee cup was empty and I looked across the restaurant and the waiter was already heading my way, a plate in one hand and a coffeepot in the other. He arrived and set my eggs and rasher of bacon before me and as he poured my coffee, he asked, "Are you Mr. Cobb?"

"I am," I said.

"The front desk has received a Western Union delivery. I'll fetch it for you."

"Thanks," I said.

He moved off briskly and I was feeling American again, surrounded by briskness.

I took a sip of coffee, watching, as I did, the tiny, innocuous birds flying in a delicate little flock over the plaza. I looked sharply away. If I was getting nostalgic about the *zopilotes,* then I was in serious trouble. I barely got a taste of egg and bacon before the waiter brisked back to me and I gave him a dime for his trouble and his haste, and I laid two telegrams before me. One was from Vera Cruz. One was from New Orleans. None was from Chicago. But of course not. Clyde was only barely beginning to look at the story right now.

Bunky first. I opened the wire, and he said: *Vera Cruz gets cleaner and cleaner. The boy does not. My hand is steady, since you are wondering. Otherwise, we're fine. Bunk*

I was wondering, of course. He sounded so like the authentic Bunky in the wire that I actually believed him. As for the boy, I found myself inordinately pleased. Not only that he was fine but that he was no cleaner. I realized I did not want that boy to change.

I ate some eggs. I ate some bacon. I let my mother's telegram lie there: I was afraid that if I did my eating afterward, she would upset my digestion. She might anyway, but at least I'd have a few minutes of American food in me without it roiling around.

After thoroughly running a crust of bread in the last bit of egg yolk remaining on my plate and after drinking some more coffee and even watching the little birdies in the placid American sky, I picked up my mother's telegram and I opened it.

She wrote: *I am full aware you know the city I am in from my clearly having said too much already in a previous wire. So for you now to ask me where I am means you ask too much. Where are you? Western Union Laredo Texas? Did you elope with that sniper girl you wrote about? Be careful. She doesn't sound your type. But that was in another country.*

She was angry. No signature to the wire at all. Not even an et cetera. She just threw the lines from Marlowe back in my face. At least she didn't quote the whole thing. There was just too much going on below the surface of this telegram. I had no desire to figure it out. That may have been fornication, but there was no guilt in the thing at all. And the wench wasn't dead.

51

A Laredo doctor was cleaning and rebandaging my wound and tossing me odd little looks like he'd never seen a gunshot wound before in Laredo, Texas—though it was true the stitching was a little unorthodox and maybe I needed to shave and certainly I needed to stop wearing my sombrero—and as he was doing his business, I was thinking about New Orleans. But merely to wonder which of the New Orleans papers was picking up the *Post-Express* syndication. I was all work. I was wishing there was a doctor who could heal my Corona Portable Number 3, who got stabbed between the **5/T/t** and the **-/G/g** and whose wounded body I hopefully jammed into my saddlebags and carried on my three-day dash for the border. But when I arrived, my Corona refused to allow not only any "t" or "g" to be used in my story but several vowels, as well, and had thus left me stuck with a hotel-rental Underwood table model. As for the two stories I would write on that machine today, the leads were already bristling in my head. All work.

So I wrote my stories and it was mid-afternoon, and I stopped at the hotel front desk on my way out to the telegraph office, expecting, ironically, to find a wire that had been delivered to me from that very office. Huzzah. What a story.

Nothing. I went out. I filed. I wanted to check to make sure that, in fact, they hadn't delivered something to the hotel, which the hotel then, obviously, misplaced. I wouldn't complain. I just wanted the damn wire.

It wasn't misplaced. They hadn't delivered.

I wandered through the plaza on the way back to the hotel. In the center was a very odd circular brick platform, large enough to be a bandstand, but it wasn't. It had no apparent function at all except to support, around its edge, eight brick pedestals, each of which supported a concrete column, at the top of which was a white, globular, electrically lit ball. What were they thinking in this city? Where was the band playing Cohan and Sousa? Where were the girls in summer lingerie dresses promenading around with each other before the lounging, leering boys? When Gerhard threatened to slide back into my head and start tooting his alto horn, I beat it back to the hotel.

I squeezed at my material some more just to keep occupied, trying to cobble together a profile of Villa in the context of life in his railway-bound campsites, though I'd seen very little of it, really. I did not include the boxcar full of the recently arrived, unattached women. Somebody in Chicago would try to make that the lead.

Then I sat in the hotel bar drinking whiskey till the night came on and I grew as dark as the view out the window. And I probably asked again at the front desk a time or two about a telegram and I probably went up the steps and I probably went into my room and took off my boots and lay down. Probably, because I had no memory of any of that when I woke with light coming through my window and I was on my bed and my boots were off.

My head was stuffed as full as this mattress, though the gob of felt inside my head was being heated in a furnace and it was expanding plenty and I was just waiting for it to burst into flames, though it seemed somehow resistant to that obvious next turn of events. Which was probably for the best. Still, if it was not going to burst into flames, I wished it would just cool the hell down.

But it was a new day and a new chance for a telegram from Clyde so I could receive his praise and maybe an editorial question or two and then I could figure out how best to get myself back to Vera

ROBERT OLEN BUTLER

Cruz. That was probably what was keeping him: He was going to do the huzzahing and the inquiring all in one comprehensive telegram.

I managed to get up and get one boot on, which was enough for now, and I managed to complete a few necessary ablutions, and then I was glad to find I could get the other boot on with noticeably less difficulty, and I went downstairs. Since I would want to go straight from Clyde's editorial inquiries to the typewriter and get this done with, I even had enough restraint to bypass the front desk and go to the dining room, and I sat in a shadowed corner as far away from the windows as I could and I ordered simply a pot of black coffee, which I drank searingly fast.

I realized the morning was pretty far advanced. The sun was not low outside there, and I was the only person in the dining room. I was sure to have a telegram from Clyde waiting for me at the front desk.

And I did.

I carried it back to my room unopened.

I went in.

I sat before my typewriter at my small, rattly desk.

I opened Clyde's wire, expecting him to have composed an ardent love aria for my having produced a veritable Wagnerian opera for tomorrow's front page.

Instead, he wrote: *Knockout story, champ. But this is something we need to talk about in person. Please take train to Chicago as soon as possible. Clyde*

"But"? Meaning it was not running tomorrow. Not running till I could get to Chicago. If I was working for Hearst, he'd run it first and then *he'd* be on a train, coming down here to congratulate me personally, on the spot, and to start planning how to follow this up so we could declare war on Mexico. Hell, declare war on Germany too. He'd see this as bigger than Cuba and Spain.

Maybe this was exactly that. Maybe it was just a matter of who took the train. This was certainly big enough that Clyde kicked it upstairs to Paul Maccabee Griswold himself. This was as secure a beat as you could find. No one else would get it in the next few days.

Or ever. So let's confer about the best way to roll it out. Griswold was capable of that.

And yet. I had a bad feeling. Knockout stories got rushed into print. No matter how secure they were. Still. I could come up with a plausibly optimistic scenario. But I'd be damned if I could dream up what the problem might be.

Then one problem led me to another, where the dreaming up was easy. And I thought of an opportunity.

I'd route myself through New Orleans.

52

So I got ready to leave Laredo. And it felt as if I were truly leaving Mexico. Not just ducking across the border. But I had no choice. I found a livery and a big general store and I sold my horse and saddle-bags in the one, and the Mauser and *bandolera* in the other. I bought a couple of white shirts and a ten-dollar blue serge suit and a fedora. I bought an oversize cowhide traveling bag. I kept the Browning and the holster and Luisa's knife, and before dawn the next morning I packed them away, and after staring at the sombrero lying on the center of my hotel bed for a long few moments, I folded it as best I could and wedged it into the bag.

By noontime the International and Great Northern Railway had dropped me in my blue serge suit and fedora in San Antonio, Texas, where I cooled my heels till sunset. I did think for a time about how I just came up the train tracks that Germany was urging Villa to use in his attack on the United States. But I didn't dwell on that. The story was written. There was no more for me to do about that for now other than ride these trains to Chicago. And I exchanged wires with Clyde, sending him my schedule and getting not another word from him about the face-to-face meeting other than I should come straight to the office when I arrived.

And then the Southern Pacific carried me on to New Orleans Union Station. We were due to arrive there by the next sunset, but things went slow out of Houston and again out of Lake Charles,

Louisiana, and it was past nine when we got in. Which was okay by me. I had a ticket on the next train to Chicago on the Illinois Central and it didn't depart till 9:40 tomorrow morning, and my arriving late in New Orleans meant Storyville would be going strong when I got there. Before I headed out, I went to the baggage room, and there I hesitated. Should I take my Browning? I did not. But I removed Luisa's knife and scabbard and I strapped it on my belt in the middle of my back, and I stored my bag and went out.

The air smelled of old fish and a recent rain. I got into an automotive taxicab—a Model T with a limousine body—and I told the driver I wanted to go to Storyville.

He cranked the engine and I got in the back, and when we drove off, he tossed me a look over his shoulder and said, "Your first time?"

"Yes," I said. Which was a lie.

"You in search of a sportin' house? I can do you a good one where they'll treat you specially nice at the dropping of my name."

"I'm interested in music," I said. "High-class singers. You know anything about that?"

"I don't know nothing about that," he said in a clipped tone as if he'd offered a good place to hear music and I'd asked for a whore.

At least it shut him up, which I was happy for because the truth about my first time in Storyville slipped into me as we headed downtown on Rampart.

I was born in this town, backstage at the Pelican Theatre in the early morning, as Mother tells it, and she opened as Shakespeare's Juliet that night without having to add a whole new dimension to the role that the producers, however, had been only too willing to do. Not that we stayed around after the run. But whenever we toured back to New Orleans over the years, I treated the place like my hometown, and then, in 1901, her leading man in some melodrama or other—a silver-haired warhorse named Gilbert Russell Whitaker—had laryngitis such that he could make himself heard but he couldn't emote, and he took the night off. I'd recently turned seventeen and he decided it was high time for me to lose my virginity in my own hometown. I happily agreed and he took me to Storyville and he spent a very generous five dollars on my behalf for one of Willie V. Piazza's octoroons, an angel-faced girl wearing opera-length striped stockings—the only thing, indeed, that she was wearing when I trembled my way into her room—and she was not much older than me and she lay down on the mahogany four-poster and said, "You're a fine, strapping boy and I don't care it's your first time, I want you to do me like you should and like I deserve, which is to say I want you to make me scream from the pounding." And this I did. And the son of a bitch Whitaker, a few years later, drunk one night in his dressing room in St. Louis, squealed on my mother, revealing that the whole idea and the five dollars were from her. Of course I'd never mentioned any of it to her when I got back from Storyville that night. And she was a consummate actress. I'm certain I would have found suspicious the slightest clue in her face, a little smile, a little glance. I would have known she knew. But there was nothing. And neither did I ever speak of what I learned about her complicity.

And so I found myself now on Basin Street, the southern boundary and main thoroughfare of Storyville, with a run of bordellos three and four stories high and a block deep, but all of them with mansion facades, a mash of cupolas and towers and balconies from Queen Anne and Queen Victoria and Second Empire styles. And among them were the lower-slung saloons and dance halls and cabarets, most of them selling women too, a bottom floor providing song and dance and whiskey to smooth the transition to the upper floor. And on the opposite side of the street, just about everything done on this side was illegal, with a three-block passenger shed running into the Southern Depot on Canal Street, everyone stepping off a train of the St. Louis & San Francisco Railway getting a vivid introduction to the city of my birth.

And I jostled through the men who staggered and drifted and prowled on Basin: the lonely soldiers, and the slumming parties of uptown boys, and the pairs of pals or of brothers or of fathers and sons, and the isolated ones, alone and full of desire that they could express nowhere but here. All of these men working up to a woman. And I just walked for a time from the Canal Street end of Basin—if

Mother was singing in Storyville, it would be on Basin Street, I was sure—and the music from inside the establishments jumbled together outside, the Negro *perfessers* with upright pianos and the cornetists and the brass combos, and from out here in the street, the spasm bands, with washboards and wooden-box fiddles and Confederate bugles. All of them playing jazz over the din of male voices.

And now and then I heard a fragment of a singing voice. A woman singing. From a cabaret. From a saloon. None of them Mother. And I was thinking I'd made a big mistake to come here. I thought if I did find her, I'd just pay back her five dollars and go. But no. I'd just slip quietly away. I'd been happy for the chance to be with the octoroon girl. My mother had known what I wanted, what I needed, and she made sure I had it. And if now she saw herself cast in a role in the vast melodrama of Storyville, I was not going to cast myself in it with her. She was not asking me to. She'd even warned me not to come here. But what did she think she was doing?

And maybe I was entirely wrong. Maybe I'd misread the clues in her telegrams. Maybe she was not even here. Maybe she was somewhere else in New Orleans.

Still, I walked on, going "Down the Line," as they called the cruise in this direction along the brothels of Basin. I crossed Bienville Street into the last block, which would end, I knew, at St. Louis Cemetery Number 1, where everyone lay above the ground, in concrete or marble, so when the heavy subtropical summer rains came, as they did in this town, the bodies wouldn't rise from the earth and float away. I passed Willie V.'s place without looking at it. And halfway along the block, from a wide-fronted vernacular building with no stoop and made for music and booze and sex, came a piano and a voice that I knew, even as a hawker stepped from the doorway into the midst of the passing gaggles of men and said my mother's name. Just the one name. He said, loud enough to be heard by all the men around him but still conversational, persuasive, "The famous Isabel is singing right now, gents. Straight from Broadway. And backing her up are the prettiest cabaret girls in The District. Just step through that door."

I stepped through. Others did too. The place was jammed with men front to back. They were remarkably quiet for Storyville. I slid immediately away from the door but parallel to the street, not going any farther inside. On the wall to my right was a long cherrywood bar with a mirrored top. On the opposite wall was a wide staircase. Like showgirls on a stage set, the house girls were draped all the way up the balustrade. They wore ruffled camisoles and high stockings and nothing in between. Over everything and everyone stretched a ceiling full of electric bulbs making it bright as Louisiana noontime. And at the far end was a raised platform with an upright piano where a Negro in a pearl-gray derby and checkered vest played sweetly and sadly, in the solo moments putting in half a dozen notes for every one note you'd expect.

And at the front edge of the platform was my mother, her hair stacked high on her head and sparkling with jewels, and she was wearing a long, jade-green gown, her décolletage fringed in black feathers. And she was why the men were almost entirely silent. Her voice—she had a lovely, rich, vibrating singing voice, my mother—her voice filled the place. She sang, "Baby won't you please come home, 'cause your mama's all alone." And my mother didn't mean *Mama*. She honky-tonked up her voice, rasping that word, picking out some man I couldn't see in a table close to the platform: It was to him she sang *your mama*. And it was as if she had just given this audience that she utterly commanded permission to laugh. They did. From the street front of the place all the way to the stage, they laughed raucously and then instantly went quiet again to hear her. And she came down off the platform as she sang, "I have tried in vain never more to call your name."

I lost sight of her. Men immediately before me stood up, trying to see my mother as, I imagined, she played the crowd, moved among them, brushed against them, smelled them, these men who were out simply for a buzz and a whore but were surprised and excited to find Isabel, a great Broadway actress, singing as if for each of them individually, "When you left, you broke my heart, because I never thought we'd part."

This was a mistake, coming here. And why should I have begrudged her this audience adulation? It was what she lived for, always.

And if it was a selective audience, if it was not an easy one to win over—or even to silence—then all the more satisfying. And for them to be entirely riveted on her even as half-naked young women decorated the stairway nearby, waiting to open themselves to any man in this audience at any time: This was a standing ovation, a dozen curtain calls, an armful of long-stem red roses; this was eternal youth.

She sang the growling, heartfelt climax, "Every hour in the day, you will hear your mama say, Oh, baby, won't you please come home."

I was not a baby any longer. She was not a mama. We neither of us had a home to wait in or to come home to. We never had.

The song was over. The crowd was cheering now. They all rose and they cheered, and derbies were flung into the air, rising into the bright perpetual day of the electric lights above us.

I wished to move. I wished to walk out the door now and go find a hotel and sleep in a bed and put all this out of my mind. I also wished to make my way toward the stage and guide my mother over to the bar—start there, if I must—buy her a drink and then persuade her to leave this place. But those two opposite impulses seemed to have exactly the same motive force, because I did not move at all. In either direction. I simply stood there watching as some of the men settled back into their tables and some of them headed for the staircase.

I could see her again. I watched her, still near the stage, as she bent to a table, the one she'd pointed to, she bent to the derbies there and talked with her typical post-performance animation. She said something grandly and the derbies laughed. And she watched them laugh. And she watched one of them particularly. And when they were finished laughing, she leaned close to that man, very close, almost as if to kiss him, but at the last moment she moved her face to the side of his and she said something directly into his ear. She drew back and he was rising instantly, and the other men had watched this and I could not hear the sounds they were making but they were clearly in envious awe of the man, who shot the most animated of his companions a sharp, silencing look and they all abruptly turned their heads away.

The man took his place beside her, and my mother slipped her hand into his arm, and they walked this way, heading for the door. I pulled the brim of my fedora down, but Mother did not look in my direction. She gave the man beside her a glance—so did I, and he was a thick-necked, ruffian-shouldered man with a long-ago-broken nose and tiny eyes—and it was only the one glance she gave him, and after that, she was focused on the door. They passed by and out and I stepped to the door myself and through and onto the sidewalk, and I looked to my right, Up the Line. I didn't see them. I looked Down the Line, and they were walking together, leaning into each other.

I had only one impulse now. I turned away and headed off in the opposite direction, hustling as fast as I could through the crowd of horny men.

53

Thirty-six hours later I was arriving at the Illinois Central Railroad Station at the south edge of Grant Park. And an hour after that I was standing in Clyde's office and I was holding the postcard of Luisa and me and the two dead Mexican snipers and I was stuck on her all over again, just like I was when Bunky snapped me from behind, and Clyde had just lit his cigar and I was feeling hotter standing here ten stories above Michigan Avenue than I had at any time in the past few weeks in the *tierra caliente* of Mexico.

And he had just said, "So what became of your señorita, do you suppose?"

And I had just answered, "Did I get drunk and send a telegram I don't remember?"

And he had just responded to that, "Nah. Call it a newsman's intuition."

And I had just shrugged and looked away from him.

And now one of Griswold's endless supply of young stenographers, a redhead in a white shirtwaist and a long black skirt, showed up in Clyde's door and said, "They're ready, Mr. Fetter." She was clearly a little fluttery, as if Clyde and I were very special characters, and since we were not, in her eyes—she'd sassed us both a couple of times each in the last few months—since this fluster was about whoever she'd just left, I was very curious indeed about the meeting.

So we followed her down the hall and into the electric elevator, whose metal doors she yanked open and shut behind us and whose power handle she operated herself, as if she already had the vote and was moving on to any job she'd like to do. We ascended. We followed her again, down the heavily carpeted hall, and she passed a door in the left-hand wall and abruptly stopped and turned and faced us. She nodded us in. We stepped through, into the publisher's conference room.

At the far end of the table, backdropped by the horizon line of Lake Michigan, sat Paul Maccabee Griswold and a tall, thin man in a bespoke, black, three-piece suit with a gray pinstripe.

Clyde and I didn't know where to go. Since they were at the end of the table, perhaps we were to sit here, at this end, far away, and face them. But the man in the black suit motioned for us to come down to them. He pointed us to the closest chairs, which were at a right angle to theirs, directing me with a "Mr. Cobb" to the one on the long side of the table, closest to him.

I sat, and Clyde sat beside me. Though the air in this room was smotheringly hot and palpable with barely hidden moisture, the man in the black suit did not appear to have a single drop of sweat on him. He pushed back a bit, angled his chair to face me. Griswold moved himself only minimally, only so he could hold his face on us without getting a crick in the neck. I got the feeling he'd rather have us at the other end of the room and was not happy with the stranger seeming to run the show.

A silence followed. The man held his eyes unwaveringly upon me, large, black eyes that had something wrong in their stare—like the eyes of a prostitute—though that impression may have been an aftereffect of my recent evening in Storyville—and that was wrong, actually, for these eyes, though they were certainly impenetrable, were not like the eyes of anyone who was submitting to anything. He had a bit of Richard Harding Davis about him, a brick of a chin, like a prizefighter who could take a punch, and him making me think of Davis made me consequently think that this was a newspaperman, that Griswold had hired some star editor away from Pulitzer or Hearst and wanted his new man to massage my story.

And Griswold was saying, "You've written a surpassingly good story here, Cobb. Three surpassingly good stories."

The guy in the black suit and I were still looking at each other. He had some of the face lines of a prizefighter, too, of a younger man looking prematurely older because his face was a focal point for aggressive attention. But just a hint of that, really. And his hair was as black as his eyes and Brilliantined into absolute obedience on each side of a right-hand part. He had no mustache, no beard, and the nakedness of his face should have made him seem more open, in a way, but it only emphasized his opacity. And yet, opaque though he was, he was clearly conveying a keen interest in me. I was not sure exactly how. His implacable attention was part of it, certainly. But there was something else.

"In fact," Griswold said, "your stories are so surpassingly good that much larger issues become involved."

I looked now at the long-jowled, wide-girthed Griswold, who seemed to be working on expanding his vocabulary with a word-for-the-week. This week: *surpassingly.* He paused to let the possibility of those larger issues sink in and he pushed his lower lip up and drew the sides of his mouth down, thus putting on his characteristic seriously-silent mask.

I was aware of the prickly mood that was coming over me.

Then he said, "This is the man to speak to those larger issues. Gentlemen, meet James P. Trask, special assistant to the Secretary of State of the United States."

Trask rose from his chair. "I will stand to shake your hand, Mr. Cobb. To offer all due respect."

I stood as well, trying to flip the throw bar in my head and switch tracks in this new direction. The Federal Government was why I'd been called back to Chicago. The *Federales.*

We shook hands, firmly.

"Please," he then said, pointing to my chair.

I sat. He did too.

He took an envelope from the inside pocket of his suit coat. He handed it to me.

"This is first," he said.

I opened the envelope, which was sealed in red wax with the American eagle spreading its wings in bas-relief. I unfolded the letter and found the eagle again, in a familiar form: the letterhead of the President of the United States. It was dated two days ago. Written as I was somewhere between Lake Charles and Baton Rouge.

"I saw one of these recently," I said.

"So I read in your surpassingly good story," Trask said, smiling slightly. His back was to Griswold and I had no doubt he was asking me to quietly share our mutual assessment of the man. Trask was manufacturing a little bond between us. Instantly he made the smile vanish. "This one is real," he said.

And so I found that the President of the United States had written this to me:

Dear Mr. Cobb,

I am a great admirer of your work. Not only do you keep the President and his cabinet informed on the status of battlefields around the world, you make a crucial contribution to our democratic society. The free press makes sure all ideas can be expressed, all institutions, all public officials, can be held accountable. It is the freedom upon which all our other freedoms rely.

Sometimes, however, a democratic society might humbly and carefully request a different sort of contribution, one that is rarely required but is, nonetheless, just as crucial.

I hereby introduce you to James P. Trask, who is acting as my personal representative and who will speak to you on my behalf. I hope you will give the matters he will discuss and the favors he will request serious consideration. Your country calls you to a high service, Mr. Cobb.

Sincerely,
Woodrow Wilson

And there was his sharp-edged, forward-slanting signature. It was vividly black from a broad-nibbed pen. I'd been traveling for more than three days and all the while had to keep myself from considering why the biggest scoop of my career, the biggest scoop for this newspaper in many years, hadn't been rushed into print. They were going to kill the story. That much was clear to me now. But in spite of all this, I was looking at a personal appeal from the president of my country, and though I was bucking and snorting inside at the thought of my story being spiked, I had a powerful urge to put a fingertip on the signature, to touch this barely dried ink which he himself put there to endorse his regard for me. To ask something important of me. As critical as I sometimes was of Woodrow Wilson, he was still the man who tried to watch over us all, look after our needs, tried to lead us all. We empowered him to do that. I needed to yield to my good reporter instincts now. I needed to hear what the President would say through his Mr. Trask, hear it without my intervening and influencing or obscuring the words. I had to listen.

Trask turned his body around in his chair to face Griswold as much as possible. "You have the thanks, Mr. Griswold, not only of the Secretary of State but of the President himself. Would you be so kind as to affirm that what I will ask of Mr. Cobb has been endorsed by you?"

"Yes, of course," Griswold said. "I take it that letter is from the President?"

Trask looked over his shoulder at me. "Would you mind?"

I leaned forward and extended the letter in Griswold's direction. He was used to having someone on hire to reach for things on his personal behalf, but it was clear Trask wasn't going to intervene, and so Griswold collected himself and made the effort. He even lifted his butt off his chair to reach out and take the letter from me.

He sat and put on his wire-rim reading spectacles. He opened the letter and gave it a careful look, pushing that lower lip up as far as it would go. When he finished, his mouth loosened, and he looked at me and nodded. Here was another goddam old man whose approval gave me a little goddam lift. Now that I was in this goddam mood, I even retrospectively basked a bit in his praise for my story.

I had to remember who I was. I had to get back into character.

Griswold was lifting his butt again—twice in two minutes—to return my presidential letter. This time Trask played go-between, taking the letter and passing it on to me while Griswold said, "Of course. The *Post-Express* and all of Griswold Enterprises are prepared to answer the call of our country."

"Thank you," Trask said. He waited for Griswold to settle back down in his chair, and then he said, "Now if you two gentlemen don't mind, I need to discuss some things with Mr. Cobb in private." He paused a moment, let Griswold thrash a bit at being dismissed from the room. Griswold was showing evidence of the thrashing in jowl and mouth and eye. Then Trask said, "Per the President's specific request."

Griswold rose from his chair, harrumphing and of-coursing. I looked at Clyde, who was a good soldier and stoic in his dismissal. Once on his feet, he gave me a little nod of sympathy and he headed for the door and waited there for Griswold, who grumbled at him to go on, go on. The Boss wanted to assert himself over some situation here, even if it was simply who would be the last one out the door, which he closed behind him.

Trask reached into his inside coat pocket once again. "Smoke?" he said.

"Sure," I said.

He withdrew a yellow pack with a veiled woman's face in the center. Fatimas.

"You kept those next to the President's letter," I said.

Trask gave me that little conspiratorial smile again. "He's fussy about not smoking."

"So you're saying 'To hell with you'?"

"Now, would I say that to the President of the United States?" Again the little smile.

"Covertly."

"Good word," he said.

He wanted me to know we were private here. He wanted me to know he was operating in a world where he made the rules. This was an interesting man for the President to send.

He struck a safety match and lit his cigarette first and then mine.

"And your boss?" I asked. "He's surely even fussier."

"*He's* my boss," Trask said, nodding at Wilson's letter, which sat on the tabletop between us.

"I thought you worked for the Secretary of State."

"Technically speaking. But in reality, the President doesn't consult with Bryan on anything of importance. I work for the President."

"You get a baseball card?" I asked, nodding at the pack, which he'd placed on the table before him.

"Fatima only puts them in the tins."

"Too bad."

"I buy the tins at home."

We looked at each other for a few moments in silence, each of us blowing smoke. Then Trask said, "These aren't the questions I expected, now that we're alone."

He was right. But I was taking a few moments to let him know I operated in my own world as well. I said, "You expect me to ask 'What's happening?'"

He shrugged an "of course."

I said, "I figure you'll tell me."

"But first a little 'To hell with you'?"

I gave him the same shrug. "You're going to kill my story. Already have, in fact, judging from that thinly veiled exchange you had with Griswold. I'm not in a good mood."

Trask gave me that small smile. But this time there was a different point to it. "I like you, Cobb," he said. "I like the curves and fadeaways you're throwing at me."

"Who do you root for?"

"The Giants."

"Oh brother," I said.

"We can get past that."

"So what's happening?" I asked.

"The President—not lightly, you understand; on the contrary, quite reluctantly and gravely—is asking that you not run this story."

"And Griswold, who *will* run, for the Senate this fall, is fine with banking some favors."

Trask nodded. "We're glad you work for a rare newspaper Democrat."

"Grover Cleveland wing. He'll need all the party favors he can collect. Especially from a new-breed Democrat."

Trask squared his shoulders to me. We'd postured enough, the two of us. He was right. "Look, Cobb," he said. "This is a major story you've uncovered. And it was news to the White House as well. Now, needless to say, we all want to thwart an invasion of America by a bunch of Mexican bandits. And you're right. Germany's right. There's a chance Villa could pull *all* the bandits of Mexico together behind this and the Federals too, all the men in arms in that country. And that is a very large number. They might indeed find a common cause in this, especially at the present moment, with us in Vera Cruz and nobody thanking us for it. Backed by German arms? This could get very nasty. And protracted."

"Banner headlines could stop that," I said.

"You're right," Trask said. "You're right. It could. Villa's first strike would have to be a surprise and the spotlight of the free press would take that away. And you're going to make him look like a puppet of the Germans if he tries anything. Okay. Let's say he backs off. But how does it play out from there? Europe is working up to a war. We think it could happen any time. And if it does, it will be Germany on one side and Britain and France on the other. We think it can get out of hand. If you look at all the collateral alliances, it's hard to imagine anyone in Europe staying out of that war, on one side or the other."

Trask stopped for a moment. He wanted me to think about a massive, comprehensive war in Europe. He had a reasonable next point to make and I could probably guess it, but I tried to break his hold. I looked away from him, out the window, as if concentrating on the next drag of my Fatima. From where I was sitting, Lake Michigan stretched to the farthest horizon and vanished there, as if the world were flat and it dropped off the edge. From this conference room table, the lake seemed as vast as any ocean. It wasn't. Far from it.

Which seemed significant in the present discussion. But I sure as hell couldn't figure out how. I was just a reporter. A news writer. I was merely toying with a metaphor. Put it in. Make it fit. Play to the balcony. But there was a real world out there. I still had Hernando's stitches in my arm. Itching like crazy. I killed four men. Recently. Men were dying in Mexico even as I sat here fiddling around with a metaphor about how something could seem way bigger than it is.

Trask said, "Every country loves to find an external enemy. It helps you understand who you are. You are *you*, as opposed—violently opposed—to *them*. We love that as much as anyone else, us Americans. Fifty years ago, we tried to do *us* versus *them* inside our own house. Fifty years later, we are in deep need of a viable new *them*. Your man Hearst knows that. He tried to give us Spain. And from how much he succeeded with as stupid a setup as that was, you can understand how deep that need must be. The Germans are perfect. There's so much to hate about their regimented tight asses. They are very much unlike us, very much unlike the spirit of this country. And if you trumpet this story of yours about the Germans trying to stir up a Mexican invasion of the U.S.A., you will work up such widespread, mouth-foaming anti-German feeling that at the first opportunity, everyone from the senators in the capital to the boys in the bar down the street will demand we march off to Europe to make war on Germany. No President is strong enough to resist that. You publish your story, Mr. Cobb, and you will force the President's hand. You will send our country to war when there may be some other way for us. Even if you personally think we should go to any war, any time, just let us at it, do you really want to make that decision for us all in tomorrow morning's newspaper?"

He stopped talking. I'd more or less watched him while he spoke, though at the moment I was looking back out at the lake. What did I want? What was my real desire, not just the conventional objective of the character I'd decided to play from the script I was improvising as I went? That this story be published because every truthful news story needed to be printed no matter what? Not exactly. That Friedrich von Mensinger and the German government should be prevented from provoking a Mexican invasion of the United States?

I looked at Trask. "So who's going to stop the Germans in Mexico? Mensinger's making his case to Villa right now."

Trask smiled. Not the little one. A big one. He said, "You are."

54

I was. By personal request of the President, no less. And who would that require me to be?

I waited to hear. Trask took a drag on his cigarette and blew the smoke toward Lake Michigan. I stubbed my cigarette out in the table ashtray, even though it had a couple more puffs in it. And this much I felt keenly: A great, two-ton, plushly upholstered, crimson stage curtain had just fallen. It would shortly rise again, and I was in the midst of an actor's recurring dream: I was about to go on stage and I had no clue even what the play was, much less what my lines were.

I supposed Trask was waiting once more for me to ask what was going on. He was my dark, opposite twin. I controlled a conversation by asking questions. He controlled it by making you ask. I was not doing it and he said, "Why do you think I've come here to carefully explain the killing of a story that is already dead?"

Which was a rhetorical question that simply squeezed me harder to inquire. And why didn't I? Control, I supposed. I asked, "What does the 'P' stand for?"

This stopped him for only the briefest of moments. His eyes did not even flicker. "Polk," he said.

"James Polk Trask," I said.

"My grandfather insisted. He knew a good president when he saw one."

"Do you ever use all three names?"

"Never," he said.

I didn't think so. Okay. I asked, "So what can I do for you?"

"Go back to Villa."

"I'm not exactly *persona grata* down there anymore."

"Why's that?"

"I coldcocked the German emissary just before I vanished."

Trask lifted his eyebrows and stubbed his cigarette next to mine.

"The typewriter's mightier than the sword," I said.

"Who started that?"

"He did."

None of this made it into the stories I filed.

"Why?" Trask asked.

"He knew I was a journalist. He knew somebody'd searched his bags."

"That's how you discovered the contents of the documents."

That wasn't in the story either.

"My sources," I said, flexing my fingers in the air before me.

Trask smiled. Then, upon further reflection, he laughed. This somehow didn't surprise me. He said, "Tell me. When you rode with the *Villistas,* and the *colorados* attacked. Did you just watch and take notes?"

"No."

"Did you fight?"

"Yes."

He looked at me steadily, and I had the distinct impression that something behind those dark, flat eyes had awakened. Was he going to ask the next question? I waited. He knew the answer, but I'd make him ask, if he wanted me to say it.

"I do like you, Cobb," he said. "You are the man for us, no doubt. Not just for me and for the President. For the country."

And I wondered if he could see something awaken now in my eyes, which, I suspected, were usually as opaque as his.

"Did you respect Mr. Vogel?" he asked.

"Yes."

"Do you understand that he was serving his country?"

"Yes."

"The thing the President would have you do will yield no public story. But it will do a great service to your country. Far more than a newspaper story would do."

He paused again. But he was not expecting a question now. He was choosing his words. I felt in my own pocket for a cigarette. I didn't have one. He saw what I was doing and pushed his pack of Fatimas across the table toward me. I took up the pack and removed a cigarette and put it in my mouth. I pushed the pack back toward him. He leaned across the table and lit the cigarette for me.

He said, "Vogel was a reporter of sorts too. All such men working for our country are reporters. But their reporting methods are more diverse—as yours have become—and their readers are very selective, very elite. Your Christopher Cobb story wasn't killed. It had the most important life of all. It informed the President of the United States. We are already on the alert about the plot, so your work has not been in vain. Far from it. They can no longer surprise us. But it would be much better still to prevent even the attempt, discredit the Germans in Mexico and win over Pancho Villa to us."

"You and the President think I can do that?"

He said, "We think you will be very good at this sort of work." He gave me that little smile of his.

I understood.

And the curtain rose.

55

And so I was flying two thousand feet above the very ground I crossed by horse a little over a week ago, the northern desert of *estado* Nuevo León. I was sitting on the leading edge of the lower wing of a Wright Model B aeroplane. Behind me the four-cylinder vertical engine pounded away and the two great pushing propellers spun in near invisibility; and around me the struts and rigging wires strained to keep our wings from flying off; and below me the long fall to the desert beckoned. My legs hung out over the empty air but my feet pressed hard against the shiny nickel-plated foot bar, as that and the mere friction of the wales of my corduroy-covered chair were the only things holding me in the machine.

Sitting to my left and constantly fine-tuning us in the air with two tall levers was Birdman Slim, Tallahassee's old pal. His flying services, paid for by the U.S. government, and this specially outfitted Model B were the immediate gifts I was bearing to Pancho Villa, and they were a small down payment on the military supplies and logistical support I was authorized to promise. Trask explained to me in Chicago, with impeccable logic, how my mission to arm a man even as we occupied a part of his country, a man who we had good reason to believe hated us, a man who we would otherwise reasonably expect to invade us, was clever foreign policy.

Villa was in Saltillo now, vanquisher yet again of the *Federales*. He
was, however, still far enough away from Laredo, whence Birdman and
I began to fly, that even with a special 15-gallon fuel tank in our Model
B, we could expect to be using our last drops as we landed. This was
something that the chill buffeting of air from our fifty-mile-an-hour
rush helped to press away from my thoughts. I had to assume I would
arrive safely, though we and our Model B dipped and lifted and dipped
again in the eddies of air, and Birdman, a wiry-muscled mule driver of
a man—he indeed once was a mule driver, he explained to me when
we met in Laredo, adding that aeroplanes were different from mules,
though he did not elaborate—this estimable Slim seemed anything
but confident as he worked intensely and gruntingly at the rudder and
elevator and wing-warp. I suspected if he had elaborated, it would turn
out that an aeroplane was unlike a mule in its being very much like a
bronco, and flying it was—each time—like the first time on the back
of the most headstrong mustang straight from the wild. Only you rode
it half a mile above the ground.

And higher. We rose at the little outbursts of the Sierra Madre
Orientals, ascending to a mile high and higher to thread a pass, the air
going as cold as a corpse pressing against us, and then we descended on
the other side. We did this once, and once again, and yet again before
he nudged me and nodded his head forward—daring not to take hand
or eye from his business of flying—and I looked, and in the distance I
saw a clumping of tiny shapes that I presumed he meant was Saltillo.
I hoped his Laredo declaration about the bare sufficiency of our fuel
took into account these ups and downs with the mountains.

We were coming in north of Saltillo, bearing southwest, and we
kept our course out past the western boundary and then banked south
and sharply descended to about the height of Griswold's conference
room, less than two hundred feet, which, after the last four hours, felt
reassuringly low. We throttled down and flew just beyond the city's
western edge of adobe houses. And now I saw before us the familiar
snake-bodies of Villa's trains, stretching a mile or more south from

Saltillo. Directly ahead were the campsites of the *Villistas,* full of after-noon *siestistas,* and as we bore down on them, I could see them lifting up, rising up, a wave swelling and rolling on ahead of us, their hands stretching upward toward us, sombreros spinning into the air at the sight of an aeroplane.

As we reached them I looked across Birdman and down, and our shadow sprung upon the trains, familiar trains: Villa's red caboose, the train behind, the flatcar where the men were scrambling to the Maxim guns, and the boxcar where I found Luisa. Was she still there? Had she found her way to escape from this man? That question, not the brief sputter of our engine, clenched inside my chest. Though a moment later the engine sputtered again and we banked west away from the campsite and now the engine was all that was on my mind.

I looked at Birdman. He seemed no more concerned than at any other moment of the past four hours. So we sputtered our way west on our last drops of fuel till we were clear of everyone and we turned north and faced a stretch of desert scattered with low-growing creosote, and our engines cut off altogether and suddenly things were very quiet, with only the rush of air around us, and we were about the height of Clyde's eighth-floor office now, and Bird-man, the sensitive ex-muleteer that he was, said, "Don't worry. We got no brakes anyway."

So we glided and the ground rose to us and I looked out to the mountains far away until we jolted and lifted and jolted and then we ran, no more bumpingly, in fact, than in a Model T on a potholed street, until we lost all momentum and we stopped.

I sat for a moment with my skin prickling away as if we were still flying.

"Birdman," I said, "can I ask you a question?"

"Yup."

"Why is it that the absence of brakes was supposed to take away my worry about the absence of a functioning engine?"

I looked at Birdman. It was hard to read his eyes through his goggles, but I thought that he thought I was pretty stupid to ask this.

"Since we got no brakes," he said, "I have to turn off the engines anyway to stop."

"That makes perfect sense," I said.

"Sure," he said.

I stepped onto the desert floor and I looked toward the trains, and three horsemen with rifles in hand were bearing down on us in a swirl of sand and dust, and now they were upon us and they pulled up and the lead horse reared briefly and settled, and leaping from its back was Tallahassee Slim.

His landing carried him a few steps toward us and he stopped and he looked at these two men lifting their goggles, and his own eyes went wide. "If this don't beat all," he said.

56

Back on his horse, Tallahassee Slim offered a hand and I went up to ride behind him to Villa's train. Birdman went up behind Hernando, who gave me a single, firm nod that I was surprised to find lifted me far more than Clyde's "knockout story" or Griswold's "surpassingly good."

I was carrying my own leather document portfolio, though this one had the presidential Seal embossed upon it. And I was wearing the *colorado*'s sombrero, which I unfolded and smoothed out as best I could and put on a few moments ago, also having removed my suit coat and tie and stuffed them into my aeroplane-light carpetbag. I was glad to see I was showing my battle ribbon: The left sleeve on my white shirt was discolored from a bit of ooze from my healing wound, the Laredo doctor having to struggle to get Hernando's stitches out before Birdman and I took off. I thought now to untuck my shirt so as to hide Luisa's knife, which was in its scabbard at the small of my back.

Slim and I headed off at an easy trot. "So how's your German visitor doing?" I asked.

"It took him a couple of days to clear his head," Slim said. "But he's had Villa's ear for nearly a week."

I grunted at this.

Slim said, "I thought word of your story would've gotten here by now."

We were still a good three hundred yards from Villa, but I needed to ask some more questions. I gave Slim the five-inch, single-column summary of what had transpired. It was condensed, but I got all the basics in. Trask would disapprove of my saying even this much, since he'd impressed upon me that what I was doing was secret government business intended for Villa's ears only. But here was another little lift I found myself feeling: I trusted Slim—with my life and whatever else—more than I trusted anyone in Chicago or Washington, D.C.

When I finished, Slim whistled, low. Before he could comment I said, "What's Villa's mood about me?"

"I'm not sure. I told him that you and Mensinger had some kind of personal beef, but I didn't know anything about it. He does understand personal beefs. But I don't know what Mensinger might have said about you. Lies of some sort. So with those lies and you taking off so quick—which *Jefe* really couldn't understand and I didn't know how to explain—I don't know what he'll do."

We rode on for a few moments and I was quiet, thinking what those lies might have been, hoping that Villa would lay them out to me openly.

"He may try to shoot you," Slim said.

This comment came into my head as I was deep in thought and I didn't quite grasp it at first.

"We need to talk about that," Slim said.

We were down to two hundred yards to go. It sank in. "Yes," I said. "Let's."

Slim said, "Don't forget. He's been known in the heat of the moment just to draw his pistol and shoot someone. Even men he's friendly with up to the last second."

Slim paused. We'd talked about this much before. I believed him.

Slim said, "If I somehow can end up behind him and if he draws and doesn't shoot instantly, I might could get the drop on him. Though I guess I'd just have to go ahead and plug him, since at that point we'd be pretty much up the *Rio Mierda* anyway."

I knew Slim would be willing to do that. I said, "Thanks, but forget it."

"You sure?"

"We wouldn't even make it to the horses," I said.

"We could go out in a blaze of *gringo* glory."

"What's the use? We'd never be able to tell the story in a bar."

"In hell," he said.

"If they got bars, it ain't hell," I said.

"Now, don't go taking away my last hope in the hereafter."

"Just see if you can bury me somewhere instead of feeding me to the *zopilotes.*"

A few more moments of silent riding, and the red caboose was getting close. Who expected to die in a goddam red caboose?

"He may not do it," Slim said.

We said no more. Slim pulled his horse up. He and I both got down. "At least let me try to clear the way," he said.

I nodded and was about to follow, but he had another thought and turned around to face me. "He's always testing for *cojones.*"

"Let me go first," I said.

Slim hesitated. "That's not what I'm saying."

"I know."

I pushed past him and went up the steps of the caboose with heavy feet and I arrived in Villa's open door.

He was standing over his desk in shirtsleeves, a map spread out before him, two of his Mexican officers on his far side, wearing ersatz military tunics. And there was Mensinger. He was ramrod-straight at the end of the desk, the only one of them facing the door, though his head was angled slightly downward, as he watched Villa point to the map. In the center of his forehead was a tomato-red welt the size of a leghorn egg. He was back in his linen suit, but without the jacket. His tie was knotted tightly.

They were unaware of me. I knocked at the doorjamb. Mensinger was slow raising his face, and as interested as I was in him and his reactions, Villa instantly turned his face at my knock and I could see nothing but him. He straightened up sharply. His restless animal's eyes fixed on me, and I was glad I was coming into this trying to be aggressively confident, because he did know how to intimidate. He straightened without taking his eyes off me; he squared around without taking his eyes off me; he said "Step into the room" without taking his eyes off me.

Without hesitating I made one strong stride into the room, and not far from his right hand I saw the Smith & Wesson .32 lying on his desk just as it was when I first met him. I took a second step, which was still pretty firm but not quite as strong as the first, and I stopped because somewhere in that process, faster than I could honestly say I was able to notice, Villa had snatched up his .32 and was pointing it square between my eyes. He took one quick stride toward me and everything suddenly slowed down, though I was sure he was still going fast: He began another step, the muzzle growing in my sight, the very tip of the muzzle, the black hole from which I expected a bullet to hurtle as soon as he finished bringing his right leg forward, which I could see happening at the lower periphery of my sight, though I was primarily focused on the muzzle, and I was working hard to stand still so I could at least die without flinching and with my eyes open, which was what I expected, to die, momentarily, because his right foot landed and his upper body, which had remained perfectly squared toward me all this time, now had the lower body squared perfectly beneath it, now he was motionless, Pancho Villa, and everything came to a stop in this room and, as far as I knew, in the desert outside and in the wide world beyond, and I was not flinching, I was not closing my eyes, though I expected the trigger-squeeze and the flare and the end of my life any moment now, any moment.

But the moment passed, and then another, and then another. I let my eyes shift very slightly from the muzzle to the face behind the muzzle, and those dark, wide eyes of his—as dark as but totally unlike Trask's dark eyes—these predator eyes were anything but opaque, they were clearly aware, they were seeing, they were hiding nothing.

He advanced again, quickly. The muzzle grew suddenly larger and then it vanished from my sight. It landed coldly, heavily, against my forehead. Pancho Villa's eyes held onto me without the tiniest flicker and his pistol pressed against me only long enough for me to think once more that the end had come. Then the muzzle abruptly left my forehead and his forearm jerked upward and I felt my sombrero fly off.

He took one step back from me. Not a retreat. He was just giving himself some shooting room so he wouldn't be spattered with my blood.

I did not flinch. I did not blink. I did not breathe.

"You ran away," Villa said.

I breathed. Just that. No other movement.

And then I spoke: "I ran *away* from nothing. I ran *to* something." He was listening. I kept talking. Very calmly. Taking my time. Like over a tankard of *pulque.* Shoot me if you want, you bandit son of a bitch; listen if you want: That had to be my attitude. *Cojones.* "I knew what the German would ask you," I said, tempted to look at Mensinger when I spoke of him. But I resisted that. Better to treat him as if he did not exist. I said, "I knew what he would offer. I knew all that when I came here. I also knew my own country gave you exile not so long ago, when your entire Army of the North could fit inside this railroad car. I knew my government would do better by you than the Germans. The first proof has just landed outside. I've brought you a cavalry of the air. An aeroplane and the services of your old *compañero,* Birdman Slim. Both are gifts of the United States of America. And there will be more support for General Pancho Villa and his vision for Mexico."

I stopped talking.

The pistol remained.

I said, "The proof is in my right hand. A real letter from the President of the United States. Not a fake, like the one given you by the man standing at your desk. He and his country held you in contempt, and that made me angry. That was why I left. They brought you a fabricated lie. Any English-speaking person would see through their forgery."

Villa's pistol slowly descended now. He held it at his side, pointing at the floor, his arm straight. I moved my eyes—just my eyes—from Villa's face and past his right shoulder and across the desk to Mensinger's.

There was a faint twitching in his right cheek, affecting now that side of his mustache, now his right eye, now his mustache, now both at once. He was seething. I brought my eyes slowly back to Villa, who casually turned his head and looked over his shoulder at Mensinger.

All Mensinger could say was "Lies. This invading American swine is the liar."

Villa looked back to me. Just as casually. Keeping a straight face.

I thought to invoke the aeroplane again. But this was no longer a matter of explanations or logic or offers made and fulfilled. Ultimately the way Pancho Villa understood the world was in his right hand. I figured since I was in this deep, I had no choice but to go in deeper.

I said, "This man tried to kill me with a sword when I had nothing but a typewriter to defend myself."

I could tell from the flicker in Villa that this was not entirely a new thing to him but he had heard quite a different version.

I said, "Let him fight me again."

Villa smiled. He looked me square in the face and he was smiling the way he smiled when he heard what I did to some *colorados* on his behalf.

Good. I felt my instinct was right about this.

He looked back to Mensinger. I looked at the German too. When I saw Mensinger smiling broadly, I felt I needed to reconsider my instinct.

"A duel?" Mensinger said to Villa. "Of course. It is a point of honor. I choose sabers."

I knew Villa was not going for the "point of honor" crap. But a duel meant somebody dies.

So I was still trying to understand this new role of U.S. government secret agent I was playing. I had figured out where I was in this scene and the role had seemed to suggest a course of action and I took it. Right. But I didn't quite have my instincts fully refined. I was correct in my reading of Villa's attitudes. My mistake was not anticipating the next move: fight with what? I might even have had something like a fistfight in mind.

I was professionally stupid like this when I first became a reporter as well.

In deep. Get in deeper. Was I nuts?

I said, "Not a duel. A fight."

"A fight," Villa said, emphatically. I supposed it was too much to think that my semantic distinction might reopen the subject of an appropriate weapon, because Villa immediately said, "Sabers."

"I will kill him," Mensinger said.

No one contradicted this. In all honesty, neither could I.

Maybe a fight with sabers was better for me than a duel with sabers. But only marginally so. I thought I'd declared for something less formal. But in fact I'd invited Mensinger to try to kill me again. With his weapon of choice. And it was the saber part that I was seriously concerned about. Not that I hadn't wielded a sword plenty in my life. As I traveled with a famous actress mother through my teens and a little beyond, the many supernumerary stage roles I played often put a sword in my hand. And I was trained in this by a couple of men who were quite adept at it. But the training involved thrusting and parrying to give the impression of a killing intent while assiduously avoiding one. I was trained to miss. I would have to make a fundamental adjustment *in medias res.*

But I showed no hesitation. I turned crisply on my heel. I found Tallahassee Slim standing just inside the door, and he gave me a furrow-browed look that was hard to read. I suspected it was half "You got balls" and half "You are dead." But he also gave me a quick nod and I returned it.

I passed through the door and out onto the platform and I started to go down the steps and I stopped. A crowd had gathered. Two or three hundred. Mostly *Villista* fighters. But some of the women too, and some of the children. All keeping their distance and still only loosely cohering as a crowd, but all of them facing these steps I was standing on. The word had gotten out to them about the German and the American. The man of the aeroplane and the man of the scarred face. Mortal adversaries. I figured I better stop writing the damn story of this in my head if I expected to have a chance to stay alive.

There were footfalls behind me. I stepped down and moved away from the car. The crowd receded a bit but started to pull together. I turned. Mensinger was standing near the back of the caboose, severely upright. He unknotted his tie, pulled it off, threw it casually aside. He started to unbutton his shirt.

Villa was striding this way, running the show, calling for two sabers. All around me bets began. The cockfighters calling out "*Gringo!*" or "*Alemán!*" and showing their bets with hand signals and looking for others making the same bet, pairing up. Mensinger was stripping off his shirt. I figured I'd better keep the sun to our side; it would blind me reflecting off his whiteness. I was just standing here. A little apart from all this. Watching. Which could be the death of me. I was a reporter no longer. That was a German agent standing over there, preparing to kill me. I was an American agent. Standing here. In the middle of the action. Creating the action.

I straightened. I started unbuttoning my shirt. Fine. I'd show my fresh scar to remind Villa who I'd fought and killed for lately. Not that it would do any good if I was run through with a saber. I took off my shirt and tossed it aside. Villa was standing near me. He had a saber in each hand, both of them the older British-style, slightly curved, cut-and-thrust swords. He gave me one. Villa and I looked each other in the eyes as I took it. I said, "Who are you betting on, *Jefe?*"

"The German," he said, showing his bad teeth in a big smile.

I said, "In the spirit of my country's friendship with Mexico, I will cover your inevitable losses."

Villa laughed.

I was glad I didn't choke on the words. At the moment I was not confident.

Villa moved off toward Mensinger, bearing the other saber.

I whipped my sword in the air half a dozen times, getting the feel of it, the heft of it. It was heavier—strikingly heavier—than the stage swords. I looked toward Mensinger, who now had his saber. His heels were pressed tightly together and he was mincing his feet outward till they were at right angles to each other. He'd spent his life learning to fight with a sword on the even, stone floors of a university fencing club. He had a necessary routine. Its full effectiveness was based on his opponent fighting from the same routine.

Villa was heading back toward me, intending, I assumed, to step between Mensinger and me and give some sort of starting signal. And looking at General Pancho Villa, the bandit rebel and would-be savior of Mexico, I thought of his tactics. His men were never driven around in regimented step but encouraged to fight personally and of their free will, in contrast to the *Federales,* who fought stiffly, by the book. His army was relentless and fast-moving and full of tricks. He was always adapting to fit the terrain, fit his men's skills.

I took one sidestep to the right, placing the approaching Villa directly between me and Mensinger. Villa stopped at this. He looked me in the eyes, his face pinching in thought. What was I up to? *You should know, Pancho.* I put my sword hand in front of me, chest high, and I rotated the saber to point to the sky. An improvised present-arms. I said, "I have learned from you, *Jefe.*"

And I took off in a sprint, veering right, doing an end run around Villa and then curving back toward Mensinger at a sharp angle of approach, from off to his left, and he was slow even turning his face to me and I was almost upon him and I pulled up, raising my right arm, and I was swinging the sword as he lurched toward me off balance and he lifted his sword to parry and his saber and mine clanged between us and he stumbled away.

He was quick with his hands.

I was glad I was not fighting by his rules.

My arm was doing an independent thing—since my head was simply crying for it to attack and attack and attack—my arm was swinging back to slash again, and Mensinger had caught his stumble and was straightening and my arm stopped its backward swing and I should have been thrusting now, not slashing, I was giving him a chance to recover and he was upright and trying to set his feet, still trying to establish the only rules he knew to fight by but I was slashing and my arm whipped around and he threw his own sword arm partly across his body, awkward still but he caught my sword and my arm flinched back from his blow, and I saw him doing what I should have done, setting up to thrust, recovering his arm from the stroke and making it glide right and it glided and as I tried to refocus my own arm his gliding stopped and I knew he would thrust and my legs were still at immediate call and I pushed back hard on my feet, I leap-stepped back and away and his sword rushed forward but I was propelling backward and his sword stretched for my chest but I was just out of his reach.

I stopped my backward flight and set myself and I saw Mensinger extended there—his sword stretched into empty air—and I realized I first had to close this distance from him to do what my arm wanted to do but my arm did it anyway—too soon—I thrust at him from a slight side angle and the tip of my saber ran and ran and stopped short of his chest but I did not overextend, I knew not to lunge too far even in the middle of the thrust when I recognized the gap was too big between us, and his saber flicked and parried my blade aside and he set himself for a riposte and because I withheld a little I could sidestep again to the right, I started crabbing around him and I realized I better keep him on the defensive but I was simply moving without attacking and I would look bad to Villa if I didn't attack and I was allowing Mensinger to get his balance and keep his balance as I moved and he was deftly following my sideward movements now, waiting for me to stop, and I was looking bad, and I stopped sidestepping and I set myself and I thrust and he parried and I moved to the side as he thrust back and he was confident now and focused and I had to take some sort of stand or I'd lose Villa and I was thinking too much and I was feeling slow and Mensinger was faster than a thought and I'd stopped moving and I thrust at him and it was weak and he parried almost nonchalantly and I was even thinking about thinking now and I did not see the twist of his wrist after his parry and his blade flashed and I felt a sharp burn on my left cheek.

He was confident again, and it had kindled his arrogance. He thought he could toy with me. I'd just given him the opportunity to run me through and he hadn't taken it. Instead, he'd given me a

Heidelbergian cut to the cheek. He let his sword linger now, just a brief moment, as he happily watched me bleed. His blade pulled back ever so slightly and it dropped a little, though he thought—and he was probably right—that he could thrust it into my chest at any moment of his choosing now that he was set and I was standing flat-footed before him. My sidestepping would work for only so long since he'd regained his balance and his composure, and I was still very aware of Villa watching us, assessing us. I had to throw Mensinger off balance again and finish this.

And I thought of Mensinger's wife. What I knew from her letter.

"Quick hands to the cheek," I said to him, putting the sneer in my voice like a saber thrust. "Like the way you strike Anna."

His eyes flickered at this. He was a little off balance now in his head. His wife was suddenly here with us. He was wondering how I could know this. And my thinking of Anna made me think of someone else.

But first I needed to shock Mensinger again.

Without taking my eyes off his, I took two quick backward steps, putting a little distance between us, and before he could come forward to engage me, in one smooth unthreatening gesture I lifted my sword arm out to the side, pointing the blade at a right angle away from him, and immediately I flicked the saber out of my hand. It flew off and chunked onto the ground and I was lowering my arm and empty hand, quickly, quickly, swinging them down and then continuing on, out of his sight, to the back of me, even as he shifted his eyes very briefly to my sword lying on the desert floor somewhere off to the right, and my hand moved to the small of my back and I grasped the handle of Luisa's knife and my hand was rushing upward now—holding the knife as easily and loosely controlled as in a mumblety-peg throw—I lifted the knife upward and backward. Mensinger's eyes were returning to me and my hand rose and I felt the leather wrapping of the handle against my palm and I even had time to realize that my outward knife-throwing manner had all my life been like a Mexican's, starting from behind the neck, and my knife hand was ready, even as Mensinger's eyes fixed on me once more. He did not see the knife, and though my posture may have struck him as odd, he overlooked that in order to smile me a now-you-will-die-you-*Schweinehunde*-American smile.

And I threw the knife. It buried itself what looked to be about three inches into his chest. A little lower, however, than directly in the heart. He did not die more or less instantly. Instead, he looked wide-eyed astonished. He dropped his sword. He staggered back. He sat abruptly down, stiff-legged. He was done, Friedrich von Mensinger.

I did not intend to go twist the knife in him or assault him further. He could die on his own. Like a Mexican bullfighter, I turned my back on him. I started to walk slowly away from him. I realized the crowd was roaring. Pancho Villa was suddenly at my side.

He handed me a handkerchief from his pocket. It was, surprisingly, brilliantly, whitely clean.

I pressed the handkerchief against my left cheek.

Villa said, "You have been a good student." And he laughed.

And a gunshot cracked loud.

I thought, for a flicker of a moment, that now I was dead.

The crowd went instantly quiet.

I didn't seem to be dead.

Villa and I spun around.

Mensinger, having sat down flat on his butt with his legs straight out, was having trouble falling completely over to his side. But the right half of his face, which was sharply turned our way, was a bloody pulp, and he swayed at last and fell backward, twisting to his left. As he did, his right arm swung outward, and as he settled onto the ground, that arm fell over his right hip.

And still in his hand was a pocket Mauser, which he'd drawn and was intending to use on me. Perhaps even on both of us.

I looked at Villa beside me.

He was staring intently at the pistol.

He turned his face to me and we exchanged a look I have seen on battlefields: two comrades in a moment of shared danger that has passed. And he looked beyond me now, toward the place where the shot came from.

I turned as well, and even before I saw her, I realized from an afterimage of Mensinger in my head that the bullet taking him out had entered through his right cheek. The unscarred one. A statement shot. Her signature.

And there she stood.

Her right arm was still straight out and absolutely sharpshooter-still. In her hand was an old Colt Army revolver.

She was dressed in black. A skirt of black, but I recognized the jacket from the lamplight in Vera Cruz. She had no *rebozo* and her hair was rolled tightly up on her head. Villa was walking toward her. I thought she would turn her arm now and shoot Pancho Villa dead.

But she did not.

As Villa neared Luisa, her arm slowly fell. He stopped before her. He spoke. She spoke. I could not hear. The crowd was murmuring. I found myself thinking she might yet shoot him. They talked. The wound on my cheek burned hotly. I'd killed another man. They talked. I'd killed another man, and this was a dispassionate thought. This was the attitude of the men I'd made a career writing about. The men who went to a place away from where they were born, away from where they were children, where they were young and had never killed anyone; and in this other place they killed, they killed in service to their country, they killed because they must or they would be killed. And eventually they did it and did not feel it. Luisa and Villa talked. I had killed and I could pass the bodies by in a street and not even glance their way.

And Villa nodded, and he turned his back on Luisa, blocking her from my sight, and he raised his hand to the crowd. They fell instantly silent. And he called out to us, "From today onward, this *soldadera* will ride with the Army of the North."

The crowd cheered.

57

I do not understand women.

I walked away. I did not look back.

Later, Pancho Villa stood beside me and put his hand on my shoulder while one of his doctors in one of his hospital boxcars stitched my wound, my *Schmiss*, and I passed his final test. I did not flinch at the pain.

I executed the details of my mission, as instructed, and Pancho Villa shook my hand with a vow of friendship for the United States of America. He put my *colorado* sombrero back on my head. I paid him the amount of his lost wager. We laughed together.

Some of his men escorted me across *estado* Nuevo León to Laredo. Tallahassee Slim and Hernando Soto were not among them, as they were off robbing a train.

I boarded a train for Chicago. A train safe from bandits.

Trask and Clyde both wanted me back.

I was finished with Mexico.

Whatever I do not understand about women began with my mother. But when I boarded that train, one thing about her seemed clear to me. She needed to be rescued.

So on the way to Chicago, I found myself in another taxi leaving Union Station on a steamy May night in the city of my birth. I did not have a clear plan. I realized, though, as soon as we headed out, that I did not want to do another walk Down the Line on Basin Street. The taxis could only work the perimeter of Storyville, so I told my driver to drop me at Claiborne and Conti, The District's far corner. I could walk the quieter few blocks along Conti down to Basin, where the main street ran into St. Louis Cemetery Number 1. The direction Mother was heading the last time I saw her. I figured I could think a little on that walk. For all the time I'd lately spent thinking on the train, I'd come up with no plan whatsoever about how to save my mother from what she was presently doing. Save her to what? I had nothing to offer.

But I was on Conti and I was walking toward Basin and this was a mistake. I was at the low-price end of the street-level, short-time cribs. The older whores, the stranger ones, the ones who were simply used up, were on this block, and in the incandescence they all were jaundiced and most of them were mostly naked and in this first block they were calling at me and offering quite a lot for a dime, just a dime, a thin dime for a lush lady, a dime for a blow a poke a chunk a crack a flop. And I wondered where my angel-faced octoroon was now, thirteen years later, certainly no longer at Willie V. Piazza's house in expensive striped stockings. Did she cost a dime now? If I recognized her would I rescue her instead?

And in the next street they were two bits. And from behind every incandescent-lamp-stained body in every doorway on every tiny, bed-filled room wafted the smell of lye, which they kept in a pan under the bed to throw in the face of any customer who got rough. And I stopped considering anything at all about any of these women, and they went to four bits across Marais and they were a dollar across Liberty and then I crossed Franklin and on my left began the cemetery and I was walking fast now, just needing to find my mother and take her by the arm and whisper to her, low, *We have to go now, we have to go,* and I wouldn't even think about how every man in the place assumed I was her young man for the evening.

And I turned the corner onto Basin and I headed down the street and I was bumping past the strolling men and suddenly the curtain of bobbing heads before me parted for a moment and I saw my mother heading this way with some bowlered, thick-mustachioed Johnny on her arm. The curtain closed again briefly, but I stopped. I let the men flow past me and I waited for her, one moment and another and another and I didn't have a weapon, my knife stayed in Mensinger, who was dead in another country, and my Browning stayed in my checked bag because why would I need a weapon simply to ask my mother to go home now, even if I didn't know where home would be in this circumstance—except perhaps simply with me—and even if I didn't know how to persuade her if she said no. But now I thought it might have been a mistake not to bring a weapon.

And the shifting bodies shifted away once more, and thirty feet before me was Mother and this man and she was looking up at him and I could not wait even a few more moments for her to be in front of me. I called out "Mother," and it was loud, it was way too loud.

And her face turned to me and the man's face turned and she was such a good actress, so very good, and I knew that whatever was going on, keeping her composure would be the appropriate response for whatever character she was playing now in her life, but instead, her eyes went wide and her mouth even fell open a bit, and meanwhile the man beside her—and I could see it was not just a bowlered and mustachioed face but still another oft-beat-upon face—was this my mother's type, dear God?—was this a thing I never noticed?—this man was not astonished at the sight of me, he was pissed, greatly, and he was reaching into his coat and I took a step toward him and I wished again to have a weapon because a little damn pocket Mauser just like Mensinger's was coming out and what an idiotic irony this would be to end up dead from that and I was taking another step and this guy was used to drawing fast and the muzzle was out and starting to swing down and I was lifting a hand that I was not sure what I'd do with and suddenly another pistol appeared over the Johnny's shoulder, a big one, a Browning like mine and there were only so many good weapons in the world and I was caught in my head thinking of these same two pistols back in Mexico and I wondered if I was getting nostalgic over pistols and I wondered if nostalgia could get me killed now, except the

Johnny's head thumped forward a little and the Browning was stuck on the back of it and the Mauser paused in its track to a shot at my chest, and attached to the Browning was another bowler and mustache who I'd normally take to be part of the Johnny's gang except for the gun-and-head relationship. And now my own head dipped a little forward from the steel-heavy push of a muzzle and a couple of voices were recommending a general cessation of movement and the man behind the Johnny was reaching around and taking the Mauser.

My mother piped up quick and said, "Phil. He's okay. He's my son." And my own head was released and Mother hooked my arm and was guiding me insistently away from the others and across the street and into the shadow of the Southern Depot passenger shed.

She stopped me and she turned me and she looked up into my face and her eyes were vast and searching and deep dark—the eyes I could look at in any mirror, the part of my mother I carried most obviously upon myself—and her hand came up and hovered over my stitched-up cheek and she said, "What have you done?"

I said, "That's the question I've come here to ask you."

"You damn fool of a boy," she said. "I told you to stay away."

"Then you shouldn't have given me so much information."

She took a sudden, deep breath.

"You wanted me to do this," I said.

"No. No. I just wanted an audience of sorts."

"An audience?"

She heard in my voice now what I'd been thinking.

She said, "If my best slapping hand wouldn't land on your stitches, I'd make you pay dearly for that tone and all that's behind it."

I didn't say anything. She looked at me hard in the eyes for a moment and then she wagged her head.

She said, "It's all because my wonderful role, to be wonderfully played, can never be truly seen."

I didn't understand. I waited.

"My darling," she said, dropping her voice into a vibrant whisper, "I am working in Storyville as a secret agent for the Pinkertons."

She paused, but not for me to speak. She was playing the revelatory scene. After holding me suspended, she said, "A large number of wanted men pass through this place. Very bad men. I identify them. I peel them off. The Pinkerton Detective Agency takes them away."

I was, of course, tempted to speak. My mother and I grew up sharing secrets and ironies and a sense of the mad, unlikely scripts we were cast in beyond the footlights, but I found myself keeping my own counsel now, taking in the ironies, working up to giving her a kiss and walking away. So I remained silent and she played on, only too happy to float uninterrupted upon her dramatic pauses.

"Usually," she said, "this transpires with more discretion than in the case of Solomon Ward, bank burglar and murderer, whose face I recognized and whose apprehension you so ostentatiously interrupted."

We looked deeply into each other's eyes for a long moment. She'd spoken her line, given me my cue. She waited. I knew how to work a silence. I have learned much from my mother.

And then I simply asked, "Do you think I've compromised you?"

"No, my darling. Don't worry. I think we'll be all right."

"I'm sorry, Mother," I said. "But I'm glad I've put my mind at ease."

"Me too," she said.

And I gave her a hug and she inquired after me a little bit and I told her a little bit and we hugged again and she kissed me on my good cheek and I kissed her on both of hers, her preference, in the style of the French, and I explained that I had a train to catch and she sent me off by saying, "My darling son, I know you have always felt my place was in the great body of classic literature. But this work I am doing is great work as well. It is real. It is deeply representative of our unsettled times. It is all about life and death and the struggle for the good and the true."

I took her hands in mine and I said, "My darling mother, I could not agree more."

And I let go of her and I walked away.

On the train to Chicago the next day, rushing along the great Mississippi River outside Memphis, the past few weeks began to settle into me. No. Not settle. Perhaps decompose. I thought of Diego. How I likely would never see him again. How there was one more *papi* in this world who had vanished. I thought of Luisa. And I stopped myself thinking of Luisa. I thought of my mother and I found I did not clearly know what to feel about her. I had an explanation for Storyville, but I did not fully understand. I was happy for the vibrancy of her voice and the buoyancy in her body, but I didn't like the risks she was running. Though maybe the risks were necessary for the sense of renewed life in her. Maybe that much of it I did understand. After all, the risks of my own life were greater now, and they promised to grow greater still. And I felt strangely happy about that. As The Bard said, "All the world's a stage, and all the men and women merely players." I'd played at watching others play at the primary narratives of this world. I had a chance to do more now. I would do more.